The Sun in Splendour

Jean Plaidy, one of the pre-eminent authors of historical fiction for most of the twentieth century, is the pen name of the prolific English author Eleanor Hibbert, also known as Victoria Holt. Jean Plaidy's novels had sold more than 14 million copies worldwide by the time of her death in 1993.

For further information about our Jean Plaidy reissues and mailing list, please visit
www.randomhouse.co.uk/minisites/jeanplaidy

Praise for Jean Plaidy

'Plaidy excels at blending history with romance and drama'
New York Times

'Outstanding'
Vanity Fair

'Full-blooded, dramatic, exciting'
Observer

'Plaidy has brought the past to life'
Times Literary Supplement

'One of our best historical novelists'
News Chronicle

Further titles available in Arrow by Jean Plaidy

The Tudors
Uneasy Lies the Head
Katharine, the Virgin
Widow
The Shadow of the
Pomegranate
The King's Secret Matter
Murder Most Royal
St Thomas's Eve
The Sixth Wife
The Thistle and the Rose
Mary Queen of France
Lord Robert
Royal Road to Fotheringay
The Captive Queen of Scots

The Medici Trilogy
Madame Serpent
The Italian Woman
Queen Jezebel

The Plantagenets
The Plantagenet Prelude
The Revolt of the Eaglets
The Heart of the Lion
The Prince of Darkness

The Battle of the Queens
The Queen from Provence
The Hammer of the Scots
The Follies of the King
The Vow on the Heron
Passage to Pontefract
The Star of Lancaster

The French Revolution
Louis the Well-Beloved
The Road to Compiègne
Flaunting, Extravagant
Queen

**The Isabella and
Ferdinand Trilogy**
Castile for Isabella
Spain for the Sovereigns
Daughters of Spain

The Victorians
The Captive of Kensington
The Queen and Lord M
The Queen's Husband
The Widow of Windsor

The Sun in Splendour

JEAN PLAIDY

arrow books

Published by Arrow Books 2009

2 4 6 8 10 9 7 5 3

Copyright © Jean Plaidy, 1982

Initial lettering copyright © Stephen Raw, 2008

The Estate of Eleanor Hibbert has asserted its right under the Copyright, Designs and
Patents Act, 1988 to have Jean Plaidy identified as the author of this work.

First published in Great Britain in 1982 by Robert Hale Limited

The Random House Group Limited
20 Vauxhall Bridge Road, London, SW1V 2SA

www.rbooks.co.uk

Addresses for companies within The Random House Group Limited can be found at:
www.randomhouse.co.uk/offices.htm

The Random House Group Limited Reg. No. 954009

A CIP catalogue record for this book is available from the British Library

ISBN 9780099532989

The Random House Group Limited supports The Forest Stewardship
Council (FSC), the leading international forest certification organisation.
All our titles that are printed on Greenpeace approved FSC certified paper
carry the FSC logo. Our paper procurement policy can be found at
www.rbooks.co.uk/environment

Typeset by SX Composing DTP, Rayleigh, Essex
Printed and bound in Great Britain by
CPI Cox & Wyman, Reading, RG1 8EX

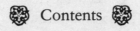 Contents

SUNRISE

I	The Meeting in Whittlebury Forest	3
II	The Secret Marriage	60
III	The Queen's Revenge	77
IV	In Sanctuary	120

HIGH NOON

V	Richard's Wooing	181
VI	Hastings in Danger	218
VII	The French Adventure	238
VIII	A Butt of Malmsey	255
IX	Death at Westminster	296

SUNSET

X	The King and Protector	337
XI	Jane Shore	363
XII	Death on Tower Green	388
XIII	'My Life was Lent'	414
XIV	King Richard the Third	422
XV	Buckingham	433
XVI	Rumours	448
XVII	Bosworth Field	461

Bibliography	467

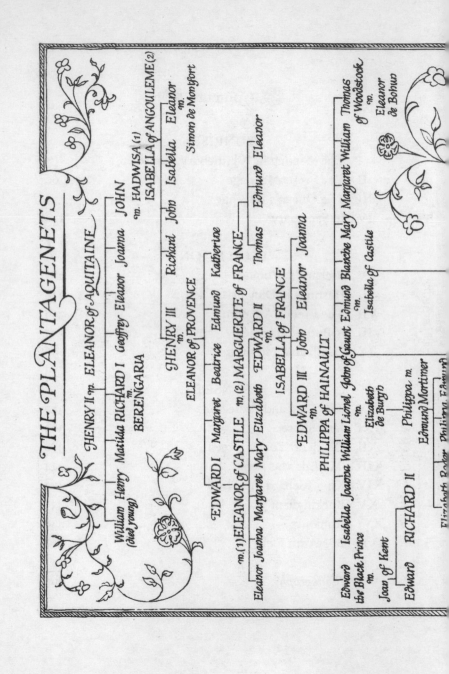

THE PLANTAGENETS

HENRY II *m.* ELEANOR *of* AQUITAINE

William Henry Matilda RICHARD I Geoffrey Eleanor Joanna JOHN
(died young) *m.* *m.*
BERENGARIA HADWISA (1)
ISABELLA *of* ANGOULEME (2)

HENRY III Richard John Isabella Eleanor
m. *m.*
ELEANOR *of* PROVENCE Simon de Montfort

EDWARD I Margaret Beatrice Edmund Katherine

m.(1) ELEANOR *of* CASTILE *m.*(2) MARGUERITE *of* FRANCE Thomas Edmund Eleanor

Eleanor Joanna Margaret Mary Elizabeth EDWARD II

m.
ISABELLA *of* FRANCE

EDWARD III John Eleanor Joanna
m.
PHILIPPA *of* HAINAULT

Edward Isabella Joanna William Lionel John *of* Gaunt Edmund Blanche Mary Margaret William Thomas
the Black Prince *m.* *m.* *m.* *of* Woodstock
m. Elizabeth Isabella *of* Castile *m.*
Joan *of* Kent de Burgh Eleanor
de Bohun

Philippa *m.*
Edmund Mortimer

Edward RICHARD II Philippa m.
Edmund Mortimer

Elizabeth Roger Philippa Edward

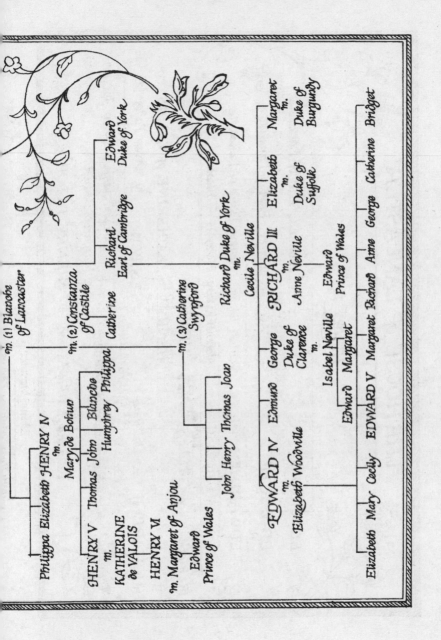

THE HOUSE of LANCASTER

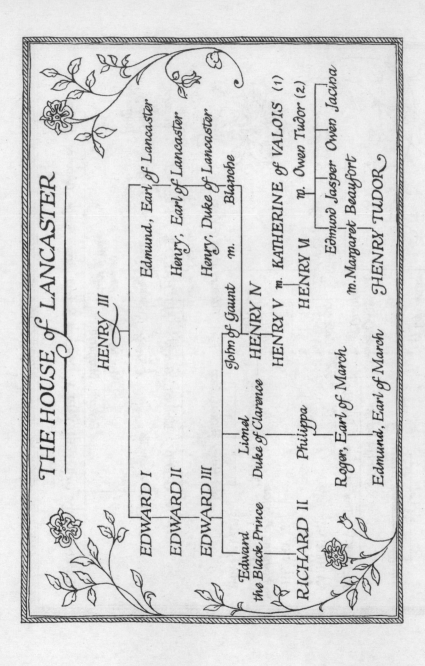

HENRY III

EDWARD I

EDWARD II — Edmund, Earl of Lancaster

EDWARD III — Henry, Earl of Lancaster

Edward the Black Prince — Lionel Duke of Clarence — John of Gaunt m. Blanche — Henry, Duke of Lancaster

RICHARD II — Philippa — HENRY IV

Roger, Earl of March — HENRY V m. KATHERINE of VALOIS (1)
m. Owen Tudor (2)

Edmund, Earl of March — HENRY VI — Edmund Jasper Owen Jacina

m. Margaret Beaufort

HENRY TUDOR

THE HOUSE of YORK

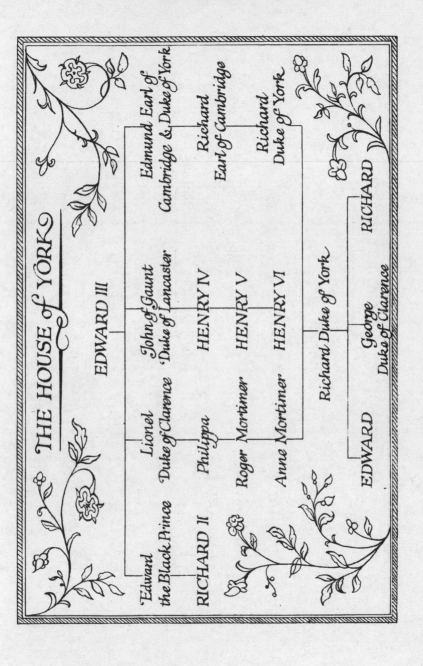

SUNRISE

Chapter I

THE MEETING IN WHITTLEBURY FOREST

Jacquetta was watching from the topmost turret of Grafton Manor for the arrival of her daughter. She herself had made sure that Elizabeth's bedchamber was ready and that it should be as comfortable as she could make it. Poor Elizabeth would be in need of comfort, sorrowing widow that she was with two young children to provide for and an uncertain future before her.

These were indeed uncertain times. The wretched war went on and on – swaying this way and that, victory one day for York and the next for Lancaster.

A plague on their wars, thought Jacquetta, which continually took a warm-blooded woman's husband away from her and robbed her daughter of hers altogether.

At least her beloved Richard was safe and had managed to send news to her after having fled with the King somewhere up to the north, for the message had come to her from Newcastle. They were the losers again, and this time it seemed that some conclusion might be reached for Edward of York had proclaimed himself King and the people favoured him. He was a young man of great charm, Jacquetta had to admit, although the Rivers were staunch Lancastrians. 'Every inch a King,' was what they said of Edward; and as he was almost six feet four there were a good many inches. He was a magnificent soldier, an ardent lover of women and the greatest possible contrast to poor Henry who was so saintly that he longed to be a monk and had on more than one occasion lapsed into madness.

Perhaps, thought Jacquetta, we are on the wrong side.

Her heart began to beat faster for in the distance she could make out a party of riders. Her daughter must be among them. She would go down at once to meet her, to assure her that she was welcome, that Grafton was her home and should remain so for as long as she wished it to be.

The sight of her daughter filled her with pride. Elizabeth was as beautiful as ever – the most handsome of a very attractive family. Jacquetta had reason to be proud of the children she had borne Richard – seven sons and seven daughters, and Elizabeth, the eldest, had made a very quiet entrance into the world for their marriage had been frowned on in high places and everything connected with it had had to be conducted with the utmost secrecy.

Elizabeth had dismounted. She was as calm as her mother expected her to be. Little ruffled Elizabeth and it had always been so from nursery days. Elizabeth had taken command which was perhaps natural as she was the eldest, and her brothers, lively young boys as they had been, could never get the better of their sister Elizabeth.

'My dearest,' cried Jacquetta, embracing her daughter. 'This is a sorry occasion.'

Elizabeth returned her mother's embrace with restrained affection.

'We knew you would offer us a haven,' she said. She led the

boys forward. Thomas and Richard Grey were pleasant looking and about ten and eight years of age, old enough to realise that the death of their father was a very tragic event and of great consequence to them.

Jacquetta kissed her grandsons with fervour, calling them her little lambs whom she was glad to have in her keeping.

'Come in, dear child,' she went on, putting her arm through that of her daughter. 'You will be weary. Your own room is ready for you, and the boys will be next to you. Welcome to Grafton, my darlings. Your home, dear Elizabeth, as it ever was and always will be while I am here.'

'My heartfelt thanks, dear lady,' said Elizabeth. 'For we are indeed in dire circumstances.'

They went into the Manor together.

'It has been a long ride to Northamptonshire,' went on Elizabeth.

'Never mind, my child. Now you are here.'

The boys were taken to rooms made ready for them and Jacquetta accompanied Elizabeth to hers.

'There, my child, just as it used to be. You'll be happy again. I promise you.'

'Have you read the signs?'

Jacquetta hesitated. Many people thought she was a witch. She was in a way, she supposed. She had on occasions foretold the future but in her heart she was not sure whether she had wanted something to happen and had made it so by her own actions. The water nymph of the Rhine, Melusina, was said to have been an ancestress of hers. It was one of those lovely legends which became attached to some families. Supernatural beings found their way into the family history by beguiling one of its members and thus infused some strain either for good or evil which appeared in the family for generations. The House of Luxembourg had Melusina, and the serpent who was said to be a familiar of that fair enchantress had become one of the devices on the shields of the Luxembourg Princes. Because she came from the ruling Luxembourg family and had the right to the device, the suspicion that she was a sorceress had been born; and Jacquetta found it intriguing and often useful so, while she did not exactly encourage it, she did nothing to deny it.

'There is a great fortune for you,' she said now. 'My daughter, your fortunes are at a low ebb but that will change. There is such a dazzling prospect before you that soon you will be looking back to this day and realising that it was only a stepping-stone to great things. It is the little dark wood which you must traverse before you reach the pastures of prosperity.'

'Oh, dear lady, is that what you wish for me or what you prophesy?'

'Elizabeth, I would say this to none but you, but sometimes I do not know the difference.'

Elizabeth threw back her hood. Then the full blaze of her beauty struck even her mother speechless even though she had been aware of it. It was always like that after she had not seen her for a while. Elizabeth knew it and there was just a hint of the dramatic in the manner in which the hood was thrown back.

The beautiful golden hair fell loose about her shoulders to her knees. It rippled and shone where the light caught it; it softened her face which in its perfect classical features might have been a little repellingly cold without it. Her teeth were white and perfect; her eyes a greyish blue fringed with long thick golden lashes; the nose straight, neither long nor short, but perfect. Jacquetta always thought that Elizabeth had inherited the best features from each parent; and they were two exceedingly handsome people.

Elizabeth, however, had inherited little of her mother's warmth. She was clever, and had been from a child, and Jacquetta had always thought: Elizabeth can take care of herself. That was why it was such a triumph to have her come home now in this time of need.

'The estates have been confiscated,' Elizabeth said. 'We have nothing at all. Dear Mother, I need to get through that dark wood quickly.'

'You will. I promise you that. These are strange times.'

'Warwick has made Edward of York King and he will remain so, they say. Henry has no heart for battle.'

'There is the Queen,' Jacquetta reminded her daughter. 'And the little Prince.'

'Margaret will fight to the death,' said Elizabeth. 'But Margaret is a fool.'

'It is well that lady is not able to hear you say that.'

'She would rage against me, threaten me with all sorts of horrible punishments, and then, when I reminded her of our friendship and service to her cause, embrace me, forgive me, and tell me she would always feel affection for me. That is Margaret.'

'You should know her. You served in her bedchamber and such service is the best way to know queens intimately.'

'Mother, we are on the losing side. The sooner we face that the better.'

'Dear child, noble families cannot change sides because they are on the losing one.'

'They all say that Edward has come to stay. Warwick will see to that and it is Warwick who makes and unmakes kings.'

'Edward has the looks of a king which is just what poor Henry lacks, but kings are not chosen for their looks.'

'They have some effect surely,' said Elizabeth. 'And while the Yorkists reign I shall never regain my estates, my children will have nothing and I shall remain a widow.'

'My dearest child, you have the greatest asset of all.'

'And what is that?'

'Yourself. Your beauty . . . I never saw a more lovely creature. There! How can you despair when you have such gifts!' She came nearer to her daughter, and spoke softly, mysteriously. 'Change is coming, I promise you. Your fortunes will be reversed. Wait, Elizabeth. Be patient. Trust your mother. Trust the old serpent of the Rhine.'

Elizabeth looked at her mother eagerly, hopefully.

At least I have managed to raise her spirits, thought Jacquetta.

She left her daughter to wash and rest while she went to her own room.

It was good to have Elizabeth and the boys with her. The trouble with children was that they went away – boys to be brought up in other noble houses and girls to the homes of their future husbands. Life was sad – and made so by absurd conventions. Families should be together. Jacquetta had always rebelled against doing what was expected of her. She believed that a woman of spirit should judge for herself.

She had been forced into marriage when she was sixteen years old. A very grand marriage in which her family had rejoiced. She remembered her uncle Louis of Luxembourg, Bishop Therouanne, coming to her rubbing his hands together

8

murmuring: 'Great good fortune, niece. Such a marriage I have arranged for you.'

There had had to be a certain amount of secrecy because the great Duke of Burgundy would have objected. Everybody then had been terrified of offending the great Duke of Burgundy, even the important man they had succeeded in capturing for her husband. And the reason was not only that Burgundy did not want the English to have fresh influence with Luxembourg but because the bridegroom had just become a widower his late wife having been the sister of the Great Duke himself.

An intriguing situation which had appealed to that arch intriguante Jacquetta. Her prospective husband was the mighty Duke of Bedford, the most important man in France at that time, some said, because he was the Regent and had been so since the death of his brother Henry the Fifth who had conquered France and married the French King's daughter. No wonder her family had been eager for the match. She was not averse to it herself apart from the fact that she was being forced into it and Jacquetta always liked to make up her own mind – then she saw him. He was in his forties and he seemed to her a very old man.

However the marriage took place. He was not unkind. He thought her very pretty and charming – and she did not see very much of him because he was always engaged in weighty matters and with the ceremonies over there was another important concern for him – the pacification of the mighty Burgundy.

The marriage did not last long. Poor old man, he died worn out by his troubles and deeply depressed because he saw that the English were losing their grip on France.

And Jacquetta had been free. She had been seventeen when she saw the most handsome man in England. He was not so only in her eyes because she had heard him called that by others. Richard Woodville of the Mote Maidstone until his elder brother died and he inherited Grafton in Northamptonshire.

Richard had served Jacquetta's late husband well and had been knighted by Henry the Sixth at Leicester about ten years before they met. Of course even with his knighthood he was only a humble squire and she was the daughter of the Count St Pol of the reigning House of Luxembourg. Jacquetta had known that if she had made known her desire to marry Richard Woodville there would be protests from her family. Protests? – More than that. It would be strictly forbidden and attempts would be made to hustle her into marriage with someone of high rank and very likely no physical attractions for her whatsoever. The fact was that after she had seen Richard Woodville no one else would do for her, so with what her uncle called a wanton lack of consideration for her rank she had married the handsomest man in England in secret, consummated the marriage with such verve that before her irate brother and her uncle knew of it she was *enceinte* with Elizabeth, which made any annulling of the marriage impossible.

Jacquetta had been ecstatically happy and had fourteen children one after the other and looked scarcely a day older than she had been when she had married her beautiful Richard. She knew it was whispered that she was a sorceress, for none but a witch could continue to look so young and beautiful and full of vitality after so much childbearing.

Jacquetta could and did. There were powders and concoctions besides lotions to help the hair retain its colour. She was knowledgeable in such arts and if that was witchcraft, then she was a witch. But she enjoyed her life, except when her husband and sons were torn from their homes to fight these wretched wars of the roses. But her nature was such that she knew the reunions could not have been so glorious but for the partings. There were great compensations in life.

Secretly she was glad that Edward now seemed firmly on the throne. He might be the enemy but the acceptance of him as king would stop the wars, and more than anything she wanted her family to be safe and with her whenever possible.

'I am proud of my Woodvilles,' she would say, 'every one of them.' And once more she would congratulate herself on her wisdom in snapping her fingers at convention and following the path of romance. It was an unwritten law that when a woman married once for state reasons, the next time – if there was a next time – she should choose for herself. And that was exactly what she had done. Poor Richard, he had been bewildered, a little fearful, but she had swept him off his feet, and he had been no match for the demanding determined Duchess of Bedford.

He had been right of course to fear there would be trouble. Her brother the Count of St Pol and her uncle, Louis of Luxembourg and Bishop of Therouanne, had sent bitter reproaches and declared they did not want to see her again. She snapped her fingers at them. She could endure the separation, she declared. They were naturally not the only ones who were angry. There was also the English royal house for in marrying the Duke of Bedford she had become a member of that.

Henry was lenient though and all that had been demanded was a fine of a thousand pounds. It was not easy to find that money of course for Richard was only a poor knight, but they had managed and very soon were forgiven for Richard was firm in his allegiance to the House of Lancaster and he had been raised to the peerage for his services and was now Lord Rivers, a name they had chosen from the old family one of Redvers. Happy years they had been saddened only by separation and the fear of what might be happening to him in those stupid wars. In common with many women Jacquetta did not greatly care which side was successful as long as there could be an end to the senseless killing.

No one was safe – but when had they ever been? At any moment a man could offend someone in a high place and some pretext would be found for taking off his head. The best life was in the country, away from the Court and dangerous affairs, and that was where Jacquetta liked to be with her family about her.

And now here was Elizabeth come home in her trouble: beautiful Elizabeth with her long golden hair and face that resembled a Greek statue, tall, willowy, still with a figure unimpaired by the bearing of children.

Jacquetta fingered the serpent's device on the brooch she was wearing.

She was certain that her beautiful daughter would find a way out of her troubles. Of all her children, Elizabeth was the one who knew best how to take care of herself.

During the months that followed Elizabeth had plenty of time to brood on her fate. It seemed worse to her because she had planned it all so differently. Being exceptionally beautiful for as long as she could remember she had expected to reap benefits from her outstanding physical perfections. She had been aware of admiration from the cradle; and although she knew that her father was not one of the powerful nobles of England, she had expected a good marriage.

Perhaps she would have been wiser to have accepted Sir Hugh Johnes. He was, it was true, of no great significance but he had been under the patronage of the great Earl of Warwick and might have risen. But she had declined, and it was only now that this calamity had befallen her that she was wondering whether she should have taken him.

Elizabeth had always felt that some special fate was in store for her. Her mother had hinted at it more than once and whether Jacquetta really could see into the future was not certain, but like most people Elizabeth liked to believe auguries that were good and only doubted when they were not.

To have been born the daughter of a mesalliance was in itself dramatic. Of course they had been poor and there were so many brothers and sisters; Jacquetta had dominated the family for their father was away a great deal and in any case was completely under the spell of his exciting wife. Warm-hearted, lively Jacquetta about whom there was an aura of mystery because of the serpent of Melusina, had formed close family ties and Elizabeth, in spite of the calculating streak in her nature, was one of them and could never forget that she was a Woodville.

Woodvilles stand together, Jacquetta had said. The good fortune of one of us is the good fortune of all and so shall it be if troubles are to come. It was the code of the family and none would ever forget it.

She remembered with excitement the day she left for Windsor there to play her part of lady of the bedchamber to the Queen.

Margaret of Anjou had liked her even though there could

not have been two women less alike. Margaret was impulsive, fiercely vindictive to her enemies and as fiercely faithful to her friends. Elizabeth was cool, and rarely acted on impulse; she was always looking for the advantage to herself as she must, being born without the means to buy a rich and powerful husband. But marriages were rarely arranged by the young people concerned; they were not the result of demanding passion, devoted love. Oh no, lands, possession, titles came into it; and the least physically desirable *parti* had far greater chance if possessed of a fortune than the most beautiful woman on earth who was without one.

Such knowledge rankled; and Elizabeth was wary. If her father was a humble knight who had managed to get into the peerage for service to a cause which was now out of favour, her mother though disowned was of the reigning House of Luxembourg. Elizabeth had decided that she was not going to throw away her chances lightly.

Margaret had become quite fond of her. Elizabeth knew how to please her, and that was to listen to her tirades against the Duke of York, to murmur sympathetically, to admire the Prince of Wales as the most perfect baby that ever had been born, and to show an interest in Margaret's gowns which was not difficult for Elizabeth herself liked splendour. We are of a kind in one way, she thought. We have both had impoverished childhoods, but she has become a queen. What a triumph – and yet now Margaret had lost her crown . . . or not exactly lost it. Margaret would never agree to that. But she was in exile and the young godlike Edward, who had so caught the people's fancy, was on the throne. To stay, some said.

And that brought her back to the ever recurring theme. And we are on the wrong side.

If only her father had sported the white rose instead of the red! He might have known that Henry was not going to prevail over York. York had had everything on his side. He was energetic while Henry was lethargic as far as war was concerned; Henry wanted to read his books, listen to music, plan buildings and pray. Oh those prayers! They went on interminably. Elizabeth was grateful that Margaret had become a little impatient with them. York was a ruler; he even declared he had a greater claim to the throne and some agreed with him. The usurpation of Henry's grandfather was a constant topic, and York's having descended from two branches of the royal tree was true enough. York had the greater claim; he was more fitted to be the king. Moreover he had the Earl of Warwick on his side. It should have been obvious to any that York was going to succeed. A clever man would have arranged something to enable him to change sides but her father had not done it; nor had her husband.

She sighed. Yes perhaps it would have been wise to have taken Hugh Johnes.

She often thought of Hugh, though she had had no deep feelings for him; nor had she a great deal for John Grey. One must, she was sure, remain calm in these matters. Her mother had been so different. She had thrown away rank and power possibly for the sake of Richard Woodville, and never regretted it. But Jacquetta was different from others. She had been a member of the royal House of Luxembourg; she had made one brilliant marriage and had been the Duchess of Bedford, a member of the royal family, before she married Richard Woodville for love. Jacquetta had had a wonderful life, she always said. She may have had. But what of her poor penniless offspring?

Margaret had said when Elizabeth arrived to be a lady of her bedchamber: 'Ah you are beautiful. I shall have no difficulty in finding a husband for you.'

Margaret's matchmaking had been something of a joke at Court. She took time off from meddling in state matters to get her ladies as she said 'settled'.

Nothing had pleased her more than to pair off people; to get them married, to watch for the children and bestow gifts on them. A strange trait in such an ambitious fiery little Queen.

It was of course not long before Hugh appeared and no sooner had he set eyes on Elizabeth than he had wanted to marry her. Elizabeth had known what was in his mind and had not been very excited. He was reputed to be a brave knight; he had distinguished himself in the service of the great Earl of Warwick, but he was without a fortune.

This had happened during one of the periods of Henry's madness when the Duke of York – the present King's father – was Protector of the Realm and there was peace – although an uneasy one – between the houses of York and Lancaster.

The Queen, being immersed in looking after her husband, had not noticed what was happening to her maid of honour. So it was that Elizabeth was made an offer of marriage. Not by Hugh himself. He was of a timid nature and he must have sensed that Elizabeth had a high opinion of herself for he arranged that others should seek her hand for him. And whom did he ask but the two most important men in the kingdom at that time – the Duke of York himself and one who was perhaps even greater: Warwick the Kingmaker.

She remembered now the letters she had had from those two men and she marvelled at their friendship for Hugh and that they should take time to plead for him.

'He hath informed me that he hath great love and affection for your person . . . I write to you at this time and pray you that you will (at this my request and prayer) condescend and apply you unto his lawful and honest desire . . . and cause me to show you such good patronage as shall hold you content and pleased . . .'

There was something about the letter which irritated her. He was telling her that he favoured her marriage with this poor knight as being worthy of her and offered his patronage in a lordly condescending manner. This was the great Warwick, friend of the Duke of York whom Margaret regarded as her great enemy.

The Duke of York had written less pompously urging the match which Hugh Johnes so desired and hinting more tactfully than Warwick had done that he would be pleased by the match.

She supposed that Hugh believed she would find requests from such men irresistible. He did not know Elizabeth.

When she had told Jacquetta about the offer Jacquetta had laughed. 'I like a man to do his own wooing,' was her comment.

And so do I, thought Elizabeth.

Margaret was pleased when she refused the match.

'Warwick's protégé!' she had cried. 'And the Duke of York's! How I hate those two. They are responsible for all our troubles . . . for the King's illness . . . everything . . . They try to snatch our crown from us. They shall never do that. So you are refusing this man they want to force on you, eh. Good. That is very good. My beautiful Elizabeth, I will find a better match for you.'

And then there had been that staunch Lancastrian.

'John Grey is a good man,' said the Queen. 'He has served us well. The King is fond of him. I have always liked him myself, and he is the heir of Ferrers of Groby. Do you know, my dear, he has a fine place at Bradgate and he is descended from the Norman nobility.'

'I am in no hurry to marry, my lady,' said Elizabeth.

'Of course you are not, but you are wise enough to see a good chance when it comes before you, eh? I believe that in life it is unwise to miss good opportunities hoping for better that may never come.'

So the Queen was in favour of the match, and she was apt to grow impatient with those who did not fall in with her wishes.

Elizabeth had thought about a match with John Grey and Jacquetta had agreed with the Queen that it would be a good one. John Grey was young, good-looking and very much in love with the beautiful Elizabeth.

So they were married and she spent several years at Bradgate. She grew to love the place which was about two miles from Groby castle and only four from Leicester. There her two boys were born and, as she had taken quite a liking to the quiet life, the marriage turned out to be quite a happy one. She would ride in the beautiful grounds enjoying the pleasaunces and the fish ponds and the well-kept gardens. It was thrilling to ride over the bridge across the moat and look up at the two towers and the battlements with their quoins and corbels; and to say to herself: This beautiful place belongs to us . . . It will be my son's in time and Groby castle as well.

She had thought at that time that she had done well on her marriage.

All went smoothly until the fighting started. More battles were fought again. Northampton and then Wakefield where the Duke of York had met his death after which his head, adorned by a paper crown, had been stuck up on the walls of the city of York. How Margaret had rejoiced then. Poor Margaret, she should have learned that she was one of those women whom Fate loved to mock. Her triumphs were short-lived and her defeats were very often of her own making.

The brilliant tactics of the Earl of Warwick turned the tables after the Yorkist defeat at St Albans, which was a fateful battle for her for in it her husband had perished and everything had changed. The wife with two boys whose future had seemed secure – or as secure as anything could be in this changing world – had become the widow.

Even then she would have been rich and able to care for her boys. How foolish Margaret could be! The Lancastrians had won the battle of St Albans for her and it was that sly strategist Warwick who had turned it into victory for York by simply taking London and setting up Edward of York as king. The Londoners had always been Yorkists. They were only interested in trading, and the good stable government offered by Edward of York – with the Kingmaker behind him – was what they wanted. They had done with mad Henry; they hated Margaret who was tactless and foreign and had never made any attempt to understand them.

And so Margaret and Henry had become fugitives and Edward of York was King; and because John Grey had fought for the Lancastrians his possessions were confiscated and his widow was forced to fall back on her parents with her two fatherless boys.

And so the months passed and there was no sign of the people's wavering from their adherence to the new King. They liked Edward. He had a charm which Henry had lacked; he was taller than everyone around him which a king should be; he was more handsome than any of his courtiers; wherever he went the women smiled on him. He had a host of mistresses and, although several marriages had been arranged for him, so far he had remained a bachelor. There were some in the country who feared his way of living was not chaste but the majority of the people laughed at his amorous adventurings and it was said that a smile from him could win even the flintiest heart.

He made his progresses through the country and wherever he went he was welcome. The country was prospering from a peaceful period. Henry was somewhere in the north – in exile or in hiding and Margaret, it was said, had gone to France to seek help.

Let her stay there, said the people. Let Edward continue to reign over them.

It so happened that at this time the King came to Northamptonshire. He very much enjoyed the chase and it seemed certain, said Jacquetta, that he would be hunting in Whittlebury Forest.

'That,' commented Elizabeth, 'is very near us. We can be sure, however, that he will not be calling at Grafton. We are in disgrace.'

'Ours will not be one of the houses honoured by the King, I grant you. But . . .'

Elizabeth looked sharply at her mother. She could see an idea forming in her mind. She was touching the serpent on her brooch as she often did when she was brooding thus.

'Well?' asked Elizabeth gently.

'I think, my dear, that you should try to see the King.'

'He would never see me. The widow of a Lancastrian and

one who served the red rose as John did. Think how many white roses he must have plucked before their time.'

'I know, I know . . . but feuds don't go on for ever and they say that the King has a forgiving nature particularly where a beautiful woman is concerned.'

'Are you proposing that I give favour for favour . . .'

'I suggest no such thing! But something tells me that you should attempt to see Edward of York.'

'How? Do you think I would be allowed to get through to him if I presented myself?'

'Assuredly you would not. Therefore I think you should meet him by accident.' Jacquetta was laughing. 'A well-planned accident,' she went on.

'My dear Mother, what do you plan?'

'We may need several plans. We could try the forest first. You might meet him there . . . by accident of course. Then you could plead for your inheritance . . . for your children.'

Elizabeth studied her mother. She was beginning to feel a growing excitement.

At the head of the cavalcade rode the King and beside him his greatest friend William, Lord Hastings. Hastings was some twelve years older than Edward but there was a strong bond between them. In fact, Edward often thought that he was closer to Hastings than to any other man. He had admired Warwick from his childhood. In fact he had regarded him as a sort of god, greater than any man, even Edward's own father; it was Warwick who had taught him almost everything he knew and but for Warwick's clever tactics Edward would not be King today. He would never forget that. But Warwick, although only two years or so older than Hastings, seemed of another generation to Edward.

William's interests were similar to his, and Edward's chief inclination at this time was involved with women. Hastings shared his exploits. They would go out together disguised as merchants and look for adventures in the streets of London. It was not easy for Edward to disguise himself, for towering above most people, outstandingly handsome, he was often recognised. Many women's eyes were brightened at the sight of him and even the most virtuous merchant's wife would find her heart beating a little faster. Edward had a quality beyond charm and beauty, for since he had become King an aura of royalty had grown up about him but, because he was none the less familiar with his subjects because of it, it added vastly to his attractions. He could mingle with the humblest and make them feel significant. Hastings often said that was the true secret of his charm, even more so than that bounding vitality and that promise of hitherto undreamed of delights amorous adventuring with him could bring.

Hastings himself was not without charm. Less obviously handsome than Edward he was still good-looking; he was fairly tall, with an air of nobility, and was not without his admirers. The trouble was, as he pointed out to Edward, we are all like pale stars compared with the sun.

'Stars are equally bright in their spheres,' Edward pointed out.

'Ah,' retorted Hastings, 'but we are in that of the sun.'

Hastings was clever, witty, a good commander and best of all a faithful friend. Edward trusted people too easily, Hastings often told him; but Edward shrugged that aside. He was easy-going, good-natured, bent on pleasure. Or he had been before he became King. He was less so now. Hastings often thought that the change had come about when he had seen his father's head wearing that paper crown on the walls of York. Perhaps it had been even more horrible to him because beside his father was his younger brother Edmund, Duke of Rutland, that boy who had grown up in the nursery with him and who had adored him as most of the family did. Edward had certainly not been the same since he had witnessed that grisly spectacle.

He had seemed to realise that the world was not merely for pleasure. There was cruelty in it, and cruelty must be met with cruelty. Before he had witnessed that terrible sight he had been inclined to forgive his enemies very easily and sweep away all thoughts of revenge.

Perhaps he had become a little more serious, more inclined to rule on his own account, for people were right when they said that Edward wore the crown but the real ruler was Warwick.

So Hastings, the King's intimate friend, was the first to realise this new seriousness. It was not a bad thing, he thought. Edward was coming into his own, trying to wriggle free of the strings which Warwick held. How far he would break away from them, Hastings was not sure. But Edward was young yet . . . twenty-two years of age and still believing that sexual pleasure was the foremost goal for him.

As they rode into Northamptonshire they were talking as they often did of recent conquests and Edward was wondering what new ones lay ahead.

'You'll have to mend your ways a little when you are married,' Hastings reminded him.

'A little, perhaps,' retorted Edward.

'You should be married soon.'

'There speaks the married man. He is caught himself and wants the rest of us to be in like case.'

'Katharine understands me,' said Hastings easily. 'She knows that I must have a little licence, being the bosom friend of our King.'

'My reputation does not stand high in the land it seems.'

'Your nocturnal adventurings are noticed.'

'But I am not averse to a little dalliance by day.'

'You are as five men in the field, they say, and as ten in the bedchamber.'

'Who says that?'

'The merchants' wives of London Town, I believe.'

'Oh come, William, you flatter me and I think you can give a good account of yourself.'

'There is none in the land who can begin to rival its King.'

'Has Warwick expressed an opinion?'

'Warwick? Why should he to me?'

'Perhaps to his sister.'

'I hardly think he would hold such discourse with Katharine.'

'They are a close family and your being his brother-in-law I thought mayhap he may have said a word to you concerning the King's indiscretions.'

'He does not frown on them. I think he applauds them in a way. It is strange how some indiscretions arouse the admiration of the people . . . but only when performed by one of irresistible good looks and charm.'

'He has never suggested to me that I should mend my ways.'

Indeed not, thought Hastings. It suits Warwick well. Let the King amuse himself while Warwick rules. Has Warwick noticed the change in the King he has set up since that fearful day when Edward had ridden into York and seen his dead father's head in its jaunty paper crown?

If Edward were ever to want to take another road than that chosen for him by Warwick, what would happen? Which one of them would prevail? But no, Edward was too easy-going, too fond of luxurious living; and he did not forget that Warwick had made him King. Edward would want to go on playing the king while Warwick ruled. Or would he?

The King loved to hunt and journeys throughout the kingdom were always enlivened by days spent in the chase. Whenever they came to forest they paused for the sport and if it were good rested for a few days to enjoy it.

So it was at the forest of Whittlebury close to Grafton Manor that the King was enjoying a few days hunting. Everyone at the Manor had been aware of the proximity of the King's party. If the Rivers had been Yorkists it was very likely that the King would have honoured them with his presence. As Lord Rivers had always been a staunch Lancastrian it was certain that he would not, for which, in a way, Jacquetta had said, they should be truly grateful. 'To entertain the King would impoverish us for the next five years. Our way of living cannot match his, I do assure you.'

But there were secrets in Jacquetta's eyes and she had managed to convey these to her daughter. Jacquetta knew something was going to happen. Elizabeth could guess that by the far-off look in her eyes. Elizabeth could never be sure whether her mother really did see into the future or whether she dreamed up a possibility and then used all her ingenuity to make it happen.

'Take the boys,' she had said, 'and go into the forest. There is an oak-tree – the largest in the area. It is just where Pury Park ends and Grafton begins. Sit there with the boys and wait.'

'Why should I do that?'

'I have heard the royal party are hunting in that vicinity today.'

Jacquetta had means of finding out these things. She surrounded herself with intrigue and her servants were drawn into it. There was no doubt that she would glean knowledge of the royal party's whereabouts through that communication between her servants and those of other noble houses.

'It may well be,' said Jacquetta, 'that you will see someone to whom you can plead your cause. You have done no harm. It was your husband who fought for the Lancastrians. He is dead. You are ready to accept the new King. It might be that you could make someone understand this.'

Elizabeth stared at her mother. Jacquetta had always been bold and sometimes her schemes had worked out. It was only necessary to consider how she had married the man of her choice in view of the opposition of powerful men.

Jacquetta had gone to the cupboard and was pulling out dresses.

'This blue is most becoming. It is very simple too. I think it suits you as well as anything you have. Looks such as yours show to perfection against simplicity. Your hair should be quite loose . . . no ribands to bind it . . . nothing . . . no ornaments of any sort except this silver girdle to stress how small your waist is. At ten o'clock the party sets out. They will have to pass the oak if they are hunting in this forest. If you are waiting there . . .'

Jacquetta had not mentioned the King but Elizabeth knew that he was in her mind.

So she must play the suppliant, something her proud nature rebelled against. But she was tired of being poor, of seeing no way out of her predicament but marriage to someone who could give her a little comfort and help her sons to make good marriages. It was a dreary prospect.

If she could regain her husband's confiscated estates she would at least be free. Then she could choose a husband if she wanted to marry again and at least her children would have what was due to them.

But why should the Yorkists reward those who had fought against them? Was it not a hopeless cause? Jacquetta did not think so and Jacquetta had that strange prophetic look in her eyes.

It was true that Elizabeth was at her most beautiful that day. The excitement of this project had set the faintest colour in her cheeks so that she looked like a statue that was just coming to life. That touch of animation enhanced her charm and even Jacquetta who was more than prepared for it was again astonished by the beauty of her daughter.

'None will be able to resist you,' she said, 'if you play your part well.'

It was a short walk to the oak-tree.

The boys were asking questions. Why were they going there? Was it some game?

'We shall see the huntsmen ride by if we are lucky.'

That pleased them. They were both eager to see the huntsmen ride by.

She came to the oak-tree. It was a great sight, that tree, standing apart as it did from the others. It had a majestic air, an air of grandeur almost as though it had set itself apart and forbidden others to approach.

The morning wore on. The boys were getting impatient when suddenly they heard the baying of the dogs and the galloping hoofs of the horses.

With a fast beating heart she stepped out from under the shade of the oak. She saw them emerge from the trees. They were coming this way.

She took her sons by the hand and stood waiting.

Edward was slightly ahead of the others. He saw her standing there with the sun gleaming in her golden hair and glinting on the silver girdle at her little waist.

She looked like a goddess in her simple blue gown and Edward thought he had never seen such a beautiful woman.

He pulled up sharply.

'God's mercy,' he cried. 'What do you here, lady?'

She knelt and her beautiful hair fell forward sweeping the ground. She whispered to her children to kneel also.

'Lady,' said Edward, 'I beg you rise. I see you know me.'

She shifted her beautiful blue-grey eyes to his and said: 'My lord, who could fail to know you? You are distinguished among all other men.'

Edward laughed. 'You have not told me what you do here.'

'I am Lady Grey,' said Elizabeth. 'These are my sons. My husband was killed at St Albans.'

'Grey,' said the King, noting the sweep of golden lashes against her smooth delicate skin. 'Can he be Rivers' son-in-law?'

'It is so, my lord.'

'And you are Rivers' daughter?'

She bowed her head.

'He must be a proud man to have such a daughter . . . a proud man but a misguided one. Lady Grey, what would you have of me?'

'My lord King, I come here to beg you to restore my husband's estates to me.'

'You have a strange opinion of me, Lady Grey, if you believe I will give estates to those who have shown themselves to be my enemies.'

'*I* never was,' she said with a hint of passion. 'Nor were these innocent boys.'

The party had arrived and were waiting nearby watching. Many a covert grin was exchanged. The woman was a beauty and everyone knew Edward's inclinations. It was clever of her to find such a way of bringing herself to his notice. And she looked very appealing standing there holding the boys by the hand.

'It is a sad thing,' said Edward, 'when widows and orphans must suffer for the sins of their husbands and fathers.'

'My lord, if you can see your way . . .'

Edward leaned forward and touched her hair. He let a strand of it linger in his hand.

'I can consider this,' he said. 'I do not care to see beautiful ladies in distress.'

He was gone. She stood there under the oak-tree watching him ride away. Then she walked slowly back to the manor.

Jacquetta was waiting for her.

'Well, well?' she asked eagerly.

'I saw the King.'

Jacquetta clasped her hands. 'And what said he?'

'He was kind.'

'And will restore the estates?'

'It was a sort of promise. I daresay he will forget he made it within the hour.'

'My heart tells me that we shall hear more of this,' said Jacquetta.

❀ ❀ ❀

It was late afternoon when a rider came clattering into the stables of Grafton Manor.

He leaped from his horse and called to a bewildered groom to take it. Then he strode into the house.

He stood in the hall and his voice echoed up to the vaulted ceiling.

'Is no one at home?'

Jacquetta appeared.

'A traveller?' she said. 'Are you seeking shelter, my lord?'

'The answer to both those questions is Yes, dear lady.'

Jacquetta descended. 'We are humble in our ways,' she said, 'but never turn travellers from the door.'

'I knew that you would offer me right good hospitality.'

'Do you require a bed for the night?' asked Jacquetta.

'There is nothing I desire more,' was the answer.

'Then you shall have it. We sup shortly.'

'My lady, you overwhelm me with your goodness. Tell me, is your lord at home? Have you a family?'

'My lord is from home and my daughter is with me. A widow who has lost her estates because her husband was fighting on the wrong side at St Albans.'

'A pitiful story.'

'Pitiful indeed, my lord, that she should be punished for something in which she was not allowed a choice.'

'She is a Yorkist at heart?'

'My lord, have you seen the King? One only has to look at him to know that he is the man England needs.'

Elizabeth had appeared on the stairs. She was still wearing the blue gown which she had worn in the forest and her hair was loosely tied with blue ribbons to match the colour of her dress.

The traveller stared at her.

He was smiling. 'I have met your daughter before, my lady.'

Elizabeth descended the stairs and coming to stand before the man who could not take his eyes from her she knelt.

'Elizabeth . . .' began Jacquetta.

'My lady,' said Elizabeth, 'do you not know that this is the King?'

Jacquetta, having known all the time and having expected him to do just this, feigned to be overcome by embarrassment – which she did so well that if she had not known her better Elizabeth might have believed genuine.

'Pray rise, dear lady,' said Edward, 'that I may look on your face for by my very faith I never saw a fairer.'

'We are overwhelmed by the honour of your visit,' said Elizabeth, 'and filled with hope for I think it means you are ready to give an ear to my request.'

'I would be inclined to grant any request you made to me.'

'You are gracious indeed.'

'My lord,' said Jacquetta, 'are you alone?'

'I am, dear lady.'

'I was wondering how we could feed a party. It is rare I think that you travel thus.'

'My friends are not far away. I escape their attentions sometimes and then they know better than to attempt to stop me.'

Jacquetta asked leave to retire. She must give orders to the servants. Perhaps Elizabeth would speak with the King while a room was prepared for him. He must indeed take them for what they were – impoverished by the war.

'And being on the wrong side,' added Edward with a smile.

'Not all of us, my lord,' said Jacquetta; and left him with Elizabeth.

'Would you care to sit down, my lord,' said Elizabeth. 'My mother will not be long.'

She led the way to a window seat and sat down; he was beside her.

When he took her hand and kissed it, she withdrew it with a hint of haughtiness. She was wondering whether this was a clever project after all. She might regain her estates but the King would want to strike a bargain and all knew the kind of bargains he would be likely to make with attractive women.

'I trust the hunt was successful,' she said.

'I know not whether it was or was not. My thoughts were all of an encounter under an oak-tree. By God's Faith when I saw you standing there I thought I had never seen a more lovely sight in the whole of my life.'

'I am sure my lord has seen many such pictures that attracted him. If one is to believe . . .'

'The rumours about me. Never believe rumour, dear lady. It always lies.'

'Does it not have *some* foundation in truth?'

'That must be admitted but should we not beware of exaggeration?'

'Always,' she said. 'I am one to prefer plain truth.'

'Then you are a lady after my own heart. To tell you the truth your beauty has overwhelmed me.'

'You said you would consider my poverty.'

'It is a crime that one so beautiful should be poor.'

'You could change that with a stroke of a pen, my lord.'

'So could I, and so am I inclined to. I believe we can find a solution to these matters. We must talk of it, get to know each other. It was for that reason that I called on you this day.'

'It was a most gracious act.'

He had moved a little closer to her. 'I hope we shall be even more gracious to each other.'

Oh no, thought Elizabeth, this is moving too fast. Surely this was not what my mother intended? I am not going to be one of that army of women who share his favours for a week, even if it means the return of my estates. He must be reminded that my mother is of the noble House of Luxembourg even if my father is of little account – and a Lancastrian at that.

She was relieved to see that her mother had come back to the hall.

'I have told them all what an illustrious visitor we have. My lord, you will have to forgive their clumsiness, for they are overwhelmed by the honour. We did not expect this . . . in our wildest dreams. You must I fear take us as we are.'

'There is nothing,' said Edward, his eyes on Elizabeth, 'that would please me more.'

'Would you allow us to conduct you to your bedchamber.'

'I would be delighted,' said Edward. 'Perhaps the Lady Grey . . .'

'We will both show you,' said Jacquetta.

Elizabeth realised as she had on other occasions that there was a certain royal dignity in her mother. She was after all a Princess of Luxembourg.

When they were alone together Elizabeth said to her mother:

'Did you foresee this?'

Jacquetta was thoughtful. 'I saw it as a possibility.' She surveyed her daughter. 'You are so beautiful that you could not fail to impress him. He will return your estates.'

'He has already implied that he expects me to become his mistress. That I will not be.'

Jacquetta watched her daughter slyly.

'Your refusal may well increase his ardour. Do you think he has ever been refused in his life?'

'It will be good for him to find there is someone who can say no to his advances.'

'Is he not handsome? What a fine figure of a man. I knew him the moment he stepped into the hall. Perhaps I had been expecting him. But his looks and manners are such to distinguish him anywhere. He could never hide his identity.'

'He is all you say he is. He is also a libertine. He makes sport with the merchants' wives. He will have to learn that I am not a merchant's wife.'

'I do not think you will have much difficulty in teaching him that.'

'I want a return of my estates. Do you think I shall get that?'

'I should ask for that immediately. Then when he comes with *his* request you can play the innocent and the virtuous. You can do that very well, because, dear Elizabeth, although you may not be innocent you are virtuous. I do not believe your thoughts ever strayed from John Grey while he lived.'

'I was never deeply attracted by that which seems to dominate the King's life. I assure you all his wiles and good looks will offer me no temptation.'

'That is good. That will leave your head clear and calm for reasoning.'

'Dear Mother, you will be with me in this.'

'I am always with you, and everyone of the family, as you know. If we succeed in getting the return of your estates nothing will please me more.'

'I am glad you are here. I feel safe with you near. I think he will attempt to seduce me tonight. It is a pity he is staying here.'

'I think he plans to make the attempt. It is a strange situation. He should be travelling with a party of friends. It is dangerous. How does he know that a Lancastrian assassin is not lurking in this Lancastrian household? It is clearly true that he plunges recklessly into dangerous adventures. One cannot help but admire him. Elizabeth, you will need your powers of determination to resist him.'

'If you think that you do not know me. I can resist him very well. I can assure you I have no desire to become his mistress.'

The dreamy look was again in Jacquetta's eyes.

'We shall see,' she said.

They supped and Edward sat beside Jacquetta with Elizabeth on the other side of him. That he was enjoying this was obvious. When the musicians played he applauded and called for more. He let his hand rest on her thigh but with tact she withdrew herself. He smiled at her reluctance. He had met that once or twice in his many amours, but it had never lasted and he had come to realise that it was part of the game of courtship for some women. He was not averse to playing it for a while, but not too long; he was growing more and more impatient for this fair widow.

During the meal he had promised that her estates should be restored.

She was grateful and immediately after supper she was going to take him to her mother's chamber and there he should give the necessary documents which should be witnessed by two of the esquires as well as her mother.

Yes, yes, he agreed to that. But why did they not sign it in her bedchamber? Wouldn't that be more appropriate?

'My mother would expect it to be done in hers. It is more grand than mine.'

He would like to see hers. Would she show it to him?

There was that in his eyes which told her it might be unwise to refuse to do so before the documents were signed.

So when they went to her mother's chamber she pointed out her own which was quite close. He looked in and said that it was especially interesting to him. He liked to imagine her sleeping in that bed.

The papers were signed and he was duly conducted to his chamber.

Elizabeth immediately went to that of her mother.

'He will be here shortly. It will be hard to ward him off. He might even be capable of rape which he would call his kingly rights.'

'I don't think that. He would pride himself on never having to resort to such methods with a woman. He tells himself that they are all eager to fall into his hands.'

'Even when they have shown that they are not?'

'He wouldn't accept that as true reluctance.'

'He has asked where my room is. He will be in there at any moment. I shall stay with you this night.'

Jacquetta nodded. 'But, dear child, he will know where my

room is also. That is why I have had a chamber prepared for us in the east wing of the house.'

Elizabeth laughed at her mother.

'You think of everything,' she said. 'I do believe you are in truth a sorceress.'

'If I am, dear child, rejoice in it, for every power I have will be used in the service of my family which is dearer to me than my own life. Now, we will waste no time. I have a feeling that he will not want to either. So let us go.'

Although Edward showed no sign of his frustration he was decidedly piqued. He did not see Elizabeth in the morning. Jacquetta told him that Elizabeth had been with one of the boys who had developed a fever during the night and could not leave his bedside.

'You know what mothers are,' she murmured.

It was a feeble effort to offer an explanation why Elizabeth had not been in her room on the previous night; but he knew well enough why. She had really meant it when she had hinted that his attentions would not be welcome. She was indeed a virtuous woman. But she had been clever enough to make sure that her husband's estates were returned to her. She should take care. He could easily rescind that order.

He took a cool farewell of Jacquetta and thanked her for her hospitality. She went up to the top turret and a few hours later saw the royal party riding away.

Elizabeth joined her.

'So he has gone. Do you think he will refuse to honour the return of John's property?'

'I think not.'

'Was he very angry?'

'It is hard to say. He was disappointed. But extremely courteous and thanked me pleasantly.'

'Then if I have regained my estates this will have been a good day's work.'

'It may well be that we have not heard the end of this matter,' said Jacquetta.

'I sincerely hope so. I shall claim Bradgate and Groby without delay. Perhaps I should leave at once.'

'I should wait a little while. It would be unpleasant if the King did rescind the order. And what if he came to you there and you were unprotected? Here you are in your mother's care.'

'And you think he would consider you a stalwart protector?'

'I fancy he has a little regard for me.'

'Then what?'

'Wait a little. See what happens. This may be the end and perhaps we shall hear no more of the King. In that case you will have regained your estates which was what we set out to do.'

'I should like to return to Bradgate.'

'All in good time.'

In her heart Jacquetta was certain that the King would not let the matter rest there. Elizabeth was outstandingly beautiful and men to whom conquests came easily were invariably intrigued when they did not.

She was right. Within a few days he was calling once more at Grafton.

Jacquetta saw his arrival and hastened to call Elizabeth.

'He is determined,' said Jacquetta.

'And so am I,' answered Elizabeth.

'You are going to find it difficult.'

'I shall not become his mistress. I promise you that.'

Jacquetta lifted her shoulders and went down to greet the King.

He kissed her heartily on either cheek. He found her attractive although she was not a young woman but she had great charm and vitality and Elizabeth's looks resembled her mother's in some ways.

'My lord, can it truly be!' cried Jacquetta. 'Once more you honour us.'

'To tell you the truth, my lady,' he said with a disarming charm, 'I did not want to come, but I found it impossible to keep away. Is the Lady Grey at home?'

'She is on the point of departing for Bradgate.'

'Then I am in time. Take me to her.'

'I will tell her that you are here, my lord.'

Jacquetta curtsied and left him standing impatiently in the hall.

Elizabeth was in her chamber, combing her hair, piling it up on her head; she was twisting a rope of pearls in it. Her gown was of blue and white silk; she looked regal.

'He is asking for you,' said Jacquetta.

'I will see him,' answered Elizabeth.

'Have a care, daughter.'

'You may trust me, Mother.'

'Yes,' said Jacquetta, 'I believe I can. But remember my dear, it may be a dangerous game you will be playing.'

'I will let him know that I have no intention of being his mistress. Then perhaps he will go away.'

As she came into the hall he ran towards her. He took her hand and kissed it with fervour.

'My lord,' she said coolly. 'So you have returned to hunt here. I believe there are especially good bucks in Whittlebury.'

He laughed aloud and would have drawn her to him but with an imperious gesture she held him off.

'I know not how fine the bucks in Whittlebury may be but I do know this: the fairest lady in the land lives here at Grafton.'

She inclined her head, again with a regal gesture.

'Your friends are close by?' she asked.

'Let us not talk of them. I have come to see you. I want to talk of us . . . Elizabeth.'

'What could there be to say of the King and his humble subject?'

'I am the King it is true, but you humble . . . not you, Elizabeth! You are beautiful and well you know it and one with beauty such as yours could never be a *humble* subject. My dear lady, ever since I saw you under the oak-tree I have thought of nothing but you. I want to put my arms about you and tell you of the devotion you have inspired in me. I want us to be together. I am full deep in love with you.'

'My lord, I do not see how that can be when you scarce know me.'

'I know you well enough to know my feelings. Come, let me show you. Tonight we will rest here in your parents' home and tomorrow you and I will go away together. You will join me. You shall have apartments of course. Ask anything and it shall be yours.'

She opened her eyes very wide and regarded him with a display of astonishment.

'My lord, I do not understand your meaning.'

'Have I not made myself clear? Have I not told you in a hundred ways that I love you?'

'Then I am sorry,' she answered. 'For naught can come of

that in view of our different stations. You must go from here, my lord . . .'

'Indeed I will not. I will not be cheated as I was last time I was here.'

'Cheated, my lord?' She retreated from him and opened her eyes very wide with reproach.

'In what way, I beg you tell me, were you cheated?'

'I came to your room. You were not there. I did not see you again.'

'My lord, I think you are mistaken in me.'

'No. You are the most desirable and beautiful woman I have ever met. There is no mistake about that.'

'Even here in the country we hear rumours of one so prominent as the King,' said Elizabeth coolly. 'I know your customs, my lord. You have a deep interest in my sex. But allow me to assure you that we are not all alike. There are some of us who have a respect for morality and I am one of them. I do not enter into light amours.'

'By God's blood, this would be no light amour. I swear to you that never in my life have I been so affected.'

'That is often the impression at early encounters, and if you do indeed feel strongly drawn towards me it could not be love you feel, since you do not know me. If you had, my lord, you would never have expected me to become your mistress on a first meeting.'

Edward saw a glimmer of hope. He had been too quick. Very well, he would be prepared to wait a little – but only a little – for such a prize.

Elizabeth realised what was in his mind.

She said quickly: 'My lord, you should go away from here. Pursue your light o' loves, if you must. I have been a virtuous wife to the noble Lord Grey of Groby. I am not of a nature to become any man's mistress.'

The words were ominous if taken seriously. Edward had heard them once before. He did not wish to recall that time when he had been guilty of a certain indiscretion which was best forgotten. He hardly ever thought of Eleanor Butler nowadays. She had gone into a convent . . . That matter was all over.

Now he was all impatience to become the lover of this woman.

'Moreover,' she went on, 'I am several years older than you are.'

'That is impossible.'

'Yes,' she said. 'I am five years your senior. I am the mother of two boys.'

'I find these matters no obstacle to my devotion to you.'

'My lord, do you not understand? My mother is of the House of Luxembourg. She has brought her children up to respect their honour and their virtue. My father is a baron, but he was not born to high station. My mother married him for love, but she married him, my lord. I beg you, put all thought of me from your head. I am not for you by nature of my upbringing and my convictions. Never will I become your mistress and no other relationship is possible between us.'

'I will not accept this,' he cried.

'I fear you must; I shall forever remember you with gratitude. You have restored my estates and for that I give you my heartfelt thanks. Alas, my lord, it is all that I can give you. And now may I have your leave to retire.'

He caught her hand as she rose but she withdrew it gently.

'Goodbye, my lord. It is the only way.'

He sat staring after her as she went. Wild thoughts crowded into his mind. He could abduct her, force her . . . Some of his acquaintances indulged in adventures like that. He never had. He had always jeered at them, explaining, 'My friends, I have never yet had to force a woman.'

And Elizabeth Grey of all women. There was something aloof about her. She was cool. She did not respond as most women did, and yet at the same time she liked him. He was sure of that. There was a note of tenderness in her voice when she spoke of her dead husband. She had clearly been fond of him. She was a good mother, it seemed, to her boys; he had sensed that when he saw them together under the oak-tree. In fact the boys had added a little to the charm of the picture which was engraved on his mind and which he felt he would never forget.

It was maddening that she had these ridiculous notions of morality – although he admired them in a way. She was no light of love, that was clear enough. She had looked like a queen when she had drawn herself to her full height and stood there facing him.

He would have to go away and forget her.

It was hard to do that. It was the first time he had ever been refused. Oh no . . . not quite the first. There had been Eleanor Butler. In a way this Elizabeth reminded him of her. That was why the Butler affair had been brought to his mind for the first time in several years.

Jacquetta came into the hall.

'My lord, you are alone. What happened to my daughter? She cannot have left you thus . . .'

'Alas, she has wounded me deeply.'

Jacquetta looked alarmed. 'Unwittingly I promise you,' she said.

'No, with intention.' He looked at Jacquetta. A beauty herself, with quick warm eyes and understanding of human needs. There was about her an easy friendliness, the right amount of deference for a King and yet the implication that she herself was royal. She could feel completely at ease with him as he could with her.

'Ah, you have been making suggestions to her.'

'You have guessed.'

'It did not need the powers of witchcraft to do that.'

He looked at her sharply. He had heard it whispered that Lady Rivers, who had been Duchess of Bedford, was some sort of sorceress. Was it true? he wondered. Many people were accused of that quite unreasonably.

'My lady, are you mistress of such powers?' he asked.

'Nay, nay. I am just a wise woman – at least I think I am.'

'I believe I would quickly share that view. So you know your daughter has refused me and made me utterly desolate.'

'Oh my lord, you must not despair.'

He looked at her hopefully. She said quickly: 'My daughter Elizabeth would never be any man's mistress. I know that well. You must go and never let your hunting bring you near her again. There are many other forests in which to exercise your talents.'

He looked at her, liking her more each moment, and laughed. 'Oh I do not give up as easily as that,' he said.

'Nor does Elizabeth,' She leaned towards him confidentially. 'She was the most strong-willed of my brood. Did you know that I had seven girls and seven boys? We are great breeders, you see. Ah, what a joy is a family. But it brings its sorrows. But knowing them, having them there in one's life . . . though they are scattered far and wide, that is a boon from

44

heaven, as you will find, my lord, when you marry and settle down.'

'I want your daughter,' he said.

She signed. 'I know it well. She is beautiful . . . incomparably so. But perhaps I, as her mother, see her through loving eyes. I tell you this, my lord, she will never give in. For your own peace of mind leave her. To pursue her will mean nothing but frustration and disappointment. You are handsome, you are royal, and there are few women who would resist you. But Elizabeth is one of them. My dear lord, I feel as a mother to you. You have come here, and graced my home. I shall feel it honoured evermore. We were Lancastrians . . . we shall be so no more. I shall not rest until my husband and every son of mine tears the red rose from his coat and his heart. From now on, the Rivers are for you, my lord. We shall stand for your cause. We shall be your good servants if you will allow us to be for I have in these few days seen a man who is indeed a king and the only one living in this realm whom I would accept as mine. My husband is away at this time. When he returns I will ask him to come to you. Will you receive him? He is a man who will be faithful to you if you will forget he once served Henry of Lancaster. He believed him to be the true King. You understand that, my lord?'

'Indeed I understand. He was faithful to what he believed right. I respect that in men. Fidelity is what I look for in those around me.'

'When I have talked to my husband, when I tell him what I have seen this day, I know he will understand. England needs a strong king and you are that, my lord. I promise you that the Rivers will serve you well.'

Edward kissed her hand. She was an unusual woman. He

was drawn to her, partly for herself and partly because she was Elizabeth's mother. And she was his friend. Somewhere in his mind was the thought that she would help him if she could.

She was implanting that thought there, trying to draw him into the family, visualising a glorious prospect for Elizabeth without giving him a glimmer of what it was . . . in fact, she scarcely admitted it to herself, because it seemed impossible.

'We shall serve you,' she said. 'Elizabeth will be your faithful subject but never never anything else.'

'My lady, I believe you to be my friend. You will make my cause yours.'

'The King's cause shall be mine,' she answered solemnly. 'Bless you, my bonny lord. I shall wish for you everything that will serve you best.'

He rode somewhat disconsolately away from Grafton. He was beginning to believe that Elizabeth meant what she said. She was a virtuous woman. She would not take a lover outside marriage.

Marriage! But he was the King. That was impossible.

Edward was so quiet in the days that followed his visit to Grafton that his friend Hastings was quite concerned for him.

He enquired how the King had fared with the beautiful widow lady.

Edward shook his head.

'She was a disappointment,' said Hastings. 'I thought she might be. There was a frigidity in her. A plague on frigid women.'

Edward was not pleased to hear Elizabeth discussed lightly as though she were the participant in some ordinary brief affair.

He said shortly: 'She is the most beautiful woman I ever saw.'

'Oh, I grant you that. But I personally have no fancy for statues.'

'It would avail you nothing if you had,' said Edward shortly.

'Do you mean to tell me that it did not come to fruition?'

'Lady Grey is a virtuous widow.'

'A plague on virtuous women . . . widows especially.'

'I have no wish to discuss the Lady Elizabeth Grey with you, Hastings.'

God in Heaven, thought Hastings, what has come over him? The lady refused him. It must be the first time that has happened. Well, it will do him no harm. But it has affected him considerably.

He did not mention the visit to Grafton Manor after that.

At Westminster the Earl of Warwick was impatiently waiting. Edward always felt a slight deference in the presence of Warwick, who was known by the soubriquet of Kingmaker. Everyone was aware, and Edward would be the first to admit it, that but for Warwick's prompt action in marching on London after the Yorkist defeat in the second battle of St Albans Edward might not be king today. Warwick was not going to let anyone forget it. Nor did Edward want to. He was grateful for his friends and Warwick had been his hero from childhood. Ever since his early days in Rouen where he and his brother Edmund had been born he had known he was destined for greatness. His mother Cecily Neville had made him aware of that; and Warwick's father was her brother, so there was a bond of kinship between him and the great Earl, and Warwick had always been part of his youth. Warwick was fourteen years older than Edward and had seemed almost godlike to the boy.

If Edward had the bearing of a king, Warwick had an even more powerful image. Kings were glorious but they depended on kingmakers and Warwick fitted without doubt into the second category.

Warwick spoke with authority. Ever since the first battle of St Albans which had been won by his strategy he had been distinguished throughout the country; and when he had become Captain of Calais and had held that important port for England and the Yorkists, he had won the hearts of the English by his exploits against the French; he had seized their goods and played the part of pirate-buccaneer with such verve that he was accepted as a great hero, one of that company of men of which England was in need since the disastrous losses in France.

The Earl had never been one of Edward's boon companions such as Hastings and men of that kind. It was a serious relation-ship between them. Warwick did not frown on Edward's adventures. They had kept the young man occupied while Warwick ruled. That was all very well when Edward was in his teens, but he was now twenty-three years of age and Warwick had plans.

They embraced when they met and Edward's affection for his cousin was obvious.

'You are looking pleased with yourself, Richard,' he said. 'What have you been doing? Come, tell me. I know you are longing to.'

'I am as you notice rather pleased with my negotiations at the French Court. We must have peace with France and, Edward, you must marry. The people expect it. They love you. You look like a king. They smile at your pursuit of women. They expect a young king to have his romantic adventures. Not too many though, and they want a marriage. The people want it, the country wants it . . . and that is a good enough reason. What say you?'

'Well, I am not averse.'

Warwick looked at the King with affection. He had made him and he would keep him on the throne. Edward was amenable. He was the perfect puppet; and while this state of affairs remained Warwick could rule without hindrance. It was what he had always wanted. Not for him the heavy crown of office; how much more comfortable to rule behind the throne, to be the Kingmaker rather than the King. And Edward was the perfect tool. His easy-going, pleasure-loving nature made him that.

'Then let us get to business. Do you realise you are one of the most eligible bachelors in the world? Not only are you King of England but the whole world knows that in addition to your crown you have an outstanding charm of person.'

'You flatter me, Richard.'

'Never will I do that. But let us face facts. I have become on excellent terms with Louis. I can tell you he treats me as though I were a king.'

'Which you are in a way, Richard,' said Edward.

Warwick looked at him sharply. Was there something behind that remark? Was Edward growing up, resenting someone else's use of the power that was his? No, Edward was smiling his affable, good-natured smile. He was merely reminding Warwick of his power and implying that he felt it was right and proper that it should be his.

'I have decided against Isabella of Castile. Her brother is eager for the match. He is impotent, poor fellow and it is certain that there will be no children, so Isabella would be the heiress of Castile.'

'But you have decided against her.'

'I think, Edward, we have a better proposition. My eyes are set on France.'

'Ah yes, you are on such good terms with Louis.'

'We must have peace with France. The best way of making peace is through alliances as you well know. So I turn away from Isabella, and back to France. Louis suggests his wife's sister, Bona of Savoy. She is a beautiful woman and one who will delight you, Edward. Louis and I agreed that we must not lose sight of the fact that you must have an attractive wife. You are very well experienced in that direction and we want you to be happy.'

'You are most considerate,' said Edward.

'She is a very beautiful girl and it will be a successful match. The great thing is heirs. We must have an heir to the throne. The people are always uneasy until they can see their next king growing up ready to take his popular father's place.'

Edward was scarcely listening. He was thinking of Elizabeth. What a wonderful project it would have been if *she* had been a Princess of France or Savoy or Castile! How joyously he would have contemplated his marriage then, for of course he must marry. Of course he must produce an heir.

If only it could be with Elizabeth!

'I see no reason why we should not complete these arrangements with Louis immediately,' Warwick was saying but Edward scarcely heard him for his thoughts were far away in Grafton Manor.

One of his squires came into Edward's chamber to tell him that there was a man who was asking for an audience.

'And who is this?'

'My lord,' said the squire, 'he is a Lancastrian, a traitor who had fought for Henry of Lancaster.'

'Why does he come here?'

'He says he has something of importance to say to you.'

'Ask his name.'

The squire disappeared and came back almost immediately. 'It is Lord Rivers, my lord.'

'Ah,' said Edward, 'I will see him at once.'

The squire replied: 'My lord, I will see that the guards are within call.'

'I do not think you need to go to such lengths.'

The squire bowed, determined to in spite of the King. He was not going to put Edward in any more danger than could be helped.

He hesitated.

'I have asked you to bring Lord Rivers to me at once,' Edward reminded him.

'My lord, forgive me, but should there not be guards in this very chamber?'

'No. I do not think Lord Rivers has come here to harm me.'

At length Lord Rivers was brought in. Undoubtedly he was handsome. Edward had been learning something about the family since the encounter under the oak. So this was the man for whom that rather enchanting Jacquetta had defied convention and given him fourteen children to boot, and among them the delectable Elizabeth.

'Well, my lord,' said Edward. 'You wished to speak with me?'

'I have come to offer you my allegiance.'

'Odd words for one who has supported the cause of my enemies for so many years.'

'Times have changed, my lord. I was for Henry because he was the anointed king. I do not change sides easily. But Henry is little more than an imbecile; he is far away somewhere in the North in hiding, but if he returned he could never give England the rule she needs. And now we have a king who has more claim to the throne than Henry had. I shall work now to keep us in this happy state.'

'What has brought this change of heart?' asked Edward. 'Tell me, I am interested to know.'

'I have been to my home at Grafton Manor and talked with my wife. You may know that she was the Duchess of Bedford before our marriage. She is astute, and has an understanding of affairs. She tells me that she had the great honour of entertaining you briefly and she was so convinced that you were our rightful lord and monarch that she wished us to change our allegiance without delay.'

Edward was smiling. 'I did have the good fortune to hunt near your place and I met both your wife and your daughter and her sons. Did your daughter agree with her mother that you should cease to be Lancastrian supporters and turn to York?'

'My daughter gave no opinion, my lord. I discussed the matter only with my wife.'

'I see. Well, Rivers, you shall take a goblet with me and we will drink to your future alliance. I am always ready to offer friendship where it is given in the right spirit.'

'You honour me, my lord.'

'I respect your courage in coming here. And I liked your wife . . . and your daughter.'

Wine was brought and as he drank Edward was thinking of Elizabeth. He could not forget her face. He had believed he would ride away and take up with some woman and in a brief time forget the aloof Elizabeth. But it was not so. She had spoiled things for him, and his desire for her showed no signs of diminishing. Rather did it increase.

Edward enjoyed talking to Lord Rivers. It gave him a certain comfort to be with someone who was close to her. Lord Rivers was astonished by the King's interest in his family. Jacquetta had mentioned nothing of Edward's passion for Elizabeth for she knew that would have alarmed him. He would have had no wish for their daughter to become one of the King's mistresses. They enjoyed too short a reign and Edward's reputation with women was such that no woman who valued her good name should be involved with him. She would immediately be classed with the army of merchants' wives who had pandered to the King's lust, and satisfied him temporarily until he passed on to the next.

Jacquetta had told her husband that the King had called briefly and she had seen that their adherence to Lancaster was a mistake. Edward had obviously come to stay on the throne and Henry was quite unfit to rule, and she believed that, for the good of the family, they should turn from a cause which was dead in any case and offer their services to the crowned and reigning King. She had in due course convinced him as she invariably did.

So he had called not expecting this warm welcome and he was really astounded when Edward wanted to know much about the intimate details of his family life.

Edward asked about his marriage with Jacquetta.

'A bold action to take,' said Edward. 'I'll swear her family were planning some grand marriage for her.'

'They were indeed, but Jacquetta had made up her mind and in the family we have all learned that once that happens, there is no gainsaying her. Jacquetta is a wonderful woman, my lord.'

'I gathered that in our brief acquaintance. And you were happy in this marriage?'

'My lord I have never regretted it for one moment. We have a fine family of beautiful children.'

'I have seen your eldest daughter. Her beauty is remarkable.' The King spoke with an emotion which Rivers did not notice.

'There are Anthony, John, Lionel and Edward, my sons who have survived. Then there are my daughters, Elizabeth whom you have met, Margaret, Anne, Jacquetta, Mary, Catherine . . .'

'You indeed have a goodly brood and a handsome wife into the bargain.'

'My lord, I have been a very happy man and most singularly blessed when Jacquetta came into my life. We risked a great deal to marry and I never cease to thank God that we did.'

'Boldness often pays in life. So I have found and I am glad to welcome you to our side, Lord Rivers. I trust I may see you often. I liked your place at Grafton. When I am hunting that way . . . for there are fine deer at Whittlebury, I will call on your family.'

'My lord, you overwhelm us.'

When Lord Rivers took his leave of the King he was quite bewildered. He had expected to be called on to prove his loyalty before he was admitted to such a favour. He had heard that Edward was an easy-going man, not in the least vindictive. But such a reception was strange indeed.

The King's friendship with Lord Rivers was noticed, and not without a little rancour. He seemed to have taken more to this man who had fought against him in several battles than he did to his friends.

Warwick said: 'What is this intimacy with Rivers? I should hardly have thought he qualified for such favour.'

'Oh, he is a pleasant fellow,' replied Edward. 'I like his company.'

'And his son's too, it seems.'

'Lord Scales.'

'Is that what he calls himself now?'

'He is Lord Scales, Richard. He married Sir Henry Bourchier's widow and got the title of Scales through her.'

'You seem to have made rapid friendship with them. I never thought much of the Woodvilles.'

'Did you not?' said Edward coolly.

'No. It is not so long ago that we made them look silly . . . very silly indeed, Rivers and his son Anthony. It was Dynham, you remember him?'

'I have heard something of this exploit. It was well talked of, I believe. You saw to that.'

'They were the enemy. Stationed at Sandwich preparing a fleet for Somerset to come and drive me out of Calais. Dynham landed at Sandwich and caught the pair of them in their beds. He brought them over to me . . . just as they were.'

'Had they not been in their beds it might not have been so easy to surprise them. It does not need a great deal of valour to surprise a man asleep and unprotected.'

Warwick was quite unaware of the asperity in the King's tones.

'I let them know how I scorned them when they arrived in

Paris. Low-born traitors I called them. Rivers's father was just a squire . . . Henry the Fifth knighted him on the field of battle so I think. They gave themselves airs I told them and they should be careful how they conducted themselves in the presence of their betters.'

'There are many,' said Edward pointedly, 'who attain their honours through brilliant marriages, or some such turn of fortune. Perhaps one should not probe too much into how people rise. Suffice it that they have the wisdom or the bravery to do so.'

This was a direct hit at Warwick who had acquired the noble title of Earl of Warwick and vast lands through his marriage with Anne Beauchamp, Warwick's heir. But Warwick did not see this. He had determined to warn Edward against showing too much favour to the Woodvilles and he had given that warning as he had on so many other occasions when he thought the King's conduct was not quite what it should be.

Warwick was becoming overbearing, thought Edward. Indeed, one would think I were a child instead of the King.

'You'll be pleased to know,' Warwick was going on, 'that negotiations with Louis are going on apace. He's delighted about Bona of Savoy. We shall soon be able to make an announcement.'

But Edward was not listening.

It was impossible to stay away. He had to be there again. He could find no delight in any other woman. He had made several attempts. They all ended in failure.

He would go hunting, he said, in Whittlebury Forest. He

had found the game there as good as anywhere in England. Hastings said that he could remember nothing special about it and had thought their efforts had been even less rewarding than usual.

Edward looked sharply at his friend. He was not amused.

Heaven help us, thought Hastings, he is taking the widow very seriously indeed.

Usually Edward liked to laugh and was prepared to do so, within reason, against himself. Now, he was very definitely not amused.

Caution, Hastings warned himself.

Of course he left the party and Hastings knew well enough not to try to follow him. Let him go alone to Grafton and call on the reluctant lady.

Edward felt frustrated and wretched to discover that Elizabeth was not at Grafton. She had gone to Bradgate. Lord Rivers was also absent. But Jacquetta was there. She received him with a great warmth and declared that she was honoured indeed.

'Elizabeth went off to Bradgate with such joy,' she told him. 'She lived there with her husband, you know. Both the boys were born there. She says she could never be grateful enough to you for your goodness in restoring her estates.'

'She did not seem to be over grateful.'

'Oh, my dear lord, you mean because she would not be your mistress. It is quite impossible for a lady of her upbringing. You are not still thinking of her in that respect, are you?'

'I shall never cease to think of her.'

'You must. It is the only way. I daresay she may marry again in due course. She will marry for love, I do believe. There is no other reason why she need now that you have been so good to her.'

'Do you really think she had some regard for me?'

'Some regard! My lord, she thought very highly of you. She admitted to me that she had never seen a man so handsome, so kingly . . . so much to be admired save in one respect.'

'And that respect?'

'In making suggestions to her which she considers immoral, you hurt her a little.'

'*I* hurt her! I would rather lose my crown than hurt her.'

'Do not speak of losing your crown. That is unlucky talk. Let us talk sensibly as people such as we are can do. The fact is, my lord, you are the King. When you marry it must be a royal Princess and you must take her because my lord Warwick will choose her for you and it will be for the good of the country.'

'Why should my lord Warwick choose my bride?'

'Because my lord Warwick makes all the decisions for the good of the country, does he not? And he would consider the marriage of the King a matter of the greatest importance to the country and one which only he could decide.'

Edward was staring blankly ahead of him. There was a certain twist to his mouth which was not lost to Jacquetta. She laid a hand on his knee and then withdrew it with an apology.

'Forgive me. I forget my place. I have grown so fond of you. I am beginning to look upon you as a son . . .'

She turned away and then stood up. There was a faint pinkish colour in her face.

'My lord,' she floundered, 'I think you must excuse me . . . I am overcome by the honour you do us. I . . .'

'Pray sit down. Your affection moves me. Do not apologise for it.'

She smiled at him. 'Then I will be frank. You must not try to see Elizabeth again. She is my daughter and you know I am of the royal House of Luxembourg. I have brought her up to have a great regard for herself. I married as they said beneath my station. I did not consider it so. I married one who was the best husband in the world to me. But in doing so I lost my standing. I was no longer considered royal. And that is the plain fact. Elizabeth will never be your mistress and you could never make her your wife . . . which is the only way that you could be together. It is a cruel hard fact, my dear. Listen to an old woman whom you yourself have called wise. Go away from here. Make the marriage Warwick will arrange for you and try to be happy. I know you will find it very hard to forget Elizabeth. But it cannot be, my dear dear lord. The only thing that could make her yours is that which you, in view of your position, cannot give her. There, I have said it and now I am overwrought. I have spoken too clearly. I have forgotten to whom I speak. I pray you forgive me. Give me leave to go and you, my lord, must join your friends. It is better for us all if you never come here again . . .'

With that she rose and kneeling before him kissed his hand. Then she left him.

She went to her bedchamber and from her window watched him ride away.

I wonder, she thought. Is it possible? No, Warwick will never allow it. But if it did come to pass, what great good fortune their beautiful Elizabeth could bring to the Woodvilles!

❁ Chapter II ❁

THE SECRET MARRIAGE

There was an air of suppressed excitement in the household of the Duchess of York. The King was coming. He had promised his family that he would be with them for a while and he was always one to keep his promises. Cecily, the Duchess, now mother of the King, was said to be the proudest woman in England. She would naturally have been happier if her husband had lived and taken the crown, but that Edward should have it was the next best thing of course. Cecily's greatest ambition had been to become Queen and when she thought how narrowly she had missed it she was filled with regrets.

But now she revelled in her new state. She would never forget that there was royal blood in her veins for her mother had been Joan Beaufort, daughter of John of Gaunt and Catherine Swynford. It had seemed only right that her husband should take the throne, descended as he was from two branches of the royal family, and it had been a great tragedy when he had died at Wakefield. She could not bear to think of that day when she had heard that they had stuck his head on the walls of York with a paper crown perched on it. Ah, it was different now; and their son, their beautiful Edward, was King.

Handsome Edward had always been her favourite. He had always been a big boy and now growing to his full height he towered above all those about him. He had not taken after his father who had been dark and rather short in stature. Edward was the golden Plantagenet born again. It was wonderful to contemplate that he took after his ancestors the sons of Edward III, Lionel and John of Gaunt. Edward was the perfect Plantagenet. He was a popular king. He looked like a king; and while he had good advisers like her nephew the Earl of Warwick he would act wisely and well.

She was proud of her son. It had turned out well for the family — if only Richard had not been so foolish at Wakefield in taking an unnecessary risk. He would not have done that if she had been there. But he had lost a battle and his life and deprived her of the title of Queen. But her glorious son had taken that honour and she lived now with the state of a queen even if she had failed to win the title. Everyone must treat her with the ultimate respect. Her women must kneel to her; they must behave in every way in which they would had she been a queen in name.

She knew that behind her back they called her Proud Cis. Let them. She *was* proud. Proud of herself and her family and most of all proud of her beautiful son who was the King.

She had three of the children with her in London now and it was rarely that they were together. There was Margaret who was eighteen. They would find a husband for her soon, and that should not be difficult as she was the sister of the King; George was also with them; he was fifteen, her least favourite among her sons. George was inclined to be plump, self-indulgent and somewhat arrogant but she had to admit he had his share of the Plantagenet good looks; he was fairish and tall of stature but not as tall as Edward of course. Next to Edward her favourite was young Richard. Richard was quieter than his brothers, a serious boy given to learning. He was shortish and dark, taking after his father in looks. He lacked that gaiety which was a characteristic of Edward and George; he lacked their impulsive ways. He was serious, thoughtful and she had always believed cleverer than the others. He would always hesitate before giving an answer and one felt he wanted to weigh all points of view before speaking.

Sometimes she was a little worried about Richard. His frame was delicate and now that he was growing – he was twelve years old – it seemed to her that one shoulder was a little higher than the other – almost imperceptible but detected by a maternal eye. She had spoken to Warwick about it for she feared that at Middleham Richard might be set strenuous martial exercises which were too much for him.

Like all boys of noble houses Richard had been sent into another noble house to be brought up and Edward had thought Warwick's castle of Middleham was the right place for Richard. Edward doted on Warwick. No wonder. It was Warwick who had made him King. So to Middleham to be brought up in Warwick's household Richard had been sent. Warwick himself would almost always be away somewhere, but he would have laid down the rules of conduct for the noble boys who came into his castle. Cecily was glad that the Countess of Warwick was there for she was a gentle lady. It was strange to think that through her Warwick had received his wealth and titles. Richard was very fond of the Countess as he was of Warwick's two daughters Isabel and Anne. So perhaps she should not worry too much about Richard's health. When she had mentioned it to Edward he had laughed at her.

'Richard has to grow up as a man, dear lady,' he said. 'And I can tell you there is none more qualified to bring out the best in him than my cousin Warwick.'

Even when Edward spoke his name she could hear the reverence in it. She was glad he felt like that. She, too, had the utmost faith in Warwick, for Edward, she was fully aware, much as she loved him, was too fond of pleasure. This continual pursuit of women was all very well while he was so young but when he married he would have to give it up, or conduct his adventures more discreetly.

Perhaps she should have a word with him about that. He would be a little impatient, but he would never silence his mother of course. He was too well mannered to do that.

Margaret, George and Richard were awaiting the King's arrival with great excitement. Richard was thinking: As soon as I hear the horses I shall be down there to greet him. I will stand and wait and perhaps he will notice me.

Richard adored Edward. From the time he was a child this great and glorious brother had been like a god to him. He had followed his adventures avidly. When Edward was defeated Richard was sunk in melancholy; when Edward was victorious none rejoiced more than he.

'You are besotted about our brother,' George had said contemptuously.

'Our brother is the King,' Richard had replied with dignity.

George had shrugged his shoulders. It was only an accident of birth. If he had been the eldest he would have been King. He would have been the one everyone came out to cheer and all the women beckoned into their beds. Life was rather unfair, he thought. It could so easily have been George.

Margaret also admired Edward. He was always good-natured and made everyone feel slightly more important than they were. Perhaps that was the secret of his charm. It might be, but even if he did not mean it it was pleasant to pretend for a while that he did.

Soon he would find a husband for her. It was inevitable really now that he was King. Her two elder sisters Anne and Elizabeth were already married; Anne to Henry Holland Duke of Exeter and Elizabeth to John de la Pole the Duke of Suffolk. Yes, it would certainly be her turn next and now that Edward was King – her sisters had been married before that happy event – hers might well be a very grand marriage indeed.

But what they were all discussing now was the King's marriage. Her mother had told her that the bride would very likely be Bona of Savoy, sister to the King of France. It would be a very grand wedding of course and after that there would be the new Queen's coronation.

It was hardly likely that there would be time to give any consideration to the marriage of the King's sister just yet. So there would be some respite.

And soon Edward would be here. Margaret smiled, wondering how her mother would act with the King. She would hardly expect him to kneel to her, as they all had to do.

Dear mother, so ambitious for them all. . . and for herself!

The time had come. The King was arriving. Richard hurried out to meet the party. If he were quick enough he would avoid his mother who would want to insist on some sort of ceremony.

To see him again, this wonderful brother who had dominated his life! It had been hard to be sent to Middleham and to

64

be so far from him and to hear of what he was doing from other people. He would have been really unhappy at Middleham if it had not been for the kindly Countess and her daughters, particularly Anne. There had been a very special friendship between them. They were of a kind – both a little shy of the world, unable to mingle freely with people and express themselves easily. But when they were together that was different. Oh yes, he had been very grateful to Anne and she to him, he believed.

His had been a childhood of uncertainty. He had been born just at that time when civil war between the houses of York and Lancaster was brewing. He had heard talk of the red and white roses and he knew that the white roses were worn by the good people and the red by the bad.

He remembered very well the terror of Ludlow when his father had had to fly because the Lancastrians were at the gates of the castle. He remembered his proud mother holding him close to her on one side with George on the other while the soldiers burst into the castle. There was death in the air then and young as he was he sensed it. But his mother was proud and noble and he had believed after that invincible; for when they burst into the room and she stood there with her sons held close to her and spoke to the soldiers in those commanding tones of hers, they hesitated. He noticed that there was blood on their swords . . . and he saw it too on the men's jerkins. But they did not harm them. Instead they were taken away and put in the charge of his aunt the Duchess of Buckingham, who strangely enough was not on the same side as they were.

Then of course there was the battle of Northampton and they were free again; they were brought to London and lodged in John Paston's house. It must have been less than six months that they were there but Richard remembered vividly the terrible dark day when news came that a battle had been fought in Wakefield and during it his father had been killed.

His mother's grief had been terrible. She vowed vengeance on their enemies. Richard was not told that his father's head had been stuck on the walls of York with a paper crown on it, but he heard it whispered by the attendants and servants and he was very good at picking up whispers.

But their mother recovered a little after the second battle of St Albans which oddly enough was won by the bad Lancastrians, but Warwick – the great Earl who had decided how he should be brought up at Middleham – marched to London, took it and proclaimed Edward King.

Then their fortunes had indeed changed. Richard would never forget the coronation – a grand occasion when a nine-year-old boy – which was what he was then – was so honoured by his mighty brother that he was made the Duke of Gloucester. George had become Duke of Clarence at the same time.

'Now you are Dukes,' said their mother, 'and that means you have a great responsibility to yourselves and the family and most of all to your brother. Never forget that your brother is the King and you must serve him with your lives if necessary.'

Richard wanted to say that he would have been ready to serve Edward with his life even without a dukedom, but he did not. One was careful what one said to Dame Cecily.

And then to Middleham Castle to learn to be a great fighter so that he would be ready if there was need to defend the crown. To spend long hours carrying arms which were too heavy for him and made his shoulders hurt and then to creep into the castle and lie down on his bed to rest making sure that none – except Anne – knew that he needed to rest.

Now the King had come. How magnificent he was – even taller than Richard remembered him. His mother was there first. She was about to kneel, for as she insisted on deference to her she was ready to pay it where she considered it due. But Edward would have none of that. He seized her in his arms and kissed her on both cheeks.

'My lord . . . my lord . . .' she murmured in protest.

But all those watching loved him for his easy manners.

Cecily was pale pink with pleasure at the sight of him. He looked more handsome every time she saw him after an absence. Oh she was proud of him. They all were.

'Margaret, sister . . .'

He embraced her and then his eyes were on his brothers and Richard noticed with a thrill of delight that they rested on him.

'Richard . . . George . . .'

Richard's eyes were full of devotion which was not lost on Edward. George's were a little clouded. Edward understood that there was a streak of envy there. He made a mental note. He might have to watch George.

'Richard . . . how are you, boy?' He had his hand on his shoulder. Richard felt uneasy. Was it noticeable then? It clearly was when he was without his cloak.

'Growing up,' said Edward. 'By God, you are almost men.'

And when he went into the palace he kept his hand on Richard's shoulder.

Cecily was longing to talk alone with her son. She wanted to know how far the negotiations for the marriage had gone. She would need to know well in advance of the ceremony. There would be a great deal to plan and she intended to have a very firm hand in that planning.

She noticed his profligate friends in attendance, Hastings

among them. There was one other she saw. She had a vague idea that it was Lord Rivers, the man whom Edward was favouring, so she had heard. She had her friends everywhere who brought her news of Edward. This friendship with Rivers and his son Scales was most strange. It was not long ago that they had been fighting the House of York. They had been staunch Lancastrians. Why, he'll be making a friend of Margaret of Anjou next, she thought. It was rather foolish with Henry of Lancaster, the man whom some people believed was the real king, wandering about somewhere in hiding in the North. How could Edward know that Rivers and his son were not traitors?

She would have a word with him about that.

She sought the first opportunity. She went to his bed-chamber and imperiously dismissed those who were in attendance.

'Edward, we must talk alone.'

'Indeed we must,' said Edward, who had no wish to listen to her probing questions but would not have dreamed of telling her so.

'I am a bit uneasy.'

'Dear Mother, when have you not been?'

'The times are not so easy that we can allow ourselves to shut our eyes to danger.'

'As usual you speak with wisdom.'

'What of these men . . . this Rivers and this Scales?'

'Good men, both of them.'

'Good men, who fought for the red rose!'

Edward put his hands on her shoulders and smiled down at her. His towering height gave him the advantage he felt he needed when dealing with his strong-minded mother.

'They are good men, my lady. I like them. I trust them.'

'Why should you do that? How long is it since they were our enemies?'

'They supported Henry because they had taken vows to do so. Henry was anointed and crowned King. They realise now that he is unfit to rule so they have given their allegiance to me.'

'*I* would not trust them.'

'You do not have to,' said Edward with dignity. 'As long as I do that is all that is necessary.'

This was a new Edward, smiling affectionately as he spoke but with a firmness in his voice.

Cecily decided to drop the subject and turn to that of his marriage.

'Warwick is on excellent terms with the French King, I hear.'

'Warwick has told you that?'

'My dear Edward, Warwick does not talk to me. But I hear these things. I know that arrangements are very far advanced for the wedding.'

'Wedding? What wedding?'

She stared at him in astonishment. 'Whose wedding would be of such importance . . . but yours.'

'Oh, mine . . .' said Edward with an attempt at vagueness.

'The sister of the King of France. That is fair enough. I believe Bona of Savoy is an attractive woman.'

'That may be,' said Edward.

'After the wedding it will be necessary for you to be more discreet. No one expects a man such as you to be faithful . . . but all this open adultery will have to stop.'

Edward remained silent. She did not notice that his expression had hardened.

She went on: 'The people laugh at your adventures. They like to think of you as the charming libertine. "Our wives are not safe," say the merchants, "when the King passes by." And they say it with a laugh, glad I suppose that you consider these women worth seducing. But it will have to change.'

'It will change,' he said. Then suddenly he said: 'My lady, I am of a mind to choose my own bride. Why should Warwick decide for me?'

'Warwick is negotiating as he knows so well how to. We can be sure that he will get the best possible terms from Louis.'

'I shall not marry Bona of Savoy,' said Edward.

'What! After it has gone so far? Is there someone else Warwick considers will bring more good to the country?'

'I have chosen my bride myself, and I shall marry her if it pleases me to do so.'

'You must tell me,' said Cecily.

'Why not,' replied Edward. 'She is Lady Grey, daughter of Lord Rivers.'

Cecily was speechless and Edward went on: 'She is a widow with two sons; she is a few years older than I. I love her dearly. She is the only woman I will marry and I am going to do so without delay.'

'Edward, you like to joke.'

'Yes,' he agreed, 'I like to joke. But this is no joke. This is reality. I am going to marry Elizabeth Woodville.'

'Rivers' daughter you say. A woman of no rank!'

'Her mother is of the noble House of Luxembourg.'

'Who made a mesalliance! Her father is the son of a chamberlain to King Henry the Fifth.'

'You have discovered that. Why did you?'

'Because of your friendship with Rivers which I did not like at all and which I did not understand, but now I do. Of course you are joking. You have met this woman and you are attracted to her. Perhaps she is rather pleasant to look at.'

'She is the most beautiful woman I have ever seen.'

'They all are . . . for a night or two. I have seen you affected by the looks of some women many times. This is just another. A widow with two children!'

'By God's Blessed Lady, I am a bachelor and have some children too. Why cannot you see what a good sign this is? We have each given proof that neither of us is likely to be barren.'

'You joke,' insisted Cecily.

Edward was faintly alarmed. He had not meant to tell his mother but it had come out. Perhaps because he had made up his mind. But who knew what action Cecily would take? He had been rash to speak.

He did not answer and he saw the relief in her face.

She slapped his arm playfully.

'You always did like to tease your mother,' she said.

There was news from Warwick in the North. The Lancastrians were by no means beaten there and until they had made Henry their captive there would continue to be risings.

Warwick was with Lord Montague and the former thought Edward should join them.

Edward therefore took leave of his family and set out. Cecily watched him go with pride. She had stopped thinking about that strange conversation. His latest inamorata was this Elizabeth Woodville she supposed. There would be another before long. Strange that talk about marriage! But she suspected it was because she had said something about Warwick's choosing his wife for him. No man liked to have another do that and that was why Edward had made this ridiculous suggestion.

It was nothing more than that. Edward's position was too unsettled for him to take such risks.

'There he goes,' she said to her sons. 'Are you not proud to be his brothers?'

Richard declared with fervour that indeed he was, but George said nothing. He was wishing he was in Edward's shoes.

'There was never a man more fitted to be king,' said Cecily and Richard heartily agreed.

Edward rode out of London. He had made up his mind. He was going to do it. He could wait no longer for Elizabeth and if marriage was the only way, then marriage it must be.

He sent a messenger on to Grafton with the news that he wished specially to see Lady Rivers. He wished her to arrange everything. She would understand.

As soon as Jacquetta received the message she went to Elizabeth who fortunately was at Grafton, for it would have meant delay to have to send for her.

'He is going to marry you,' Jacquetta told her daughter.

'I can't believe that.'

'I tell you he is. He has sent to me commanding me to make the arrangements.'

'It will have to be a proper marriage.'

'Do you think I will not see to that! I never dreamed of such triumph. I hoped of course . . . but that he should really give way, that is hard to believe.'

'You don't think there is some trap in it?'

'Of course not. I shall not tell your father.'

'No, he would be alarmed.'

'Yes, he would see all sorts of trouble. As for ourselves, we will get the marriage celebrated and think of difficulties afterwards.'

'They will never accept me . . . men like Warwick . . .'

'My dear Elizabeth, you will have the King yours to command.'

'For how long?' asked Elizabeth cynically.

'For as long as you both live – if you act wisely.'

'There will be other women.'

'Of course there will be other women. Our stallion cannot be faithful to one mare. None but a fool would expect that. Let him have his women, Elizabeth. Understand his need for them, as long as you keep command of him and let none of the others do that. Think of what this is going to mean to the family.'

'I am afraid there will be some hitch.'

'I tell you there will be none. The ceremony will take place and then you will go to bed with him. You should get pregnant as soon as possible.'

'That is a matter over which I shall have no control.'

'You will give him many children. A good fine lusty son is what will set everything to rights. And when you have that the people will forgive you . . . if some of the mighty lords don't.'

'There is Warwick. What will he do?'

'As I see it Warwick's power is on the wane. This marriage will show others that as well as Warwick.'

'And do you think they will stand aside and give up their power?'

'They will have no alternative. We shall create new lords to stand by the King. They will be the ones who have the power.'

'New lords?'

'The Woodvilles, my dear daughter. We have a large

73

family. This marriage is going to bring good . . . not only to you but to us all.'

'I shall not believe it until it happens.'

'That will be very soon. Now I must make sure we are ready when he comes.'

It was the end of April. Never had the trees flowered more richly. The horsechestnut, the hornbeam, the alder and the birch with the wild cherry were bright with springtime blossom. The birds seemed to have gone wild with joy as though they knew this was a time for rejoicing.

So thought Edward as he left his company at Stony Stratford and rode over to Grafton where Jacquetta was waiting for him.

'All is ready?' asked Edward.

'My dear lord, I have forgotten nothing.'

'Where is Elizabeth?' he demanded.

'She is waiting for you.'

'Take me to her.'

There she was in a blue robe looking very much as she had under the oak in Whittlebury Park, her long hair falling about her shoulders.

Edward took her eagerly into his arms.

'My love,' he said, 'at last. It has been long waiting for this day.'

'My dear husband,' replied Elizabeth. 'I too have waited for this day.'

'Let us get on with the ceremony,' said Edward. 'There must be no more delay.'

Jacquetta was well prepared. She led him and Elizabeth to a chamber where a priest was waiting. There were also present two gentlewomen of Jacquetta's household and a young man who would sing with the priest.

The ceremony was performed and there at Grafton Manor, Elizabeth Woodville became the wife of Edward the Fourth.

As soon as the ceremony was over Jacquetta conducted the married pair to the bridal chamber which she had prepared.

Cursing because he must leave Grafton Edward rode back to Stony Stratford.

Hastings was astonished to find him so preoccupied.

'You have enjoyed good hunting, my lord,' he said. 'I see that.'

'Yes, Hastings, yes,' said Edward shortly and returned to his own chamber.

He was married. Elizabeth was his. There would be consequences but he did not care. It was worth it. It was the only way with a virtuous woman like Elizabeth. She was wonderful; she was beautiful; and he cared nothing for Warwick or any of them. He had said he would marry where he wanted to and he had.

The next day he said casually to Hastings: 'Before we move I shall send a message to Rivers and tell him I would like to stay a while at Grafton to enjoy some hunting in Whittlebury.'

'A pleasant spot,' replied Hastings and thought: So the Lady Elizabeth has been amenable after all. It must be the case. So many of them were reluctant at first. They thought it added to the pleasure of the chase.

And so to Grafton.

There Lord Rivers greeted him and there was an especial warmth in the greeting his lady gave to the King.

Elizabeth did not appear. I believe the virtuous lady is not at home, thought Hastings. In which case he probably does like the hunting. He seems on special terms with the lady Jacquetta but she is a little too mature to interest him I should have thought.

So discreet was Jacquetta that no one guessed that when they had retired she conducted the King to her daughter's bed-chamber.

'I pray she is pregnant before the storm breaks,' said Jacquetta to her husband. 'The people will at least be more lenient at the prospect of an heir.'

Her husband, less adventurous than his wife, was very alarmed by what they had done without consulting him.

But Jacquetta shook her head. 'You will see what good comes of it for the family,' she told him.

And so Edward spent four days at Grafton where he was conducted every night to Elizabeth's chamber.

It was with great reluctance that he tore himself away. It was necessary. Warwick was waiting for him in the North.

He would tell no one — not even Hastings. As yet the marriage should be a secret; and although it could not remain so for long, he must choose the right moment to make it known.

In the meantime he could think of Elizabeth, long for Elizabeth and take every opportunity of being with her.

He was deeply in love as he had never been before. He regretted nothing.

❀ Chapter III ❀

THE QUEEN'S REVENGE

Edward paused at Leicester where he received news of battles in the North.

'It will be necessary for us to gather together more men,' he said. 'We should tarry here awhile until we have a larger army. I should think that in a week or so we should be ready.'

Hastings was amused. Groby Castle was not very far – an hour or so's riding and of course Groby Castle was part of that estate which Edward had so nobly returned to the widow of his old enemy Lord Grey.

Hastings smiled inwardly. So the ice maiden *had* relented. She had melted before the warmth of kingly passion. He was not surprised. It had happened that way before. He would help his friend all he could in his adventuring.

So they rested awhile at Leicester while Edward enjoyed a clandestine honeymoon riding over to Groby every day and staying there until early morning of the next.

It was charming, thought Hastings, but really there was no need for the lady to be so coy.

Warwick of course was getting impatient and they could not

77

rest for ever and they had to go all too soon for Edward, whose passion was growing instead of abating. A very unusual state of affairs, thought Hastings. The lady must indeed be a real charmer. Perhaps when Edward tired of her – and he inevitably would – he, Hastings, might make her acquaintance.

Poor Edward, he was indeed downcast and it was impossible to lift his spirits. One thing Hastings had observed and that was that references to Lady Grey were coldly received, which indicated that the King undoubtedly was emotionally involved.

By the time the party reached York, Montague had won the battles of Hedgley Moor and Hexham and he and Warwick had suppressed other small risings in the area.

Edward congratulated Montague and created him Earl of Northumberland. His victories had been spectacular. He had completely defeated Somerset at Hedgley Moor and at Hexham had been confronted by an army with which rode King Henry himself. The victory there seemed to have crushed the Lancastrian cause. Many of its leaders were killed. Unfortunately Henry himself had managed to escape.

'We must find Henry,' said Warwick. 'While he is at large there will be men to rally to his cause and that means danger. I shall not be happy until we have him in our hands.'

'He is too feeble to fight,' said Edward.

'Aye, but he will find others to fight for him. I like it not that he should be free – fugitive though he might be. Then there is the Prince, his son.'

'A boy!'

'Boys grow up. Let it be known that there will be big rewards for any who deliver Henry to us. I wonder what is brewing in Margaret's mind? I'll rest better when you have an heir which brings us back to the subject of your marriage. It must take place soon. We should let nothing stand in its way.'

Edward nodded. The moment for revelation had not yet arrived.

They came south. Warwick was intent on preparations for the French marriage. It seemed as though he were thinking of nothing else. It could not be long before he must be told for Edward could not allow him to go to France and draw up the contracts.

There was a matter for concern over the currency. There was a scarcity of bullion in the country and it was agreed that new coins must be minted. Hastings who was Master of the Mint had made Edward see the necessity for the changes and Edward threw himself into the scheme with enthusiasm. It was a success and in addition to the mints in London, Canterbury and York new ones were needed and were set up in Norwich, Coventry and Bristol.

The people did not like getting used to the new values of nobles, royals, angels and groats; but they accepted the changes as necessary; and Edward found that the matter took people's minds off the vexed one of a foreign marriage for a while.

But it could not be delayed for much longer and the moment came at a council meeting which Warwick had called at Reading, Warwick's main purpose being to settle the final details before the embassy left for France to make the last arrangements for the King's marriage.

Edward was ready. I am the King, he thought. And I will let them know it – all of them and in particular Warwick.

Warwick spoke at length as usual. Everyone was in agreement that it was time the King was married. The country needed an heir and the King would agree that it was his duty to provide it.

Edward said with the utmost grace that he was entirely in agreement with them. There was nothing he wanted more than to give the country an heir and he had already chosen his bride.

He was conscious of the tension in the room. Warwick was studying him with some puzzlement.

'I will have Elizabeth Woodville, the daughter of Lord Rivers, and none other.'

There was an astonished silence. At length one of the councillors spoke. 'She is a beautiful and virtuous lady, but not suitable to be the Queen of England.'

'Not suitable!' cried Edward. 'Why not? She is the one I have chosen for my Queen.'

'She is not the daughter of a duke or an earl.'

'Her mother was the Duchess of Bedford. She is of the noble House of Luxembourg.'

'The Duchess of Bedford married a humble squire, my lord.'

'Have done,' cried Edward. 'There is nothing you can say that will move me, for I have already married the lady.'

The astonishment in the council chamber was so overwhelming that no one had anything to say.

The King walked out without looking at the Earl of Warwick who was sitting staring ahead.

So the King was married! First the Court, then the country was agog with the news.

How had she managed it? She had bewitched the King. Stories were circulated. He had tried to seduce her; she had threatened to kill herself with a dagger if he approached her; he had been trapped into marriage. How could an accomplished libertine be so securely trapped? There was one answer. It was witchcraft. Jacquetta, Lady Rivers – the Duchess of Bedford that was – had brought this about and all knew that she was a sorceress. There was wild conjecture as to how she had slipped a potion into his wine when he visited Grafton; how he had been led as a sleepwalker to attend that ceremony which had made humble Elizabeth Woodville a queen.

Yes, that was the favourite theory. It was done by sorcery.

The people were inclined to smile at their King. They did not like foreigners. Heaven knew the last King's marriage had brought them the virago from Anjou. They wanted no more like her.

'It is a love match,' said the people of London. 'God bless his handsome face. He has fallen in love with her and why should these mighty nobles try to spoil his happiness by bringing over a French woman for him. God bless the King and God bless the Queen if she is the one he wants.'

But whatever was said everyone was talking of the King's marriage.

Richard was back at Middleham. He liked the fresh northern air and it was good to see the Countess and his second cousins again.

Francis Lovell, son of Lord Lovell who was also being brought up at Middleham, was there and he and Francis were great friends. There was a warmth of affection for him at Middleham which he had not quite found in his own home.

There was always a great deal to talk about when he returned after being away. He, Francis and Anne would ride out on the Yorkshire moors and sometimes lie stretched on the grass while their horses drank from a stream and they could talk of what they would do in the future. Sometimes Isabel was with them, but she was delicate and tired rather easily. So did Anne, but she was so eager to be with the boys that she tried to forget her weakness. Richard often thought how strange it was that a strong man like the Earl of Warwick should have only two weak daughters, and not one son to bear his name.

How different it had been in his family. Of course some of them had died. There was Henry William and John and Thomas among the boys. The girls had taken a stronger grip on life except little Ursula who was the last and had been born some five or six years before the death of their father.

Then there was Edmund who had been slain in battle. Richard would never forget the day when the news had been brought to him of his brother's death, because it had been at the same time as that of his father, and Edmund's head had been stuck up on the walls of York with that of the Duke.

Edward had said they must forget all that. There were three of the boys left: himself, George and Richard.

'We must always stand together,' Edward had said. 'Do you think anyone could harm us then?'

'No one would ever challenge you, brother,' Richard had replied.

Edward liked that. Edward was so magnificent in every way. He was good as well as great, and yet he had always had the time to think about his brothers and sisters.

Richard had told Anne that while Edward reigned they need never fear anything.

82

Anne had replied that while her father and Edward stood together none could come against them.

Francis Lovell pointed out that some had tried to do that and there had been battles.

That was true, agreed Richard, who hated to diverge from the truth just to win a point. But his brother had won in the end and it was the last battle that counted.

'The last battle,' he said, 'has been won at Hexham. Poor Henry is wandering from place to place fearful of capture. They will get him of course and then . . .'

They looked at him wanting to know what would happen when Henry was captured.

Richard said: 'My brother will know what to do.'

His brother always knew what to do. How wonderful he had been at his coronation – but not aloof by any means. Ever ready with a smile and a nod of approval every time his eyes fell on his young brother. Looking a little anxious as he touched the boy's shoulder, wondering whether his armour was too heavy for him, asking how he fared at Middleham.

Richard remembered how, after the second battle of St Albans, he and George had been sent to Utrecht by their mother. That had been one of the most unhappy times of his life because he had known that Edward must be in difficulties for them to be sent away. But it had been a short stay – they left in February and as soon as Edward was proclaimed King he sent for them.

What joy to see him again! He was even grander than before – a King indeed. When Richard spoke his name – and he invariably said 'My brother' – George had said it was as though he were talking of God.

Edward was a god – Richard's God.

Richard would never forget the time when he and George had been sent to the house of John Paston when their mother went to join their father at Hereford. It had been sad to part from their mother and go into a strange house; but Edward had been in London and every day he had called at the Paston house to see his young brothers.

George had said: 'So he should. We're his brothers, are we not?'

'But it is wonderful that he has time to see us . . . that he makes time to come,' Richard pointed out.

George shrugged his shoulders. Richard read the thoughts in George's eyes. He was jealous. He was always talking of the perversity of fate which brought people into the world at the wrong time. George thought that if he had been the first-born he would have been as wonderful and as suitable to be King as Edward.

What nonsense!

They lay on the grass together – he, Anne and Francis Lovell; they looked lazily from the wide expanse of sky to their horses standing quietly by. This was contentment. These were the people he loved. If Edward came riding over the rough grass now he would be completely content. Francis and he understood each other; he had made Francis aware of Edward's greatness and Francis, being his very good friend, accepted what he said. Anne's father, the great Earl of Warwick, was Edward's staunchest supporter. It was a lovely cosy feeling to be among friends.

'Dickon is so proud of his new badge,' said Anne. 'You kept touching it, Dickon,' she added.

'It is a rather nice one,' said Richard.

'Read it out to us,' said Anne because she knew he liked to do that.

Richard read loudly and clearly: *'Loyaulté me lie.'*

Anne clapped her hands. 'It is the most honourable thing in a man,' she said. 'Loyalty to what he believes in.'

'It means,' said Richard with a faint colour in his usually pale cheeks, 'Loyalty to the King. That is my brother Edward. My loyalty to him will never falter.'

'You are so proud of being brother to the King,' she said, smiling at him.

He nodded and she thought: I suppose I must be proud to be the daughter of the Kingmaker. But one did not mention the Kingmaker to Richard. He did not like the suggestion that his godlike brother owed anything to anyone – even Anne's father.

But she knew that he delighted in the friendship of her father and his brother.

Francis looked at the louring clouds and said he thought they should go back to Middleham.

When they reached the castle there were signs of activity there. There had been important arrivals. Richard's heart leaped with hope. Perhaps it was Edward.

It was not, but it was the great Earl himself.

He was in a strange mood and it was clear that he was displeased about something. The mood of the great man must affect the entire castle and everyone was clearly rather unhappy.

Richard wondered whether he might ask what was wrong. He was about to but the Countess threw a warning glance at him, and he was silent.

He did say: 'My lord, have you seen my brother of late?'

'I have indeed,' was the answer, and it sounded like a growl. It was clearly forbidding Richard to say more.

The Countess was eager to discover what had happened and when the Earl told her she could scarcely believe it.

'It's true,' he said. 'We're going to have a coronation. Richard should prepare to leave for London at once.'

'Elizabeth Woodville! I cannot believe it.'

'Nor could any of us until it was shown to be true. We thought he was joking.'

'But he has had so many mistresses . . . why marry this one?'

'By all accounts marriage was a condition of surrender and he was so bemused he gave way to it. I begin to wonder whether I have put the right man on the throne.'

That her husband was more disturbed than he betrayed himself to be, the Countess was fully aware. He had governed the King for so long that this was a bitter surprise when the King turned on him and made it quite clear that in future he would manage his own affairs.

'It's disaster,' said Warwick. 'The Woodvilles . . . the woman's rapacious mother . . . You'll see what happens. We shall have the Woodvilles everywhere and they are a large family.'

'The King will quickly tire of her. He always tires of them.'

'That is our hope. Then of course we must see about arranging a divorce and a new marriage which will bring good to the country.'

'Richard, what are *you* going to do?'

He looked at her steadily. He was not accustomed to discussing affairs with her. He was very fond of her. She had been the best possible of wives. He should be grateful, for as one of the biggest heiresses in the country she had brought him the title of Warwick and the vast wealth which had helped to make it possible for him to rise to his present position.

He said: 'I do not know. So much will depend on what comes from this.'

That was the truth.

He sent for Richard.

'You must prepare yourself to leave for London,' he told him. 'A most distressing thing has happened. Your brother . . .'

Mists swam before Richard's eyes. He grasped at the table by which he was standing. Something had happened to Edward and the way in which Warwick was looking might indicate that he was no longer the King's friend.

'My brother . . .' he murmured, for Warwick had hesitated.

'It is so grievous that I can hardly bring myself to speak of it. Your brother has married . . . without consulting the Council . . . without consulting *me*!'

'Married to . . . to Bona of Savoy?'

'Good God no. If only it were so. He has married a woman of low birth. A most unsuitable alliance. His wife is Lady Grey, Elizabeth Woodville daughter of Lord Rivers.'

'But I thought it was to be a French marriage.'

'So did we all. So should it have been. But your brother has taken this rash act.'

'What will happen?'

'That remains to be seen. At this time we have this marriage. It is a true one and cannot be denied. So now we have a Queen . . . Queen Elizabeth Woodville.'

Warwick managed to force a great deal of contempt into his voice.

'I am sure my brother . . .'

'There is one thing you can be sure of. He has made a great

mistake and we do not know what the outcome of this will be. And now we have to attend her coronation, God help us. God help the nation. God help the King. The folly of it is past understanding.'

Richard was angry. He hated Warwick in that moment. He drew himself up to his full height which was not very great and fingering the badge on his jacket he said: 'I am sure that whatever my brother has done is right.'

Richard was dismayed on arriving at Baynard's Castle where he was to join his mother to find that she was in a furious mood.

George, who was already at the castle, told him that she had been so since she had heard the news of Edward's marriage.

'She says she will never take second place to the low-born Elizabeth, even if she is the Queen.' Clarence was amused. Richard had always known that he enjoyed discomfiture in others.

'And why should she?' he demanded. 'She is of our royal blood. And this woman . . . she is a nobody. I cannot understand what possessed Edward.'

'Edward would not have married her unless he had a very good reason for doing so.'

That made George laugh. 'He has his reasons most certainly. She must have something very special to tempt him.' His eyes were speculative. 'I wonder what.'

Richard hated any references to Edward's sexual life. It did not quite fit in with the noble qualities with which he had endowed him.

'I am sure,' he said staunchly, 'that Edward has acted wisely. We shall discover that to be so in due course.'

'You are a foolish boy, Richard. You see no further than your nose. What are all the noble families going to say? What is the King of France going to say? And what is Warwick going to say?'

'He will serve the King as all good men should.'

'There is one thing I know. Edward's most faithful subject is his brother Richard. You're going to wake up one day, brother, and you will find that your god is only human after all.'

Richard was silent. There were times when he heartily disliked George. He himself was certainly uneasy about the marriage but he had made up his mind that if Edward wanted it he was going to want it too.

He turned away from George and looked out at the Thames flowing by just below the castle walls. He gazed along the water to the grey walls of the Tower and prayed fervently that all would go well for Edward and a resentment arose in him against George who seemed so pleased at the prospect of trouble, at his mother who was so haughty and declared she would not see the lowborn Queen, and towards Warwick who dared to think he knew better than the King!

Edward meanwhile was delighted with his bride. He was relieved too that the secret was out. If he had a chance to go back he would do exactly the same again. It was hard to define what it was about Elizabeth which so enthralled him. She was by no means passionate; she was aloof, cold even; he sometimes wondered whether her hold over him was that she presented a continual challenge. He was always attempting to arouse something which was not there. And of course she was incomparably beautiful – strangely enough in a different mould from beauties who had attracted him in the past. Her clear-cut features were as Hastings had once said, like those of a statue; and he was never quite sure what was going on behind those beautiful blue-grey heavy-lidded eyes. With her long luxuriant hair falling about her firm white body she moved him as he had never been moved before and he could say to himself: A plague on Louis. A plague on Warwick. Neither of them is going to stop my having Elizabeth.

Rather unexpectedly Warwick had decided not to offer any reprimand and long lecture on the harm that had been done. That was wise of Warwick. Edward would have been ready for him and Warwick would have learned once and for all that the King was no longer his to command. Warwick stayed silent, and when presented to Elizabeth showed all the respect that Edward, or even Elizabeth, could have asked.

Warwick had given his anger time to simmer down and it was no longer at boiling point and therefore dangerous. It was there, as deep and strong as ever, but under control. He could see what had happened and blamed himself for not realising it was coming. Edward was on the point of breaking away and would do so on this delicate matter of his marriage. The weakening chain must be repaired quickly and an appropriate moment chosen to slip on the leading-reins.

In the meantime he would show Edward that he accepted Elizabeth as Queen and would do his best to repair any damage that had been done to relations with France. He would try not to show how bitterly he resented having been made to look foolish in the eyes of the King of France who by this clandestine marriage had proved that he, Warwick, was not in the King's confidence.

'I made him. I put him on the throne. He would be nothing without me.' So he had ranted to his Countess.

To Edward he smiled affably and discussed the arrangements for the Queen's coronation.

First Edward wanted to present her to the nobles of the land and he would do that in Reading Abbey.

'It is meet and fitting,' he said, 'that Clarence should lead her in. As heir presumptive to the throne it is his place to do that.'

Edward was smiling complacently. He was certain that soon there would be an heir to push Clarence aside. Both he and Elizabeth had proved – as he had told his mother – that they were not likely to be barren.

Warwick smiled grimly to himself. He could imagine Clarence's feelings. That boy had ambitions. He had half hoped that Edward would never marry and then his own great ambition would be realised.

Not you, thought Warwick. I would prefer Richard – a good serious boy, loyal to his brother. I could mould him. But Clarence . . . no, too vain. Too much superficial charm that is soon shown to be worthless. Clarence is no good. But that woman and Edward will have a brood of children I doubt not, for Edward will go to the making of them with an enthusiasm he has for little else. So Clarence was to lead her in. His mother was furious, but he had to do it. He had to obey the King rather than his mother. It was an amusing situation. They'll not endure it, he thought. Warwick is seething. So are some of the others. They are setting up together against the Woodvilles already.

And here was the Queen. There was no doubt of her beauty. It was breath-taking. She was the sort of woman who was naturally regal. She was tall and therefore looked well beside Edward. He dwarfed most women. Her glorious hair fell about her shoulders and down to her knees and on her head was a crown of gems the points of which were formed in the shape of fleur-de-lys. She held her head high but her heavy lids were drawn down over her eyes and she looked at no one. Her gown was of blue, that colour which suited her above all others, and it was decorated with stripes of gold brocade; the sleeves were tight and the bodice close-fitting; and there was an ermine border about the skirt. Her shoes were very pointed and she picked her way daintily but with sure-footed resolution towards the nobles who were waiting to do homage to her.

Everyone's eyes were on Warwick. He knelt before her. He took her hand and kissed it.

Clarence was disappointed. He was hoping for trouble.

Warwick could not have behaved more agreeably if the bride had been of his choice. No one would guess from his attitude how deeply the resentment was smouldering within him.

Just over a year after the secret marriage Elizabeth was crowned in Westminster Abbey.

It was Whitsunday and Elizabeth had been staying at Eltham Palace. Edward was keeping Court at the Palace of the Tower where he awaited the arrival of the Queen. As she came into London the mayor and the city leaders in all their colourful uniforms met her at Shooters Hill in order to form part of the procession which conducted her through Southwark to the Tower.

Edward was so proud of her, and he was delighted, too, that Warwick had after the first shock accepted her. If it occurred to him that Warwick might not be quite so reconciled as he appeared to be, Edward dismissed the thought. He hated trouble and all through his life he had pretended it did not exist, until the last minute when it had to be faced. Then he faced it with a nonchalance which was characteristic of him. He believed he could overcome every difficulty with his charm and grace – and often he did.

Elizabeth was carried from the Tower to the Abbey in her litter and the Londoners came out to marvel at her beauty and to look at the King whom they so much admired; and they thought the marriage was so romantic and just what they would have expected of their handsome King.

Edward was delighted that the Count of St Pol, the brother of Jacquetta, had accepted the invitation to attend the coronation because he gave a certain standing to the bride and reminded the people that although her father was a humble knight, her mother came from the noble House of Luxembourg. As for the Count who had vowed he never wanted to see his sister again, he was completely reconciled; his sister's daughter having become Queen of England completely expiated her sin in marrying beneath her.

And after the coronation there was the grand banquet in Westminster Hall where the King sat beside his Queen and showed by his demeanour his immense satisfaction with the proceedings.

Jacquetta looked on with the utmost satisfaction. Who would have believed she could have brought Elizabeth to this?

It was wonderful. Already her daughter was bringing good fortune to the family. She and Elizabeth discussed at length the grand marriages there should be for the members of the family. There, close to the King, sat her daughter Catherine, now the Duchess of Buckingham, elevated through her marriage to the Duke into one of the richest and most important families in the land. So should it be for the others.

Very soon the Woodvilles should be the leading family in the country, outdoing even the Nevilles.

Perhaps the most satisfied woman in the country that day, apart from the bride, was the bride's mother. It was a very different case with the bridegroom's mother.

She had refused to attend the ceremony. She, Proud Cis, who at Fotheringay when her husband had been Protector of the Land had lived in the state of a Queen, with a receiving room where she gave audiences and where she had enforced royal etiquette on all those who came into contact with her – must now stand by and watch the low-born daughter of a chamberlain's son take precedence over her!

No, Proud Cis would not accept Elizabeth Woodville as Queen.

Edward, however, was delighted with life. He was still in love with Elizabeth. There had already been minor infidelities it was true but they did not seem to matter. Elizabeth never asked about them. He wondered if she heard rumours for he had been rather indiscreet with a certain lady of the Court. Their affair had lasted a week before he was longing for the cool, aloof charms of Elizabeth.

He had discovered that he did not want his relationship with his Queen impaired in any way and he had suffered a qualm or so of uneasiness; but if she knew, and he thought she might, for those cool hooded eyes missed little, she gave no sign. When he muttered some excuses about his absences, she waved them aside.

'I know full well that you will always have matters which take you from my side. I never forget that you are the King.'

He loved her more than ever. No reproaches! She just gave him cool calm understanding.

Her mother was often with her. He liked Jacquetta. There had always been a special friendship between them since she had been so helpful at the time of the marriage. People might say that it was her witchcraft which had made him so determined to get Elizabeth that he married her. He didn't care. If witches were like Jacquetta then he could do with them in the kingdom.

There was good news of Henry the King who had been captured in the North. He had been in hiding for some time, living in fear of capture, resting at times in monasteries so Edward had heard. A life which Henry must have found most suitable. Warwick had met him when he was brought to London by his captors and so that all should realise the depth to which he had sunk they had bound his legs under his horse with leather thongs while he was conducted to the Tower. There he was handed to his keeper.

Edward rejoiced, not only that Henry was his captive but because Warwick's actions showed that he was still the same strong and firm supporter of the Yorkist King.

They would all be relieved, of course, if Henry died, but they must not hurry him to death or he would become a martyr. Henry was perfect martyr material with all that piety. In the North some of them believed he was actually a saint. Moreover if he were to die there was still his son.

'Let matters rest as they are,' Warwick had said, and he added, looking steadily at Edward: 'They have a way of working out for what is right.'

Warwick's mind was busy. He had stepped back into his role of chief adviser; he had made a pretence of accepting the Queen. But in truth he hated the Queen. Not because in marrying her Edward had humiliated him in a manner such a proud nobleman would never accept, but he could see that the Woodville family would become more and more important with every passing year. The leading family was the Nevilles – made so by him. And why should it not be so? Who had put the King on the throne? Should not the Kingmaker gather a little for his own family?

And if they were going to be ousted by the upstart Woodvilles this could not be tolerated.

Elizabeth and that diabolical mother of hers were putting their heads together and enriching and empowering their family by the old well tried method – which was the best in any case – of marrying into the greatest families. And they were doing very well.

Anthony was already married to the daughter of Lord Scales and had that title. Anne Woodville had become Lady Essex having married the Earl; Catherine had married the Duke of Buckingham; Mary was the wife of the Earl of Pembroke; Eleanor was married to Lord Grey of Ruthin, Earl of Kent, and the youngest, Martha, was the wife of Sir John Bromley.

Warwick seethed with rage when he thought of Elizabeth's efforts so far. Those were the Queen's sisters, already exerting a Woodville influence in the greatest and most powerful families in the country.

This is something I will not tolerate, he thought. It is a decided threat to the Nevilles. We are the leading family. I have upheld and made the King. I will not be supplanted by these upstarts. Not only will they ruin the country, but they will ruin me.

Moreover the Queen had brothers.

Elizabeth was at this time considering her brothers. She was delighted with her sisters' marriages. Her mother was right. That meeting under the great oak had been inspired. From that all their blessings had begun to flow.

She was at this time concerned about her brother John who was now nineteen years old. She wanted the best possible for him. The girls had all married well but the boys were even more important.

When Jacquetta made the suggestion to her Elizabeth could scarcely believe it for the suggested bride was the Dowager Duchess of Norfolk. True she was one of the richest women in the country, but she was almost eighty. Jacquetta, however, was serious.

When Elizabeth broached the subject to Edward he burst into laughter. He thought it was a joke. But Elizabeth was not given to joking on sacred matters.

'I really mean it,' she said. 'John will take care of the old Duchess's estates.'

'Oh he'll take good care of them, I doubt not,' said Edward.

'Edward, my brother should be married. Please grant me this. I want it to be.'

He put his hands on her shoulders and kissed the heavy lids. He had still not discovered what this extraordinary power she had over him really meant. Perhaps he loved her; it was strange, for he had played at love so many times, but again that might be why he was bewildered by the real thing when he encountered it. In any case he was fiercely glad that he had married her. And if she wanted the old lady of Norfolk for her brother, she should have her.

Everyone thought it was a joke at first. How could it be

otherwise – a boy of nineteen and a woman of nearly eighty. The Duchess was distressed but too old and tired to care very much. She doubted the handsome young man would bother her. In any case it was a royal command, and the Duchess had no alternative but to submit.

It was the joke of the day. People talked of it in the shops and the streets.

Some said it was a marriage of the devil. Such an old woman . . . such a young man. It was done for the money, the estates, the title. This was often the case but surely never quite so blatantly before.

Jacquetta was beside herself with glee.

'You know how to manage the King,' she said to her daughter. 'Be careful not to lose your place in his affections. Be lenient with his misdemeanours, never criticise or reproach. Accept everything and he will deny you nothing.'

So the marriage of young John Woodville and the ancient Duchess was celebrated.

Warwick said: 'This is the last insult. I cannot accept this woman and her overbearing family. They are making the throne a laughing-stock. I made a King. I can unmake one.'

The King was in a contented mood when Thomas Fitzgerald, Earl of Desmond returned from Ireland to report on events there.

He liked Desmond. A handsome man of immense charm. As an Irishman he was a good man to govern there. Warwick had chosen him and was pleased with him. Desmond and Warwick were on the best of terms.

A few years earlier when George Duke of Clarence had

been made Lord Lieutenant of Ireland – a title for the King's brother because Clarence was neither of an age nor ability to be able to conduct the affairs of that troublesome island – Desmond had been made Deputy, which meant that, in the circumstances, he was in full command.

Warwick had seen him on his return to England and had confided in him his horror and disgust at the King's marriage.

'Not only is this low-born woman on the throne but she is now so enriching her family that we are going to find ourselves governed by Woodvilles if we do not take some action.'

'What action?' asked Desmond with a certain alarm.

'Some action,' said Warwick mysteriously. 'Edward is not so firm on the throne as he would appear to think. Do not forget that Henry, the anointed King, languishes in the Tower and across the water is a very bold and ambitious Queen with a son whom she calls the Prince of Wales and reckons to be true heir to the throne. Would you not think that a King who reigns in such circumstances should not be careless . . . particularly in his dealings with those who have put him there?'

'He should rid himself of the lady and her tiresome relations.'

'So think I,' said Warwick. 'And when I consider the humiliation I was forced to suffer to put a crown on that woman's head, it maddens me so much that I would do myself some harm if I gave way to my anger.'

'I can understand your feelings,' said Desmond. 'I know that while the King was married he allowed you to negotiate with France.'

'That is the truth,' said Warwick. 'The country cannot afford any more of these disastrous marriages. At the moment they are amused by this diabolical match between John Woodville and the old Duchess of Norfolk. But in truth it is no laughing matter.'

Desmond was grieved to see Warwick in such a mood; and what seemed to him most disturbing was that there was a rift between him and the King.

Desmond was devoted to Warwick whom he admired more than any living man; he was well aware of the part the Earl had played in affairs, but at the same time he was fond of the King. This was a very distressing state of affairs and he feared trouble might lie ahead.

When he presented himself to Edward the King was most affable. They discussed affairs in Ireland and Edward congratulated Desmond on what he had done.

'You must get in some hunting while you are home,' he said. 'How was the game in Ireland?'

It was very good, he was assured. But Desmond would greatly enjoy hunting with the King.

When they were riding through the forest, they found themselves apart from the rest of the company. Edward was affable and disarming. He was so friendly that Desmond quite forgot as people often did that he was the King.

Edward mentioned Warwick and asked how Desmond had found him.

'As ever,' replied Desmond. 'Full of vitality . . . as clever as he ever was.'

'I have a notion that he does not like the Queen.'

This was dangerous ground and Desmond should have been prepared for it.

He was silent. He could not say that Warwick had not mentioned this to him for Warwick had made his feelings very clear. He hesitated. Then the King said: 'And what do you think of the Queen, Desmond?'

'I think she is remarkably beautiful.'

'Well, all must think that. What else?'

'She is clearly virtuous. It is amazing that she who was a widow with two children should look so . . . virginal.'

The King laughed.

'I think I have been wise in my marriage. Do you, Desmond?'

It was difficult to answer. To give the reply the King wanted would have been so false and Desmond was sure that that would have been obvious.

Edward noticed the pause and burst out laughing. 'Now, Desmond, you can be frank with me. I know you would not be the only one to think my marriage unwise, would you? You do think that, eh Desmond?'

'My lord, I cannot deny that. It would have been wiser to have chosen a bride who could bring you an alliance which the Queen, beautiful and virtuous as she is, cannot do.'

'Well, 'tis done now, Desmond. Tis irrevocable.'

'No, my lord, not so. You could divorce her and make a match which would be more acceptable in the eyes of many of your subjects.'

Edward laughed. 'That I have no intention of doing, Desmond.'

'I am sure you have not, my lord. But you asked and I have told you what is in my mind.'

'My dear fellow, of course I respect your frankness.'

The King was in a mellow mood when he returned to the palace. It had been a good day's hunting. He went straight to the Queen who received him as always with that quiet pleasure which he found so comforting.

'You have had a good day's hunting?' she asked.

'I have. With Desmond. He's a pleasant fellow.'

'He has done well in Ireland, I hear.'

'Very well. As Warwick said, it was good to have an Irishman there. They understand their own far better than they do others, and the Irish need a bit of understanding I can tell you.'

'So you are well pleased with the man.'

'He is a good honest fellow. I like a man to speak up for himself.' Edward began to laugh.

'Something amuses you.'

'Yes. You'll like this, Elizabeth. I asked him what he thought of you.'

'Oh?' The lids had fallen over her eyes and he could not see the expression in them.

'He thought you were beautiful and virtuous, he said. So you see he appreciates your looks.'

'That is good of him.'

'Not so good. Do you know what he told me? He said that I ought to divorce you and marry someone who could bring good to the country.'

Edward laughed loudly.

She hesitated only for a very short time before she laughed with him.

He was beside her, putting his arms about her. 'Needless to tell you I have no intention of taking his advice.'

'I am glad to hear it, my lord.'

She spoke lightly but there was a cold fury in her heart. Edward was amused now but the very idea was dangerous, and men who planted such were menacing her.

While Edward embraced her she was thinking of Desmond.

I will remember you, my lord, she thought.

The Queen was pregnant and the King was overcome with joy.

'Give me a son,' he cried, 'and we will laugh in the faces of all our critics.' He told her of what his mother had said when she had first heard of the marriage.

Elizabeth laughed with him and showed no surprise or emotion when he mentioned his own offspring. She knew of them of course. They were the children of a certain Elizabeth Lucy: Grace and Catherine. He was very fond of them and visited them now and then, taking an interest in their welfare. The relationship with Elizabeth Lucy had been one of his more enduring. There was no doubt that he had other illegitimate children, but as he had a real affection for the mother of these two he felt more tenderness towards them.

Elizabeth had discussed the matter with Jacquetta and they had come to the conclusion that when she had children of her own she might bring the Lucy girls into the royal nurseries. It would be a gesture to enrapture the King and it would bind him even closer to his tolerant, quietly loving Elizabeth. But not yet, of course. It would be an error of judgement to bring another woman's children into the nurseries while she herself had none.

But now the great day was approaching. The whole nation was delighted. Edward was popular. Even his wife was not disliked, for anyone coming after Margaret of Anjou would seem a welcome change. Moreover Elizabeth was English and if she was not so highly born as a King's wife was expected to be, at least she had great beauty and as much — if not more — dignity than a Queen was expected to have.

Jacquetta was constantly beside her daughter and everyone was certain that the child would be a boy.

The King was even speaking of 'When my son is born . . .' and the physicians had given their opinion that the child was male.

There was one Dr Domynyk who claimed to have prophetic powers. He could tell the sex of a child in its mother's womb, he said, and he assured the King that the Queen carried a Prince.

So there could be no doubt and all preparations for a Prince proceeded.

Elizabeth's time came. Calm as ever she retired to her apartments. The King was in an agony of impatience.

Childbearing was no new experience to Elizabeth and her mood was one of exultation for the child she bore would be royal, perhaps a King.

She endured her pains with amazing fortitude and she was rewarded it seemed by an easy birth.

The excitement was intense when the cry of the child was heard. Dr Domynyk could not contain himself. He was determined to be the first to carry the good news to the King that he had a son and to remind him of his prophecy.

Impatiently he tapped on the door which was opened by one of the Queen's women.

'I beg you . . . I pray you . . .' panted Dr Domynyk, 'tell me quickly, what has the Queen?'

The woman regarded him through half-closed eyes. 'Whatever the Queen has within it is surely a fool who stands without.'

Then she shut the door in the doctor's face.

He could not believe it. A girl! It was impossible! He had prophesied . . .

The stars had lied to him; his signs and portents had misled him. And he was bitterly humiliated. He hurried away. He could not face the King.

Edward was disappointed when he heard that the child was a girl, but not for long. He went immediately to Elizabeth's bedside, and when he saw her so calmly beautiful in spite of her ordeal, with her beautiful hair in two luxuriant plaits over her shoulders, he knelt by the bed and kissed her hands.

'Don't fret, sweetheart,' he said. 'We'll have boys yet.'

While it was a disappointment for Elizabeth it was a triumph in a way because it showed the unabating strength of Edward's enslavement to his cool goddess for within a few hours he was delighting in the child. 'I wouldn't change this girl for all the boys in Christendom,' he declared.

The words of a proud father! Edward had always been fond of children.

The Duchess of York surprised everyone by arriving at Westminster Palace. Proud Cis had kept aloof since the marriage to show her disapproval and her refusal to take second place to that upstart Woodville woman as she called her.

It was a year and nine months since the clandestine marriage and the Duchess felt that she had remained in the shadows long enough.

They could show their contrition by naming the child after her, and she herself would attend the christening of Baby Cecily.

Edward was pleased to see her; he embraced her warmly. She had been foolish, he thought, over the marriage but if she was going to behave reasonably now he was not one to remember that.

'A beautiful healthy child, dear lady,' he said. 'We are delighted with her.'

'A boy would have pleased the people,' commented Cecily.

'Dear Mother, I am glad you are at last concerned with pleasing the people.' He was smiling inwardly. He had always known Cecily to be concerned with pleasing herself.

Cecily ignored the comment. 'An heir. That is what you need. All kings need heirs. It has a settling effect.'

'Well, I have one. My little girl.'

'The people do not want to be ruled by women.'

Edward laughed again. 'But they often are,' he said, 'without knowing it.'

'I trust,' said Cecily, 'that that is not the case with our present King and Queen?'

'Nay, Mother, Elizabeth is no meddler. In fact more and more I rejoice in my marriage. If you would only give yourself the chance to know her . . .'

'I should like to see the child.'

'Well, come to the nursery.'

'I wish to see . . . just the child. You can have her brought to me.'

Edward lifted his shoulders. He wanted no confrontation between the two women in the lying-in chamber. Elizabeth would be calm, he knew, and he also guessed that his mother would construe that as truculence or antagonism towards her. Elizabeth and Cecily were quite dissimilar. Cecily was explosive like a volcano always threatening to send out fire; Elizabeth was calm as peaceful meadows . . . where one could lie down and forget irritations, offering absolute peace.

So the Duchess went to the nurseries and there she seated herself on a throne-like chair and sent for the chief nurse. She signed for the woman to kneel before her and told her that she desired to see the baby.

The woman rose, bowed and retired and came back with the child.

Even Cecily softened as she took the baby into her arms. A healthy child indeed, with a look of Edward, she thought. She commented on this. 'This is a Plantagenet,' she said. 'No hint of Woodville here, praise be to God.'

'If she is only half as good-looking as her mother she'll be a beauty,' said Edward.

Cecily was silent. Foolish lover's talk! she thought. Is he not over that yet? Now the woman has produced a child it will be more difficult to get rid of her. Still, one never knew, and Edward had always been fickle in his relationships with women.

She said: 'I should be pleased if the child was named after me.'

Edward bowed his head. He had said to Elizabeth only that day that he thought the child should be called after her mother and Elizabeth had smiled and said she had thought the same.

He said nothing now. He always avoided trouble. There was no point in creating scenes which might not be necessary.

The Duchess said that she would consent to be godmother to her granddaughter and Edward replied that that would give him and Elizabeth great pleasure.

Later, he sat by Elizabeth's bed. The baby was sleeping in her ornate cradle.

'So your mother came,' said Elizabeth. 'Did she not want to see me?'

'Oh, she thought you might be a little exhausted.'

Elizabeth smiled faintly. Never question unless of course there was something to be gained from it. Edward was uneasy about his mother and as Jacquetta had said her task was to set him at ease . . . always.

'She suggested that she would be pleased if the baby were called Cecily.'

This was one of those occasions when a little firmness was necessary.

'But we had decided on Elizabeth, had we not? You wanted Elizabeth.'

'There is no name which would please me more but . . .'

'Then if it is your wish I am going to insist. The child shall be called Elizabeth.'

He kissed the lids of her eyes which gave such distinction to her face. Elizabeth used them sometimes because she feared her eyes might betray those innermost thoughts which she wished to keep from the world.

Now she did not wish Edward to see the triumph. The Duchess of York must learn that she could not insult the Queen and then condescendingly present herself and make demands.

Cecily indeed! After the Duchess who had made such an obvious show of her disapproval of the marriage.

Indeed not. The baby would be named Elizabeth after her mother.

The Princess Elizabeth was christened with a great deal of pomp and ceremony. Everyone was delighted that the King had a legitimate child. A son would have been a greater matter for rejoicing, but never mind, everyone was sure there would be a son in due course.

What was so comforting was that the baby's godmothers were the mothers of the bride and bridegroom. Jacquetta let it be known that she was of as high birth as Cecily Neville and that the Queen's mother had as much right to royal treatment as the King's had.

But the greatest relief of all was that the Earl of Warwick was her godfather. This must mean, it was said, that he was completely reconciled to the marriage. There would have been some perturbation if people could have guessed the inner feelings of the Earl of Warwick. Plans were forming in his head; and he rather welcomed this occasion for it enabled him to allay suspicions. He was not yet ready to act but he was not going to stand aside and see the Woodvilles take over the government of the country which was what they were beginning to do with so many of them placed in the greatest families in the land.

The christening was performed by George Neville, Archbishop of York. Warwick had scattered his men throughout the country which was what the Woodvilles were now attempting to do and it was maddening to contemplate that he, Warwick, was being defeated at his own game.

A few days after the christening came the churching. This should be a grand occasion, because the people must be made to realise the importance of Elizabeth the Queen; those remarks about her low birth and her unsuitability for her new role must be suppressed for ever.

The Queen looked beautiful; her pallor became her; she was exquisitely dressed and as usual she wore her magnificent hair flowing about her shoulders as she walked under an elaborate canopy and there was a grand procession from the Palace of Westminster to the Abbey with priests, ladies, nobles, trumpeters and other musicians. Jacquetta walked immediately behind her daughter, her eyes dancing with memories and anticipation of greater glories to come. Jacquetta often said to her husband that they had been right in everything they did. They had loved rashly, married even more rashly and produced the finest family that was ever granted to a man and woman. 'And it was because we were bold,' she insisted. 'We took what we wanted. We chose each other without thought of riches or greatness and you see riches and greatness are pouring into our laps.'

This marriage of her daughter's was of her making – so she believed. She had been its instigator. Oh, she was happy on that day. Her daughter Queen! All her children in high places! Oh happy happy day when she had conceived the idea of sending Elizabeth into Whittlebury Forest to meet the King . . . by accident.

The ceremony over they were back in the palace for the banquet. There was a golden chair for Elizabeth. How wonderful she looked! How regal! Her ladies, her mother among them, knelt before her while she ate very sparingly, neither looking nor speaking to those who knelt so humbly before her.

In spite of the lack of a longed-for boy, Elizabeth had turned it into a triumph. And a few months later she was pregnant again.

It was August when Elizabeth gave birth to her second child.

To her disappointment – and that of the King – this was another daughter. But Edward was as deeply enamoured of Elizabeth as he had ever been. Her cool beauty was so refreshing after the hot passion of his other encounters. These were continuing, though not with the same frequency as they had in his bachelor days. He had no need to make excuses or invent lies for Elizabeth. She never asked about his extra-marital love affairs. They were unimportant. She was the Queen.

As long as he never lost his taste for her, no one could replace her. That was the only thing she need fear and it seemed very unlikely. Edward was polygamous. No one woman would ever satisfy him completely. He could not have chosen a wife more suited to him and as the years passed he became more and more devoted to her.

He quickly recovered from his initial disappointment over the second girl. The boy would come, he was sure. They were fertile both of them and they might have a girl or two perhaps before they got their boy. But the boy would surely come. Elizabeth already had two to prove it.

Elizabeth was already thinking of Thomas, the elder of her two sons by John Grey, because for him she wanted Anne, the heiress of the Duke of Exeter. Warwick had already decided on the girl for one of his nephews but Elizabeth had won the day. Warwick was annoyed about this, but he was still not showing what was in his mind.

The new baby was sent to the Palace of Shene to be in the nursery there with her sister Elizabeth who was her senior only by sixteen months. The Queen was determined that they should have a household worthy of Princesses who were heiresses to the throne. Therefore the babies' nursery was conducted in the utmost state and presided over by Margaret, Lady Berners, the governess their mother had appointed.

There must be more children and most of all there must be a son, and Elizabeth was as confident as the King was that in due course they would have that boy.

Elizabeth never forgot old scores which she had decided should be settled; and as she rarely acted in haste she was always prepared to wait for revenge.

There was one remark which had been repeated to her by the King himself which she had never forgotten. It was Lord Desmond who had made it before the birth of the Princess Elizabeth, when he had suggested to the King that he should divorce Elizabeth and make a more suitable marriage. Edward had laughed the idea to scorn, but Elizabeth did not forgive it for that reason. He had planted a bad seed in the King's mind and who knew in what dark spot it was sprouting. A little ill fortune, a suggestion which to an ambitious man would be irresistible . . . and before she and her mother could do anything about it, her enemies would be descending on her.

Therefore she was interested when she heard a criticism of Lord Desmond's rule in Ireland. It came from John Tiptoft, Earl of Worcester. Worcester said that Desmond's rule appeared to be succeeding because he favoured the Irish. It was natural that the Irish should like him. Of course they did, he was an Irishman himself and Worcester believed that none could be so great a friend of the Irish without being a traitor to the English.

Worcester had always been a staunch supporter of the King. There was a family connection for his wife was the niece of Cecily, Duchess of York. Worcester's character appealed to Elizabeth. He was a man who would calculate long before he struck. In fact, he had a reputation for inflicting unnecessary cruelty on enemies who fell into his power.

He had been a deputy in Ireland and therefore knew what he was talking about. Later he had been sent out to see the Pope on a mission for the King and had stayed for a while in Italy, and his sojourn had had a great effect on him. He was said to have imbibed a great many Italian ways and was as much Italian as English now.

Sure of his loyalty Edward had honoured him, and since there had been criticism of Desmond, the King was considering sending Worcester out to Ireland again.

When the Queen heard this she cultivated Worcester. She invited him to one of the banquets she so enjoyed giving and during it kept him at her side. But it was private conversation that she wished to have and when the opportunity arose she wasted no time in coming to the matter which was of utmost interest to her.

'I am so glad you are going to Ireland,' she told him. 'I know there are great needs for reform there. The King has a fondness for Desmond, but I never trusted him.'

Worcester was only too pleased to hear his rival in Ireland denigrated. Any failure which could be attached to Desmond would enhance his own successes. He lent a ready ear to the conduct of Desmond and added something of his own.

'Such men are a danger to the King,' said Elizabeth. 'They should not be allowed to live.'

Worcester was interested. For some reason the Queen wanted Desmond out of the way, and it would certainly suit Worcester's purpose well to remove his rival.

'When I am in Ireland I will discover what traitorous action Desmond may be engaged in,' he promised.

'And if you discover . . .'

'My dear lady, if I discover treachery I will wipe it out. There is only one price that should be asked of a traitor. His life.'

The Queen nodded.

'I fear for the King. He is so easy-going, so blind sometimes to danger. He does not like to hear ill of those for whom he has some regard.'

'If he were presented with the accounts of infamy . . .'

'Even then . . .'

'Well, my lady, we shall see. I am leaving for Ireland shortly and I swear to you my first duty will be to rout out the traitors.'

'I shall look forward to hearing from you, my lord.'

'It would not surprise me if I soon have news for you. My lady, *you* are alert to danger, and we say this in no disloyalty to the King but I agree that he is apt to believe the best of people. This gives his enemies the chance they need. I am speaking too boldly.'

'My lord, you could not speak too boldly where the King's safety is in question.'

'Desmond is a close friend of Warwick's and, I suspect, my lord of Warwick is not quite the good friend the King believes him to be.'

'I, too, am watchful of Warwick.'

'It is good to know the King has you to look to his interests.'

'You may rest assured I shall do that. And I shall hope to hear from you before long.'

Worcester was as good as his word. He had not been long in Ireland when there was news of an action in a court at Drogheda.

A merchant was accusing Desmond of extorting money and livery and worse still of joining with the natives in a treasonable action against the English.

'I never trusted Desmond,' said Elizabeth.

Edward laughed. 'My dear, he has always been my good

friend. You know what these Irish are. They look for trouble and if they can't find it, they invent it.'

'Is that really so?'

Her eyes were downcast; she was demure again. He must not think that she disagreed with him or bore any grudge against Desmond, for if he did, he would know it was because of that unfortunate remark and, as Jacquetta and she had decided, to have shown resentment about that would have suggested fear. Edward must not think for one moment that she doubted his satisfaction with their marriage.

Walk warily, Jacquetta had said. And Elizabeth's temperament had well equipped her to do just that.

She said no more of Desmond to Edward, but she sent warm thanks to Worcester and waited for the next step.

It was not long before it came. Desmond had been tried on the charges brought against him at Drogheda and they had been proved to be true; he was therefore sentenced to death by the court. All they needed was the King's sanction to his execution.

Edward was in a dilemma. Warwick had taught him that he must have no scruples when dealing with traitors. They must be ruthlessly destroyed. Hadn't the battle cry always been: 'Go for the leaders. Leave the common soldiers.' It was the leaders who made trouble, the leaders who were to be feared. And now Desmond. He couldn't believe it, but according to Worcester's report Desmond had tried to rouse the Irish against English rule there and that was a direct attack on the King.

But Desmond had always been his friend. He liked Desmond. Had he been overfriendly with the Irish? He was Irish himself! But had he conspired with them? Even if he had Edward would find it hard to put his seal on the death warrant.

It was typical of Edward that he shelved the matter. He put

the order out of sight and forgot about it. They could not execute Desmond without his seal and if he did nothing the matter might blow over. Then he could perhaps recall Desmond and sift the matter himself. In due course Desmond could settle on his estates and Worcester could take care of Ireland.

It might be true that Desmond was a traitor. Men did turn for the sake of gain. But it was hard to think of Desmond doing that and in any case, he could forget it. Ireland was far away.

Elizabeth had said nothing of Desmond. But she knew where the death warrant was. She also knew that all it needed was the King's seal.

Edward had other matters with which to occupy himself for he was deeply shocked when he heard that Warwick had suggested to Clarence that he marry his eldest daughter Isabel.

This was one of the matters which he did discuss with Elizabeth.

'What does Warwick mean, think you?' he asked.

'It means that my lord Warwick is an ambitious man,' said Elizabeth.

'That, my dear, is no news. I never knew any man with more ambition. Why have I not been consulted? What does it mean?'

'That Warwick believes himself to be too high and mighty for consultation with the King to be necessary.'

'By God, there shall be no marriage. I want Clarence to strengthen the Burgundy alliance. I want this match between my sister Margaret and Burgundy's heir to go forward and I thought Clarence could have the Count's daughter Mary.'

'Of course she is only a child.'

'Clarence is not old. He can wait, I daresay. But Clarence

and Isabel Neville . . . never! For one thing they are second cousins. They need a dispensation from the Pope. I'll see they don't get that.'

Edward was so incensed that he completely forgot the case of Lord Desmond.

But Elizabeth had not forgotten. She had promised herself revenge for that remark of his and she would not be content until his head was parted from his body.

She awoke one morning early. The King lay beside her sleeping. She looked at him critically. He had lost a little of those outstanding good looks he had had when she had first met him. There were slight pouches under the fine eyes and a tendency to corpulence. She shrugged her shoulders. He was still a handsome man but his looks were not important as long as he retained his power and she must keep her hold on him.

She slipped off the bed. On a small table lay the King's ornaments which he had put there the previous night before disrobing.

She went to it and immediately found what she wanted: his signet ring.

His papers were in an adjoining chamber and she had made sure that the one she wanted was among them.

It was all done in a few moments.

She had sealed the death warrant.

She hid it in a drawer and went back to the bed.

The King was still sleeping. She lay there watching him. Then she moved closer to him and he put out an arm and held her close to him.

He had no notion that she had left the bed.

The Queen was pregnant once more.

There was no question of her fertility. This time, said the King, it must be a boy.

News came that Lord Desmond had been executed – more than that, Worcester had seen fit to kill his two younger sons with him. This had shocked many people because the boys were still in the schoolroom and it was hard to see how they could have been implicated in their father's treason. There was a story that one of the boys had a sore place on his neck and he had pathetically asked the executioner to be careful of it when cutting off his head. This story was repeated and people were beginning to hate the Earl of Worcester and to say that he had learned his cruelty in Italy and it would have been better if he had stayed there and never brought his wicked ways to England.

Edward was distressed that Desmond had been executed and was especially so when he heard what had happened to the boys.

'Worcester is too harsh,' he told Elizabeth.

She did not agree nor disagree; she just sat with her eyes downcast.

'*I* did not give my signature to the death warrant,' he said.

'He is dead now,' was all Elizabeth answered.

And so he deserved to be, she was thinking. How dared he advise the King that it would be a good thing for the country to rid himself of his Queen.

He had paid dearly for that remark. And so must all pay who tried to harm Elizabeth Woodville.

The King shrugged the matter aside. Whatever he did now Desmond was dead. At least he had not been forced to make a decision.

At the end of the year Elizabeth gave birth to another child. Once more it was a girl and they called her Cecily.

Three girls in a row was disconcerting when each time they had believed there would be a boy. But the King loved his children and to the astonishment of everyone he continued to be devoted to his wife. He was perhaps straying more to other women but he always went back to her and he did not appear to regret his marriage in any way; and cool, aloof, more regal than any of royal birth, Elizabeth held sway.

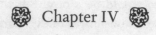
IN SANCTUARY

Warwick was growing impatient. He had endured enough. He had seen the Woodvilles rise from their humble station to become the most powerful family in the land. The King had insulted him by marrying this upstart widow while he, Warwick, was actually in the process of arranging a match for him with the French King.

Nothing could have been calculated to wound him more. Yet with superhuman control he had buried his resentments. He had attended the Queen; he had not reproached the King.

But what he would endure no longer was the power of the Woodvilles.

Almost immediately after the marriage he had sounded the King's brothers. Richard was a young idealist and Warwick quickly realised that there could be no shifting him from loyalty to his brother. It was different with Clarence. Clarence was shifty, envious, grasping and it would not be difficult to make him change his allegiance; on the other hand he would be an untrustworthy ally, ready to turn his coat according to which way the wind blew. But even a momentary betrayal of his brother would be worthwhile.

He had tempted Clarence by offering him marriage with his elder daughter. His two girls, even dividing the vast Warwick estates between them, would be the richest in the kingdom.

Clarence thought of what marriage with Isabel would mean and he liked what he saw. Moreover he liked Isabel. Neither of the Warwick girls was as physically strong as their father would have liked them to be, but they were attractive, both of them. Anne and Richard of Gloucester were close friends; and George and Isabel had always had a fondness for each other. The girls were worthy brides for the two dukes, and before the Woodville marriage Edward would have agreed with the Earl on this. Now he was trying to stop Isabel and George marrying. That should not be so. Warwick had decided on the match.

Moreover the King wanted marriage between his sister Margaret and Charles Count of Charolais, the eldest son and heir of the Duke of Burgundy. This of course was the last thing Louis King of France wanted because he did not want a firm alliance between England and Burgundy. Louis had been Warwick's friend and if Warwick took action against Edward, it was from Louis that he could look for help.

He had not let Edward know that he was doing all he could to prevent the Burgundy marriage. Indeed he had ceased to confide in Edward and although he kept up a show of friend-ship, it was nothing more than a façade. Warwick had finished with Edward. He would never forgive him for his ingratitude, and was determined that one day Edward was going to be filled with regret; he was going to see the great mistake he had made in thwarting Warwick, humiliating him, and setting up the family of Woodville to outrival that of Neville. Edward would have to learn that Warwick was still a power in the land.

In the meantime the great Duke of Burgundy had died and

Charles of Charolais had become the Duke. Edward declared that there was no reason why the marriage should be delayed and the Earl of Warwick should conduct his sister on the first part of her journey to France.

Still keeping his own counsel Warwick agreed and on a June day he set out for Flanders. There had been a ceremony at St Pauls and Margaret seated on the same horse with Warwick rode through the city of London.

The people were pleased, believing this was a sign that Warwick and the King were as good friends as ever. They did not know that even as he rode to the coast with Margaret Warwick's head was teeming with plans to take the crown from Edward.

Margaret said a farewell to Warwick at Margate and crossed the sea to Sluys where she was greeted by the Dowager Duchess of Burgundy and a splendid company.

The Duke met her and they were married at a place called Damme. After the ceremony the celebrations were so grand that those who partook in them declared that they had only been rivalled at the Court of King Arthur. The bride and the bridegroom appeared to be well pleased with each other and the only incident which marred the occasion was when they were nearly burned to death in their bridal bed in the castle near Bruges.

Fortunately they escaped in time and the fire was proved to have been started by a madman.

Edward declared that the marriage was a good piece of work, for it had strengthened the alliance between the houses of York and Burgundy.

Warwick was by no means pleased but he knew he had the friendship of one who was as powerful as the Duke of

Burgundy: the King of France himself. Louis would be annoyed by the match, and he was already favouring Margaret of Anjou who was in France in exile; he would be a useful ally to his old friend the Earl of Warwick.

Ideas were teeming in Warwick's head, for the moment of action was coming nearer.

❋ ❋ ❋

The King was at Westminster and Warwick had installed himself in his castle of Middleham where he was joined by his brother George Neville, Archbishop of York, and by the Duke of Clarence who was ready, as soon as the Pope's dispensation was received, to marry Isabel.

Warwick had made up his mind. Edward had now escaped from him; perhaps he always would have done so, for he was no puppet; he was a strong-minded man who knew how to rule and he was going to rule in his own way. He had come out in his true colours at the time of his marriage and had shown so clearly then that he would not be led. Edward was a ruler. He would have no master. Warwick had been deceived by his desire to avoid conflict – except in battle – to take the easy line, which Warwick had to admit was often the wise one to take. Edward was pleasure-loving, easy-going and not unkind by nature; these characteristics had been misleading because they had overshadowed the strong man beneath them.

Well, Warwick would have accepted that. He had wanted no weakling. It was the rising power of the Woodvilles in all key places in the country which he was going to put down.

He would do it and at the same time he was going to show Edward that though he was strong, Warwick was stronger.

From Middleham he was sounding out the North. The

North had always been for Lancaster which meant it was against York and Warwick believed that if he were going to take up arms against the King it was from the North that he would get his support.

From Middleham to his castle at Sheriff Hutton Warwick watched the effect of his carefully chosen words on those men who, he thought, would side with him against the King. He was not disappointed.

His powerful brother George was for him. He had a deep grievance against Edward for giving his support to Thomas Bourchier, the Archbishop of Canterbury, for elevation to the rank of Cardinal – an honour George had long sought for himself; and when Bourchier was elected to the College of Cardinals Edward had exacerbated the sore point by writing personally to George to tell him, and in such a way as to suggest that he was snapping his fingers at the Nevilles and reminding them that they were definitely out of favour.

It was too much to be borne, and Warwick was incensed.

'I made him,' he was fond of reminding people. 'But for me he would never have reached the throne. And when I have him there, crowned, anointed, what happens? He marries that woman and the Woodvilles are everywhere. It has to be stopped.'

Well, he was going to stop it.

From Middleham he sent messengers to the Court of France. He wanted to know how far the King would support him if he took up arms against Edward.

Louis, who was alarmed by the union of Edward and Burgundy through the marriage of Margaret of York and the Duke, would be eager to see Edward defeated and Warwick thought he could be relied on. He had Clarence with him and he had half promised that ambitious young man that if Edward were deposed Clarence could step into his shoes, which Clarence believed because Warwick wanted him to marry his own daughter Isabel. It would be a glittering prospect for Warwick with a daughter Queen of England.

But the Earl was determined not to strike until he was absolutely sure of victory. He went to Calais in order to make sure of the defences and while he was there some of his supporters who were getting impatient staged uprisings.

The leaders assumed the name of Robin which was meant to imply that they were men of the people, Robin being a friendly sort of name derived from Robin Hood. The first of these outbreaks was headed by a man calling himself Robin of Holderness. It was premature and disorganised and John Neville, whom the King had made Earl of Northumberland, had no difficulty in suppressing it. It was strange that a Neville should be siding with Edward but Warwick had been unable to convince this one of the good sense in anatagonising Edward. Robin of Holderness had declared that he had arisen to set the wrongs of the people right and there was no mention of dissatisfaction with the King, although there were hints about his generosity to the predatory relations of the Queen.

Robin of Holderness was beheaded and that little rebellion was over. The uprising of Robin of Redesdale was of a more serious nature. Robin of Redesdale was suspected of being Sir John Conyers, a kinsman of Warwick, and that fact gave his insurrection a more sinister meaning.

Robin of Redesdale's grievances were heavy taxation, men being called away from their families to military service outside their areas, and victimisation by the nobles of the land. There were also grumblings against the Woodvilles. The names of Lord Rivers and the Duchess Jacquetta were mentioned together with all those who had become so important since the King's marriage because of their alliances with great families.

Edward shrugged off accounts of these troubles. 'There is nothing that we cannot handle,' he said.

But, after a while, the murmuring of what Warwick was plotting and the continued reports of the uprisings began to alarm even him.

Robin of Redesdale was still at large. He was not the amateur Robin of Holderness had been which indicated that Warwick might have a hand in this. The King decided that if Warwick were indeed behind it, he had better get his army together without delay and go in person to see what was happening in the North. Warwick meanwhile was watching events from Calais. His great insistence was that they must not move until they were ready. There was dissatisfaction in the North it was true. How much support would they who had always been Lancastrians be prepared to give Warwick, one of the great architects of the Yorkist success who was only now turning his back on the King he had made?

Meanwhile the King marched north but in no great haste, pausing to make a pilgrimage at Bury St Edmunds and Walsingham. He was accompanied by his brother Richard whom he always liked to have near him now that Clarence had defected. He relished Richard's unconcealed loyalty and rejoiced in it. He was very upset by Clarence's behaviour – not that he feared his brother, whom he had always considered in-effectual and rather stupid, but because Clarence was his brother and the infidelity of a brother seemed to him a very sad thing indeed. He kept with him, besides Richard, Lord Rivers and Lord Scales, Elizabeth's father and brother whom he had first cultivated to please Elizabeth and of whom he had now grown quite fond. The Rivers did not argue, did not seek to guide as Warwick had done; they did what he wanted them to and if they were generously rewarded for it, that bothered Edward not at all.

Elizabeth was with them and the three little girls also. They would have to rest somewhere for it was not fitting that a child as young as Cecily should travel with an army. But he liked to have Elizabeth with him and therefore she came; and as he did not insist that the children remained behind they were with them too.

He was at Bury St Edmunds when messengers came from Kent. They had news from Calais. The King's brother the Duke of Clarence had been married to Warwick's daughter Isabel.

Edward was astounded. He had expressed his disapproval of the match; in fact he had forbidden it. That Warwick – and worse still his own brother – had openly defied him was impossible to believe. There must be some explanation; it could not be true. He refused to believe that Warwick held him in such contempt that he would deliberately defy him. Warwick had been his greatest friend, his hero, his mentor. George was his brother. He could not go against him. It was all some ridiculous mistake.

Elizabeth wanted to say that it was no mistake at all. It was time he realised who his enemies were. But she said nothing.

More news came. The rebel army was bigger than had first been reported and it was now clear that this was more than just a petty rebellion.

He looked at Elizabeth and thought of the children.

'I want you to go at once,' he said. 'Return to London. If there is going to be trouble this is no place for you.'

She did not protest. She would be glad to have done with the discomfort of travel. She would call at Grafton and Jacquetta could return with her to London.

❈ ❈ ❈

Elizabeth was glad of her mother's presence but Jacquetta was uneasy. She sensed that powerful events were looming and they might be of ill omen.

'I don't trust Warwick,' she said. 'He was too powerful before your marriage . . .'

'Life changed for him after that,' remarked Elizabeth with a smile.

'A man like Warwick does not allow himself to be pushed aside.'

'If the forces which push him are strong enough he has no help for it.'

Jacquetta was silent. At times Elizabeth was a little too complacent. However, she was glad to have her daughter safe from the armies; and the children too. Cecily not yet a year old was far too young to be carried round the country.

Warwick had landed in England and there was great rejoicing in London where he was warmly welcomed. There was trouble in the north, it was said and, the King had asked Warwick and his brother George to come to his aid. Warwick had immediately responded. All was well. Warwick and the King were friends.

It was clear, Jacquetta told her daughter, from what was being said that many believed there was a rift between the King and the Earl. The people of London were really alarmed at that. It could mean civil war.

'Civil war! Never. Warwick would not dare.'

'I begin to think,' said Jacquetta, 'that Warwick would dare a great deal.'

The days were tense and spent in waiting for news. It came in frustrating briefness, so that it was not easy to piece the events together and see the picture clearly.

Warwick had been lying, it seemed, when he had said he was going to the King's aid. No such thing. He was joining the rebels.

William Herbert, Earl of Pembroke and Humphrey Stafford, Earl of Devon were marching to Banbury. They had a strong force from Wales and the West Country and they were stalwart adherents of the King. They would soon settle the rebels.

Jacquetta and Elizabeth waited for news of the battle, certain at this stage that the rebels would be crushed and peace restored.

But it was not so, for Warwick's army had joined the rebels and at Edgecot the loyal men were defeated. Pembroke and his brother were taken prisoner and in accordance with the rule of destroying the leaders were beheaded at Northampton the next day.

'Warwick has gone too far this time,' said the Queen, but now she was beginning to be alarmed. She turned to her mother. 'What is going to happen?' she demanded. 'Where will this end?'

But this time the future would not reveal itself to Jacquetta.

The situation was even worse than Jacquetta and Elizabeth in London realised, for when the news of Pembroke's defeat at Edgecot reached Edward's small army, men began to desert him and he was left with a very few followers and to his immense chagrin he realised that he had made a vital mistake.

He had delayed too long; he had refused to believe the obvious. Stubbornly he had set his mind against accepting the perfidy of his brother and the furious revenge of the Kingmaker.

There was nothing for him to do but wait in the little town of Olney. Richard was with him, Hastings too.

'Well,' he said, 'we are at the mercy of our enemies.'

'Not for long,' said Richard. 'We shall give a good account of ourselves.'

'We need cunning, brother, rather than bravery. We shall have to meet whatever comes to us with skill. I do not think Warwick or George would want to harm me.'

Richard said: 'George has always wanted to take your place.'

'George wouldn't last a day as King.'

'With Warwick manipulating him?'

'George would never have the good sense to allow Warwick to do that. Richard, perhaps you should make your escape.'

'What!' cried Richard. 'Leave you here? Nay, where you go I go. If you stay I stay here too.'

'It does me good to hear you, Richard,' said Edward. 'You have always been the best brother a man ever had.'

'You have been that to me.'

'This is no time for sentiment. I doubt not that Clarence will be here to speak with me ere long. I wonder if Warwick will come?'

'I will kill him if he does.'

Edward laughed. 'You will not get a chance and I would not allow it if you could. In spite of everything I like the old warrior. He was a good friend to me . . . once.'

'And has become a bad enemy.'

'No, Richard, still a good one.'

'I do not know how you can laugh when this is happening.'

'Sometimes I think that quality in me . . . or maybe fault . . . is the reason I have reached the top.' He put his head close to his brother's. 'And I shall stay there, Richard. Rest assured of that.'

Back at Baynard's Castle a messenger had come into the courtyard. Slowly he dismounted and made his way into the castle. He was dreading the moment when he must face the Queen and her mother. Every messenger longed to be the bearer of good news, for messengers were often rewarded when they brought it, which was nothing to do with their efforts, and they were spurned when it was the other way round. It was illogical, and yet understandable.

Now this messenger knew that what he had to tell could not be more woeful.

As soon as Jacquetta heard that a messenger had arrived she sent for him and he came to her and Elizabeth.

He bowed low and hesitated.

'Come,' said the Queen imperiously, 'what news?'

'My lady . . . my ladies . . . I . . .'

'Speak up!' cried Elizabeth peremptorily.

Jacquetta laid a hand on her arm. 'The man hesitates because he fears what he has to say will grieve us.' She spoke gently. 'Pray tell us. Take your time. We know how you hate to be the bearer of this news.'

'My ladies, forgive me . . . but my Lord Rivers . . .'

Jacquetta put her hand to her heart. She did not speak. She kept her eyes fixed on the messenger's face.

He stared at her appealingly as though begging her not to ask him to proceed.

'He is dead,' said Jacquetta in a blank voice.

'He was captured with his son Sir John when they were making their way back to London after the defeat at Edgecot.'

'How. . .' began Jacquetta.

'They were beheaded at Kenilworth, my lady.'

Jacquetta put her hands over her face. Elizabeth sat staring in front of her.

It was Elizabeth who spoke first. 'Who ordered this . . . murder?'

'It was the Earl of Warwick, my lady.'

Elizabeth nodded her head.

'Go down to the kitchens and refresh yourself,' she said.

When he had gone Jacquetta lowered her hands and looked at her daughter. Elizabeth thought she had never seen such desolation in anyone's face before.

Jacquetta said nothing. She was thinking of the day she had met her husband, of his good looks and his charm, their romance which had swept her, a not unambitious young woman, off her feet. Their marriage had been an idyll. He had been everything she had known he would be. And now he was dead. She thought of that dear head which she had loved so well, being placed on a block and wantonly and so cruelly severed from his body. And John too. Her beloved son! She loved her children none the less because of the great affection she had for her husband. They were a clan the Woodvilles, the triumph of one was the triumph of them all as they had seen on the marriage of their sister. The Queen of England had applied herself assiduously to the betterment of her family from the moment she was able to do so. This dear John who had been with his father when they were murdered had recently married the old Dowager Duchess of Norfolk and become one of the richest men in the country. Now it was of no avail. All that money, all those vast possessions which had gone with the poor old lady bride were nothing to him now.

The sorrows of one were the sorrows of all as with the triumphs and she knew that Elizabeth, sitting there so quiet, so restrained, was fighting an emotion as bitter as her own.

It was Elizabeth who spoke first: 'Curse Warwick,' she said. 'I shall not rest until his head is parted from his body. He shall answer for this. Every time I see him I shall see my beloved father and my brother and remember what he did to them.'

George Neville Archbishop of York had arrived at Olney close to Coventry and presented himself to the King.

He was most respectful. He came, he said, on behalf of his brother the Earl of Warwick and wished to conduct the King to him. With the Earl was the Duke of Clarence, both the King's faithful lieges. They were concerned for his safety and had come to guard him.

Edward laughed. 'Not long ago they were fighting against me.'

'Nay, my lord,' said the suave Archbishop, 'you are mistaken. My brother's great concern was for your safety. He told the people of London that he was riding to your aid. Your brother the Duke of Clarence joins him in this.'

Richard who was with the King said: 'You are traitors all of you.'

Edward laid a hand on his arm.

'I see,' he said, 'that you are determined to make me your prisoner.'

Richard stepped towards the Archbishop and again Edward restrained him.

'What would you have of me?' he asked.

'That you accompany me to my brother.'

Edward knew that he was in their power. He had been foolish and foolishness could be disastrous. He had been dilatory; he had refused to see danger when it stared him in the face. Well, now he must answer for his folly. It was a temporary set-back. He was sure of that. Warwick was not a great general. Edward had little respect for his performance in the field. It was cunning strategy at which Warwick excelled. He had the ability to turn defeat into victory by some action which was totally unexpected by the other side. He must try to imitate Warwick's strategy. Therefore he would go along with him. He would pretend to believe in his fidelity even though his betrayal was clearly obvious.

'I will come with you,' he said. 'I will see Warwick.'

The Archbishop bowed his head. 'Then we should leave without delay.' He turned to Richard and Hastings who had taken up their stand on either side of the King.

Richard was a boy of seventeen or so and he looked younger because of his delicate stature. Warwick had said 'Let Richard go.' As for Hastings, well he was Warwick's brother-in-law. He had always thought that with a little persuasion he might win Hastings to his side. That was if he saw that Edward's cause was hopeless. So George Neville had had instructions to send Richard and Hastings away. Let them go free, find their way to where they wished to go. It was only Edward he wanted.

Sadly Richard said goodbye to his brother and rode away with Hastings, and Edward allowed himself to be conducted to Coventry where Warwick awaited him.

Warwick was naturally triumphant.

'Here is a sorry state of affairs,' he said. 'You know, Edward, I wish you no harm.'

'Nay,' replied Edward easily, 'you only wish to make me your prisoner.'

'You and I should never have allowed a wedge to be put between us.'

'I do not put it there, Richard.'

'Oh 'twas others, I grant you. The merry Woodvilles. Edward, it is no use. You know what happens to kings who honour their favourites to the detriment of the realm.'

'What has the realm suffered?'

'The realm has suffered because power has been placed in the hands of those incapable of handling it . . . and they are concerned only for material gain.'

'So many of us are, Richard.'

'There are some of us who love our country and would serve it asking no reward.'

'Show me such a man and I will make him my chancellor.'

'You are not in a position to make or unmake at this time, my lord.'

''Tis true. So I am your prisoner. What will you do with me? Have my head as you have that of my father-in-law?'

'It wounds me that you should even think of such a thing. I am your friend. I put you on the throne and you have spurned me for a pack of avaricious nobodies.'

'You put me up and you could put me down, is that what you mean?'

Warwick looked at him steadily and did not answer.

He is a power, thought Edward. I could not have governed in those first weeks without him. It is a pity that there should be this rift but it was either him or Elizabeth. Warwick was half resentful, half admiring of his attitude. Edward showed no fear. He could take him outside to the block and have his head as he had had those of Rivers and his son, and Edward knew it; but he sat there smiling blandly, accepting defeat which he was implying could only be temporary.

And if the tables were turned, what then? What would Warwick's fate be?

He would be forgiven, that was clear. Edward never liked dealing death. He only did it when it was expedient to do so.

'We are leaving for my castle of Warwick,' said the Earl, and within an hour the King was riding out beside the Earl, Warwick's prisoner.

There was a smile of triumph about Warwick's mouth. He had shown Edward that the King could not remain the King without the help of the Kingmaker.

For a short while it seemed as though Warwick was the ruler of England. He considered what had happened when previous kings had been desposed. In the cases of Edward the Second and Richard the Second Parliament had been called and there the fall of the King was solemnly declared.

He was not sure what should be done. The ideal action would be to put Edward back but as a puppet of the Warwick regime. Edward was the man for king – providing he followed Warwick's rule. The Woodvilles were being dismissed. That should be a beginning.

But Warwick had miscalculated somewhere. History did not necessarily repeat itself. Edward the Second and Richard the Second had been unpopular kings; Edward the Fourth was far from that. Although his favouring of the Woodvilles was similar to the action of the other two kings with their favourites, Edward had that essential masculinity, those outstanding good looks, that ability to charm his humblest subjects.

The people might not like the Woodvilles but they liked Edward very much.

Events therefore did not move to the pattern Warwick had expected. 'Where is the King?' asked the people. 'The King is a prisoner,' was the answer. Then, decided the people, there was no more rule in the country. Rioting broke out in London and in some of the main cities and the country was soon in uproar.

Warwick moved the King to Middleham. Revolt was breaking out in the North; the Lancastrians started a rising of their own. This was disaster. Warwick had expected events to follow a pattern and they were making a new one of their own.

Edward, hearing what had happened, declared that he held nothing against the House of Neville. He knew his one-time friend and mentor Warwick cared deeply for the country and as Edward did too their aims were as one. When this unhappy matter was over the Nevilles should lose nothing. They should keep his respect as they always had.

He was moved to York which he entered in state as the King should and he set up residence at Pontefract Castle.

No sooner did the people see the King and Warwick together as friends than men began to flock to the royal banner in order to put down the Lancastrian revolt. They wanted no more civil war in the country. They had hoped the Wars of the Roses had come to an end when Edward seemed to be safe on the throne.

Warwick now saw that Edward could bring men to his banner as he, Warwick, could not. Edward had the hearts of the people. It was Edward the people wanted; and Warwick had learned that it was the people who finally settled who was to be their King.

The Londoners were clamouring for him. There was no help for it. Edward must be free to go to London to show the people that he was no one's prisoner and that Warwick had been right when he had said that his aim was to stand beside the King and bring him to safety.

With great rejoicing the King was united with the Queen. Warwick remained in the North with Clarence. He had learned a lesson. Just as he had turned defeat into victory at St Albans, so Edward had at Edgecot.

Well, had not Edward been his pupil?

There would be another time though, Warwick promised himself, and then he would be wiser.

It should not happen like this again.

Edward was in command of London but Warwick was in the North and with him was Clarence. It was a dangerous situation.

The country was divided and it was no use expecting the peace to last. Warwick had learned that he could not gather men to his banner; he might be the Kingmaker but he was no King. Edward realised too that he must make peace with Warwick if he was going to bring the country to a settled state. At the moment it was uneasy and people were ready to rise at the least provocation; there were riots in various places. Moreover Warwick had Clarence with him and Clarence could be a claimant to the throne.

Edward understood Jacquetta's grief for the loss of her husband; he knew how she and Elizabeth must hate

Warwick but Elizabeth never mentioned the Earl to him.

It was pleasant to escape into the peace of her company; she was there providing just what he wanted, and she did not intrude: she did not demand this and that. She was pleased he knew when he took honours from the Warwick faction and bestowed them on the Woodvilles. Her brother Anthony was close to him now. He had become Lord Rivers, having taken his dead father's title.

Edward sent invitations to Warwick and Clarence to come to the Council at Westminster. At first they were wary, demanding many guarantees of safe conduct; finally these were given and they came to London where Edward received them with affection.

There was no real quarrel between them, Edward assured them. 'Let us forget our grievances and go on as before.'

In Warwick Castle the Earl's daughters sat together talking quietly. Every now and then Anne glanced at her sister Isabel. Isabel was heavily pregnant; she looked ill and Anne was worried about her sister. So was the Countess their mother. Isabel had never been strong – nor had Anne for that matter; their health had been a constant cause of anxiety to their parents from their birth.

'I thank God,' the Countess had said to her daughter Anne, 'that Isabel will have her baby here at Warwick and I shall be here to look after her. We'll look after her together, Anne.'

Anne nodded. 'But she will be so happy, my lady, when her baby is born.'

'Ah yes, and so will the Duke. We'll hope for a boy. Your father has been so disappointed not to have a son.'

Anne put her arms about her mother's shoulders. 'I'm sorry, dear lady, that we were both girls.'

The Countess laughed. 'My dear child, I would not change either of you. But I did often wish that I could give your father the son he wanted. Alas, I shall never do that.'

Anne knew that at her difficult birth her father had been told that the Countess could not bear more children and she could imagine what a great blow it must have been for such an ambitious man; but he was reconciled. When he was with them he was as near to happiness as he had ever been, Anne believed. Some might not. He was an adventurer, a leader by nature, a ruler of men. The King owed his crown to him. He had made Edward as surely as he had unmade Henry.

As Anne had said to Isabel: 'It makes one uneasy to be the daughter of such a father. It is as though great things will be expected of us.'

'All that will be expected of us,' Isabel had replied, 'is to marry where we are bidden to. And when we are married to produce sons . . .'

'Daughters too perhaps,' added Anne, 'for daughters have their uses.'

And they certainly had, for Isabel was soon after that married to the Duke of Clarence.

She had been a little frightened at first, but George Plantagenet had grown fond of her and she of him. It was easy to be fond of Isabel. She was pretty and very gentle and of course she had a vast fortune, or would have when her father died – a fortune she would share with Anne.

Anne remembered days which seemed so long ago now when she and Richard had ridden together through the woods or played guessing games in the schoolroom. Where was

Richard now? she often wondered. There was a great deal of uneasiness throughout the country because her father and the King were in conflict, and all the time they were trying to pretend to each other and to the people that they were not. But they were, of course. She had heard such a lot of talk about the King's marriage and she knew how much her father hated it, hated the Woodvilles and was going to be revenged on them for taking all the important posts and marrying all the rich people so that they became more important in the country than he was.

It was a frightening situation, for Clarence was Isabel's husband and he was against his own brother and had whispered to Isabel that she might one day be a queen, for there was a scheme afoot to put him on the throne in place of his brother.

Anne was suddenly startled by the sound of galloping horses. Isabel looked up from her embroidering.

'Visitors?' she asked uneasily. They were always uneasy when visitors came to the castle nowadays, for they could never be certain what news they would bring.

Anne rose and went to the window where she could see the party in the distance and that the standard-bearer carried the device of the bear and the ragged staff.

'It is someone from our father,' she said.

Isabel murmured: 'Dear God, I trust not bad news.'

Anne was silent. Then she said: 'It *is* our father . . . and sister, your husband is with him. I will go at once and find our mother.'

Anne hurried out of the room while Isabel rose and went to the window. The riders were now clattering into the court-yard. Isabel saw her young husband. He had leaped from his horse and a groom had run forward. She heard her father's voice shouting orders.

The Countess was already in the courtyard with Anne. Warwick embraced first his wife and then his daughter.

Anne knew by the set expression of his face that something was wrong. He said: 'Let us go in. I have much to say and there is little time.'

Ominous words, she thought. Something fresh had happened. How she wished there did not have to be this trouble. It seemed so wrong that there should be a quarrel between her father and the King. They had always been such good friends. And Isabel's husband was actually the King's brother which made it all most unnatural.

But now something very important was afoot. Anne noticed that her mother was trembling slightly and it was not only due to the excitement of the unexpected arrival of her husband.

The Earl lost no time in explaining the situation for they must leave at once since there was not a moment to spare. He was being pursued by his enemies and if he were caught that would be the end of him, the end of them all. They must get to the coast with all haste and then sail for France, where his very good friend the King would give him temporary shelter and the means to get back to England.

'You cannot mean this,' cried the Countess. 'Do you know that Isabel's baby is due within a month?'

'My dear lady, I know that well and I know that even so it is dangerous for us to stay here. The King's men are marching to take me. My plans have gone wrong. I shall be at his mercy and that will be the end of me. Nothing less than my head will suit him.'

Anne said: 'I will go and prepare Isabel. She will have to be carried in a litter.'

'God help us!' cried the Countess.

'Now let us lose no time,' said the Earl; and he began giving orders.

While Warwick's messengers were making their way to the coasts of Devon and Dorset with orders for ships to be made ready, the party set out. Both Anne and her mother were deeply concerned about Isabel's condition for she was clearly finding the travel both irksome and dangerous.

Warwick and his family safely embarked on one of the vessels he had managed to commandeer and they all sailed for Southampton where he kept several of his stoutest ships. Unfortunately for Warwick, Lord Rivers who was more energetic and astute than his father had intercepted them and a battle ensued.

Anne sat with her sister in one of the cabins and tried to interest her in talk of the coming baby but the sound of gunfire shattered the peace and Anne greatly feared what might be happening to her father's ships. After what seemed like an interminable battle, although the Earl had lost several of his ships the one in which his family were travelling managed to escape, and with a few of the other vessels which had survived, sailed out to sea.

As they neared Calais, Warwick sent out a message to his friend and ally Lord Wenloch, to ascertain what their welcome would be in that port. The answer came back that it would be hostile and that the Duke of Burgundy on one side and the Yorkists on the other were waiting for his arrival and were standing by for his capture. He would, therefore, do better to land at a French port and throw himself on the hospitality of the King of France.

Warwick, who had on more than one occasion shown himself to be master of the sea, turned from Calais. He had always been at his best against desperate odds, and he was already making plans – plans which at first might seem quite wild and impossible; but the more outrageous they were the more they stimulated the Earl.

Meanwhile Isabel was causing great anxiety, for her pains had started and it had become clear that her child was about to be born on the high seas.

'We must get into port at once,' cried the Countess.

Warwick was overcome with anxiety for his daughter but he knew that to go into port was impossible for if they attempted to land they would be taken into captivity.

Anne was frantic. 'We need so much. There are no herbs, no soothing medicines, no midwife . . .'

The Countess said: 'We must do our best.' A storm had arisen, and the wind began to howl and the boat to rock; and in the midst of the storm Isabel's child was born.

That she lived was a miracle but the child was dead. Isabel lay delirious on a pallet while Anne and the Countess prepared the little body for burial. The child was a boy and Anne could not help reflecting that had he lived he might have been the King of England.

There was a sad little ceremony when the child's body sewn into a sheet was slipped into the sea. Anne reflected that mercifully Isabel was spared witnessing the burial.

Afterwards she and her mother went back to Isabel. She must be their first concern. Anne knew that her mother was trying to shut out of her mind pictures of Isabel's being wrapped in a sheet before *she* was dropped into the sea.

'So,' said Warwick, 'I have lost my grandson. We must look forward. There will be more.'

His eyes were on Anne and there was a new speculation in

them which she did not notice, so intent was she on her sister's tragedy. If she had she would have been very uneasy indeed.

Isabel began to get a little better and the weather had become much calmer. They were still at sea. Warwick had turned pirate; he had captured several Burgundian vessels and his men were reminded of the great days when he had made his name as Captain of Calais and they had believed that Warwick was invincible.

Warwick's belief in himself may have faltered a little, but only a little, and had returned in full force. He was going to recapture all he had lost. He could do that with the help of a king and that king was the King of France. It was Warwick's destiny to work through kings. He did not possess the necessary titles to stand on his own as ruler. He was the manipulator. He made the rules but someone else must appear to carry them out.

He had grandiose ideas as he sailed to the mouth of the Seine and reached the port of Harfleur.

Isabel's health improved and with land in sight, Anne and her mother rejoiced. The nightmare journey was over.

The party was made welcome in France. King Edward was the enemy of Louis and Louis was Warwick's friend. The King of France had flattered Warwick by his show of affection and the common enemies were Edward and Burgundy. Therefore there was hope for the Earl in France for his good friend Louis was ready to receive him and listen to his plans.

It was in the castle of Amboise that Anne learned how deeply she was involved in those plans.

They had arrived on a beautiful afternoon in May and the

château set upon a plateau was a beautiful sight with its massive buttresses and cylindrical towers mounted by their sharp conical points.

The women were always glad when they came to a hospitable castle, for the days of travelling were exhausting to all three of them and particularly to Isabel.

It was at Amboise where the party was entertained with great ceremony by the King of France who seemed determined to make them welcome and imply that he was ready to help.

The King expressed great interest in the young ladies and particularly in Anne who gained the impression that she was the subject of conversation between her father and the King. She wondered then if they had some marriage in mind for her which was usually the case when interest was focused on young girls.

She was fifteen years of age and therefore becoming marriageable she supposed, and the prospect was one to cause her some apprehension.

In those days which now seemed so long ago, she and Richard had loved to be together. They had talked of many things; they had loved books; they were more serious than Isabel and George had been. They had never discussed marrying but Anne had on one or two occasions heard the servants mention it. They had said what a nice pair they made, how fond they were of each other and how pleasant it would be for young people who had spent their early life in each other's company and got to know each other's ways to be together in their later life.

She had known what they meant and somewhere at the back of her mind there had been the thought that one day she would marry Richard.

But now Richard was far away, their circumstances had done a turnabout so that now they were on different sides and she feared that she might never see him again. She guessed that he must hate her father because Richard had always believed that his brother Edward was the most wonderful being on earth and he would naturally hate anyone who was Edward's enemy. Oh, it was all so difficult to understand, so depressing and alarming now to consider that there might be some marriage prospect for her which did not include her childhood friend.

Soon after that her father went away and she with her mother and sister was left at Amboise, there to stay until she was sent for.

It seemed a long time that they were there. Perhaps that was because after the King and the Earl had left there was a quietness about the days, and they might have been at home at Warwick or Middleham; Isabel was still recuperating from her confinement and was often pale and listless.

Once she said to Anne: 'We are only daughters, and the purpose of a daughter is to make a marriage which will be advantageous to her family.'

'Did you not love George then?'

Isabel was thoughtful. 'Yes, I love George in a way . . . But you know why he married me. It was to spite his brother and because that was our father's price for helping him to the throne. That is what George wants, you know. He has always wanted it.'

Anne knew it was true.

'Isabel,' she said, 'we are very rich, or when our father dies we shall be. We both shall have a great fortune to bring to our husbands. Perhaps it would have been better if we had been the daughters of a poor man.'

'Then we could not have had part, could we, in this battle for a throne,' agreed Isabel.

'Poor Isabel!'

'If my baby had lived I should have thought it worthwhile.''

'I daresay you will have more. That is what we are for is it not? To have babies . . . preferably sons . . . and to bring wealth to our husbands.'

'Dear Anne, you are becoming cynical. I always thought you were meant for Richard.'

'Yes, I thought so too.'

'And you would have been but for this quarrel. Our father married me to one of the King's brothers, but of course the King did not want the marriage.'

'He has always had to do what our father wished.'

'Even now . . .'

'Even now there is this trouble because he turned from our father to the Woodvilles. I wonder what will be the outcome of it.'

They did not speak for some time. They were both wondering about the future.

Messengers came back and forth from the castle, for the Earl kept his Countess informed of those matters over which he thought he should need her help. That was why he left it to her to break the news to Anne.

The Earl loved his daughters. He would expect them to obey him, of course, and do everything they could to forward the interests of the House of Warwick, but he wanted to make it as easy for them as possible.

He did not want his gentle daughter Anne presented with a prospect to which he believed she would need a little time to adjust herself. So he asked the Countess to give her an inkling of what was in store for her.

The Countess herself read her husband's letter several times wondering whether she had read correctly, for what he wrote astounded her. But finally she saw the reasoning behind his actions and realised that it was exactly what she should have expected him to do. If he could not impose his will in one way he would in another. She should have been accustomed to such surprises by now.

Poor Anne, she thought. What will she think of this? But Richard was right to want her to be prepared.

She sent for her daughter.

Anne came apprehensively, certain that she was going to be made the victim of some match which would be necessary to her father's schemes. So she was half prepared.

Her mother after kissing her tenderly bade her be seated.

'You know your father has been away some time. He and the King have been to Angers where they have visited the Queen.'

'The Queen. I thought . . .'

'No, no child, not the Queen of France. The Queen of England.'

'Queen Elizabeth is in England, I thought.'

The Countess realised she was being deliberately obtuse to give herself time. She decided to come straight to the point. 'No, my dear, I mean Queen Margaret, who has been in exile here in France for so long.'

'My father . . . visiting Margaret of Anjou! She will not receive him surely?'

'She was reluctant to. But you know your father. He is the most persistent man in the world. Now he has succeeded in making an agreement with her and you are to marry her son, the Prince of Wales.'

Anne stared at her mother in amazement.

'Yes,' went on the Countess, 'I know it is hard to believe but it is true. Your father is determined to drive Edward from the throne and put Henry back on it. My child, do you realise what this means? If he succeeds, and your father always succeeds, you will be Queen of England . . . when Henry dies and his son comes to the throne.'

'I see,' said Anne, 'that my father is determined to have both his daughters contenders for the throne.'

They regarded each other a little sadly. Both had been used to further Richard Neville's greatness. He had been the son of the Earl of Salisbury but without great prospects until he married the Earl of Warwick's daughter and through her acquired the great title of Warwick and the vast estates that went with it. The Countess had served her husband well. Now it was Anne's turn.

'Your father did not wish you to be hurried . . . He wanted you to have time . . . to get used to the idea of marriage.'

'But I shall be married to this Prince all the same.'

'My dear child, your father has made up his mind. The King of France agrees that it is an ideal match and at last they have persuaded Margaret of Anjou that it is the only way to regain her throne.'

'She has surely never agreed to ally herself with my father. They have been the greatest enemies.'

'She sees this as a way back to the throne. Oh Anne, my dear daughter, if it comes to pass, if we could go home . . . if we could be happy again . . .'

'Happy. Do you think we shall be happy? First my father has to fight. Do you think Edward will stand by and calmly let him put Henry on the throne? Will Richard . . . ?'

'Your father makes and unmakes kings. Edward would never have been on the throne but for him. He will put Henry back, you will see.'

'But Henry is little more than an imbecile.'

'He is the anointed king.'

'So is Edward.'

'But your father has decided that Edward must go.'

'And Edward will no doubt decide he will stay.'

'My dear, we know nothing of these matters. You must prepare yourself to be married to the Prince of Wales.'

'To a man I have been brought up to believe was our enemy, the son of a mad king and a mother who is . . .'

'Hush child. You must not say such things. They are our friends now.'

'Shall we ever be allowed to choose our own friends, I wonder.'

'Come now. This will be a brilliant marriage for you. A Prince! Why most girls would be overcome with joy. It is your father's plan that you shall one day be Queen of England.'

'Isabel was promised that.'

'Your father no longer trusts Clarence. Besides Henry is the true King and his son is naturally the heir. Your father is of the opinion that the people will welcome his return and that will be the end of Edward.'

'Edward has many friends.' She was thinking again of Richard: his fervent adoration of his brother, his intense and burning loyalty.

Oh Richard, she thought, we shall be on different sides.

'Your father thinks that Henry has always had the affection of the people.'

'So has Edward.'

'You are talking of matters of which you know very little, my dear. Your task is to make yourself charming so that the Prince is pleased to make you his wife. Now you may go. You should start preparing yourself at once for we shall be leaving for Angers in a few days' time.' She looked at her daughter sadly.

Poor child, she thought. She is bewildered. She always thought she was meant for Richard of Gloucester and so did we all. But the fortunes of women sway with the fortunes of war.

Anne knelt before the haughty woman whose face showed signs of great beauty now ravaged by grief, rage, frustration – emotions felt so intensely that they had left their mark on her.

Margaret of Anjou was a most unhappy woman. She had come to England with dreams of greatness; she had ruled her weak-minded husband and loved him in a way; and she had suffered the bitter hopelessness of exile, going from place to place, relying on others for even the means to live and for a woman of her nature that was perhaps the greatest ordeal of all.

Now her greatest enemy who, she believed, was responsible for her woes had come offering the olive branch. What an effort it had taken to accept it. She had wanted to fling it back in his face; and indeed had submitted him to some humiliation before she would accept. Warwick was a man of ambition and he was ready to kneel in humility if necessary to achieve his ends. And he had done so, for at last she had subdued her pride because her only hope lay in this man and what he could do for her.

She had made him swear upon the true cross in Angers Cathedral that Henry VI was the only King of England and that he would bring him back to the throne. He was to be a figurehead for all knew that he was too far gone in senility to rule. The Prince should be the Regent. And she knew who would be the power behind the Regency. That was inevitable. Why should Warwick fight for her unless he was going to get something out of it?

And that was not all. His daughter was to marry the Prince. So Anne Neville would be Queen of England.

It was a big price to ask. But what a reward it would be if they were successful. It was worth the price. To be back there, to be Queen again. Naturally she must pay highly for that.

Warwick's daughter, her daughter-in-law! It was ironical; it was comical. But she said fiercely, the marriage shall not take place until Warwick has recovered the throne for Henry.

There would have to be a betrothal, of course. But she was agreeable to that and she would quite happily give her son to this girl, though he was worthy of the most high-born princess – in exchange for Warwick's help in recovering the throne.

So here was the girl.

Pale, pretty, charming in a way, and so young. As young as Margaret had been when she came to England. How full of hope she had been then; the daughter of an impoverished man with the somewhat empty title of King, she had realised her good fortune. This girl's fate was similar yet it was her father's power and riches which had brought her to this stage.

'Rise, my dear,' she said. 'Come close to me.'

She looked into the pale oval face, at the eyes which were shadowed with apprehension and the heart of Margaret of Anjou which alternated from being as hard as stone to being as soft as butter, began to melt.

'There is no need to fear,' she said. 'You are to be with me until we can return to England. You are to be the bride of the finest young man in the world. There.'

She drew her forward and kissed her cheek.

She might hate the father – even though he was her ally now – but she could not hate this pale trembling girl.

There was a formal meeting between Anne and her husband-to-be. Edward was handsome, slim and nearly eighteen years old. He looked curiously at Anne and taking her hand kissed it in accordance with what was expected of him.

Edward had no great desire to marry but he knew this marriage was necessary and it had to be this girl because her father was the great Kingmaker who could put men on the throne and then take the throne away from them. He had been brought up to hate him because his mother had always said it was Warwick who had made Edward King. It was particularly galling to her because after the second battle of St Albans which she had won, Warwick had marched to London and claimed the throne for Edward.

That was all past history and now a glittering prospect was opening before them. To make it a possibility certain unpleasant conditions had been demanded. One was friendship with Warwick; another was the Prince's marriage to his daughter.

But at their meeting he was agreeably surprised. She looked so gentle, so eager to please. She was pale and delicate-looking but he did not mind that. Although he himself was handsome his features were of a somewhat effeminate mould. He knew this had worried his mother who had wanted to make a warrior of him. For that reason she had made him be present when he was quite young at a bloody execution. In fact she had asked him to give the verdict on two men whom she considered had betrayed her. He vividly recalled saying what he knew was expected of him: 'Let us have their heads.'

And the execution had been carried out in his sight. He had known then that heads were not only hacked off. There was blood . . . so much blood.

Yet he had sat through it and his mother had said she was proud of him. He had to do those things because his handsome face would have done for a girl as well as a boy and he had to show that he made up in warlike spirit for what he lacked in strong and masculine looks.

And now here was Anne Neville – a quiet, self-effacing girl. He was glad of that. He would have expected the daughter of Warwick to be a forceful lady . . . someone rather like his mother.

'So they are going to marry us,' he said.

He spoke in a friendly way and she sensed that he was as apprehensive as she was. There was an immediate rapport between them. Anne smiled and her smile beautified her face, wiping away the fear.

She is very pretty, thought the Prince. Perhaps it is not so bad after all . . . even though she is Warwick's daughter.

She thought: He looks kind, so it is not so bad . . . even though he is not Richard.

At the end of July the ceremony of betrothal took place in the Cathedral of Angers. The marriage would be celebrated, Margaret of Anjou had declared, when her husband Henry the King was safely on the throne.

The ceremony was binding, however, and although she was

not yet quite a wife, Anne regarded the young Prince as her husband.

The Countess was delighted that Margaret had taken a liking to her daughter and she herself was finding it easier than she had believed possible to feel friendly towards the Queen.

Warwick had left for England to put his plan into action and they were all waiting with eagerness for the result. Because it was Warwick's plan and Warwick was in charge of its success, incredible as it was, they found it easy to believe that it would succeed.

In the meantime the King of France was determined to show them that he was their friend. This of course was due to the fact that the Duke of Burgundy was Edward's ally and the friendship between those two had become stronger since the marriage of Edward's sister Margaret with the Duke.

They did not intend to stay in Angers and after Warwick's departure they left for Paris. Louis had sent a guard of honour to escort them and Margaret entered Paris as a Queen. With her were her son, Anne, and the Countess of Warwick. She was happier than she had been for years.

All she wanted now was to hear that Warwick's plan had succeeded and that she with the Prince was to return to England to take up their rightful positions there.

The streets of Paris were gaily decorated on the orders of the King and they took up their residence at the Palace of St Pol, where they lived in luxury which was all the more appreciated because of the hardships they had all so recently suffered.

Time passed slowly and each day they waited eagerly for news.

At last it came.

King Henry had been freed from the Tower and was in possession of the kingdom. Once more Warwick had succeeded.

Margaret was wild with joy; the Prince was exuberant.

'Now we shall return to England and claim our own,' he declared.

Anne was wondering what had happened to Edward and most of all to Richard.

Edward was in the North when news of Warwick's arrival was brought to him. He could not believe it. Warwick – to join forces with Margaret of Anjou! Anne Neville betrothed to the Prince! He was astounded. He had always refused to believe that Warwick could really become his enemy.

He was concerned for Elizabeth and the children who were in London and to make matters more awkward Elizabeth was far advanced in pregnancy. Cecily was merely a year or so old and even the eldest, another Elizabeth, was only five. Warwick would very likely have the South-east with him, for he had always been popular there.

Edward rejoiced that Montague could be trusted to hold the North. John Neville, Lord Montague was the only Neville who had failed to support his brother, and he remained faithful to Edward. This had been a great help because Montague was one of the most successful captains in England. It was a source of great irritation to Warwick that a member of the family should not support him. But Montague had sworn allegiance to the Yorkist cause as they all had in the beginning and he was not going to break his word now just because his brother had.

At least that was before Edward had restored estates to the

Earl of Northumberland which Montague had looked upon as his. For his successful campaigns he had been awarded the title of Marquis of Montague but of what use was that with only what had been called a 'pye's nest' to maintain it.

Edward had forgotten this and did not realise that he had committed another of his mistakes in judging the characters of men. Montague had fought for him and stood beside him against his own brother and all he had been given was an empty title. Now Warwick had landed in England.

Edward was completely shocked when news came to him that Montague had rallied his men and called for Henry and that he was now marching to join Warwick. Edward was deserted and in the direst danger.

He was dining with his brother Richard, Hastings and Rivers when a messenger came galloping hot speed from Montague's camp.

'My lord, my lord,' he cried. 'Lord Montague has turned against you. He is already on the march. There is not a moment to lose. He is calling for King Henry and his brother and his army are with him. He is coming here to capture you and take you a prisoner to the Earl of Warwick.'

So Warwick was marching from the South and Montague, the traitor who had suddenly decided to change sides, was coming from the North. If he remained here he would be caught in a pincer movement between the two of them.

Richard was looking at him waiting for his orders. The dear boy would do everything he asked of him.

'There is only one thing we can do,' he said. 'We have to escape. Come. Every second is precious. Rally the men. We must get to the coast. We'll make our way to my sister of Burgundy. But first . . . to the sea.'

Richard was wondering whether they should stay and fight.

'A handful of us against an army!' cried Edward. 'There can be no more than eight hundred of us. No, brother, all the courage in the world – and I know you have that – would avail us nothing. We will go . . . for the time. But it is only a breathing space. We shall be back. Then woe to Warwick.'

They were fortunate. They reached Lynn in safety and in a short while were on their way to Holland.

Elizabeth was preparing for the birth of her fourth child by Edward. She was certain this time it would be the longed-for boy. She must be grateful that she could bear children so easily and so quickly following one on another; it was a great asset in a Queen.

She had decided that the Tower would be a good place for the birth and she had had an apartment made ready there for her lying-in. It was very elaborate with crimson damask and fine Brittany linen – a room worthy of the King's son.

Mrs Cobbe, the midwife who had attended her before and on whose skill she felt she could rely, was in attendance already. There were a few weeks to go, but one could never be sure with babies. Jacquetta had agreed with her that every precaution should be taken. Edward was in the North and she hoped that she would soon be sending joyful news to him.

There was something strange going on in the streets. She had been aware of it all day. She had gone to the window and seen them on the other side of the river gathering in crowds. The people were getting excited.

She wondered what was happening. Was Edward returning unexpectedly? He always liked to be close when his children were born.

Elizabeth was serenely content. She had still kept her hold on Edward after nearly six years of marriage; he was as devoted and as loving as ever; it was true he had his mistresses, but as that gave her a little respite from the indefatigable man she should perhaps rejoice rather than lament. She could say that she held his affections; he found in her an ideal wife. No recriminations; acceptance of his need for mistresses; agreeing with him and only asserting herself in matters which were of the utmost importance to her and which would not greatly affect him. If he knew she meddled as she had done in the marriages of her family and the case of Lord Desmond, he said nothing. She allowed him his amatory adventures and that meant a great deal to him. Of course he would not have discontinued them however much she protested but he was above all a man who liked to live in peace and that was what she allowed him to do.

Moreover she gave him children – girls so far but the boys would come.

And this by the way she carried him, so said Mrs Cobbe, was a boy; and Mrs Cobbe would not deceive her just to please her for a while. That was not Mrs Cobbe's nature.

Her mother came into the apartment and it was immediately clear that Jacquetta was disturbed.

'There is a great murmuring going on in the streets.'

'What is wrong with them now?'

'There are rumours that Warwick has landed.'

'Warwick? He was driven out.'

'That does not prevent his coming back. They say he has landed and is bringing an army with him.'

'That's impossible.'

'No, I'm afraid not. I have kept the news from you for the

last few days because I thought it was not good for you to worry in your condition. But it is getting serious now. Do you know what they are saying? Warwick has joined with Margaret of Anjou and their purpose is to put Henry back on the throne.'

'What!' cried Elizabeth, her face losing its delicate colour.

'My dear, you must not distress yourself, but I think it is time we took some action.'

'Where is Warwick now?'

'They say he is on the way to London. They are expecting him.'

'Warwick . . . on his way here! Then what will become of us . . . ?'

'I think we are unsafe here.'

'They would not dare to harm us . . . Edward will soon be here.'

'My dear daughter, I know you will be calm. The news is worse than I have told you. Edward has fled the country. Montague has deserted and Edward with Richard, Hastings and Anthony got away from Lynn by boat. They have gone to somewhere on the Continent.'

'I can't believe it. We were so . . . safe.'

'Life changes. But what are we going to do? If you stay here you will be Warwick's prisoner.'

'And when you consider what he did to our father and John . . . I could kill him, for what he did to them.'

'I too,' said Jacquetta quietly. 'But we have to think of ourselves now; it is a matter of safety not revenge . . . just yet. Edward will come back, I know. But in the meantime we have to think of what would be best for us to do.'

The Queen looked round the apartment which she had so

carefully prepared. There was the new feather bed – quite the most luxurious she had ever seen – and she must leave all this and go . . . but where?

'We should get out of London perhaps,' she said.

'In your condition! And with the little girls. Nay, I have an idea. We will go to Westminster . . . to the Sanctuary. He will not dare to touch us there.'

Elizabeth was silent for a while. Her mother was right. They had to get away from Warwick and quickly.

'Then,' she said, '. . . to the Sanctuary. Send for Mrs Cobbe and tell her that we must go.'

Mrs Cobbe who was never far away came running in with a dismayed look on her honest face for she immediately thought that the Queen had started her pains.

She was relieved to see that this was not so for it was a few weeks too early but when she heard about the plans for flight she was very disturbed.

'The Queen is in no condition . . .' she began.

'The Queen is in no condition to be Warwick's prisoner, Mrs Cobbe. We have to go. There is no help for it. But not far. We shall go to Westminster to the Sanctuary.'

'Then we must go carefully,' said Mrs Cobbe. 'We want no early birth for this one. He's going to be a boy, that he is.'

Mrs Cobbe gathered together all she thought they could take with them and Elizabeth with Jacquetta and Lady Scrope, who was in attendance, Mrs Cobbe and the three little girls made their way out of the Tower to the water's edge.

Mrs Cobbe lifted little Cecily into the waiting barge and Lady Scrope helped Elizabeth and Mary while Jacquetta gave her attention to her daughter.

The barge started up the river to Westminster.

'I pray we shall be in time,' said Lady Scrope.

They had reached the tall square keep beside St Margaret's church near the graveyard and west door of the Abbey.

It looked cold and uninviting and Cecily began to whimper.

'Hush my precious,' murmured Mrs Cobbe and Elizabeth said in a shrill voice: 'I want to go back. I don't like it here.'

'I don't like it,' added Mary, who repeated everything Elizabeth said.

'Now now children,' said Lady Scrope, 'we are all very happy to be here. It is nice and safe and that is the best of all.'

'*I* don't think it's best of all,' said Elizabeth. 'It's cold and I want to go.'

'Be silent, children,' said Jacquetta. 'You will do as you are told and you are all going to sleep soon.'

They were a little in awe of Jacquetta and said nothing more.

But all the adults could well understand the children's revulsion. The Sanctuary was not made for comfort.

There were two storeys in the Sanctuary. On the upper floor was the church and the lower floor had been turned into a dwelling for fugitives who feared that they were in danger. It was considered to be holy ground and no one would dare touch them while they sheltered there. The place was dark and cold and the only light that came in was through narrow arched windows of which there were only two cut into those thick stone walls.

Mrs Cobbe looked round. She wondered if she could go back to the Tower and bring a few more articles with her which they would need. She had managed to bring a certain amount but she would need more.

Elizabeth was reluctant to let her go but Mrs Cobbe

overruled her objections. 'Who would harm a poor midwife?' she asked.

'Warwick would . . . if he knew you were mine.'

'Trust me, my lady. And who knows, your pains could start at any time after all this upset. I shall go back.'

And go back she did, for which Elizabeth was to be grateful for the good woman brought back several articles without which their sojourn in the Sanctuary would have been even more uncomfortable . . . and possibly dangerous. Moreover she brought food with her for on the way she had met the good butcher who supplied the Tower, one William Gould with whom she was on particularly good terms. He told her that Warwick's army was on the outskirts of London and that they had escaped from the Tower just in time. They were going to be hungry in the Sanctuary, so he had given her some beef and mutton and some of his very special pork pies.

'He is a good man, my lady,' said Mrs Cobbe. 'He has promised me that he will keep an eye on us while we are here and see that we do not starve.'

'And you are a good creature, Mrs Cobbe,' said the Queen.

'I do not know what we should do without you,' added Jacquetta.

They tried some of the excellent pork pie and to their astonishment found they could eat even overcome by anxiety as they were. Elizabeth was wondering what could have happened to Edward and if she would ever see him again, and whether her brief glory was at an end. Jacquetta was silent. She hated Warwick. There was a very special fear in her heart for he had tried to accuse her of witchcraft and just after the death of her dear husband and beloved son had shown an image to the King which he had said she had made of him.

Warwick had implied that Edward had been forced to marry Elizabeth through witchcraft which was practised by her mother and that the image was meant to be the King and that she was plotting against his life.

Edward had laughed that to scorn. It was all so ridiculous. Why should she plot against his life when all the blessings the Woodville family enjoyed came from him? It showed though how Warwick hated her. How she hated them all! Indeed this war between Warwick and Edward was about the Woodvilles. It was because they had ousted the Nevilles from the King's favour. So assuredly Warwick hated them – her, her sons and Elizabeth . . . Elizabeth most of all . . . and all the little children.

How wise they were to throw themselves into Sanctuary. They must remain here. Warwick would never dare to touch them then. But how vulnerable they would be . . . here in Westminster while Warwick took London.

We must be safe, though, she thought. Elizabeth must have her child. Warwick would never dare to harm us.

It soon became clear that they had come just in time. Warwick reached London where he was well received, and Mrs Cobbe, having paid another visit to the butcher Gould, came in with the news that King Henry had been taken from his prison in the Tower.

'They say he was in a terrible state,' she said. 'Not as a king should be by any means. They say he was dirty and frightened in a way, wondering what it was all about and muttering prayers and things like that. The Earl had him washed and fed and put into purple and ermine. They've put him in the royal apartments, my ladies. They say his bedchamber is the one that was made ready for our little baby.'

Elizabeth closed her eyes. She was filled with rage to think of all the care that had gone into the making of that apartment – the damask hangings, the feather bed . . . for Henry of Lancaster! It was infuriating.

'Gould says there's to be a procession to St Paul's. He is to be the new King, my lady, so they say. Don't you fret. My lord King Edward will not stay long away from you.'

Jacquetta was tight-lipped, seeking to see good omens and refusing to accept bad ones. But the future looked dark indeed with Edward in exile and Warwick back in command putting a new King on the throne.

But soon for a while they ceased to think about what was happening outside for Elizabeth's baby was about to be born.

In spite of all that had happened it was a comparatively easy birth and to the delight of Elizabeth and her mother the child was healthy and a boy.

It was ironical that this longed-for event should come while Elizabeth was in Sanctuary and Edward far away.

'We'll call him Edward,' said Elizabeth.

She would look back on those days as some of the strangest in her life. Jacquetta perhaps suffered most. She was getting old and was unused to discomfort. Elizabeth was better able to endure them. Her calm nature was a great asset in such circumstances and she was firmly convinced that Edward would soon come back and defeat the traitor Warwick and put imbecile King Henry back where he belonged. The children grew accustomed to life in the Sanctuary very quickly and Mary at any rate could scarcely remember anything else. As for Cecily she was quite unaware of the change in her surroundings. Young Elizabeth now and then asked when they were going home, but at length she too accepted the Sanctuary as home.

Elizabeth the Queen declared she would never forget the services of Mrs Cobbe and the butcher. One she declared had saved her child and the other had saved them from starvation.

Warwick had quickly shown that he was not going to concern himself with them. He would be very unpopular if he attacked a woman and her little children. He regarded Elizabeth as of no importance now that Edward was in exile.

He could go straight ahead with his plans which meant that he would be ruling through Henry. Margaret would in due course come to England with her son the Prince of Wales and Anne; and in due course his daughter would be Queen of England. A notable achievement for a Kingmaker.

So why bother with Elizabeth Woodville? Let her stay in Sanctuary with her brood. She was no concern of his.

It was not dificult for messengers to get to the Sanctuary. Elizabeth was considerably heartened to hear that Edward had reached Bruges and was being given shelter there by his sister Margaret, the Duchess of Burgundy. She should be of good heart for he would soon be back with her where he belonged.

It was cheering news.

Warwick raised no objection to the little Prince's being baptised in the Abbey. There was no ceremony attached to the proceedings and Elizabeth compared this with the baptism of her girls. How strange that this should be the lot of the long-awaited son!

But Edward's words were with her. It would not be long. Jacquetta assured her that the signs were that Edward would indeed be back.

Christmas came and went. The little Prince who had been born on the 1st of November continued to thrive. They tried to celebrate the festival as well as they were able and because of the goodness of the butcher they were not without food. Mrs Cobbe and Lady Scrope managed to get some warmer clothing for them all and so they struggled on.

'God send the spring quickly this year,' said Jacquetta. Her eyes were shining with a strange prophetic light. 'With the spring will come escape from this sad state, I know.'

Elizabeth believed her. It helped her to bear the hardships.

Margaret of Burgundy welcomed her brothers to her Court at Bruges. She was delighted to be of service to them but distressed at the cause of their visit. Margaret had already made her mark at the Burgundian Court. She had inherited her strong character from her mother and she seemed more than ever to resemble Proud Cis; but there was a kindliness in her nature which her mother lacked and this trait had already made her loved and respected at her husband's Court.

Charles, the Duke, was pleased with his wife. Margaret was a good stepmother to his son and daughter of his first marriage. She was devoted to her own family and she put herself absolutely at the disposal of her brother in his need. It was fortunate that Burgundy was Edward's ally and that relations between Louis of France and the Duke were very antagonistic. Louis of course was Warwick's friend and had helped him to return to England, so it was only natural therefore that Burgundy should help Edward; and since the Duchess of Burgundy was Edward's sister that made it all the easier.

Strangely enough what distressed the Duchess almost as much as Edward's loss of his throne – though they all insisted that that was temporary – was the defection of Clarence. That one member of the family should proclaim himself the enemy of another, was to her intolerable.

Secretly she made up her mind that she would try to persuade George to stop this nonsense. She had always been rather fond of George – more so than she had of Richard. She knew that Richard was perhaps more worthy, that he was good, studious and devoted to Edward. She knew too that George was too fond of eating, drinking – particularly drinking – and generally indulging himself. He was vain, because he had a certain charm; he was handsome though they all suffered by comparison with Edward; he was clever in a way, sharp, crafty rather than brilliant. But how could one explain one's likes and dislikes? George had always been a favourite of hers.

He must be made to realise the dishonour of turning to Warwick against his own brother.

Edward was astounded by the splendour of the Court at Bruges. He had always known that Burgundy was not only the most powerful man in France but the richest, but this far surpassed his own Courts at Westminster and Windsor and he had been considered somewhat extravagant in his love of tasteful decorations and furniture.

But this was no time for such comparisons. His great aim was to get help which would enable him to sail back to England, to rout out Warwick and when he had done so . . . What? The idea of beheading Warwick could arouse no enthusiasm in him. There was so much he could remember of Warwick. How he had adored him in the old days! And to think it had come to this was so distressing. One of the worst aspects of being driven out of his kingdom was the fact that Warwick had done it.

Although Margaret was passionately devoted to her brother's cause, her husband was reluctant to support Edward outwardly.

'Louis is waiting for a chance to attack me,' he said, 'and if he and the Lancastrians joined up against me . . . I should be in a difficult position. Louis is treating Margaret and her son as very honoured guests . . . friends even. I have to go carefully.'

He was willing to help Edward in secret but he would not come out in the open and do so. This was frustrating, for the acknowledged support of the Duke would have gone a long way.

However, Edward was optimistic. Each week brought new help. The merchants had always been aware of Edward's superior qualities as a ruler and were ready to support him and money came to him from the Hanseatic towns. As the months passed he could see the day coming nearer when it would be possible for him to land with an army which could win him a victory over his enemies.

During those months he became very interested in an Englishman who had taken service in the Burgundian Court under the patronage of his sister. This was a certain William Caxton who had begun his career as a mercer to a rich merchant called Large who had been Lord Mayor of London. Caxton had gone to Bruges on the death of the Mayor and became associated with the merchant adventurers. He became a successful businessman and did much to promote trade between England and the Low Countries. But as he grew older – he must have been about fifty years of age when Edward arrived at his sister's Court – he became interested in literature, and when Margaret suggested he join her Court and continue his writing, Caxton gladly accepted the invitation.

Edward talked to him of the merchant adventurers with whom he had had some dealing but he was more interested in his literary work, particularly a book which he was translating called *Le Recueil des Histoires de Troye*.

They discussed together the interest of such a work to many people and how unfortunate it was that so few could read it as there was only one copy and it took so long to make another.

Caxton had heard of a process which had been invented in Cologne and which was called a printing-press. He had seen this and had been most interested in it. Edward listened and agreed that it would be a very good thing to have and he wondered whether it would be possible to bring it to England. Caxton was sure it would be and when he had finished his translation he intended to go again to Cologne and then possibly set up a press in Bruges.

'I will remember that,' Edward told him, 'and I hope that when we are in a happier state in England you will visit the Court there.'

Caxton said that it would be an honour to do so, for although he had lived long abroad and had been made most welcome in the Duchess's Court he did often long for his native land.

The weeks passed quickly and during them Edward worked indefatigably building up arms and men in preparation for crossing the Channel. By March he had accumulated a force of some twelve thousand men and with Richard of Gloucester and Earl Rivers he set sail from Flushing. The weather was against him and it was ten days before he reached Cromer. Some of his men landed to test the state of opinion in that area and discovered that it was solidly in Warwick's control; he sailed on northwards and finally landed at Ravenspur.

It was not as easy as he had thought for what the people dreaded more than anything was civil war. They had favoured Edward but Edward had been driven out of the country. True, they knew Henry was weak, but Warwick was behind him and Warwick had that aura of greatness which they respected.

But as Edward came to York he found there were plenty to rally to his banner and he began the march south. He was near Banbury when he heard that Clarence was not far off and shortly afterwards Clarence sent a messenger on in advance to tell Edward that he wanted to speak with him.

Edward was pleased for there was a conciliatory note in the message and he believed that his brother was fast regretting his action in turning against him.

Edward was thoughtful. Could it really be that George was looking for a reconciliation? It was too good to be true. If it were so he would forgive him with all his heart. Not that he would ever trust him again. When he came to think of it he had never really trusted Clarence. But if he and his brother were friends again, if Clarence brought his men to fight for him, this would be a tremendous blow to Warwick.

Yes, certainly he would welcome Clarence. Let them meet without delay.

Outwardly it was an affectionate meeting. Clarence looked at Edward shamefacedly and would have knelt, but Edward laid a hand on his arm and said: 'George, so you want us to be friends again?'

'I have been most unhappy,' said Clarence. 'It was all so un-natural. I was under the influence of Warwick and I want to escape from that influence now.'

'We have both been under the influence of that man – you so far as to go against your own brother and marry his daughter.'

'I regret all I have done . . . except my marriage to Isabel. She is a good creature and I love her dearly.'

Edward nodded, thinking: She is a great heiress and you also love her lands and money dearly.

Clarence went on: 'I no longer wish to stand with Warwick. I want to be back where I belong. Our sister Margaret has written to me most affectingly. I have suffered much.'

'I too suffered from your desertion,' Edward reminded him.

'And can you forgive me?'

'Yes,' said Edward.

'By God, together we will fight this traitor Warwick. We'll have his head where they put our father's.'

'It was not Warwick who put our father's head on the walls of York and stuck a paper crown on it, George. That was our enemies . . . our mutual enemies. But yes, we are going to defeat Warwick.'

'I will bring him to you in chains.'

'Your father-in-law, your one-time friend! I want him to be treated with respect if we have the good fortune to capture him. I can never forget how he taught me, how he showed me how to fight and win a crown. Sometimes I think I am more hurt that he should take his friendship from me than my crown. I would always treat him with honour. He had his reasons you know for doing what he did. Warwick would always have his reasons. He is my enemy now but he is one I honour.'

Clarence thought what a fool his brother was. But there was a hard side to Edward, he knew; he could be ruthless but where his affections were concerned he was soft. He had married Elizabeth Woodville; he was ready to forgive the man who had taken his crown from him and his own brother who had deceived him. No wonder he had lost his throne! He would lose it again and if Henry were driven out there was one who would stand in to take it: George, Duke of Clarence.

Well, there was reconciliation between the brothers and as Edward had predicted Clarence's desertion of Warwick and return to Edward had the desired effect. Edward marched without hindrance into London.

Warwick was in Coventry when he heard of Clarence's defection. There was even more bitterness to come for Louis had signed a truce with the Duke of Burgundy and so was making terms with Warwick's enemy. Clarence he despised. He had never trusted him but his greatest hope had lain with the French King. Margaret of Anjou had left France and with the Prince of Wales and Anne and Warwick's Countess was about to land in England. He, Warwick, was heading for some climax. Meanwhile Edward had reached London. His spirits rose as he saw the grey stone walls of the Tower and he assured himself that Elizabeth was not far away.

First he went to St Paul's to give thanks for his return. Then he must see Henry who was at the Bishop of London's palace close by. Warwick had ordered that he should be taken there and put in the charge of Archbishop Neville and that Neville should let him ride through the streets in an attempt to arouse people's enthusiasm for him.

This was difficult for the people could not feel very much for the poor pathetic creature. There was nothing kingly about him. And when the Archbishop thought of Edward soon to arrive – so handsome with that special charm which had taken the people by storm in his youth and was still there – it seemed to him that the wisest thing was to take Henry back to the palace.

When Edward arrived and Henry was brought, Henry

blinked up at him and said: 'Cousin, you are welcome. My life will be safe in your hands.'

'I mean you no harm,' said Edward. 'You shall go back to your prayers and your books.'

'Thank you, thank you. It is what I have always wanted.'

'And now,' said Edward, 'to the Sanctuary.'

Elizabeth was there with her beautiful hair hanging about her shoulders as he liked it best. They looked at each other for a few seconds before they gave themselves up to a fervent embrace.

It was an emotional moment and even Elizabeth felt the tears in her eyes. He was back, as she always knew he would be.

'You have been my brave Queen,' he murmured.

'I am so happy that you are back. It all seems behind me now. It does not matter, if you are to stay with me for ever.'

'As long as God will let me,' he said.

'Edward, we have lived here in Sanctuary all these months. We could not have survived but for our good friends.'

'They shall be rewarded. All will be well now. I am going to be victorious.'

Jacquetta came to him and was warmly embraced. He would never believe the stories that she was a witch and had captured him for her daughter through witchcraft. He was fond of Jacquetta and he knew that she would have been a great help and comfort to Elizabeth during his enforced absence.

'You have not seen your son,' cried Elizabeth.

'My son . . . the boy I have always wanted! Bring him to me. I long to see him.'

'He is Edward . . . after you.'

'It is a good name.'

He gazed at the child in wonder. His beloved son – a perfect healthy boy to delight any father's heart, most of all a king who must be assured of the succession.

He took him in his arms and tenderly kissed his brow. The baby opened its eyes and regarded him solemnly for a moment before closing them again while the little girls were clambering round him. He handed the baby to Elizabeth and embraced his daughters all together so that one should not feel favoured more than the other.

'Are you going to stay with us?' asked Elizabeth. 'When are we going home?'

'This is home,' said Mary.

'Nay, my dearest,' said Edward. 'You are going back where you belong. There shall be no more of this place. You are going to be surprised when you are taken back to your real home, sweetheart.'

The little girls watched him with wide eyes. They were happy. He was back with them – their big laughing handsome father and if Mary could hardly recognise him and Cecily not at all, they all knew that the best thing that could happen to them was his return.

Edward said they should go at once to Baynard's Castle and must prepare to leave. There they would stay until he had made everything secure in the land.

So to Baynard's they went, riding along by the river while the people cheered to see Edward with his beautiful Queen and their lovely children. Elizabeth herself carried the child. She sat in her litter holding him, her lovely golden hair like a halo about her perfect features and the people cheered Edward, the baby Prince, the little girls and yes, they even cheered Elizabeth, although it was due to her rapacious family that the Earl of Warwick had turned from the King.

Never mind; she was so beautiful and she had given the King all those handsome children and he clearly loved her dearly even though he was not the most faithful of husbands.

Cheer then for the return of Edward, the strong man, the King they preferred to poor mad Henry. They fervently hoped Edward and the Earl of Warwick would settle their quarrels.

At Baynard's Castle the Duchess of York was in residence. When she saw her son the tears streamed down her cheeks and she fell upon him kissing his face and his hands. There was little sign of Proud Cis at that moment.

'My dearest boy,' she called him, forgetting the dignity owed to the King even though dignity was something she had always been so insistent on. 'Oh a thousand welcomes . . . This is the happiest day of my life. You are here with us . . . and the people want you . . .'

He let her talk. Then he kissed her tenderly and said: 'Elizabeth and the children have come to stay here. I shall leave them in your care.'

For a few seconds the two women looked at each other. Proud Cis who could not like her son's marriage to this commoner and Elizabeth Woodville who knew that Edward's mother would have done everything possible to stop the marriage.

The Duchess's eyes softened. Elizabeth Woodville was an exceptionally beautiful woman and she could not but be moved to see her standing there beside her own handsome Edward. Surely a more good-looking pair could not be found in the whole of England.

And Elizabeth had done her duty. Edward still wanted to keep her after all these years so there must be something special about her. And she had produced those lovely children – and now a Prince of Wales.

The Duchess went forward. She could not expect a Queen to kneel to her, but she held out her hand and Elizabeth took it.

'Welcome to Baynards, my dear,' she said. 'It makes me happy to have you here . . . you and my grandchildren.'

Edward put an arm round her and the Queen; he held them tightly against him.

'Thank God you are back,' said the Duchess.

'Yes, I am back. But there is work to do. I shall not stay here long now. But at least I shall know that you are together. Look after each other, my dear loved ones.'

Edward stayed at Baynard's Castle for a day and a night. Then taking Henry with him, he rode out to Barnet.

HIGH NOON

✿ Chapter V ✿

RICHARD'S WOOING

S o Warwick was dead. Killed in battle and against the
one whom he had taught to command armies.
Edward was sad.

He should be rejoicing, of course. Warwick was his enemy . . .
No, he could never accept him as such. They were fighting
against each other but it never should have been. He should have
talked to me. We should have reasoned together, thought
Edward. It was either him or Elizabeth for it was my marriage
that turned him from me. He was never the same after that. The
sore had been opened and it had continued to fester although
Warwick had pretended that it had healed. Warwick wanted to
be supreme. He *was* supreme in his way. He had learned so much
in a life dedicated to the getting of power. It was power Warwick
had wanted. Not a crown as so many men did. But power. He
wanted to be the one who set up kings and brought them down.
He had been, for that was exactly what he had done.

But no more, my one-time friend and erstwhile enemy. No
more.

It was foolish of him to feel thus. He should be rejoicing. He
must tell no one of his true feelings . . . not even Elizabeth.

Certainly not Elizabeth. She would think him soft and foolish. He was not soft. None could be more ruthless when the occasion demanded, but Warwick . . . Warwick had been his friend, his ideal, his god. He could not stop thinking of the early days when he had been a young boy. He listened to Warwick; he tried to be like Warwick. He was Warwick's. That was why Warwick had made him King.

But boys grow up. They have wills of their own. They change, Warwick. You hated the Woodvilles but the Woodvilles are Elizabeth's family, Warwick; it is natural that she should wish to advance them. You saw them becoming more powerful than the Nevilles . . . so you turned against me who had made them so.

And now it has come to this. Dead . . . No more to harass me as once you helped me. Dead, dear friend and enemy.

He went to see the dead body. It was harrowing. Once so proud, once invincible . . . but we are all vulnerable. There comes a time in our lives when death beckons and kings and even kingmakers must obey.

His body would have to be on show for a while so that there should be no rumours that he still lived. He would have his enemies but legends and in particular living legends were always the hardest to overcome.

He looked so vulnerable stripped of his fine armour. Soldiers had robbed him of it. His own guards had found them engaged in that when they rode up to save his life, for Edward had been eager to save him. He would have forgiven him, as he had forgiven Clarence, and he believed that they could have been friends again.

But they had come too late. He was already dead, and there was nothing that could be done but take the corpse to St Paul's

Cathedral and there let it lie for those two days that all who wished might assure themselves that Warwick was dead.

'Let him be buried with all honour and respect with his parents and brother Thomas in Bisham Abbey,' said Edward.

So all knew that the great Kingmaker had died in deadly combat with the man whom he had made King.

It was the passing of an era.

So he was back in London with Elizabeth and his family – the triumphant victor. He had brought Henry with him and had now installed him in the Wakefield Tower. Poor trusting Henry who seemed happy to be back within those constricting walls. Edward had felt a little shamefaced when poor Henry had expressed his trust in him. Henry was an encumbrance but to have him removed would make him an even greater threat. Moreover there was still the young Prince Edward. If Henry were gone people would only transfer their loyalty to him. While those two lived Edward would always have to be watchful.

But in the meantime victory. Warwick was dead and although he could not rejoice wholeheartedly none could doubt this was in his favour.

He savoured those few days in Baynard's Castle with Elizabeth. He was glad of her coolness and the irresistible urge to break it down was possibly what had kept his passion so alive. He might go with others but he would always return to her. She was unique. Moreover she was the mother of the royal children. Sometimes he had uneasy thoughts of Eleanor Butler and that ceremony through which he had gone. But Eleanor was dead now and that was all in the past. But he had discovered that she had been alive at the time of that secret ceremony at Grafton. And if that ceremony were binding then what of Elizabeth and the children?

Oh it was long since forgotten and if anyone started to probe into that woe betide them.

So he put it out of his mind and savoured these few days of respite for it was pleasant to be shut in with this happy family atmosphere even if it were only temporary. Elizabeth had quickly filled the nursery with people whom she considered necessary to the Prince's rank. There was a widow named Avice Wells who was nurse to the Prince; and there was Elizabeth Darcy who was mistress of the little Prince's nursery. That was not enough and Elizabeth persuaded Edward that their little son should have a chamberlain.

That had amused Edward.

'At his age, my dear. Why should a baby not a year old need a chamberlain?'

'To carry him in ceremonies . . . for the people must get to know their Prince. And they must be aware at once, Edward, of the importance of the Prince.'

So to please her he had appointed one of his own best servants, Thomas Vaughan, to attend the Prince at all times.

Young Edward lay contentedly in his cradle unaware of all the fuss that was going on around him.

Into this happy domestic scene the news burst. Edward had been waiting for it and now that it had come immediate action was imperative.

Margaret of Anjou and her son Edward, calling himself Prince of Wales, had landed at Weymouth.

Anne was waiting in the small religious house outside Tewkesbury, well aware that the battle was raging between the troops of Edward of York and those who had rallied to the banner of King Henry. She knew that her father had been slain at Barnet and in her heart she felt there was little hope of victory without him.

She wanted nothing more than an end to this war. They had betrothed her to the Prince and she believed that they might live in some sort of harmony together. She was not forceful like Margaret and would not attempt to impose her will on anyone. She often thought of Richard of Gloucester and this odd turn of fate which had set them on different sides. Richard would be beside his brother whatever happened; and she of course had to be on her father's.

Yet I care nothing for their wars, she thought.

How different was Margaret. A pleasant relationship had grown up between them which was strange because they were so different – she so docile, Margaret so fierce. Poor Margaret! It had been a fearful blow to her when she had heard that Warwick was dead. She was rather frightening in her rages, when she cursed everything and everyone in sight.

And now she had gone off with the troops to fight against Edward, and that other Edward, Anne's betrothed, was with her. Anne herself was bewildered. To wish them success would be to wish Richard defeat and in her heart she could not do that. She did not know what to pray for, what to hope for; she felt lost and bewildered.

At this moment the battle was raging and at any time she might know the result.

She went to the top of the house and looked out on the road. She sat there for a long time . . . waiting.

Then at last she saw them coming . . . a bedraggled party . . . and riding with them was Margaret and she knew that tragedy had struck.

❁ ❁ ❁

Margaret was overwhelmed by her grief. This was the end. It was painful to see a proud woman so bereft of everything but her sorrow.

Her son was dead . . . killed in battle, and she would never be the same again. Much of the fire had gone from her and she had become an old woman.

Anne tried to comfort her, but there was no comfort for Margaret.

'All that youth . . . all that beauty . . . gone . . . gone,' she mourned. 'They murdered him. They could have left me my son. We are lost. There can be nothing more. They have my husband in the Tower . . . they have killed my son. All my hope was in him . . . I have lost my beautiful boy and you my child have lost your husband.'

Anne did not know what to do. She tried to soothe Margaret; she took her to a quiet room and somehow induced her to lie upon a bed. Poor Margaret lay still for a while staring up blankly into misery.

But she could not remain passive for long. She rose. She began to call curses on everyone, but most of all on the man she called the Usurper. 'Edward who calls himself King . . . he has murdered my beautiful son and may his soul rot in hell.'

It was foolish to give way to her anger for there were those to carry an account of her curses to Edward. He was usually lenient to his enemies but she made him uneasy with her curses; and the death of the Prince had brought about new complications which were occupying his thoughts. Henry had been safe while Edward lived for to have removed Henry would have been of no avail while his son was there to step into his shoes. But now there was no Lancastrian heir. There was only a half-imbecile recluse between Edward and safety.

All the same Margaret must be silenced. Fortunately the people had always hated her and without her son and her husband she would be no danger at all.

While he was considering these matters news came to him of an insurrection which had broken out in the North. He started to march north but had only got as far as Coventry when he heard that the Bastard Falconbridge had landed in England and was marching on London. This man was an illegitimate son of William Neville Baron of Falconbridge whom Warwick had made Captain of his navy, the duty of which was to cruise about the Channel and intercept any ships which Edward might be sending to France. This was far more serious than any rising in the North and Edward immediately turned and began to march south.

Hearing that Falconbridge had come through Kent recruiting men to follow him and fight for King Henry, and that he had reached Aldgate and when refused admission by the Londoners had set fire to the eastern outskirts of the city, Elizabeth was terrified. Her brother Earl Rivers advised her not to go into Sanctuary this time but to stay in the Tower which was well fortified for he was sure that Edward would soon arrive to quell this petty revolt.

He was right and when the Bastard realised that Edward's mighty and victorious army was marching against him and that the battle of Tewkesbury had decided that the cause of the Red Rose was lost, he knew that his only chance lay in flight.

He scattered his followers and they escaped as well as they could, the Bastard himself reaching Southampton where he was captured, taken to Middleham and there beheaded.

It was the end of resistance, and Edward could now count himself victorious. There was only Margaret, whom he intended to hold captive, and poor mad Henry in the Tower.

Margaret and Anne were brought to London where the King was planning to make his triumphant entry into the city. He could not forget the curses Margaret had uttered against him and he wanted her – and everyone – to realise that she was finally defeated. He gave orders that she and Anne Neville should ride in the procession; they should share the same chariot and it should be made clear that they were prisoners. Instead of riding in triumph as no doubt Margaret had imagined herself doing, she should come in humiliation. She should listen to the jeers of the people for her, the humiliated captive.

Edward was cheered wildly by the people of London. This procession, this triumphant entry meant that the war was over. This big handsome man was their King and he was the King they wanted because he could bring prosperity and peace back to the country.

And there were the captives – arrogant Margaret who brought trouble from the moment she stepped ashore as Henry's bride and with her poor pale little Anne Neville, heiress daughter of the great Earl who had hoped she would be Queen of England.

There were jeers for Margaret and no great sympathy for Anne. They had a handsome Queen. It was true she had sought favours for her family; but she had lived through the difficult days in Sanctuary and while there had produced the all-important male heir. Moreover she was beautiful and never could a more handsome King and Queen have graced a throne.

So all was well. Peace had come. Edward had vanquished his enemy. Was this the end then of the Wars of the Roses?

They believed so and as they were heartily sick of wars they cheered the man who had brought them peace.

Back to the Palace of the Tower. There to rest after the procession. Margaret and Anne were taken into separate apartments while the King and his company went to the dining-hall to the feast which had been prepared for them.

Richard was on one side of the King, Elizabeth on the other. Edward felt a deep affection for this brother who had never shown anything but loyalty to him; it was wonderful to have someone whom he could trust.

But Richard was sad. The sight of Anne seated beside Margaret in the chariot had touched him deeply. Poor little Anne, who had done nothing but what she had been made to. He could not forget her and memories of childhood days were flooding back to him.

Edward was saying: 'Young Edward is dead. There is only Henry now.'

'And he is a near imbecile,' murmured Hastings.

'A figurehead still!' mused Edward. 'They were rising in the North in his name. There will never be complete peace while that name can be used to give traitors a reason for rising.'

There was a deep silence about the table which lasted for some moments. Edward was staring thoughtfully ahead.

That night Henry the Sixth was murdered in the Wakefield Tower.

So Henry was dead. There were rumours of course for he had died at a most convenient time. His body had lain at St Paul's with the face exposed so that all might see him, and the talk continued that his body had bled as he lay in his shroud. Afterwards he was kept for a while at Black Friars and then taken by barge to Chertsey Abbey to be buried in the lady chapel there.

It may have been, said the people, that his death had been arranged on the King's orders, but even so, it was an end to strife and if it did mean that a few ruthless actions must be performed to bring about peace, then so must it be.

Within a few weeks people ceased to talk about Henry. The war was over. Edward had come to stay.

But Richard could not stop thinking about Anne seated in the chariot with the fierce Margaret of Anjou – not fierce any more. The death of her son had subdued even her revengeful spirit and left her with no energy for anything but to mourn.

He did not know whether Anne considered herself as a wife to Prince Edward, but whether she did or not he was dead and she was free now. Free for what, to remain Edward's prisoner in the Tower? Free to marry perhaps if a husband could be found for her?

Richard went to Edward for he had been making up his mind to speak to his brother from the moment he had seen Anne in the procession.

Edward was always pleased to see his brother, and as Richard entered his private chamber he studied him thoughtfully. How different he was from the flamboyantly handsome figure Edward knew he cut. Richard was of middle stature – perhaps a little lower, his face very serious, with the open looks of an honest man. So far he had not been called upon to dissemble. It would come, Edward guessed. But perhaps it did not to all men. In any case he smiled warmly and asked what troubled his brother that he looked so serious.

'I have been wanting to speak to you for some time, Edward. There is a matter which is much on my mind.'

'Well?'

'It's Anne . . . Anne Neville.'

'Ah,' said Edward. 'You have a weakness for the girl. I always knew it.'

'I cannot bear that she should be here . . . a prisoner in the Tower.'

'Poor girl! She could not help being Warwick's daughter.'

'I want to marry her, Edward.'

'Yes, I thought so. Well, what are you waiting for?'

A great smile crossed Richard's face making him look so different.

'My dear Dickon,' said Edward, 'why do you not go ahead? You wanted my blessing eh, good brother that you are! In these matters you should follow my golden example and marry where you will.'

'I intended to,' said Richard.

'Good for you. I like a man to know his own mind. But being you, you asked me first. I say go ahead. Our brother had one girl and you are to have her sister. And the greatest heiresses in the kingdom. Warwick was a very rich man! He had a genius for collecting wealth. I know he regretted not having a son largely because of those vast estates he managed to accumulate. Well, your Anne is a wealthy woman, co-heiress to the Warwick estates with her sister Isabel.'

Edward stopped and looked intently at his brother.

Then he said slowly: 'There may be trouble from George.'

'George . . . why should there be?'

191

'My dear Dickon, you know George. He married Isabel for her fortune. He believes that now that Anne is in the Tower and was betrothed – some say married – to Henry's son she is our enemy and should forfeit her estates. In which case Isabel will become doubly wealthy with a whole share instead of a half.'

'Oh, no.'

'Perhaps not. However, dear brother, go ahead and good luck attend your wooing.'

It was late afternoon of the next day when Richard went to Anne's apartment in the Tower. He had thought what he would say to her. He was remembering that she had undergone an ordeal and he was certain that she would be shocked. What her feelings had been for Prince Edward he did not know; he had heard that she had become friendly with Margaret of Anjou; she would have witnessed that lady's overwhelming grief . . . perhaps she had shared it. He did not want to hurry her. It may have been that her feelings had changed since they were children. She was not much more than fifteen now. He wanted to proceed with gentleness and tenderness. He would feel his way cautiously, reminding her of long ago days at Middleham, try to awaken those feelings they had obviously felt for each other. He was longing to see her and yet he wanted to be prepared. He felt their first meeting would be very important to them both.

He knew where her apartment was. Both she and Margaret had been given fairly comfortable lodgings; Edward was never vengeful . . . and although Margaret had caused him a great deal of trouble he shrugged his shoulders and thought that just in the nature of things.

When he reached Anne's lodging he was surprised to find it empty.

He called one of the guards.

'Where is the Lady Anne?' he asked.

'My lord,' was the answer, 'she was taken away this morning.'

'Taken away! But who had the right to do that?'

'It was the Duke of Clarence, my lord. He said he was taking her to her sister, and that he would have charge of her in the future.'

Richard was astounded. Why should George suddenly have decided to take Anne away?

However, he would go to his brother's London residence and see Anne there.

As he made his way to the Clarences' house a thought occurred to him. Had his brother guessed what he was planning? How could he have known? Because he was aware that Richard was fond of Anne? Because Anne was now free? Had one of his spies overheard Richard talking to Edward about his intentions? That was possible. George had spies everywhere. George lived dramatically and made drama where it need not exist. George was up to something. Why should he suddenly express an interest in Anne to whom he had been quite indifferent before?

Richard would find out.

He arrived at his brother's house where he was received with great deference by his servants, and he said that he understood the Lady Anne was there and he wished to be conducted to her.

If he would kindly wait for a moment the servants would go and do what was necessary.

It was not Anne who presented herself to him, however, but George.

George came hurrying in, an affable smile on his handsome face, a little bloated nowadays through too much good living especially excessive drinking, charming in a way, a pale shadow of Edward.

'Richard, dear brother, how good of you to call on me.'

Richard was always direct. 'You look well, George,' he said. 'I have in fact come to see Anne.'

'Ah,' said George, looking serious.

'What is wrong? She is here is she not?'

'Y . . . yes, she is here. She is in her sister's care.'

'Why?'

'Why, brother. Who else should look after her but her sister? You know what good friends Isabel and Anne always were.'

'Does she need . . . looking after. Is she ill?'

'I fear so. You see, she has suffered a terrible ordeal. She lost her father, and then the Prince . . . It is too much for the poor girl.'

'I wish to speak to her.'

'I'm afraid you cannot do that. She is not well enough to receive visitors.'

'Visitors! I am no ordinary visitor! Anne may want to see me. Please tell her that I am here and that I have come for the very purpose of talking to her.'

George's face hardened. 'No, brother. You cannot see her.'

'I demand to see her.'

'It is no use demanding here, my lord of Gloucester. This is my house. Anne is my ward. I am the one who shall say whom she will receive.'

'What is the matter with you?'

'I am her brother-in-law . . . her nearest relation through Isabel. Isabel and I will look after her. She is in my hands. You have come here to ask her to marry you, have you not?' George was always unable to control his anger and he was angry now. He had meant to be subtle, to ward off Richard but when his brother stood before him and he realised how strong Richard could be in his quiet way, his anger flared up. He had been informed that Richard intended to marry Anne and he thought his motive was the same as his own had been in marrying Isabel: the Warwick fortune.

'Yes,' said Richard steadily, 'I intend to marry Anne if she is agreeable.'

'You intend to marry a fortune, eh? That is what you are after. You think you'll have your share of Warwick's estate.'

'I was thinking of Anne . . .'

'Oh brother, how noble you are! I know you well. Quiet, serious, loyal always to brother Edward. Well it paid to be so, eh? And now you think you will come along to that poor desolate girl and tell her she must marry you . . . not for her fortune . . . oh no, no, but because you were always such good friends at Middleham. But you will not say no to the Warwick estates, will you? My dear brother, Anne has been on the side of the enemies of our brother the King. For that she may well forfeit her estates.'

'*You* fought with the enemies of the King, George. Will you forfeit your estates? And Anne has never fought. She did what she was obliged to. You know it and Edward knows it. Now I will see her.'

George was facing him. 'You cannot see her. She is too sick to be seen. Only Isabel is with her.'

'You're lying, George.'

'You are my brother and I do not want to quarrel with you but if you attempt to invade my house against my wishes my guards will stop you on my orders.'

'I have not come here for a brawl.'

'Then go, brother, before you provoke one.'

George's face was scarlet, his slightly bloodshot eyes bulging with rage. Richard knew George. When he was angry he lost control. He would be capable of anything.

The last thing Richard wanted was a quarrel with his brother which in George's present mood could result in the death of one of them. He turned on his heel and walked away.

He would put the matter to Edward and demand to see Anne. He was sure Edward would be on his side. Edward was devoted to him and was always suspicious of George. He knew what Edward's verdict would be and even George would have to consider very carefully before going against the wishes of the King.

Edward listened thoughtfully to what had occurred.

'It is clear what this means,' he said. 'George wants the entire Warwick fortune. He thinks by keeping Anne in his control he will get it through Isabel. Where George is, there is always trouble. Sometimes I wonder where it will lead us in the end. How dare he talk about Anne's fighting against me! He is completely brazen. Consider how he went to Warwick and actually took up arms against me. I don't know why I am so lenient with him. It is because he is my brother, I suppose. He was such a bright little fellow when he was young, and then his little wickednesses seemed amusing. But no longer so. I will let George know that he shall do nothing to impede you.'

'I fear he may be keeping Anne there against her will. If I could see her . . .'

'You shall. I will let George know that Anne is to receive you at his house and you can talk to her and make your plans.'

Richard thanked his brother and Edward immediately sent off a messenger to George to tell him that when Richard called he was to see the Lady Anne and if he, George, prevented this he would have to answer to the King.

Giving George time to receive the King's order Richard rode out to Clarence's house where his brother was waiting for him. George looked complacent and for a moment Richard thought he had decided to accept Edward's decision.

'I have come to see the Lady Anne,' he said. 'I pray you have me conducted to her apartments at once.'

'Alas,' said George, holding his hands together and looking piously up at the roof, 'you are too late, Richard. The Lady Anne is no longer here.'

'No longer here? Why . . . she *was* here . . .'

'She was but now she is not.'

'Then where is she?'

'I have heard from my brother that I do not hold the wardship of the lady and therefore her whereabouts can be no concern of mine.'

'You lie.'

'Indeed not. I assure you she is no longer in this house.'

'I do not believe you.'

'Dear brother, you may search the place. You may question my servants. You must discover for yourself. In fact I wish you to. I cannot have you spreading stories that I have the lady in secret hiding here.'

Richard said: 'I will search your house.'

'Go ahead. Feel welcome to ask anyone in the house to help you.'

Richard went to the staircase. He found Isabel in one of the corridors and he wondered if she had been listening to the altercation between himself and George.

'Isabel,' he said and took her hand and kissed it. She looked frightened. He had always liked Isabel although naturally his feelings did not go as deep for her as they did for Anne. 'Where is your sister?'

'I do not know, Richard,' she said. 'She has disappeared. I went to her room to talk to her and she had gone.'

'Gone! But where to?'

'I have no idea. It is as though she left in a hurry. I believe she has run away.'

'But where could she run to?'

'I thought perhaps to our mother.'

'Your mother is at Beaulieu is she not?'

'Yes, in Sanctuary there on the King's orders.'

Richard nodded. It was a sad state of affairs but the Countess was of course the wife of Warwick who had brought an army against the King. All the Countess's lands had been confiscated. That was probably due to George who naturally wanted the whole of the Warwick inheritance to go to Isabel.

'Isabel, can you assure me that she is not hidden away somewhere in this house?'

'I have searched for her and cannot find her. Oh Richard, what do you think has become of her?'

'Do you think she is running away from George?'

'He has not been unkind to her.'

'He tried to keep her a prisoner here and when I called he would not allow me to see her. Did she know that?'

Isabel shook her head. 'Unless George told her. *I* did not know you had been here.'

'Edward has commanded that nothing be put in the way of my seeing her.'

'But she is gone, Richard.'

'I believe George has sent her away,' said Richard tight-lipped.

'I do not know. He tells me nothing. Oh Richard, Anne would be so pleased if she knew you wanted to see her. She talked of you often. I think she thought you had deserted her after all that happened.'

'My God, Isabel, it was no fault of Anne's! Did she not think I knew that! But I'll find her. I swear I will. Now I am going to search this house . . . every room . . . every nook . . . every-where. You understand, Isabel, I must satisfy myself that she is not here.'

'I understand, Richard. Go and search. I do not think you will find her. I myself have looked everywhere. I am so worried as to what has become of her.'

Isabel was right. He searched but there was no trace of Anne.

❀ ❀ ❀

Richard visited the Countess at Beaulieu. He found a very sad woman. She was very anxious for her daughters and the greatest hardship she had to bear was separation from them.

Richard decided he would speak to Edward about her being kept in Sanctuary there. It was of course because of the Warwick estates and George's obsession with them. While the Countess was here she could claim nothing. Edward knew that George wanted those estates. Sometimes Richard thought Edward was afraid of George. Not exactly afraid. There was very little Edward feared. But Edward had always been one for peace and what he loathed above all else was strife in the family. While he was deeply suspicious of George he did not want to upset him so he turned his back on what was a form of captivity for the Countess.

Poor woman, what had she done except be heiress to a large estate! Warwick had married her for it and so became the great Earl and the owner of vast possessions and because of these Isabel had been married to George and now Anne was persecuted.

The Countess was frantic when she heard that Anne was missing.

'She did not come here,' she declared. 'How I wish she had!'

'I will find her,' declared Richard.

The Countess seized his hand. 'And when you do, please let me know.'

'You shall be the first to hear, I promise you.'

He was going to search everywhere. He would follow every clue however ridiculous it might seem.

He made enquiries in every noble house, starting with those she would have turned to most naturally.

Was Anne there? Had she sought refuge with them?

But he searched in vain.

Anne herself was bewildered. She could not understand why her brother-in-law had done this to her. She had always been afraid of him, and never understood how Isabel could love him. Oddly enough he loved Isabel. He was gentle with her and always seemed different in her company. Of course they had known each other in their childhood and had been friends, but not as friendly as she and Richard for Richard had been so much at Middleham.

She had hoped that she would see Richard. It would have been wonderful to talk to him, to explain how hurt she had been to have been forced onto the side of his enemies. But there would be no need to explain. Richard would understand.

And now she was afraid she would never see him again because this terrible thing had happened to her.

George had come to her room and with him were two people whom she had never seen before, a man and a woman.

George had said: 'Anne, you are in danger. These friends of mine will look after you. You must go with them at once. You will take nothing with you . . . there is no time for that. They will give you everything you need.'

She had cried out: 'But I want to know where I am going . . . and why.'

'It is because you are in acute danger and there is no time to waste now. You have to leave with all haste.'

'Where is Isabel?'

'She knows you are going and have to hurry. You can speak to her later.'

The woman came forward and put a cloak round Anne. She was very strong Anne noticed as she took her arm.

'It is all clear,' said George. 'Come this way.'

He led the way through a part of the house which was rarely used, down a short spiral staircase to the courtyard where a carriage was waiting. She was firmly placed in it. The man started up the horses and they were away. It had all happened so quickly that it was only when they were driving through darkened streets that Anne began to feel really afraid.

'I want to know where I am being taken,' she said.

The woman put her finger to her lips. 'Now we must be

calm, mustn't we,' she said, speaking, thought Anne, in the tones one would use towards an imbecile.

She looked out of the window. Suppose she ran away? Where would she go? To the King perhaps, to throw herself on his mercy? But he would send her back to George. Isabel would help her but Isabel was George's wife . . . Then to her mother. Could she find her way to Beaulieu?

The woman had her by the arm and was hustling her into a house. They went up a dark staircase and she was in a room alone with the woman.

'Now take off those fine clothes,' she said. 'You will not need them here.'

'Where am I? I don't understand.'

'Never mind.' The same soothing voice. 'You won't need to. You'll be safe here.'

'Safe . . . from what?'

'From those who seek to harm you.'

'Who?'

'Now then. Take off this beautiful gown. You see you are not going to be the grand lady here.'

'Please leave me alone. Let me go to my mother.'

'No, you are staying here. We are going to care for you.'

Her dress had been removed. She was in her petticoats. 'Such fine linen,' said the woman. 'Most unsuitable now.'

Everything was removed and the woman slipped a ragged gown over her head.

Anne stared down at it in revulsion. 'What is this? What are you doing?'

'My dear, you are mistaken. You think you're the Lady Anne, do you not? I found you wandering in the streets. I took pity on you. I am going to take you down to my kitchens and there you will be fed for the work you do.'

'Kitchens! You are mad.'

'No, my dear, it is you who are so afflicted. You see you have these ideas. You have heard of the Lady Anne Neville and you have been dreaming of her. You dream that you are that lady. Now what would she be doing in such a gown!'

'But you have just taken my clothes and forced me into this.'

'It is all a dream. Part of the delusion. Never mind. We'll look after you here. You should be very grateful to us. We have taken you from the streets out of pity.'

'Stop,' Anne cried. 'What nonsense are you talking? Give me back my clothes and let me go from here.'

'Your clothes . . . my dear sad child . . . those were the clothes I found you in, wandering the streets pretending to be a great lady . . . and I'll say this, you did it very well.'

Anne turned to the door but she was pinioned by the strong arms.

'Careful, child. I do not want to hurt you. Don't provoke me.'

'I want to get out of here. This is all such nonsense. Let me go. Let me go.'

Anne received a stinging blow on the side of her face. She reeled back and stared at the woman in horror.

'There now,' said the woman, 'no harm done. You've just got to behave yourself, that's all. No nonsense, see. I mean to be kind to you. You must let me be. Look at you, all skin and bone and weak as a kitten, I'd say. Never done a hand's turn of real work. Never mind. You just be quiet and you'll get along all right. But any defiance . . . and you'll be sorry. I'm taking you in . . . doing you a good turn . . . Now come with me.'

It was a nightmare. She must be dreaming. Who was this woman who had taken her clothes and given her these rags in substitute, and who was saying such mad things to her?

She was led to another room. They went in and shortly afterwards a large woman appeared in a gown which was splashed with grease.

'This is the poor girl I've been telling you to expect,' said the woman who had brought her to this place. 'She is suffering from what they call delusions. Thinks she is some great lady. Lady Anne something. Gives herself airs. She does it rather well, speaks and acts it. Must have been in some grand house sometime. Well, it's turned the poor thing's head. She could get into real trouble wandering the streets saying she's all sorts of people.'

Anne went to the fat woman and took her sleeve. 'I am Lady Anne Neville,' she said. 'Take me back to my family . . . to my sister . . . to my brother. You will be well rewarded.'

'See,' said the woman, 'she does it very well. That's why it is a little dangerous. Take her to the kitchen. Don't make her do too much . . . just at first. Have a little pity on her. She'll want showing how to do things. Keep her in the kitchens. She might try to get away. Don't let her do that. I can trust you to look after her.'

The fat woman nodded. 'I'll see to her. I've seen these loonies before. Think they're all sorts of people they do. I'll look after her.'

'Thank you, Cook,' said the woman.

The nightmare continued. She was taken to the kitchens. There were pots and pans everywhere and a great fire was burning.

'Sit down and watch the pots,' said the woman who had

been called Cook. 'Come on. Stop dreaming. Have to work to eat you know . . . even if you are a grand lady in your dreams.'

Anne sat on the stool into which she was pushed.

She could not understand why she had been forced into this nightmare.

Richard gave himself up to the search. He could not imagine where she could have been taken. He went to Isabel and talked to her when George was absent but she could offer no clue. She had thought that Anne had run away in which case she would go to their mother. Where else? And if she were not there, she had no idea where she could be.

'I believe George to be concerned in this,' said Richard.

'He has always said that he would look after her and that she and I should be together.

'We know George. He loves you, but he does want the whole of your father's estates for himself.'

Isabel was silent.

'Therefore I believe my brother has hidden her somewhere. Where, Isabel?'

'I do not know.'

'Isabel,' he caught her hands and held them tightly. 'If you knew you would tell me, would you not?'

She was silent again.

'I beg you, Isabel, for Anne's sake . . . for my sake. I love Anne. I always have. When we were children I used to think when we grew up we would be married. We talked of it once. You know how I care for her. You will tell, Isabel.'

'Yes, I would of course if I could, but I simply do not know where she is. George tells very little and I swear on my soul that I do not know where she is.'

Poor Isabel. Torn between her husband and her sister. But he was convinced that she did not know.

Somehow the conviction came to him that Anne was in London for the big city would be the best place in which to hide her. She could not have gone to any of Clarence's friends because the news would assuredly leak out as to where she was.

In addition to his noble friends Clarence had an army of hangers-on. People who spied for him and worked for him in many devious ways. Richard knew his brother well. He was one of those men who surrounded himself with drama. He was a born intriguant. Where intrigue did not exist he created it. He was always working on some twisted project. Edward was right not to trust him. For one thing George always had his eye on the throne. He was resentful against a fate which had not made him the elder brother. Richard knew he had to be watchful of George not only for his own sake but for that of Edward. Edward was well aware of George's perfidious nature of course, but being Edward he pretended to ignore it, to preserve the peace and a show of amity between them.

Then if Anne were not hidden in one of the noble houses she must be in one of the lesser ones.

He would search every one of them. He would set his own spies to discover who was on the payroll of his brother in however small a way, and if necessary he would take an armed guard to search their houses. He knew that Edward would approve of what he was doing for he understood his feelings for Anne. His had been as strong for Elizabeth. Moreover he might take whatever action he cared to as long as he did not involve the King. In quarrels between his brothers Edward would wish to stand outside. But Richard knew that Edward's support would be for him against George.

He decided to call in the help of a woman he had once known very well indeed for whom he still had a great regard. Katherine had borne him two children during their relationship – a boy John and a girl Katherine. Richard visited her now and then and had always made sure that the children had every advantage. It had never been a grand passion between them, and Katherine had become a true and grateful friend.

Katherine lived modestly in the city of London and would perhaps have knowledge and access to places which were denied him. There could never have been any question of marriage between Katherine and the Duke of Gloucester and he had often talked to her about Anne and explained to her that he would probably marry Anne in due course.

So to Katherine he took his problem and he knew that she would do everything she could to discover if Anne were indeed in London.

It was a forlorn hope for indeed she might have been removed from the city; but Richard was determined to make quite sure that she was not in London before he abandoned the search there.

It was Katherine who discovered that there was talk among the servants.

There was working in one of the houses a strange crazy girl who imagined that she was really a great lady.

She was, so the story went, a poor waif who had been found wandering in the streets and given a home by a magnanimous lady. The girl worked in the kitchens and was practically useless and it was a wonder she was not driven out into the streets, but in spite of everything the mistress kept her there. She was quite crazy. She had even said that she was the daughter of the great Earl of Warwick.

Richard could hardly contain himself.

'Find out where the house is,' he said. 'Let me know at once and I shall be there.'

One day seemed to merge into another. Anne was bewildered still. Sometimes she wondered whether she had imagined another life, whether she was indeed the crazy waif who believed herself to have been a great lady. But that was rarely. She remembered so much . . . Middleham, Richard, Isabel, her mother and Isabel's husband George who was gracious to her and yet whom she feared.

No, she must cling to sanity. She must try to turn attention from herself. She must try to do these kitchen tasks for which she had no aptitude and which she never knew had to be done until she came here. She must try to be patient and quiet and wait until some way of escape was offered to her.

It was an ordinary morning. She was roused from the pile of rags on the floor which was her bed and in the room which she shared with six others she awoke to a new day.

She endured the usual teasing from the kitchen girls. She never agreed with them that she was mad and although she did not insist that she was the Lady Anne, she never denied it. They laughed at her fancy ways, at her manners of speaking and eating. Some of them even inclined to think that there might be something in her story, but any suggestion that there was would be reported to the mistress and that meant a threat that they might be driven out into the streets for talking such nonsense. 'We can't do with two loonies in one kitchen,' the cook had once said threateningly.

How long she had endured this wretched life, Anne did not know. She lost count of the days. She seemed to sit for hours watching the spit – the task usually given to her. 'It's all she's fit for,' said the cook.

And so the morning began to pass and was like any other until suddenly there was commotion without. She heard a voice which seemed to her familier but it could not be. She was dreaming. She had fancied she had heard that voice before.

'I demand to see your kitchens. Stand aside.' Then the door was flung open. She stood up, pushed her lank and dirty hair from her face to stare. Then she cried out shrilly: 'Richard!'

He strode across the kitchen. He could not believe this dirty creature was Anne; but it was her voice.

'Anne! Anne! Have I found you at last?'

She ran to him and threw herself against him. He held her tightly, her greasy dress soiling the richness of his jacket.

'Anne . . . Anne . . . let me look at you. I have searched and searched. Who would have thought to find you thus. But let us get out of this place as quickly as we can.'

The woman who had brought her here and taken her clothes had come into the kitchen.

'What is happening here?' she demanded while the cook and the maids looked on in astonishment. They had never seen anything like this in their lives – and never would again. The rich and noble-looking man had come for their loony kitchen girl and it was dawning on them that she had been speaking the truth all the time.

'This is the woman who brought me here. She has my clothes,' said Anne.

'You will bring the Lady Anne's clothes.'

'My lord . . . I have commands . . .'

'I know. From my brother the Duke of Clarence. So I can hardly blame you, though you deserve to be hanged for what you have done. No matter. Let us have the clothes and bring us water in which the Lady can clean herself.'

'My lord . . . I dare not . . .'

'You will obey me with all speed or you will be arrested without delay. Obey me. At once.'

The woman muttering that she had acted on orders hurried away.

Richard held Anne's hands tightly in his own.

'Anne,' he said, 'stop trembling. You are safe now. No one is going to hurt you again.'

'It has been like a nightmare, Richard. I could not understand. They thought I was mad. I began to think so too.'

The woman had returned with the clothes and hot water was brought. Anne was taken away from the kitchens to another part of the house and the clothes and hot water were put in a small room. Anne went in and Richard said: 'I shall wait here for you and I shall not move until you come out.'

When she emerged with her beautiful hair still hanging limply about her face, but washed and in her own clothes, she looked more like herself although Richard was shocked by her fragile looks.

'Let us get away from this evil house,' he said.

They went out together. He lifted her onto his horse and mounted behind her.

'Anne,' he said. 'I am taking you into Sanctuary. There you will stay until we can be married. There'll have to be a dispensation first. But never fear. I have found you at last. There is nothing to be afraid of now. That is, of course . . . if you will marry me.'

She laid her head against him. 'I am so afraid,' she said, 'that I am going to wake up and find myself in that house. Oh Richard, so often I have dreamed of your coming like this . . . I am not dreaming now, am I? I could not bear it if I were. It would be even worse after this.'

'Nay,' he said. 'You are wide awake. Anne, you will take me then?'

'With all my heart,' she said.

'Then the future is ours.'

Anne remained in St Martin's Sanctuary, relieved to have come out of her nightmare, to awake every morning and sometimes be afraid to open her eyes lest she should see that dark room with the servants lying on their pallets on the floor beside her. Sometimes the nauseating smell of fatty foods would seem to be there and she wondered whether it had become part of her until she realised it was only imagination.

She was free now. Richard had freed her. He had visited her in Sanctuary and said that as soon as he could get the King's consent to their marriage and the necessary dispensation from the Pope – for they were cousins – they would marry.

She was waiting for that day. If in the meantime she could free her mind of memory and of evil dreams she could be content, but she knew it would take some time to wash the grease out of her hair and to cleanse herself of the odours of that fearful kitchen where the rats frolicked and the cock-roaches scuttled across the floor and where she had been taunted as the crazy girl who thought herself a fine lady.

Edward was sympathetic, as Richard had known he would

be but at the same time he did nothing to alienate Clarence. Clarence had proved himself a rogue and a criminal. He had submitted Anne to the utmost degradation. He had in any case fought against his own brother – yet Edward deceived himself into believing that he could be placated. Strife in the family was something Edward could not bear to contemplate – even though it was there. But even though he was eager not to upset Clarence, his sympathy was with Richard.

He showed this by granting Warwick's northern estates to his younger brother as well as lands which had been confiscated from rebels like the Earl of Oxford. Clarence retaliated by insisting that he was Anne's guardian and as such must give his consent before she married.

Edward's answer to this was that the two brothers should take the case before the Council. He thought that Richard's calm statements were certain to win over Clarence's angry harangues.

This, however, was inconclusive for although Richard put forward his case with a calm precision, George waxed eloquent and declared that Anne's sister Isabel was the one who should be nearest the girl in this dilemma. The Council not wishing to offend either Clarence or Gloucester suspended judgement and the quarrel was no nearer conclusion than it had been before the Council sat.

Christmas came and Richard was at Court while Anne remained in Sanctuary.

It was a dreary festival for Richard. Nor did Edward enjoy it. He hated to see the enmity between his brothers, and as always he felt an inner perturbation when he thought of Clarence's defection and wondered what he would do next.

He had loved his brothers – both of them. Richard had been such a serious little chap and how could he help favouring one who bestowed that abject adoration on his big and handsome brother? Richard had made him feel like a god and Edward had liked that. But George had been such a bright and amusing little fellow. Always pushing himself forward, strutting, boasting, lively and handsome.

Families should never quarrel but what could he do to solve this difference between his brothers? Richard was determined to marry Anne; Clarence was determined that he should not. He was certain that Richard loved Anne but George of course had as intense a passion for Anne's estates.

Edward discussed the matter with Richard.

'George should be punished,' said Richard. 'Consider what he did to Anne. You have no notion how she suffered. To put a girl who has been so tenderly nurtured into such conditions . . . it's criminal. Why should he not be brought to judgement for that?'

'Listen Richard, he is our brother. He has power as such. I cannot afford strife in this country. He joined Warwick once. I watch him closely for I never know what he will be at, but I do not want to anger him. Help me to settle this matter. If you agree to share the estates and give him the lion's share, we might be able to settle it. I have a mind to put you in the North. I know your heart is there. You would leave Court and settle up there. You are the only man I would trust to keep the North faithful to me. You would have Middleham which you could make your chief residence and Warwick's northern estates. You and Anne could marry as soon as the dispensation comes through from the Pope. I feel sure that I could get George's agreement to this. What say you?'

Richard did not hesitate. To go north, to Middleham, the home of their youth, to have the North at his command, to marry Anne. To hold the North for Edward . . . Oh yes, he would agree to that.

'Then,' said Edward, 'it only remains for me to show George what a good settlement this is.'

George considered the proposition with no great show of eagerness.

Secretly he saw that he would come out of the arrangement better than Richard. Richard was to have Middleham Castle – let him. He had no desire for that place right up in the North. He wanted to be at Court where everything happened. Richard was to have Warwick's Yorkshire estates. Very well. But he would give up the manor of Warwick to George and George would have the earldoms of Warwick and Salisbury.

George had indeed the greater share of the Warwick estates but Richard did not mind that. He was longing to take Anne out of Sanctuary, marry her and settle in Middleham.

'Now,' said Edward, 'all you have to do is wait for the Pope's dispensation.'

There was a twinkle in Edward's eyes. He knew that Richard was contemplating acting without that. Why not? It would come in due course. There was no reason why it should not.

He was right. Richard went to the Sanctuary where Anne was waiting for him. He took her hands in his.

'Our troubles are over,' he said. 'We have made an agree-ment – my brothers and I. George will put nothing in the way of our marriage. He has taken most of yours and your sister's inheritance, but I think we have enough in each other.'

'I care nothing for the lands,' said Anne.

'I thought not. I wish Clarence joy of them. And now we are only waiting for the Pope. But I will tell you this, Anne, I do not intend to wait longer for His Holiness. Do we need ceremonies? Do we need a grand wedding? I believe you are in agreement with me when I say we do not.'

'I am in complete agreement.'

'Well then, tomorrow we shall be married. And Anne almost at once we are going to leave for Middleham. Does that make you happy?'

'Very happy,' she said.

'Yet you are a little downcast?'

'I was thinking about Isabel . . . who has grown so weak . . . and my mother. I think of her often. She must be very lonely.'

Richard nodded.

He said he would return for her the next day when they would be quietly married.

And so they were; and they made immediate preparations to leave for the North.

Edward was amused. 'So you decided to flout His Holiness then?'

'There is only one man whose command I have ever obeyed.'

Edward looked at him affectionately.

'I know it and I am grateful. Richard, let us take a brotherly oath and swear that it shall always be so.'

'There is no need for swearing,' said Richard. 'You know my motto. I will serve my King while there is life in my body.'

Edward embraced him.

'We shall see little of each other from now on. You will be in the North but know that my thoughts are with you and that I shall sleep more soundly in my bed at nights for knowing you control the North. It has always been a source of anxiety to me, Richard. But it will be so no more. The one I trust beyond all others will guard it for me.'

'With my life,' said Richard. 'And my lord, there is one request I would ask of you before I go.'

'I promise you before you ask it that if it be in my power to give it, it is yours.'

'It is the Countess of Warwick. She is alone at Beaulieu. Anne grieves for her. I ask your permission to take her out of Sanctuary at Beaulieu that she may live with us at Middleham.'

'How like you, Richard, to make such a request. I grant it with pleasure. God bless you, brother. I wish you all the happiness you deserve. And there is one thing I would ask. From time to time you must tear yourself away from Middleham and come to see me. I shall send for you and I know you will not dare to disobey your King's commands.'

Once more they embraced and the next day Anne and Richard set out for Middleham. They were happy for they were in love. They were young – Richard but twenty, Anne sixteen – and they had their whole lives before them.

So they came to Middleham. It was springtime and the country at its most beautiful. Anne was overcome with emotion when she saw the castle on its high eminence with the moat surrounding it filled with water which came from the spring on high ground which she and Isabel used to ride to, when they were children.

Here she could forget the dirty kitchens, the greasy smell, the terrible fear that after all she might be as mad as they had made her out to be.

And she had Richard too. This was how they both imagined it in those early days. They were together now as they had been then. Her mighty father was dead; her sad mother was coming to them for the King had promised it, though the Duke of Clarence was trying to put obstacles in the way.

But she would be with them soon.

During that first year Richard had to go south to attend Parliament but he did not stay long and was back by Christmas which they celebrated with the old traditions in the great castle hall.

By that time Anne had discovered that she was pregnant so there was very special rejoicing and how delighted she was when during the following year her child was born.

Richard wanted to call him Edward after her brother whom he so admired and Anne was eager to agree.

In due course the Countess of Warwick arrived at Middleham and Anne felt that she needed nothing more to complete her happiness.

All that had happened before was worthwhile since it had brought her to this.

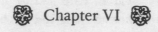

Chapter VI

HASTINGS IN DANGER

The Queen had watched the controversy over Anne Neville with a certain cynical amusement. She could well appreciate Clarence's point of view. Naturally he would want the whole of the Warwick estates if he could get them and the manner in which he had concealed Anne was to say the least ingenious. She and her mother laughed over it.

Jacquetta had been with her a great deal since her last confinement which had been slightly less successful than usual, for the child, a little girl, was less robust than her brothers and sisters. Because of her concern for the child she had sent for Jacquetta who had come with all speed and together they concerned themselves with the welfare of the little girl who had been christened Margaret.

The child seemed to be getting stronger but Elizabeth noticed with apprehension that Jacquetta was looking tired and seemed to have lost a little of that bounding energy which had been one of her main characteristics. When she asked tentative questions about her mother's health Jacquetta waved them aside and said that her recent confinement had made her fanciful but Elizabeth continued to be faintly uneasy. She had relied so much on Jacquetta. It was her mother who had first suggested that she plead to the King for the restoration of her estates and that had started her amazing prosperity. Sometimes she wondered if the rumours about Jacquetta's special powers were true. Was her mother a witch? No, that was absurd. Did she have communication with supernatural powers? No. She was just a wise woman and being devoted to her family she planned all the time for their advancement.

There was one subject which Elizabeth wished to discuss with her mother and that was the Captaincy of Calais. Warwick had held that post with such flair and it was in fact his daring exploits there which had begun his startling career; but now he was dead and this most important and lucrative of posts had to be filled.

Jacquetta listened intently while Elizabeth put her plan before her. She wanted the post for her brother Anthony who had become Earl Rivers on their father's death.

'Anthony will do well there. I shall hint to the King . . .'

Jacquetta nodded. 'Be careful,' she said.

'Be careful? What do you mean?'

Jacquetta hesitated for a moment. Then she said: 'Well, my dear, I believe the King is very much taken with the wife of a merchant.'

'Dear Mother, he is constantly being very much taken with the wives of merchants.'

'But this one I believe a little more so than usual.'

'I have always found that the best way of dealing with Edward's adventures is to ignore them.'

'Heaven alone knows how many mistresses he has,' said Jacquetta.

'Then Heaven may keep the information to itself. I do not

want to know. Dear Mother, I have kept my hold on the King by never reproaching him, never refusing him when he comes back to me, being an understanding wife and mother of his children. That is why he stays enamoured of his wife however many mistresses he has.'

'I have heard that she is a woman of exceptional charms and that Hastings has aspirations with this woman but Edward claimed her first.'

'Well, he cannot marry her.'

'No, not even if she says, "Your mistress I cannot be and I am unfit to be your Queen."'

'Of which you already have one.'

'Elizabeth, you treat this matter lightly. Perhaps you are right.'

'Who is the woman?'

'Her name is Jane Shore. She is said to have great physical beauty and a merry wit and to be quite unlike most merchants' wives. She has left her goldsmith husband and settled into apartments the King has found for her.'

'May he have good sport with her. It will put him in the right mood when I ask for Calais for Anthony.'

'I hear that Hastings found her, boasted of her and so the King saw her.'

'I wish Edward would not be so friendly with Hastings.'

'Hastings is a rake of rakes, second only to the King.'

'I know. I should like to remove Hastings. I will, one day. But the least little whisper against him and the King shuts his ears. You know I never impose my feelings on Edward . . . at least not so that he will know . . . so it is hard to tell him what I think of Hastings.'

'Hastings has been a good friend to him. I daresay Edward

is more friendly with him than with anyone. He is closer to his brother Richard perhaps, but in a different way. Richard is his loyal henchman. Hastings is his companion in profligacy.'

'Undoubtedly so. I believe there would not be so many of these adventures with merchants' wives but for Hastings. Hastings shows what a fine fellow he is with the women and Edward regards it as a challenge. How I wish I could break that friendship!'

'There is no need to tell you to go carefully,' said Jacquetta, 'for you always do.'

'Always,' replied Elizabeth. 'But when I make up my mind I usually get what I want in the end. Desmond thought he was very clever. . . but look what happened to him. I sealed his death warrant while Edward slept. He must have known it was done . . . yet he said nothing and he was quite fond of Desmond. Mother, what has happened to you?'

Jacquetta was lying back in her chair, her face deathly white, her lips blue.

Elizabeth rose in horror and summoned her women to come at once.

They took Jacquetta to her bed and Elizabeth immediately sent for the doctors.

Her mother was very ill and had been so for some time, they told Elizabeth, and the manner in which they spoke alarmed the Queen. Jacquetta looked so wan now that she was lying in bed and was no longer pretending that this was just a slight indisposition. She took Elizabeth's hand and looked at her appealingly, almost apologetically. She was thinking: Perhaps I should have told her. It would have been better to have warned her rather than give her this sudden shock.

But Jacquetta had known how unhappy that would have

made her daughter and she could not bear to disturb her with impending tragedy. She had worked for Elizabeth, lived for Elizabeth as she did for all her children and her great fear now was that Elizabeth would miss her.

There was little time left, she feared. At least she had seen her daughter safely on the throne; she had seen the rest of her children make brilliant marriages and take up important posts. The most influential family in England had ceased to be the Nevilles and had become the Woodvilles. She need not have worried about Elizabeth and this Jane Shore. Elizabeth knew how to handle the King.

So Jacquetta could say: Lord now lettest thou thy servant depart in peace.

My house is in order, she thought. She died peacefully in her bed a few days later.

Elizabeth was stricken with grief. Devoted to her family as she was, she loved her mother intensely. She saw in her the wise woman, the founder of their fortunes.

And now . . . she was dead.

Elizabeth remained deeply affected. Cold she might be to the world but she was devoted to her family and she had always been particularly close to her mother but only now did she realise how much she had meant to her. Edward was sympathetic. He too had been fond of Jacquetta but it was characteristic of him that he avoided unpleasantness. He preferred to forget rather than to brood.

As the weeks passed she saw less of him. Perhaps he was completely entranced by this new mistress. That might be a bad or good sign. She was not sure which. It was sometimes better for a king to have one mistress than many; yet on the other hand if he became too devoted to the woman, might not his love for his wife wane a little?

Elizabeth was determined that it should not. But she realised that with such a menace as the goldsmith's wife she must tread more warily than before.

He was as loving as ever when he came to tell her that Louis of Bruges, Lord of Gruthuyse, who had sheltered him when he had been obliged to fly to the continent and had therefore proved himself to be such a good friend, was to visit England. Edward wanted him to be entertained with all the splendour of which the Court was capable.

Elizabeth threw herself into making the arrangements. It helped her forget the loss of her mother and the health of baby Margaret which was growing less and less satisfactory; moreover it kept the King at her side.

When Gruthuyse arrived at Calais he was welcomed by Lord Howard who was the deputy Captain and there he remained for nearly fourteen days while he was entertained with every show of honour and respect. In due course he arrived at Windsor where the King was waiting to greet him. Edward conducted him to the Queen's apartments assuring him of Elizabeth's impatience to greet him and to thank him in person for his goodness to Edward during his enforced absence from England. It was at such times, Edward commented, that a man discovered his true friends.

Elizabeth, prepared for the coming of this honoured guest, was waiting, looking very beautiful, her golden hair loose about her shoulders and a circlet of jewels about her forehead. She was gratified to see Edward's eyes gleam as he looked at her and she asked herself what she had to fear from any merchant's wife. She had been playing at morteaulx, a bowls game, with her ladies while waiting, and her eldest daughter was present. Like all the royal children six-year-old Elizabeth was very good-looking and there was no doubt of Edward's pride in his wife and daughter when he presented them to the Lord of Gruthuyse.

There followed dancing and games in which the King joined and during the dancing he took the young Elizabeth as his partner at which everyone applauded.

The next morning de Gruthuyse must meet the Prince of Wales and the little Edward was carried in by Thomas Vaughan his chamberlain, and when de Gruthuyse had complimented the King on his charming family, Edward presented him with a gold cup which was decorated with pearls, and on its cover was an enormous sapphire. Nothing was spared in the entertainment which went on for several days. There was hunting in Windsor Park when the King insisted on his honoured guest riding his favourite horse; and when de Gruthuyse was seated on it he was informed that the horse was his. Not content with giving his friend these valuable gifts Edward also presented him with a crossbow and silk strings and a cover of velvet for it which was embroidered with the King's arms and devices.

De Gruthuyse particularly admired the rose-en-soleil which combined the White Rose of York with the blazing Sun and, as Hastings had done, likened the King to that very sun. 'You are the sun of your people,' he said. 'You have brought them peace and prosperity. They bask in your radiance.'

Edward graciously accepted the compliment for indeed it seemed to him that it was so.

There at Windsor de Gruthuyse was given his own

apartments which were called chambers of pleasance; the walls were hung with silk and there were carpets on the floors. There were three chambers and in one was the bed which had been prepared for him. The down was of the best; the sheets of rennes and finest fustian and the quilt of cloth of gold, edged with ermine. The tester was of the same cloth of gold as the quilt and the curtains of white sarsenet. In the second chamber was another fine bed and in the third chamber two baths which were covered with white cloth in the shape of tents.

The whole company escorted the visitor to these apartments and there they left him with Lord Hastings who would stay with him for the night, to care for his comfort in the name of the King. Hastings was, of course, well known to de Gruthuyse and had reason to be grateful to him as had the King, for Hastings had enjoyed hospitality at Bruges when he had shared the King's exile.

They bathed together and while they did so they were served with refreshments which consisted of green ginger, sweetmeats and spiced wine.

A week or so later the company were in London where the investiture of de Gruthuyse with the earldom of Winchester took place. The King was a magnificent figure in his crown and state robes and it was a brilliant assembly that assisted at the ceremony. The Duke of Clarence had been assigned to carry the guest's train and after the ceremony the King led the new Earl back to Westminster where the Queen was waiting to greet him. She was beautiful in her splendid robes wearing the crown on her golden hair and she had rarely felt so confident. Her great regret was that Jacquetta was not there to see her.

Yet another tragedy was awaiting Elizabeth. December had come and little Margaret was growing steadily worse, and on the eleventh of the month, when the child was only eight months old, she died.

They buried her in the Chapel of the Confessor in the Abbey. So there were two deaths in one year. Elizabeth deeply mourned her loss, but she was cheered to know that she was once again pregnant.

Edward grieved with her but he was, like herself, delighted to know they could expect another. Although he was very satisfied with what he had, he longed for another boy. Young Edward was a delight but kings always liked to know that there was at least one other son should anything happen to the first.

Occasionally Elizabeth thought of Jane Shore. She did not know why she should bother about one of his women, except that her mother had mentioned her with a touch of uneasiness during their last real talk together.

She certainly would not mention the woman to Edward but she did find what she thought an opportune moment to mention the Captaincy of Calais which she had heard discussed recently with the comment that the King could not wait much longer before appointing Warwick's successor.

She knew why he delayed. It was because thinking of the post reminded him of Warwick and strangely enough in spite of all that scheming Earl had done, he was still fond of him. Edward's moods might seem strange to some but she understood them. She knew of his devotion to his family; this had been proved by his weakness – she could only call it that – in forgiving Clarence who was only waiting for a chance to betray him again. She understood the force of family ties – none better – but the Woodvilles worked for each other

whereas Edward's brother and some of his kinsmen had their
eyes on what brought them the greatest reward.

'You will have to appoint a Captain soon,' she reminded
him.

He was silent. His thoughts seemed elsewhere. Were they
with the goldsmith's wife?

'Anthony has served you well. He loves you dearly. I was
wondering if you would . . . '

Edward was smiling at her benignly. He is going to agree,
she thought.

His words were shattering: 'I have already bestowed the
Captaincy,' he said.

She stared at him in amazement. If it had been given to
Anthony she would have known at once. She had seen him
only that day.

'I wanted to reward Hastings,' went on the King. 'He has
been a good friend . . . and he was eager for it.'

Hastings! Her enemy! She had the greatest difficulty in
curbing her anger.

She was not looking at the King at that moment, because she
was afraid to; she could have slapped his handsome, smiling
face. Calais . . . for Hastings, her enemy! That man who
accompanied Edward in his adventures with women and urged
him on to greater lechery.

Hastings! The man she hated. She would be his bitter enemy
from now on.

When she turned back to the King she was smiling and all
the bitterness had been wiped from her face.

She was remembering Jacquetta's warning. Perhaps she
must be doubly careful now.

Elizabeth discussed the matter of Hastings', appointment to the Captaincy of Calais with her brother Anthony. He was about a year younger than she was and perhaps the most able of her family. He had married well and through his wife had gained the title of Baron Scales. Being the eldest son he had become Lord Rivers on the death of their father and had advanced rapidly since his sister became Queen of England and was always watchful for improving his state. The King had become quite fond of him; he had his share of the Woodville good looks and had distinguished himself at the jousts where he was considered to be a champion.

Elizabeth knew how he had set his heart on Calais and she guessed what a great disappointment the selection of Hastings must be to him.

'Of course Hastings is as debauched as the King himself,' said Anthony, knowing it was safe to speak so to his sister. Elizabeth had never attempted to deny Edward's flagrant infidelities within her family circle and Jacquetta had always complimented her on her treatment of them.

'There could not be such a complacent queen in history,' Jacquetta used to say. 'Oh how wise you are, my daughter. Your attitude to his philandering makes you irresistible to him.'

She was right. Edward would never have endured a carping wife.

He had always seemed ready to reward her for her attitude to his way of life by granting her requests as long as they did not interfere with his intentions. This matter of Hastings and Calais had been settled before she could as much as hint where she wanted the Captaincy to go.

'Is there no way of turning his favour from Hastings?' asked Elizabeth.

'They have always been friends. They have roamed the streets of London at night together; they have urged each other on to more and more outrageous adventures . . . long before you came on the scene, sister.'

'I know it well. I blame Hastings for much of the King's night adventures. Hastings is a profligate, a rake and a philanderer.'

'Well, Edward knows that as well as any and he continues to give him his friendship.'

'They are two of a kind,' said Elizabeth vehemently.

Anthony was alarmed to see his sister so intense, fearing she might betray her feelings to the King. They owed their prosperity to Elizabeth's relationship with the King; it must not change. No, there was no need to remind Elizabeth of that. She was as much aware of it as any of them.

'So,' said Anthony, 'we should not turn the King away from him by a complaint against his immoral way of life.'

'You mean . . . there could be some other way?'

Her eyes were alight with purpose and again Anthony felt that tremor of disquiet. He laid a hand on her arm. 'There might be a way.'

'How?'

'He has a large household of retainers. There are many who serve . . .'

'Well?'

'There may be some member of that retinue who is a little dissatisfied . . . a little envious of another . . . one who feels he has not been justly treated.'

'And if he were found?'

'He might discover something against Hastings . . . some little plot involving the King.'

'Edward would never believe a thing against Hastings.'

'It might be possible to remind him that once he was loth to believe Warwick was a traitor to him.'

'First you must find something against Hastings.'

'I will,' Anthony promised.

Elizabeth nodded. And once Hastings was proved to be a traitor it would be a simple matter to suggest that the Captaincy should be given to one whom he could trust and whom could the King trust more than his own brother-in-law?

Hastings could not believe it. There was whispering about him. What had he done? He could find no answer to that. Who should be his enemy? Perhaps a husband of one of the women he had seduced? But which one? There were too many of them for him to guess.

It was a strange feeling.

Clarence looked at him slyly, almost invitingly. What did he mean? Hastings had always suspected that Clarence was looking about him, seeking some way of destroying his brother. Hastings wanted none of such matters. He was Edward's friend; he had always been Edward's friend and he wanted to remain so.

Sometimes he laughed at this shadow which was beginning to grow bigger. It was ridiculous. Who had started such rumours?

He suspected the Queen. She did not like him because he often shared the King's nocturnal adventures. He supposed it was natural for a wife not to care for her husband's companion in debauchery. They often went out together in some sort of disguise, usually dressed as merchants. Edward had a childish pleasure in keeping his identity secret and then suddenly revealing it. It was hard for him to remain incognito. He was so tall for one thing; he was outstandingly handsome and if he were growing somewhat too fat and there were pouches beginning to form under his magnificent eyes, he was still very good-looking. He would be known in merchant's clothes as surely as if he wore one of his favourite devices – the rose-en-soleil emblazoned on his cloak. Hastings had once remarked how appropriate that one particularly was. 'You are like the sun in splendour, Edward,' he had said. 'You arose on the dark world of poor mad Henry's country and you took the crown and dazzled us all. And here you are high in the sky . . . in all your splendour.'

Edward had laughed and called Hastings a romantic poet. But he had liked what he had said; and Hastings noticed he used the badge – a combination of the blazing sun and the rose of York – more than any other.

And how could Edward ever believe that he, William Lord Hastings, was not the truest friend he had ever had?

Sometimes he wondered what the Queen whispered to him in the connubial bed at night. What poison did she drop into Edward's ear about his faithful friend? It was said that the Queen never meddled, never advised the King, never mentioned state matters or questioned his decisions. But there were ways, of course.

Once he caught Edward regarding him very coolly indeed as though he were assessing him, suspecting him, and he felt himself go cold with apprehension. Edward had changed from the golden youth who used to slip out into the streets of London with his good friend, looking for adventure. Edward still sought adventures; his appetites were as voracious as ever; but he was different. Warwick had deceived him. Warwick had pretended to be his friend so that he had no notion that he was planning to rise against him. And then Edward was forced to flee into exile.

He never recovered from that. Who would? It had changed the light-hearted trusting young man into a hard one . . . a suspicious one. Clarence had deceived him too. But perhaps he had never thought very much of Clarence. But that Warwick should have turned against him had done something to Edward which would leave its mark forever.

He was ready to suspect his best friend.

Warwick, he would say to himself. And now . . . Hastings!

So when Edward looked at him with that cold assessment in his eyes Hastings trembled. He had noticed for some time that Edward had chosen other companions and Hastings was now never alone in the King's company. There always seemed to be some member of the Woodville family with him – either his Queen's brother or young Thomas Grey, her eldest son by her first marriage. What had Edward been told? Who were Hastings's enemies?

He did not have to look far. He knew it was the Woodvilles. The Queen herself. They disliked anyone to be in favour with the King; and it suddenly dawned on him that they might have been angered by his appointment to Calais. The post was one of the most important that could be bestowed on a man; that trading post, the centre through which passed so many goods: leather, wool, tin and lead to be exported to Burgundy, graded and taxed, meant prosperity to the country and who should reap the reward of all this more than any, but the Captain. Yes, it must be the Captaincy of Calais. When he came to think of it this suspicion had grown up since his appointment.

He brooded; he fretted; he walked the streets of London

asking himself what he should do. He roamed along by the river and looked at the gloomy fortress of the Tower and thought how many men had entered those dark walls never to emerge again except to the scaffold. Was that the fate they were preparing for him?

Each day he awoke with a heavy cloud upon him. He could not enjoy food, wine, nor even women. He was realising how alone he might be in a hostile world.

He thought a great deal about Edward. Their friendship dated back for years. Edward had always been so genial, so good-tempered, so easy-going; a perfect companion for one built in the same mould, though, Hastings would be the first to admit, lacking that aura of splendour. 'I am like the moon,' he had once said, 'reflecting the glory of the sun.'

Edward had laughed at him telling him that such verbal adulation would profit him nothing. 'It's deeds, William,' he had said. 'Deeds that impress me.'

He had joked but he meant it. Now of what deeds had he been accused?

Hastings realised that he could not continue in this way. He was going to the King, and presuming on their long-standing friendship, ask him what was wrong, why he was regarded so coldly, what had been said against him.

Edward had always been affable and amenable. Why should he change now? But he had changed, Warwick's disaffection had changed him. He would never be the same easy-going trusting golden boy again. The sun could be fiercely dangerous as well as benevolent.

But he could not go on in this way. He decided he would speak to Edward. He went to his private apartments and because of their old friendship he found his way to the King.

He was gratified to discover that Edward was alone. Edward looked up in surprise and said: 'What do you want, Hastings?'

'A word with you . . . alone.'

The King hesitated and for a moment a terrible desolation swept over Hastings, for he thought he saw himself doomed. On false evidence of course, but how many men had been condemned on that? He most certainly would not be the first.

He went forward and on impulse kneeling he raised agonised eyes to Edward's face. 'I must speak with you alone. I can endure this state no longer.'

Edward's expression changed. He burst into laughter. 'Get up, William,' he said. 'You look ridiculous in that position.'

Hastings rose and found himself laughing with the King, albeit the laughter was somewhat hysterical.

'Well,' said Edward, 'what is it you have to say?'

'I want to know what has come between us. If I am accused of something . . . I beg you let me know what.'

Edward hesitated. This was William, his old friend, and he could not believe that he would plot against him. At least he should have an opportunity to clear himself.

'My lord . . . my friend . . . Edward,' cried Hastings, 'then I have not been mistaken. There *is* something . . . '

Edward said: 'You have been working against me, Hastings.'

'Never,' said Hastings.

'I found it hard to believe that you had,' began Edward.

Hastings burst into impassioned speech. 'My lord, my King, have I not always served you well? Have I not stood with you . . . always . . . in failure as well as success? We have been in exile together . . . we have adventured together in beds and in battlefields. Edward, you cannot seriously believe that I would ever plan to do you ill.'

'I must tell you that I would not believe . . . for long . . . I refused.'

'Tell me of what I am accused.'

Edward said: 'You know that I have my enemies. My own brother . . . You are friendly with Clarence, I believe.'

'My lord, I am on good terms with your brother as you are . . . because he is *your* brother. For no other reason. I beg you tell me who has brought these accusations against me.'

'It is some who served you once and are no longer in your employ.'

'Disgruntled servants, my lord?'

'Just so. But . . .' Edward looked at Hastings through narrowed eyes. He saw it all clearly. He knew who had trumped up charges against Hastings. It was Lord Rivers and the Queen. And it was because of Calais. He laughed inwardly, trying to remember what Elizabeth had said about Hastings . . . nothing definite of course. She was far too clever. But she, with the help of Rivers, had managed to sow seeds of distrust in his mind about his best friend.

He was remembering now all the exploits they had shared together, the merry evenings, the days of adventure. And he suddenly knew that the suspicions against his old friend were false and he understood what anguish he had been submitted to over the last weeks.

Elizabeth had not said a word against Hastings but subtly when his name had been mentioned she had referred to the treachery of Warwick and Clarence, knowing that when those two were mentioned he would remember how they had both betrayed him and how astonished he had been that they could do so.

She was clever, his Elizabeth. And how well she suited him. So calm, so secret, so fascinating always . . . But she knew that she must never attempt to persuade him or influence his decisions . . . outwardly. But she could act in her own secret way. Sometimes he thought of Desmond, whose comments about a divorce she had received so quietly. But they had rankled and how had Desmond come to be so swiftly executed?

He did not want to think too much of that incident. It was unpleasant. It was unpleasant also to think of Hastings betraying him. Hastings betray him! Never. He had allowed himself to be persuaded. But never again. Everyone, Elizabeth, Rivers, every Woodville among them would have to learn that it was the King who made the decisions, the King who said: 'This shall or shall not be.'

Let them try if they would; but they should not succeed.

'William,' he said, 'I know you well. You have always been a good friend to me. Are you still? Just tell me that.'

'My lord King, I swear on everything I hold most sacred that I have never swerved from my loyalty to you. The gossip which has suggested otherwise is slanderous, evil . . . and has no place in reality.'

The King looked at his friend and said: 'I believe you, William. Let us forget this slander. Let us be together as we always were and I pray God always will be.'

Hastings fell on his knees and kissed the King's hand.

Edward was laughing. 'Get up, you fool,' he said. 'Have I not told you already you look ridiculous down there.'

And so the affair was at an end. Hastings was back with the

King. They laughed together at table; they rode out together. And Elizabeth realised that her attempt to separate the King from his friend had failed.

🌹 Chapter VII 🌹

THE FRENCH ADVENTURE

Elizabeth was enraged to realise that her plot to destroy Hastings had failed; in fact the King was more affable than ever to his friend and seemed eager to make up for suspecting him.

Hastings had quickly recovered and was his old merry witty self and he and Edward were hardly ever out of each other's company. She had discovered too that his passion for Jane Shore had not abated; rather it had increased; it seemed as though it were likely to become a permanent relationship. She wondered what view her mother would have taken of that. Perhaps she should ask the woman to Court to keep an eye on her and let her believe that she was ready to be a friend. How would Edward react to that? She would have to tread warily. In any case she was now faintly disturbed by the long-standing nature of the liaison and she deeply wished that Jacquetta was with her so that they could discuss it together.

But now she was preparing for her confinement and decided that the birth of the child should take place at Shrewsbury. Edward was eagerly awaiting the day and she knew that he longed for another boy. They had their three beautiful girls,

Elizabeth, Mary and Cecily, and little Edward. Now if they could have another boy Edward would be so delighted with his Queen that surely he would forget this Jane Shore . . . for a little while at least.

The death of little Margaret had upset him. He hated anyone to mention the child, which was characteristic of him. Edward wanted only to think of what was pleasant. She was grateful again to Jacquetta who had taught her the wisdom of understanding what would please and what would depress him and making sure that no unpleasantness marred the hours they spent together.

She bore her child without a great deal of discomfort and to her great delight it was a boy. Moreover a healthy child; she had been a little nervous after what had happened to Margaret.

Edward came to her bedside, knelt and kissed her hands. He was gracious, grateful, loving and tender. She wondered how long it was since he had been with Mistress Shore.

'What do you wish the boy to be called?' she asked.

'Richard,' he replied promptly, 'after my brother who has always been a good friend to me. He will appreciate the honour.'

'He named his son after you, Edward,' she said, 'so it is only right and fitting that yours should be named after him.'

So the child became Richard and Elizabeth promised herself that she would keep him close to her for a year or so.

Elizabeth loved her children dearly and she did not forget the two she had before her marriage to Edward and although she could not do as much for them as she would have liked, she was determined that they should share in her good fortune. A landed endowment had already been provided for them and Thomas was doing well; he was a favourite with the King and often joined him and Hastings in their adventures, for Thomas was only some ten years or so younger than the King and as the time passed he was becoming more and more of a companion to him. Thomas showed the same tendencies she feared. She had no doubt that her son, like Hastings – or so she had heard – had cast lascivious eyes on the desirable goldsmith's wife.

It had been a wrench for her to allow her little son Edward to be taken to Ludlow Castle and put into the charge of his chamberlain, Thomas Vaughan. The boy was so young – only three years old – but she had arranged that members of her family be appointed to the important posts of his household. Her brothers Edward and Richard were his councillors; and she had found a place there for her younger son by her first marriage. Richard Grey was Comptroller of the Prince's household. His governor, however, was her brother Anthony, for close as the bond was which bound the whole family together it was at its strongest between her and Anthony.

Her little son Edward would be brought up to be a good Woodville. There was no doubt of that; and if Edward knew this he raised no objection.

It was at this time that the King began to think of settling affairs in France. England had enjoyed a few years of prosperity but with a little prompting from the Duke of Burgundy, Edward was of the opinion that an invasion of France providing it were successful would inspire the people to greater enthusiasm for him. The people liked their kings to be warlike; Edward Longshanks, Edward the Third and Henry the Fifth had all waged war satisfactorily. He could see no reason why the same should not apply to Edward the Fourth.

To raise an army he needed money and that must come from the people – every man and woman in the land. Taxation was never popular and it had laid the seeds of downfall for several of his predecessors. But Edward believed it would be different with him.

For one thing he was built in the mould of the great conquerors. He was meant to ride through the streets — acclaimed as the hero returning from his conquests. The situation in France had been such a humiliation when people remembered the glorious days of Henry the Fifth, and they looked to him to bring back glory to England.

But money! Where to find the money? Perhaps he should collect it himself for he was sure people would give more willingly to him than to some tax levied on them by the Parliament. Suppose he make a progress through the country explaining to the people what he needed the money for. Would they not then give willingly?

He sent for Richard to come down from the North. The reunion was affectionate in the extreme. Richard had the same admiration as ever for his splendid brother; and Edward made it clear that he was grateful to Richard who had kept good order in the North so that for the first time Edward had had no need to worry about what was happening up there.

Richard talked of his pleasant life at Middleham, of his wonderful son Edward. The only thing that marred his happiness was his concern about Anne's health. Like her sister Isabel she suffered from a weakness of the lungs which on certain days made it difficult for her to get her breath. He had had the best doctors and they were sure the keen fresh northern air was good for her, so he was more hopeful now.

Edward took him to see the new baby Richard.

'Your namesake, brother,' he said. Richard admired the baby and as he had visited the young Prince of Wales at

Ludlow on his way down was able to assure the Queen that her son was in the best possible health.

When Edward talked to him of the proposed war he was less happy.

'Think of the taxes you will have to raise to get an army which can do any good in France.'

'I have already thought of it and how I will raise the money. Burgundy will be with us. We will give Louis a fight and it may well be that we shall regain all the territory we have lost in the last years.'

'Are you sure that Burgundy does not want you to fight his battles for him?'

'If he does,' said Edward, 'he will be disappointed. Come, Richard, prepare. Very soon I shall have Louis suing for peace.'

'First you must raise the army.'

'I intend to,' replied Edward, 'and such an army that Louis will tremble at the sight of it and mayhap we shall come to some terms — most advantageous to us — without much fighting. Battles do not always go to the best fighters, Richard. Strategy is more important than strength sometimes. Warwick taught me that . . .'

Edward was silent suddenly thinking of Warwick . . . Not a great warrior really, but a strategist of genius . . . a man who could turn a defeat on the battlefield into a victory in diplomacy.

He was constantly remembering what Warwick had taught him, and there was always an element of sadness when he did. He had to stop thinking of Warwick the traitor and remember Warwick the teacher and all the golden rules he had taught his pupil.

Richard said nothing. He knew the trend of Edward's thoughts.

Edward had meant what he said when he had declared he would collect the money himself and very soon was setting out on a tour of the country. In all the towns and villages, people flocked to hear him speak and they marvelled at his handsome looks.

A king to be proud of, they said. They decorated the market-squares with flags and prominent among these was the badge of the white rose in the heart of the blazing sun. The white rose at the very heart of the sun of York. But the King himself was more splendid than any device.

They rejoiced in him; in his excessive good looks, his affable manners, his smiles, his willingness to share a joke, his laughter which rang out wherever he was, his splendid garments all in exquisite taste, made of him a king to be proud of.

And if he wanted money in order to bring the French King to his knees, he should have it. If they had to give there was no one on whom they would rather bestow it.

He visited the houses; blatantly, but so charmingly, he asked for money – and he got it.

There was one case which people were to talk of for years to come because it was so typical of what happened on that progress through the country.

A widow of certain means was asked for twenty pounds which she graciously gave. She was not uncomely and to express his gratitude for her ready compliance with his request, the King kissed her, whereupon she was so overcome that she immediately said she would double her contribution: the first twenty pounds were for the war, the second for the handsomest man in England.

There were few who could have toured the country asking for money and made a triumphant progress of it but Edward did, and emerged from it ever more popular than when he had set out. The people deemed it well worthwhile to have paid their money to receive a smile and a friendly word from such a king – and in the case of the comely widow – a kiss.

In due course Edward was ready to cross the Channel at the head of a considerable army. He had fifteen hundred men at arms, fifteen thousand archers on horseback, and innumerable foot soldiers. In addition to this army he had equipped another smaller one to go to Brittany in order to aid the Duke whom the French were threatening to attack. He had a reason for wishing to make the Duke of Brittany his ally, for sheltering there was Jasper Tudor with his nephew Henry. Jasper had been one of the leading Lancastrians and although if he were to return to England now there would be little support for him, Edward liked to know where these Tudors were and he could at any time if he remained friendly with the Duke of Brittany ask for their extradition.

Edward was well aware that so many men had rallied to his banner because they hoped to bring back to their homes some of the spoils of war. They wanted French booty. Edward, however, had other ideas. To fight the French would be to embark on another war such as that which had taken one hundred years to settle, which had swayed back and forth over those years, costing blood and money and eventually had ended by driving the English almost completely out of France.

No, Edward wanted something, but it was not war. He wanted some alliance, some monetary reward for holding off a war . . . bribe some might call it. But that was all part of the fortunes of war.

So if these men whom he had gathered together were

spoiling for a fight, Edward was not. It was almost as though Warwick were at his shoulder. He would have liked to discuss this matter with Richard but it was something of which Richard would not approve. Rivers . . . ? Well, Rivers agreed with him whatever he did, which was comforting almost always, although there were times when a man wanted an honest opinion.

As soon as he had landed in France he wrote a letter to Louis couched in formal terms. He must give up the crown of France to Edward or face a bitter war.

Having written the letter he called one of his most trusted men to him.

'What I have to say to you,' he said, 'is too important to be trusted to writing. You must swear secrecy on this. Do so now.'

The man swore that nothing should prise the secret, or whatever it was, from him.

'You will take this letter to the King of France and when he has read it you will ask to speak to him in private. He will see you and you will tell him that you know I have no wish to invade France, but that I have threatened to do so to satisfy my people and the Duke of Burgundy. If the King of France would come to some agreement which would be to the advantage of the King of England, your master would graciously consider it. Now is that clear?'

'Absolutely so, my lord.'

'You should also say that I shall not be prepared to listen to any proposition until my entire army is landed on French soil and as it is so large that will take at least three weeks.'

'I understand, my lord.'

'Tell the King that he will have that time to decide what he will be able to offer me to avert this long and destructive war on French land.'

The King's messenger bowed his head and went off to do his mission.

Edward's suspicion that the Duke of Burgundy had wished the English to fight his battles with the French was confirmed when the Duke came to meet him, not at the head of an army but with nothing more than a personal bodyguard and in the first meeting explaining, with some embarrassment, that he had to leave at once for the defence of Luxembourg.

Louis in the meantime had followed Edward's lead in sending a herald to the English camp who was more than he appeared to be. This man told Edward in a private interview that Louis was prepared to consider the suggestions which had been put to him and suggested a meeting at Picquigny.

Edward called together a council of his commanders. This included his brothers Clarence and Gloucester, the Dukes of Norfolk and Suffolk, his stepson Thomas, Rivers, Hastings and a few others. Edward laid the proposition before them. The Duke of Burgundy had gone to Luxembourg and had therefore deserted them; the King of France was ready to treat for peace. It seemed to Edward that they might come very well out of the excursion without having been engaged in the smallest battle.

Richard spoke up. 'The people paid their benevolences to win victory in France. The soldiers have joined your banner in the hope of capturing booty to take home. The people want to hear of victories. You have taken their money under false pretences if you do not fight.'

Edward looked at his brother quizzically. 'My dear brother,' he said, 'you are over-concerned with this scrupulous reckoning of yours. Wars have done no good to our country. We have lost all we won. Now we stand a chance of getting something very substantial from the King of France without bloodshed or the loss of our equipment.'

'I see your point,' said Richard. 'But what will the people say? They will not get what they paid their taxes for . . . call them benevolences if you will, they are still taxes.'

'I tell you great good will come from this. You will be surprised what the King of France is ready to pay for peace.'

'To pay to whom?' asked Richard. 'To the soldiers who have come for booty? To the people at home who have paid for a war?'

Edward laid his hand on his brother's shoulder. 'Richard,' he said, 'the others among us see my point. They will follow me in this.'

'And you would do it if they did not,' said Richard with a shrug of his shoulders.

'You will see,' said Edward.

He then discussed the terms he would put before Louis. First there should be a truce of seven years duration; there should be free trading between the two countries. Louis would pay Edward seventy-five thousand gold crowns immediately and fifty thousand a year; the Dauphin should marry Edward's eldest daughter Elizabeth.

These terms seemed very harsh but to the amazement of the English Louis accepted them. It had all been so much easier than Edward had thought and he could not see that the arrangement was anything but a triumph of strategy. He had amassed an enormous army which seemed invincible; he had come to France and so frightened Louis that he had been eager to make terms at once.

When Charles of Burgundy came riding with all speed to Edward's camp he demanded to know why Edward had made such terms with the enemy.

'The King of France is no longer my enemy,' said Edward. 'My daughter is to marry his son.'

Burgundy sneered. 'And you think Louis will ever allow that to come to pass?'

'We are coming to an amicable agreement about the matter . . . and others.'

Burgundy was furious. 'So you come with your armies like a conqueror and slink away like a paid lackey of the King of France.'

Edward retained his imperturbable good humour. 'Not so. Not so. I shall leave as triumphantly as I came – a richer man and my armies intact to make sure the peace stays with us.'

Burgundy left in a rage and Edward could not repress his gratification to see the mighty Duke so nonplussed.

There followed the meeting with Louis. The two Kings made a startling contrast. Edward was splendid, wearing a gown of cloth of gold lined with red satin. Out of compliment to the French he wore a black velvet cap aglitter with jewels in the shape of the fleur-de-lis. Louis was very soberly clad and so drab did he look beside the brilliant King of England that Hastings murmured that he looked like a mountebank.

The terms were agreed and the King of France was extremely affable not only to Edward but to all those who, he thought, would be important to keeping the peace.

There was one notable absence and this disturbed him. Richard Duke of Gloucester had declared that he would have none of the treaty and therefore he would not be present on the occasion. Louis made up his mind that he must talk to Gloucester and see if it were not possible to offer him something which would be irresistible to him.

He was alert watching for those who were against the peace, even though they dared not come out in the open – as Gloucester had – and say so. There was Louis de Bretaylle, one of the English King's foremost captains who it had been reported to Louis had been heard to comment that the treaty was a disgrace to England. It was important to have the support of such men so Louis entertained him personally and offered him a high post in France which de Bretaylle immediately refused. However, when Louis came up with a gift of one thousand crowns, this was irresistible and de Bretaylle did accept them. Money was always so hard to refuse; and all Louis asked in return was that the captain should work for continued peace between the two countries.

But Louis's chief anxiety was of the Duke of Gloucester. Richard could be a power in the land and he had showed his disapproval more openly than anyone. Louis invited him to dine – not a great banquet but a personal meal when they could talk together as good friends and come to some understanding of each other's actions.

Richard could scarcely refuse such an invitation but he went along determined not to be bribed as his brother had been.

Louis surveyed the young man shrewdly. A strong young man, thought Louis, and obviously one of principles, loyal to his brother always, even when he did not approve of what Edward was doing. Edward was fortunate to have inspired such devotion.

Louis asked Richard questions about his life at Middleham,

enquired after his wife and young son and in due course came to the point of the meeting. Louis was delighted to be on such good terms with the King of England and he was happy that they had settled their differences without loss of life. War brought miseries to thousands and if it could be avoided that was a matter for rejoicing. He believed that it was the duty of all to do everything to maintain peace between the two countries.

Richard agreed that peace was desirable . . . honourable peace, he stressed.

'Indeed you are right,' said Louis. 'Your brother is astute, my lord. He knows how to strike a good bargain. But I want to show you some very fine horses which have come into my stables. I venture to think they are the best in the world. And what think you of this plate? It is some of the best to be found in France. My lord, I am going to ask you to accept a gift from me . . . Plate such as this and some of those new fine horses which have come into my stables.'

Richard did not employ the finesse of his brother. He came straight to the point.

'If these are meant for bribes to bring me to your way of thinking, if in accepting them I am to announce that I think my brother was right . . .'

'My lord, my lord, what can you be thinking of me? These are gifts to an honoured guest. I ask nothing in return for *gifts*.'

Etiquette demanded that Richard accept the plate and horses for when they were offered in such a way there was no alternative, but he made it clear that he did not approve of the treaty and would never say he did.

One to be watched, thought Louis. Men with high principles were dangerous.

Richard went away a little sorrowfully. He would never ride the horses nor use the plate for to do so would make him think sadly not of Louis, but of his brother.

Always he remembered with clarity the days of their childhood, those brief visits of Edward and how he had descended on them with his dazzling good looks, his laughter and his obvious affection for them. They had been the outstanding days in Richard's life; and when there was trouble and he with George and Margaret had been sent to lodge at the Pastons' house in London, Edward had come every day to see them and to remind them that the fortunes of the House of York though temporarily in decline would soon rise and then they would see their parents again.

He had been so entirely under Edward's spell that he had never escaped from it and he knew he never would. But of late there had appeared a few clouds in the sky to obscure the splendour of the sun. The hero was flawed. He was as strong as ever – perhaps stronger because of the flaws. But Richard was faintly disillusioned. Not that his affection had changed. His loyalty would be there until his death. He would stand by Edward no matter what he did; but this latest affair was an indication to him. He had actually refused to sign the treaty, and Edward had not attempted to force him. It was typical of Edward that he respected his brother's views.

When Richard was ready to depart for the North, Edward made it clear that their difference of opinion over this matter would make no change in their relationship. Edward explained to Richard that they had come out of the expedition richer and without shedding a drop of blood. They had had the honour of frightening the King of France into parting with a great deal. Edward was considerably richer because of it. So were many of his friends.

'Did you know that Hastings has a pension from France of two thousand crowns a year?'

'Because he is your close friend. Because he is expected to work for France.'

'As I am, dear brother. Well, there is no harm in that. This will be good for the country. French money coming into it and not a drop of English blood to buy it.'

'You and your friends have profited indeed,' said Richard. 'But the men will be disgruntled. They came back empty-handed.'

'With their limbs intact. Oh come, Richard, when you are as old as I you will know that diplomacy and sound good reason bring more good than battle cries.'

Richard could not be convinced that the treaty was an honourable one and he was not going to say so.

Edward looked at him steadily and said: 'A difference of opinion does not change the feelings between two good friends, I hope.'

'Nothing could challenge my loyalty to you.'

'So thought I,' said Edward. 'I trust you, Richard. You have always been my good friend. I need your friendship particularly as I cannot rely on it from George. He troubles me, Richard.'

'What is he plotting now?'

'I do not know what. But I know he plots. I would I could rely on him as I do on you.'

'You will never be able to.'

'Nay. But you and I shall stand together, Richard, eh? Never shall we forget that we are brothers . . . whatever may befall.'

Richard was comforted to know that the bond between

them was as strong as ever, even though they had disappointed each other, even though they could not always act in unison, they could rely on the loyalty – one to the other.

Edward showed that Richard's attitude had made no difference by bestowing new lands on him and Richard returned to Middleham pleased to be away from the vanities and insincerities of Court. Back with his wife and his son the apprehensions would be blown away by the fresh northern air.

Richard had been right when he had said the men would be disgruntled because they must return without booty. There was grumbling among the soldiers who had thought to come home rich; they would not have minded a scar or two, they said. They had joined the army to fight and what had happened? They had been to France and come back again . . . just as they went.

The people who had paid good money for victories were disappointed too. The King had come riding through the country charming the money out of their pockets, asking most graciously for benevolences and what had happened? He had just gone to France and come back again!

Disappointed soldiers roamed the countryside. If they could not loot French villages they would loot English ones. The roads had become unsafe.

Edward's reaction was immediate. He set up judges all over the country and he himself made a pilgrimage from north to south. Anyone caught robbing, raping or murdering would be hanged at once. There should be no mercy for offenders. He would have law and order throughout the land.

His action was immediately effective and the outbreak of violence died down as suddenly as it had risen.

In the market-squares Edward explained to the people what

had happened. He had taken an army to France, yes, and they in their generosity had enabled him to do this with their benevolences. 'My friends and loyal subjects,' he said, 'we have humbled France. What think you would have happened if we had fought great battles . . . and even won them. What good would that be to you? You cannot live on glory. Conquest is great and good when there is no other way of achieving the best for a nation. But I have taken my armies to France and the King of France has paid me highly to desist from making war. I did desist. I return your men to you . . . your husbands . . . your brothers . . . they are with you again. I have come back with a full purse and that means that with this money I can strengthen my country. All this good I can bring you with no cost to you, my friends. The King of France is paying *your* taxes. Was that not worth raising money for? You have won these concessions which I have brought to you through your benevolence, good people. From here we go on . . . to greatness.'

They listened. They loved him. How could they help it? He was so handsome. Many said they had never seen a more handsome man. He was clever; he was shrewd; he was the King they wanted. The sun was high over England in all its splendour. The people loved their King.

Chapter VIII

A BUTT OF MALMSEY

Isabel, Duchess of Clarence, was feeling very ill. She dreaded her confinement which was now imminent. She would never forget the first of all which had taken place when she was at sea with her father, mother and sister Anne. Her father had been forced to leave England with his family and although she had been eight months pregnant at the time and in no condition to travel, she had been obliged to go.

The misery of that time, the agony she had suffered only to produce a dead child had remained with her ever since and although she had had two healthy children, Margaret and two years later Edward, she still was fearful.

She wished that Anne or her mother could be with her. But they were at Middleham. The Countess was ageing and Anne she believed did not enjoy robust health.

No, she would try not to worry, try to fight the terrible weakness which overcame her, try to forget the discomforts of her condition and remind herself that they were normal.

She had a very good attendant who had been sent to her by the Queen. The woman was not young and seemed to have a great deal of experience. The Queen had been most affable and

Isabel supposed that Edward had suggested she should be for the King was anxious to show that he bore George no malice for those days when he had joined with Isabel's father and fought against him.

The woman Elizabeth had sent was Ankarette Twynhoe and she had been in the Queen's service for some time. Isabel welcomed not only the woman but the goodness of the Queen in sending her.

Isabel sighed for peace. Often she remembered the days at Middleham when she and Anne with Richard and George used to ride together and play games and gave no thought to the future. Or perhaps George did. He was always wanting to win in everything, to ride faster, to shoot his arrows further . . . it had always been the same with George. He had enjoyed showing his superiority over them all which he could do quite easily, being older and definitely taller and more handsome than Richard. George was boastful, exaggerating his successes, ignoring his failures. He was very different from Richard. People liked George better though. George was always the most handsome person present except in the company of his brother Edward, who outshone everyone. Isabel, who had come to know George very well after being married to him, realised that he hated his brother. Not Richard . . . he had nothing to hate in Richard considering himself superior in every way, but Edward. She had seen his eyes change colour when his elder brother's name was mentioned; she had seen that clenching of his hands, that tensing of his muscles and she had known how the hatred rose within him, because sometimes in the privacy of their apartments he had let it loose in all its fury.

George could never forgive fate for making Edward the

elder. But for that George would have been King; and what George wanted more than anything on earth was to be King. It was for that reason that he had sided with Isabel's father against his brother. Warwick must have promised him that he would be King, but she guessed her wily father would never have allowed that to happen. She herself had been very disconsolate when the feud had arisen between the King and her father. She knew that Warwick was called the Kingmaker and it was no empty title; but it had been his great mistake she was sure to part from Edward.

Poor George! Oddly enough she loved him, and what was perhaps stranger still, he loved her. Her weakness appealed to his strength perhaps, but he had always been tender with her, and she would listen to his grandiose schemes. She encouraged him. She wanted to know what was in his mind. He would talk to her sometimes about the wildest schemes and they were all tinged with his hatred of his brother and the goal in the plans led to that one thing – the crowning of George, no longer Duke of Clarence, but King of England – in the Abbey.

She often wondered what the outcome would be and in the last few days she had doubted whether she would be here to see it.

That was wrong. Women sometimes felt like this when they dreaded a pregnancy. Her cough was worse and she had a pain in her chest. She and Anne had both caught cold easily. In Middleham Castle their mother had coddled them and at the least sign of a cough they were put to bed with hot fomentations on their chests. But her mother was with Anne now and they were in the North and she was here in Gloucestershire which was one of their favourite counties. George liked it, so she did.

She called to Ankarette who came at once.

'You are feeling unwell, my lady?'

'It is my chest. I have a pain there. Oh it is nothing. I have had it before . . . often.'

'My lady, I think perhaps you should go to bed. Will you allow me to call your women?'

Isabel nodded. 'I think perhaps, my lady, you should go into the new infirmary at Tewkesbury Abbey. You would be well attended there.'

'Yes, I believe these monastic infirmaries are very good.'

'My gracious lady the Queen has great faith in them, as you know.'

'Indeed, yes,' said Isabel. 'Perhaps I should go.'

'Shall I make the arrangements, my lady?' said Ankarette.

It was pleasant enough in the infirmary at Tewkesbury Abbey. Ankarette was with her for she had expressed her desire that the Queen's woman should attend her until the child was born and Elizabeth had said that Ankarette was to stay as long as Isabel needed her.

George came to visit her at Tewkesbury. He was alarmed at the sight of her. She looked so pale. She was shortly to give birth to a child and she had never been strong but she certainly looked very ill. He was fond of Isabel, not only because she had brought him vast estates but she soothed him; she listened to his ramblings about his dreams and the glittering prizes he would have; she always seemed to believe him and he needed such an audience. He could not say to anyone else what he said to Isabel. It would be rank treason; but with his wife he felt safe. She would never betray him; she was always on his side. He needed Isabel.

Because he was worried he looked about to blame someone for her state.

'What woman is that who is always in attendance?' he demanded.

'You mean Ankarette? The Queen sent her to me. She is very good and has been in the Queen's service for some time.'

George grunted. 'I cannot see why the Woodvilles want to send us a woman.'

'It was only the Queen . . . from one woman to another. She knows I have not been well and she says that Ankarette is an excellent nurse. She insisted on my having her.'

George nodded and went on to ask about her heatlh. He was not satisfied with the place. It was cold and a monastery was no place for a confinement especially one of such importance.

George could not contemplate his children without seeing them as heirs to the throne.

'I am going to take you back to Warwick Castle,' he said. 'There we shall look after you as you should be looked after.'

Isabel smiled. She did not greatly care where she was.

It was November when they reached Warwick Castle. Her baby was due in the next few weeks and all was in readiness. But as the weeks passed Isabel's cough grew worse and Ankarette and the other women became gravely anxious.

Three days before Christmas the child was born and it became clear that not only had the baby little chance of survival but Isabel was also in grave danger.

She did not recover from the birth. That was a gloomy Christmas at Warwick Castle. In his cradle the baby lay small and shrivelled, refusing nourishment, just lying quiet and still.

On the first of January he joined his mother.

George came to Warwick and was overcome with grief.

Isabel dead! He was desolate. He had wanted to tell her of

his plans; he had been looking forward to greeting the new child. Dead, both of them!

Life was cruel to him. It had denied him a crown and now it had taken his wife and child.

He wept genuine tears. He would miss Isabel. There would never be anyone for whom he could care as he had cared for her.

He looked with narrowed eyes at the women of her bed-chamber. He felt resentful towards them because they were alive and she was dead.

He went back to Court. The place was buzzing with the news of the Duke of Burgundy's death. George's sister Margaret was a widow now and the Duke's son had died before he did but he had a daughter, Mary, and she would be heiress to the vast estates of Burgundy, surely the richest heiress in France, or the whole of Europe for that matter.

It was an interesting situation.

No one would replace Isabel in his heart, of course, but a man in his position was expected to marry and when he did he should marry in a way which would be advantageous not only to him but to his country.

It was perhaps too soon to be thinking of marrying again with Isabel scarcely cold in her grave, but matters such as this would not wait. The heiress of Burgundy would be snapped up with all speed. That was one thing they could be certain of.

He mentioned the possibility to Edward. 'It would be to England's advantage to get the Burgundian estates in English hands,' he said.

Edward was pensive. The last thing he would give his consent to would be a match between his brother and Mary of Burgundy. He knew that the Duke of Burgundy believed that he himself had a claim to the English throne . . . a flimsy one admittedly. His mother Isabel of Portugal was a granddaughter of John of Gaunt. This claim, slight though it might be, would strengthen Clarence's. Certainly there should be no match between Clarence and Burgundy.

He discussed it with Hastings. 'My sister Margaret, the Duchess of Burgundy, has always favoured George. Heaven knows why. But he was an attractive child when she knew him and you know how people in families have these favourites. She might try to influence Mary into taking him.'

'You will never allow it,' said Hastings.

'My God no. I should like to get him out of the country . . . but not to Burgundy. With this extra claim you can imagine what he would be planning.'

'I can indeed,' said Hastings.

While the King was considering this and preparing the refusal he would give to Clarence, Elizabeth mentioned the matter to him.

'A union between England and Burgundy would be an advantage,' she said quietly.

'It would depend, my dear, very much on the bridegroom.'

'So thought I. Have you . . . ?'

'Selected him? It is hardly for me to do that. Mary I believe is a strong-minded young lady and will want some say in the matter.'

'She will marry where it is best for her to do so, I doubt not, and your sister Margaret will have some say in the matter perhaps. I believe they are very good friends.' Elizabeth hesitated and looked sharply at the King. He was smiling slightly. He knew what was coming. Dear Elizabeth, she was full of schemes for bettering her family. Who had she in mind now? He could guess. Anthony. For recently, like George, he had lost his wife and was in the market. Trust Elizabeth to try to pull down this very important prize.

He had to admire her. What hope had Earl Rivers of marrying the heiress of Burgundy, but since Elizabeth herself had married the King of England she believed anything was possible.

'It would seem,' he said, taking one of the tendrils of golden hair which hung over her shoulder and twirling it round thoughtfully in his fingers, 'that my Queen has a husband in mind for this fortunate child.'

'I would not presume to suggest . . . '

'Then whisper to me, my love.'

'Well, Edward, I think that if Anthony were to have the girl it would bring great good to this country.'

'Anthony! Did you know, Elizabeth, that my brother George is after her?'

'You will never allow that.'

'No,' he said. 'Never.'

'Then Anthony?'

He was still smiling at her. He did not answer. To what lengths did her ambition for her family go? Did she really think the greatest heiress of the day would be allowed to marry a mere Earl and one who had inherited his titles because of his sister's relationship with the King?

Yet she looked so appealing. Why not grant his permission? Nothing would come of it in any case. The suggestion would be laughed to scorn in Burgundy and perhaps it would teach Elizabeth not to aim quite so high for her family in future. It was different with herself. She had won her place through her outstanding beauty and her determination never to irritate her husband with criticism of his actions.

'Well,' he said, 'let Anthony try. Nothing will come of it, I assure you. But there is no harm in trying.'

That was it. He would not refuse her. He would please her as always. Let someone else do the unpleasant part, which was of course inevitable.

It was different with Clarence. When he came and asked permission to put forward his suit to the heiress of Burgundy he was met with a blank refusal.

As Edward had expected scorn was poured on Anthony's hopes; but when George realised that Rivers had been allowed to try while he himself had been refused even that, his fury knew no bounds.

He had had enough. The King and the Queen were now his bitter enemies and he would act accordingly.

Sulking he went back to Warwick Castle. He was in deep mourning, he said, for the wife he had loved so well.

He was lonely. He might have been contemplating another marriage if all had gone smoothly with the Burgundy project. Not that that would compensate for the loss of Isabel, but it would take his mind off this miserable lonely state.

Edward had refused him that consolation. And what was more had given it to Anthony Woodville. My lord Rivers! That upstart! Where would he have been if his sister had not attracted the King and had the cunning to refuse him till he married her.

A curse on the Woodvilles. And that sly woman the Queen had tried to pretend she was Isabel's friend by sending her the woman . . . Ankarette somebody. Curse curse curse the Woodvilles and in particular the Queen who was responsible for their rise. Edward was a fool to have married a woman of no standing. They were always the worst when it came to grabbing titles and lands.

He ground his teeth in rage and wished with all his might that he could raise an army and destroy Edward.

How dared the Queen send a woman to serve Isabel! And why had she done it? Why?

Pictures were darting in and out of his fevered mind. That woman . . . sent by the Queen! For what purpose? Why should the Queen send Isabel a woman to serve her?

There was something behind this. The more he thought of it the more excited he became. He revelled in his excitement. It took his mind off the disappointment in the loss of Mary of Burgundy.

The woman had come . . . sent by the Queen . . . and Isabel had died. He did not trust the Queen, so he did not trust any of her women.

He sent for one of his menservants. He said to the man: 'Send the woman Ankarette to me. I would speak to her.'

'My lord,' was the answer, 'she has left us. She went after the Duchess's death. She said she had come to serve her and now she and the child were dead there was no reason why she should stay.'

'Oh she did, did she? I understand. Yes, I think I understand very well. Where has she gone? Has she returned to her mistress the Queen?'

'I think not, my lord. She has a home in Cayford.'

'And where is Cayford?'

'It is in Somerset I believe, my lord.'

'Ah, that will do. I will find her.'

The manservant looked astonished but George waved him

away. The plan was already there in his mind; and he never paused to consider consequences. He summoned eighty of his guards and told them that they were to go with all speed to a place called Cayford which was in Somerset. There they would find the home of Ankarette Twynhoe, and they were to arrest her and bring her immediately to Warwick Castle where he would be awaiting them.

The Captain of the guard looked somewhat dismayed. It was a well-known fact that none had the powers of immediate arrest except the King; and although Clarence was the King's brother that was not the same thing.

'Why do you hesitate?' asked Clarence.

'We are to arrest this woman . . . in the name of . . . '

'You are to arrest this woman. Have I not told you? I command it. I command it . . . '

When Clarence was in such a mood it was wisest to obey him and the Captain remarked that he would leave at once for Somerset.

When the soldiers arrived Ankarette was at home with her daughter and son-in-law, who were visiting her for she had been long from home nursing the Duchess of Clarence. They were sitting peacefully at dinner when Clarence's guard appeared.

As the Captain came into the dining hall Ankarette rose from the table in astonishment.

'You are under arrest,' she was told.

Her son-in-law had risen with her. 'What means this?' he demanded. 'What right have you to burst in on us thus . . . ?'

'We are ordered to take her to Warwick Castle.'

'For what reason?' cried Ankarette. 'I have just left Warwick.'

'On the charge of poisoning the Duchess of Clarence and her child.'

'This is madness,' said Ankarette.

'You must nevertheless come with me to answer the charge.'

Ankarette's son-in-law laid a hand on her arm. 'You should not go. They have no right. Only the King can arrest a person in this way . . . and these men do not come on the King's orders.'

'We come on the orders of the Duke of Clarence,' answered the Captain.

Ankarette said: 'It is such nonsense. I shall be able to prove my innocence without the least trouble. I will go.'

'My dear Mother,' said Ankarette's daughter, 'I think you should refuse to go until you know more of this ridiculous matter.'

The Captain of the guard had called in his men. 'It would be better not to resist,' he said.

They all saw the wisdom of this. What chance had three of them against eighty?

Ankarette said: 'I will come peacefully and I shall want a very good explanation of this violation of my home, I warn you.'

'So be it,' said the Captain of the guard.

'We are coming with you, Mother,' said Ankarette's daughter.

So the three of them were taken to Warwick Castle where Clarence was waiting for them in a fever of impatience. He had worked himself to even greater fury convincing himself that Isabel and his child had been murdered at the instigation of the Queen. This was not so much a case against Ankarette

Twynhoe as against Elizabeth Woodville. He had been thinking a great deal. This was going to be the first step on his journey to the throne. He was going to expose these Woodvilles as jealous murderers and people would see how foolish the King was to have given them the power they had. He had been drinking heavily of his favourite malmsey wine while he awaited the arrival of the party from Somerset, and he was intoxicated not only with the wine but with dreams of the great triumphs which lay ahead.

First he must deal with this woman – the Queen's woman as he thought of her, the Woodvilles' assassin.

He was down at the gates of the castle when the party arrived.

They had the woman, he gleefully noticed. She looked truculent, very sure of herself. And who was this with her? he demanded to know.

Her daughter. Her son-in-law. But he had not wished to see them. They came uninvited. The man was subservient as became him in the presence of the great Duke of Clarence.

'My mother-in-law is no longer young, my lord. We do not care for her to travel alone.'

Clarence laughed. 'She is not too old to do the bidding of her masters and mistresses, it seems. Take the woman into the castle and send the others away.'

'My lord . . .' It was the daughter.

'Take this woman,' cried Clarence, 'and remove her from my castle. It is only Ankarette Twynhoe that I am going to bring to justice. Of course if these people want to make trouble they will be arrested without delay.'

Ankarette was now beginning to feel alarmed. She knew Clarence's temperament: it was impossible to have lived for a while in his household and not discovered something of him. What did he mean? Of what was he accusing her?

She turned to her daughter. 'Go at once,' she said. 'I see his mood is ugly. I shall be all right. There is nothing of which he can accuse me.'

'Stop this whispering,' cried Clarence. 'Take the woman into the castle.'

Ankarette turned to smile reassuringly at her daughter and the younger woman, after hesitating for a moment, went off with her husband. They would have to find their way to the nearest town to see if they could find a night's shelter.

Ankarette meantime was conducted into the hall of the castle.

Clarence had seated himself at a table and he signed to the guards to bring her to him. He looked at her angrily and said: 'You will stand trial tomorrow.'

'Trial, my lord . . . for what?'

'Your pose of innocence is useless, murderess. I know what you have done and at whose instigation.'

'My lord, I beg you, tell me what it is you think I have done?'

'You know. You murdered my wife, as your mistress instructed you to.'

'Murdered! The Duchess! My lord, how could you possibly have thought such a thing!'

'I know it,' said Clarence. 'The Queen gave you instructions. You are her woman, are you not?'

'I served the Queen.'

'Most effectively I see.'

'You are very mistaken, my lord. The Queen wished nothing but good to the Duchess and she sent me to help her. I loved my lady.'

'I see through lies, madam. Do not imagine that you can outwit me.'

'My lord . . . This is monstrous . . . this is . . .'

'Take the woman away.'

Ankarette lay on a pallet in one of the small rooms of the castle. This was like a nightmare. What could it mean? The poor Duchess had been weak before her confinement. She had never been a strong woman. The doctors had shaken their heads over her condition and Ankarette knew that they feared that she might not come safely through. And now she was accused of murdering her! It was such nonsense.

And yet . . . there was a wildness in the Duke of Clarence, a determination to prove her guilty. Why? Why select her? What harm had she ever done him?

She tossed on her pallet. Sleep was impossible. A glimmer of understanding was coming to her. This was not an attack by Clarence on her . . . but on the Queen.

It must be solved. It was nonsensical. The Duke was intoxicated. He often was. In the light of morning he would have recovered and realised the ridiculousness of this accusation.

It was a relief when dawn came. The guards came to her. They were losing no time and were taking her to the court without delay.

The proceedings were quickly over. The Duke of Clarence accused Ankarette Twynhoe of murder. She had come ostensibly to serve the Duchess but in fact to bring about her death. The Duchess had sickened from the moment Ankarette entered the household and all knew that she had died. Her death had been brought about by poison which had been administered by Ankarette Twynhoe.

That was Clarence's case against her. He ordered the jury to find her guilty and they did.

'This woman deserves a fearful death,' said Clarence, 'but we will be merciful and let her die by hanging.'

Ankarette protested her innocence. She was still bewildered by the suddenness of this accusation. Two days ago she had been in her own home entertaining her daughter and son-in-law, and now here she was face to face with death.

There was no point in delay, Clarence said. Let the hanging take place at once. Everything was in readiness. They would leave the hall and the deed should be done.

They took her out. She stood for a few moments looking up at the blue April sky. Suddenly she heard the song of a chaffinch and the realisation came to her that she would never hear that again.

One of the jury who had condemned her was standing close by looking at her.

'Forgive me,' he said.

She bowed her head; she was amazed that the anguished look in his eyes could touch her at such a moment.

He went on: 'You are innocent. It is wicked. I dared not say so. I despise myself. But I was afraid of the might of the Duke of Clarence. He wanted this verdict and we had to give it.'

'I understand,' she said.

A man was at her side. 'They are waiting,' he said. And he led her to the hangman.

It was impossible for Edward not to hear of what had happened to Elizabeth's one-time serving woman Ankarette Twynhoe.

He did not discuss the matter with Elizabeth although he knew that this was meant to be a blow at her because she had actually recommended Ankarette to the Duchess of Clarence. He did, however, speak to Hastings about it for it was very much on his mind.

'What do you think of my brother's latest exploit?' he asked his friend.

'He has usurped your powers in arresting that woman and in hanging her immediately after the trial.'

'And we know the trial was no real one. The jury are saying that they believed the woman innocent and were forced to bring in a verdict of guilty because my brother demanded it.'

'There will be trouble with Clarence, Edward.'

'There has always been trouble with Clarence. But this is a flagrant abuse of rights. To kill the woman for no reason but ... but what, William? What motive had he for this foolish and wicked act?'

'To discredit the Queen and perhaps yourself.'

Edward nodded. 'How long can it go on?'

'As long as you allow it.'

'He is my brother. I have forgiven him again and again, but William, the time has come when I can endure no more. I have begun to think that he would plot against my life.'

'Only just begun to, my lord? Don't forget he sided with Warwick and fought against you when he believed there was a chance of displacing you and taking the crown for himself. He would do so again ... given the chance.'

'And this is the brother I have favoured! I have forgiven him time and time again; and all the time he seeks to stab me in the back.'

'At least you now realise it.'

'Always knew it but wouldn't face it. You know my nature. I want to think well of everyone.'

'Even when they prove themselves to be your enemy? I know you well, Edward. You doubted me once . . . I who have ever been your faithful friend. It would be well now to direct a little more watchfulness towards the Duke of Clarence, for I have a notion, my lord, that we must be careful indeed.'

Edward nodded. Hastings was right.

Clarence rarely came to Court. He wanted to give the impression that since his wife and child had been poisoned on the instigation of the Woodvilles they might well turn their attention to him.

He made a rule of never eating while at Court. He would make such elaborate excuses which said as clearly as though he had uttered the words: 'I fear that I may be poisoned.'

Edward was losing patience with him; moreover people were talking about the end of Ankarette; the fact that she was so hastily despatched and several members of the jury had declared that they deeply repented having pronounced her guilty, for guilty she was most certainly not and they had given their verdict out of fear of the Duke of Clarence.

Rivers was very watchful of Clarence. Edward could understand that. Who could know what wild plots were even at this time forming in Clarence's mind? The case of Ankarette Twynhoe was an indication of what great lengths he would go to – however absurd – to point a finger at his enemies. Clarence was a fool, thought Edward, but fools could make a great deal of trouble, and he could never be sure what Clarence was plotting and what turn such plots would take. Of one thing he was sure: Clarence had always wanted the throne and had resented Edward's being the elder, and whichever way he looked he must see Clarence as a menace.

He should have taken some action over the case of Ankarette, for it was so clear that the woman had been completely innocent and the case against her had been trumped up by Clarence. If he could behave as he had, wreaking vengeance on an innocent woman just to prove that the Queen was really the guilty party, he would be guilty of any folly. Elizabeth said little as was her wont but she had been greatly disturbed over Ankarette's death and understandably so.

Hastings learned from one of the women with whom he consorted that certain soothsayers and necromancers were drawing up horoscopes of the King and the Prince of Wales, to try to discover how long they had to live. Hastings thought it wise to report this to Edward, because when soothsayers and such like acted so it was usually at the request of someone who was interested in the death of a certain person.

Hastings had traced the horoscopes to a Dr John Stacey of Merton College, Oxford, and he suggested that the King look into the matter and discover why this man was casting these horoscopes and at whose instigation.

A law had been made forbidding that anyone set up horoscopes of any members of the royal family without first asking the King's permission, and Dr John Stacey was arrested for having done this and he was conducted to the Tower.

The King gave orders that he was to be questioned and if he refused to betray his clients he should be requested to do so with a lack of gentleness. Edward awaited the outcome with a great longing in his heart that nothing should be proved against his brother.

However the rigorous questioning brought forth an

interesting piece of information. Stacey had been asked for the horoscopes by a certain Thomas Burdett, and Thomas Burdett happened to be a member of Clarence's household.

So the King had discovered what he had suspected and hoped not to find. Clarence was eagerly awaiting his death and he knew his brother too well not to guess that if it did not come quickly he would grow so impatient that he would attempt to assist nature.

Edward was in a dilemma. He must show Clarence where this foolish careless plotting was leading him. He had over-looked the Ankarette Twynhoe affair although he knew that he should not have done so. He longed for Clarence to act in a brotherly way towards him, to be like Richard, to help him, not to threaten him as he was constantly doing.

Elizabeth was very uneasy. Edward had come back from France with Louis's pension and what pleased Elizabeth more than anything, the promise of the Dauphin for her eldest daughter. Making grand marriages for her family had always been her delight, now with the daughter of a King there was no end to her ambitions. She had announced that in future young Elizabeth should be known as Madame le Dauphine. But the death of Ankarette Twynhoe had upset her a great deal. Not only because she had known and liked the woman but because of what it meant. Clarence was her enemy and, because of his rank, a deadly one. He was a fool, she knew, but he was powerful; and men such as he was would always find those to follow him.

Stories came to her ears of rumours that were circulating, and she knew they were set about through Clarence and those who served him. One which disturbed her deeply was the story that Edward was a bastard. He was, according to this particular account, the son of an archer of great height and exceptional good looks who had charmed the Duchess of York during one of the Duke's many absences. The story was ridiculous, of course. Anyone who had ever known Proud Cis would see how ridiculous it was to accuse her of taking an archer lover; moreover if any member of the family had the Plantagenet looks it was Edward; he was very like Edward Longshanks only considerably more handsome. No, it was a ridiculous story and would be discounted by most people as the jealous fabrication of an ambitious brother who was so eager to get his hands on the crown that he was ready to think up the wildest tales. All the same, it was dangerous, and an indication of the way Clarence was moving.

It was against Elizabeth's principles to talk of state matters with her husband and her persuasions had always been of the most subtle kind, but she was really frightened now. It occurred to her that if anything happened to Edward, her little son would be in a very dangerous position indeed.

Clarence must be removed.

The King noticed her depression and asked what ailed her. She burst out that she was tortured by anxieties. She feared for their children and in particular for the Prince of Wales.

'It's Clarence,' she said. 'Oh Edward, he is your enemy. You know he is saying you are not your father's son. That means that you have no right to the throne.'

'Nobody takes any notice of Clarence's drivellings.'

'A jury did and that cost an innocent woman her life.'

Edward was silent, and Elizabeth caught his hand and lifted her fearful eyes to his face.

'I am frightened for our little Edward. He is so young.'

'No harm shall come to him. I shall see to that. Nor to any

275

of the children. The country is with me, Elizabeth, as firmly as it ever has been beside any king. Clarence has his followers it is true, but they are nothing compared with those who would support me.'

'I know . . . I know. But he is dangerous, Edward. And I think of the children . . . and of you too. I fear for us all.'

Edward was thoughtful. He said: 'Something must be done. Something *shall* be done.'

Edward began by sending Dr John Stacey and Thomas Burdett with Thomas Blake, a chaplain at Stacey's college, for trial. They were found guilty of practising magic arts for sinister purposes, and condemned to be hanged at Tyburn. As was usual in these cases the sentence was to be carried out immediately. However, the Bishop of Norwich interceded for Blake, who he said was involved simply because of his association with Stacey's college and it had not been proved that he was actually aware of what was taking place.

Blake was pardoned. The other two, protesting their innocence to the last, were hanged. It was clear from what had happened and the fact that Burdett was a member of Clarence's household that the King meant to teach his brother a lesson. Edward suspected the source of the rumours which were circulating about him. If Clarence thought that after having been forgiven once he would be so again he would be mistaken. Edward's feelings towards him were hardening every day.

Edward went to Windsor after the trial. Clarence stayed in London and he took advantage of Edward's absence to seek out a preacher, one Dr John Goddard, to force his way into a council meeting at Westminster to read the declarations of innocence made by Stacey and Burdett before their deaths.

This was a wild and reckless act, for John Goddard was the Franciscan who had declared Henry the Sixth to be the true King in 1470 when Warwick with Clarence had come to oust Edward from the throne.

After the protestations had been read before an astonished council Clarence then began gathering men about him; he declared that not only was the King a bastard but that he practised black arts and was planning to poison him, his brother Clarence, because he knew too much. He went to Cambridge-shire and declaimed in the market-square that the King had no right to the throne and if men would rally to him they would soon have the true King on the throne and the imposter replaced.

The people listened open-mouthed. Why should they rise against a king who had brought the country to a state of prosperity which it had not enjoyed for a very long time. It was exciting to listen to Clarence; a few hotheads joined him; but even they did not stay.

Meanwhile Edward in Windsor received news of what was happening. He returned to London and summoned Parliament for the purpose of bringing charges of high treason against his brother.

The King spoke with eloquence and sadness. They would all remember that he had been notoriously generous to his enemies even those who were guilty of heinous treason. His clemency had not been well rewarded. Now a much more malicious and unnatural treason was conspiring against him.

'My own brother's hand is against me. He, above all others, owes me love and loyalty. I have rewarded him most generously, with grants, goods and possessions, yet he plots to destroy me and my family. He has urged his servants round the country to tell the people that Burdett had been unjustly executed; he declared that I am a bastard; he holds in his possession an agreement made in the year 1470 which stated that if Henry the Sixth died without heirs he should be the next in the line of succession. My lords,' went on the King, 'you see the dilemma in which I am placed. Many times have I forgiven the Duke, my brother; and again and again he has flouted my friendship. I am considering now the safety of the realm and I think that my brother is a danger to us. I therefore ask you to pass upon him a sentence of high treason and to deprive him of all his estates and properties which have been granted to him by the Crown.'

None stood against the King's accusations and consequently Clarence was arrested. Clarence blusteringly offered to settle the matter by single combat which offer was ignored by the King. There was no one who came forward to defend him or to show that there was not complete agreement with the King's request.

The Duke of Buckingham, as steward of England, pronounced the death sentence and Clarence was lodged in the Tower.

Now that Clarence was under lock and key Edward found it difficult to bring the matter to conclusion. Clarence had been sentenced to death; he was undoubtedly guilty; and yet he was Edward's brother. There were so many memories of the bright little boy. He had been so handsome in his youth before dissipation and in particular heavy drinking had marred his good looks. He had had a certain charm too. He was wild and reckless; he said whatever came into his mind without considering the consequence. Edward had loved the boy. He had always been aware of the sterling qualities of Richard but it was George who had had the charm, the power to draw people to him which Edward himself had to an even greater extent. Of course he had been more fond of Richard because of Richard's admiration for himself and he had quickly realised that his younger brother was loyal and to be trusted. But that did not mean he did not love George. They had been a devoted family. How then could he give the order for his brother's execution? Yet to fail to do so might bring disaster to the country. While he himself lived in all his strength, Edward could not believe that anything could go wrong. But what if he were to die? And who knew from one day to the next when the call would come? He had a young son, a minor . . . what would happen to him if Clarence were to claim the throne declaring that Edward had been a bastard. No, Clarence had to die. He must steel himself. Forget he was his brother, remember only that he was a traitor.

But he put off giving the order.

Elizabeth was clearly pleased because Clarence had been judged guilty. It was a great weight off her mind, she said; and she could now concentrate her thoughts on the betrothal of her second son by Edward Richard Duke of York. Richard was five years old – young to be a bridegroom; but then the bride was only a year older. She was Anne Mowbray, one of the richest girls in the kingdom, and it was for this reason that she was marrying the Duke of York.

Elizabeth excelled at such times. She was delighted with the marriage; her eldest daughter, Madame le Dauphine as Elizabeth insisted she be called, was most happily destined for the throne of France. Her eldest son by Edward would be King,

279

and dear little Richard was going to collect a handful of titles and estates through his rich marriage. Clarence was disposed of. She wondered how she could prevail on Edward to give the final word. It was folly to wait. What if Clarence escaped from the Tower? It was difficult though to work on Edward, and to appear to suggest to him what he should do. She only resorted to that in cases of dire necessity and she had already helped to make Edward aware of how dangerous Clarence was.

But first the wedding, and after that Clarence must die.

The little girl was now at Westminster Palace in the apartments of the Queen's chamber, and she would be led to St Stephen's Chapel by Lord Rivers. Elizabeth was always anxious that her family should play big parts in these affairs.

The beautiful chapel was decorated with blue hangings spattered with golden fleur-de-lys. The King and the Queen were with their children about them – all beautiful and golden-haired like their mother, and it would have been surprising if they had not been good-looking with such handsome parents.

Elizabeth took her little son by the hand and led him to the altar. The little girl was taken there by Lord Rivers and the King himself gave her in marriage to his son. Richard of Gloucester was present and when they came out of the chapel it was his task to scatter gold coins among the crowd.

The children looked a little alarmed because all this fuss and ceremony was for them. They held hands as commanded to and surveyed each other with a hint of hostility. Richard did not want a bride and mildly resented having one forced upon him; Anne who was a year or so older thought him something of a baby and if she had to have a bridegroom would have preferred his elder brother who not only was a more mature age but was the Prince of Wales.

However, the last thing that was considered was the feelings of the bride and groom, and the ceremony over, the rejoicing began. There were to be days of tournaments and knights were coming into London from all over the country, and some from abroad, to share in this.

Elizabeth was very contented to see members of her family compete with distinction. Anthony was already a champion, but Dorset, her eldest son by her first marriage, was fast becoming known as a man to be reckoned with at Court.

He was profligate it was true, but then so was the King and his greatest friend Hastings; in fact the three of them went roystering together which in Elizabeth's eyes was somehow unpleasant. It seemed wrong that a man and his stepson should indulge together and she had been faintly alarmed to hear that Dorset had cast his lascivious eyes on Edward's goldsmith's wife. Now that could cause trouble. Perhaps she should speak to Dorset about it.

But worries could be shelved at this time for the glorious ceremonies were about to begin and a nice gesture would be when the little Anne Mowbray, the new Duchess of York, presented the prizes. Elizabeth had told Madame le Dauphine to sit beside her and help her for the bride was very young.

It was a great and glittering occasion but all through it the King was thinking of his brother.

Clarence was in the Bowyer Tower! He had been sentenced to death. Edward could not remember being so disturbed and undecided in the whole of his life.

Clarence free was a menace and yet how could he give the order that his brother be put to death? He knew if he did he would be haunted by what he had done for the rest of his days.

He, who had always liked life to flow pleasantly, now must face this terrible problem. He could not kill his own brother; and yet to let him live was danger. Was he afraid of danger? Not for himself, no! He had fought his way to the throne; he was strong; he had even stood against Warwick and won. No, he could deal with Clarence. But there was that haunting fear that he might not be here for ever. What if he died while his son was young? Who would look after him and what match would he be for Clarence?

Clarence must die for the Prince's sake. Elizabeth wanted that. But then Elizabeth was sly and cunning. She had her own reasons for wanting Clarence out of the way. He was the self-confessed enemy of the Woodvilles, and the Woodvilles were sacred in Elizabeth's estimation.

If Clarence would only repent. He had talked of the matter with Richard who was in the South for the Mowbray wedding. Richard said that he could not kill Clarence.

'He is our brother. You would never forgive yourself.'

'And the alternative, Richard?'

'You can keep him in check.'

'Can I? If he raised an army against me I could defeat him, yes. It is these sly rumours. He now says I am a bastard. What think you of that? What an insult to our mother! He should lose his head for that alone.'

'He should,' agreed Richard. 'But you cannot kill him, Edward. It would haunt you for life.'

'Not if I could convince myself that it is the only way.'

Richard said: 'Go to the Tower, Edward. Talk to him. Try to make him see reason.'

'Would you go?'

'He would not listen to me. He has never forgiven me for marrying Anne. No. But you mayhap could strike fear into him for I believe that is the only way to get him to act reasonably.'

'I will go to him,' said Edward. 'I will try to make him see reason. I will make him see what the consequences will be if he does not.'

'It is the best way,' said Richard.

Edward made his way to the Bowyer Tower. They were just taking in a vast butt of malmsey.

He stopped the men and asked where they were taking it.

'To the Duke of Clarence, my lord,' he was told.

'Someone is going to have a drinking party, I should think. There is enough there to last one man a year.'

'My lord, not the Duke of Clarence. He is very partial to the stuff.'

'So, for my brother,' said the King, and he went his way.

Clarence looked sullenly at Edward.

'So my lord King has taken to visiting the poor prisoner,' he said.

'George, I have come to talk to you.'

'I am overcome by the honour.'

'Listen, you know you are in danger of losing your life.'

'I know that you have condemned me to death.'

'Not I. The parliament.'

'At your command. You are afraid of me, Edward. That is why you want to get me out of the way.'

'If I had been afraid of you I could, as you put it, have got you out of the way long ago. I will not hesitate to tell you that many people to whom I should have been wise to listen would have done just that.'

283

'I know. You have your cronies. You have the Woodville clan whom *you* have created, brother. You have made them the great family of England and all because you wanted the widow.'

'I ask you not to speak of the Queen.'

'Indeed not. Holy Elizabeth! Clever Elizabeth! A witch if ever there was one.'

'I have not come here to talk nonsense, George. I have come to give you one last chance. Stop this foolishness. Be my good brother as you were once when we were young. That's all I ask. Do this and you shall be free. But I warn you, George, that if, after you are forgiven, I find you out in one treasonable act the death sentence shall be carried out without further trial.'

'Oh magnanimous brother, beloved of his people! The handsomest man in the kingdom . . . in the world some say. A little worse for wear just now, eh. Too many nights of love, too much romping with the ladies of the town. Have you had any attacks of the fever lately, Edward? That is what we call it is it not? You should be more careful of some of those town women, brother. You see after every fresh bout you are just a little less splendid.'

'Be silent,' said Edward. 'I can see that you are completely unrepentant.'

'What have I to repent of? Being the *legitimate* son of my father?'

'That is unforgivable . . . a slander on our mother.'

'You know our mother, Edward. She is a woman of strong character. Do you think she was always faithful to our wandering father? He was scarcely at home. It would have been surprising if she had not given birth to a son who was not sired on her by the Duke of York.'

'You know you lie. George, you deserve everything that has come to you.'

'And you, brother, do not? The crown should have been mine . . . mine . . . But you, bastard that you are, took it from me.'

'You are quite mad,' said Edward. 'I see I waste my time in talking to you. Stay here then . . . suffer your full deserts. I will try no more to help you.'

George closed his eyes. He was feeling somewhat muddled. He had finished the last of the malmsey before he had sent for the new butt. There had been more to finish than he had realised and he was slightly intoxicated. Heavy drinker that he was he was capable of taking a good deal of wine without its having any effect on him but he seemed to have taken more than usual and the effect was to dull his senses.

Edward was offering him freedom if he would swear to be a good brother in future. Had he been stark sober doubtless he would have accepted the offer. Not that he would have kept his side of the bargain. George was not burdened with a sense of honour. But he would have been free and able to work out his plan.

There was one thing he had discovered . . . only a few hours before his arrest, and he had been pondering on it during the whole period of his incarceration. It was the most important bit of luck which had ever come his way.

He had kept it to himself wondering when would be the best time and place to use it.

Now in his muddled state, to see Edward standing there, so big and strong and with all the advantages which he had always had, he could not contain that valuable piece of information to himself any longer. He wanted to see how Edward would receive it.

He stood up unsteadily.

'You . . .' he pointed to Edward, 'Edward . . . have no right to the throne . . . Bastard.'

'Be silent! If you say that again I will kill you with my own hands.'

'I'll say this,' cried Clarence. 'Your son whom you call the Prince of Wales has no right to the throne. And why not? 'I'll tell you. It's because Elizabeth Woodville is your mistress . . . not your wife . . . not the Queen . . . She's another such as Jane Shore and the rest of your merry band of women. The Queen's just one of them . . . Your children are bastards . . . The Prince of Wales is a little bastard. The Duke of York . . . '

Edward had strode to his brother and had him by the shoulders.

Clarence laughed. 'Shake me. Kill me if you will. You're strong enough, are you not? The great King . . . the mighty King . . . and what when the people know that your marriage to the Woodville witch was no true marriage, eh?'

'It was a true marriage. You utter treason. By God, George . . . '

'Aye,' he said. 'Do you remember the name of Eleanor Butler . . . Shrewsbury's girl . . . ? Do you remember that betrothal? She was alive when you went through a form of marriage with the Woodville . . . so that makes proud Queen Elizabeth just another of your women and the little Princes . . . oh and proud Madame le Dauphine . . . bastards . . . bastards all of them.'

Edward had turned pale. If he had been less drunk Clarence would have seen his pallor beneath the ruddy weather tan.

'Edward,' went on Clarence, 'I have seen Bishop Stillington . . . Just before I was arrested. Too late to act then. But I'm

286

clever . . . I keep the information locked in here . . .' He patted his chest. 'I know all about it. Bastards . . . because you had a previous contract with Eleanor Butler and she was alive in her convent when you went through a form of marriage with the Woodville.'

Edward pushed his brother back onto his pallet. He was glad he was drunk for he himself was more shaken than he wished him to see.

He turned away and went through the door. He did not notice the guards outside. He walked straight out of the Bowyer Tower and mounting his horse rode along by the river.

His mind went back years. He could see Eleanor now. She had seemed very beautiful . . . rather like Elizabeth and of the same proud nature. The daughter of the old Earl of Shrewsbury. They had met and he had desired her as desperately as later he had desired Elizabeth. There were many women, there always had been, but here and there would appear one who was completely irresistible and he must pay the price for her whatever it was. So with Eleanor; so with Elizabeth.

Eleanor had gone into a convent afterwards. He thought he would never hear more of her . . . and he had married Elizabeth.

There was no longer any uncertainty. His mind was made up now. George Duke of Clarence had signed his own death warrant.

He was to be executed but the King did not want a public execution. Let him be killed in his prison and let it seem as if it had come about by accident. The Duke had been drinking heavily . . . more so than he usually did since his entry into the Tower. It would not be difficult for some accident to befall him.

The next morning Clarence was found dead. He was hanging over the butt of malmsey which had been brought to the cell the day before.

The news spread. The Duke of Clarence had been drowned in a butt of malmsey.

That very day another arrest was made and Bishop Stillington was lodged in the Tower.

No sooner was Clarence dead than Edward was filled with remorse. He could not shut out of his mind memories of their early days when he had strutted through the nurseries and his brothers had looked at him as though he were the perfect specimen of manhood. He had been devoted to them; he had visited them when they were in London, always making time to sit with them and to answer their questions; he had loved his family, and it was he who had given the order for George's death.

Elizabeth knew that he suffered; so did Jane Shore. Elizabeth watched him covertly; she had her own reasons for wishing Clarence out of the way and although she said little she could not hide her relief that he could no longer plague her.

Jane was different. He softened thinking of Jane. She was his comfort nowadays. Who would have believed that he would have found such a woman among the merchants of the city? Jane was different from all others. That incomparable beauty for one thing and with it her tender nature. People marvelled that he had been faithful to Jane for so long – well not exactly faithful for there had been scores of others; what he meant was that Jane had continued over years to hold a fascination for him. The fact was he loved Jane. He loved

Elizabeth in a way. She was a Queen to be proud of in spite of what those of the first nobility insisted on calling low birth. She was as beautiful in her way as Jane was in hers. Elizabeth was the cold cold north; Jane the warm and glowing south. Elizabeth was aloof, secretive; Jane was intimate and impulsive. Jane never thought of holding back what she thought; she had no ulterior motives, no high honours to seek. That was scarcely the case with Elizabeth.

He was a man who needed many women and none could say he had not had his share. He needed Elizabeth — cool calm mother of his children; and he needed warm and loving Jane; and it was to Jane he would go at times like this.

Jane knew at once what ailed him. She was no fool and she interested herself in state affairs because they were his concern. She knew of the trial George had been to him and how he had to wrestle with himself before he could give the order to kill.

She stroked his hair; she was motherly on this occasion because it was what was needed. Instinctively she knew that was the phase of their relationship which was required. She must soothe him, repeat that he had been over-generous, as he had.

'How many would have despatched him long ago?' he demanded not for the first time.

Jane could assure him that few would have been so lenient. He had forgiven Clarence again and again. Had his mischievous brother not joined Warwick and come against him? He had forgiven him then, which was magnanimous.

Jane assured him that he had only done what was necessary for his own safety and for that of the country.

Oh yes, it was indeed soothing to be with Jane. He was lucky to have found such a woman. Others sought her, he knew. That rake of a stepson of his, Dorset, had his eyes on her. Sometimes Edward wondered about them. Dorset was very good-looking . . . and young. He was a cynical young man; inclined to be brutal, and he hoped Jane would never go to him.

Hastings had his eyes on her too. Well, Hastings was as profligate as Edward himself was. They had been companions in many nocturnal adventures and they still pursued them with the same gusto – or almost. Yes, Hastings undoubtedly had a tender spot for Jane. Oddly enough he believed that Hastings's feelings were similar to his own. They both realised that there was something special about Jane.

Poor Hastings! He had to keep off. Edward had made it clear that he was in no mind to share Jane.

So he felt better for a while after a sojourn with her.

But later of course the haunting returned.

The weeks were passing. People did not talk quite so often of the death of the Duke of Clarence and ask themselves whether he had fallen into the butt of malmsey or had been pushed into it.

In time even events like that were forgotten.

Edward ceased to think of his brother every morning when he awoke. It was only occasionally now when he would suffer that sudden catch of his breath as he realised he had condemned his own brother to death. Clarence deserved it, he kept assuring himself. He had to die. It was Clarence or disaster. The country was not safe while Clarence lived.

There was one other matter which disturbed him. He had imprisoned Robert Stillington in the Tower and tried to forget

him. But that was not possible of course. He had to do something about the man. It was now three months since he had
been imprisoned.

Edward made up his mind that he could not allow him to
remain there indefinitely. Questions would be asked. It was not
as though Stillington was an insignificant person.

It was on a bright June day when Edward rode to the Tower
and slipping in without ceremony ordered that he should be
conducted to the room in which Bishop Stillington was held.

When he arrived, the Bishop hastily rose and hope shone in
his eyes as he bowed low.

Robert Stillington was an ambitious man; he had chosen the
Church as his profession not only because it suited his nature
but because he saw means of advancing himself through it. He
had shown himself to be an able man and preferment had come
to him. He was now the Bishop of Bath and Wells. For a time
he had been Lord Chancellor being a strong Yorkist but on the
return of the Lancastrians in 1470 he had been deprived of his
office. Edward had reinstated him but he had resigned from the
office a few years later. Yet he and Edward had worked
together on occasions. Edward had felt uneasy about
the Tudors for they had made themselves prominent in the
Lancastrian cause and he particularly suspected Jasper of
subversive planning from Brittany. Jasper was getting old but
he had with him his nephew Henry Tudor and by the way in
which he kept that boy, nurtured him and trained him,
suggested that he might have plans for him.

Edward had considered Henry Tudor. Unfortunately his
mother was Margaret Beaufort descended from John of Gaunt
and of course the Tudors said they had royal blood because of
that connection with Henry the Fifth's Queen. It was a

mysterious relationship. Some were sure there had been a marriage, others said there had not. But in any case it was a very flimsy claim. Still, there was a strength about the Tudors, and Edward had decided that he would be more at peace if Jasper and his nephew Henry were in his care. He had sent Stillington to bargain with the Duke of Brittany to bring them out of that country and to England but as old Jasper discovered what was afoot and escaped with his precious nephew that had come to nothing. It was, however, no fault of Stillington.

Now the two faced each other and Edward studied the Bishop intently.

'So, my lord Bishop,' he said, 'you have spent the spring in this place.'

'It is so, my lord.'

'It was well deserved,' said Edward.

The Bishop bowed his head and said nothing.

'You spoke ill-chosen words where it was most unwise to do so.'

'That was so, my lord.'

'My brother is now dead.'

An almost imperceptible shiver crossed Stillington's face. By God, thought Edward, he believes I have come to murder him.

'I am a lenient man, Bishop,' he said quickly. 'Do you agree with that?'

'My lord, none could have been more so to the Duke.'

'So because I act kindly towards men, because I understand their foibles and sometimes forgive, there are those who think it is amusing to provoke me since it will bring no punishment.'

'I never thought that, my lord.'

'And yet . . . and yet . . .'

Edward's eyes had started to blaze. He was rarely angry but when he was he could be fierce. Stillington knew this and trembled.

He went down on his knees. 'My lord,' he said, 'I ask your forgiveness. I swear nothing shall pass my lips again.'

The King was thoughtful. He looked down at the Bishop's head and was thinking of that occasion . . . so long ago now it seemed. He could see them all in the little room – Eleanor, seeming so desirable then. Worth all the trouble. Virtuous, beautiful . . . the sort of woman a man had to make sacrifices for. And he had not been a king then. The Bishop had warned him, this very Bishop. Pompous old fool, he had thought. What did Bishops know of love?

And so there had been that ceremony . . . that fateful ceremony which if it were brought to light could wreak what damage? His marriage to Elizabeth no marriage at all! His son . . . little Edward a bastard and that would apply to all his children. Oh no, it must be stopped at all costs. At all costs. Clarence had paid with his life. The secret would never have been safe with Clarence. Once Clarence knew, once he had spoken of it, that had to be the end of him.

And now the Bishop . . . But the Bishop was not Clarence. The Bishop was a man of good sense. He had babbled. He had made a fatal error. He knew it now. He had learned the bitter lesson for three long months.

He would not commit such an error again.

'Get up,' said Edward.

The Bishop rose and Edward looked at him steadily.

'You have been foolish, Bishop,' he said. 'Do you agree with me?'

'Indeed I do, my lord.'

'You and I were good friends once.'

'My lord, I trust we still are.'

'When you seek to harm me?'

'My lord, what I did was done through carelessness . . . I whispered . . . I talked . . . I could cut my tongue out now.'

'And if you had the chance over again you would be silent . . . You would not talk of this matter?'

'My lord, I swear it.'

There was a silence which seemed to the Bishop to go on for a long time.

Then the King said: 'I believe you, Stillington. You acted foolishly and carelessly and without any thought of what this could mean. You will not do such a thing again?'

'My lord, I promise.'

'Then I am going to be kind to you, Stillington. You shall pay a fine and go free.' Edward moved very close to the Bishop and seizing him by the shoulder looked down on him from his great height.

'It would go so ill with you, my friend, if you ever did, that I know you will not. That is why I am going to send you away a free man – on payment of your fine, which indeed you owe. I trust, Bishop, that you will be of as good service to me as you were before this unfortunate incident occurred. Remember, that with a less lenient master, it could have cost you your life.'

'My lord, you are good and great and like all truly great men you are merciful.'

'That is so. Now I will take my leave of you, Bishop. You may prepare to leave. I will give the order.'

With that Edward left him.

He came out into the fresh air; he was smiling. He had

settled that matter. There would be nothing more from Stillington. He could put that tiresome matter out of his head for there was an end to it.

Now if only he could banish George from his thoughts he could be a happy man.

🏵 Chapter IX 🏵

DEATH AT WESTMINSTER

These were the good days. Edward could congratulate himself. When he had come to the throne the country had been in a state of disorder. He had brought it to prosperity. He was strong; while at the same time he was amazingly affable. His extraordinary good looks could not fail to distinguish him. Of late they had deteriorated from the golden glory of their youth. He had grown fat but his great height helped to disguise it and in some ways his immense bulk made him even more impressive than ever. He had the respect of his subjects and no matter what fines he levied he held their affection.

He looked like a king; he behaved like a king; and this was what the people wanted.

There was no doubt that the country was regaining its self-respect through him. He had a beautiful wife. True the people disliked her because of her arrogance and the fact that she was as they said 'low-born' but they admitted that she was very beautiful and she had done her duty in producing a fine family. There were now seven living children. George had been born within the last two years. A handsome King, a beautiful Queen and a clutch of children including Edward the Prince of Wales to follow the King – which they all hoped would not be for many years and before he was a mature man – and little Richard Duke of York who had so recently married Anne Mowbray and now little George just a year old. An unfortunate choice of name perhaps as it recalled that other George who had died so mysteriously in the Bowyer Tower but royal families stuck to certain names and so there was George.

As the months passed and the shadow of Clarence grew further away, Edward's contentment grew. He had one great wish that was as yet unfulfilled and that was to see his eldest daughter Dauphine of France. This would be the ideal marriage. Peace would be brought about between the two countries and with an English Princess Queen of France none could complain but would realise how much wiser it was to settle these disputes through such alliances than to carry on with destructive wars. But Louis was prevaricating and there was always some reason why he could not send for the Princess. Now he was saying that he must come to some settlement of his disagreement with Burgundy before the plans for the marriage could go forward.

Edward waited content. He was more independent than an English king had been for many years. He owed this to what he considered his skilful diplomacy in France. What other king would have been shrewd enough to take a mighty army to France and come away with a pension and no bloodshed? Those fifty thousand crowns were a symbol of his shrewdness. They had bought him his independence; they had set his exchequer in order and made it possible for him not to impose heavy taxes on his people. They had enabled him to shake off the yoke the barons liked to put on their kings and usually managed to because the king had constantly to ask them for money.

He had always been something of a merchant. Perhaps that was why he had enjoyed mingling with them. He was interested in their trading as well as their wives. He had learned a great deal about the exporting of wool both raw and made into cloth, and he had sought to make English cloth the best in the world. Moreover he had succeeded.

He was at the height of his power. He was the glorious sun which the house of York depicted so well on its banner. Right at the heart of the people's love for him was his interest in them. He loved his people. He could talk to them with ease; he could move among them dressed as a merchant so that they were not aware of his identity. He could talk to them of the difficulties of business and when they discovered that they had been in conversation with the King, they were his for ever.

He had the rare touch of being at one with his people and because he was at the same time so splendid, so magnificently attired on state occasions, and always, even now that he was so corpulent and showing the marks of a debauched existence, he was still handsome. He would keep this gift until the day he died.

Edward could look back on the last ten years since he had been restored to the throne and say: 'I have done well. I have given them what they asked.'

But he did not stint himself. He still had his mistresses, his rich food, his fine wines and his splendid clothes. He lived like a king; and the people wanted it that way.

The Queen was quite content that it should be as he had made it. That he had his mistresses she had known for a long time. He had slipped back into his old promiscuous ways soon after their marriage. Her wise mother had taught her that that was something she must accept and she had accepted it. Her delight in her marriage did not lie in the bedchamber. Elizabeth liked to see her women kneel before her when they addressed her; she liked all of them to remember every moment of the day that she was the Queen. Her joy had been to see her family rise to be the most significant in the land. All the important posts now – or almost all – were held by Woodvilles. There were jokes about it in the Court. They said the Rivers flowed very high now. Let them! What mattered it what they said? While her brothers had grown rich and powerful the envious lords and ladies who had lost to them might look on and gnash their teeth all they wished.

Like the King, more than anything now, she wished to see the marriage of their eldest daughter to the Dauphin. Madame la Dauphine would in due course become the Queen of France. Herself a Queen, her daughter a Queen of France, what more could Elizabeth want.

The death of Clarence had brought them peace.

They owed something too to Edward's brother Richard who was keeping order with constant efficiency in the North. Edward had often said how relieved he was to have someone up there whom he could trust. When he thought of Clarence which he still did far too frequently, he also thought of Richard. The contrast if nothing more would have brought Richard to his mind. He often said to himself: If I had but been blessed with another brother such as Richard how different life would have been. Richard he fancied had not come to Court so much since the death of Clarence. He seemed to make excuses for not coming. Was it because of George's death? Edward knew it was. With Richard's strict code how would he have felt about the removal of their brother? It was hard to say. Richard had the makings of a ruler and surely one such must realise that the death of one man was a small price to pay if it was going to prevent the blood of hundreds being shed. Yes, Richard must understand that. But he had not liked it. Clarence's execution had shocked him and Edward had to remember that Richard had been more closely brought up with him than he, Edward, had for they were nearer in age.

He must stop thinking of Clarence.

Richard then was in the North keeping the border safe, ever watchful of the Scots. He had some good men up there. He was not flamboyant like his brother but he did have a gift for binding men to him – some men that was . . . men like Francis Lovell the friend whom he had known since they were both boys, Lord Scrope and Richard Ratcliffe.

He was happy up there too – always happier in the harsh North, he had often teased him. He liked the brash manners of the northerners rather than the more gracious ways of the South. One was honest, Richard said; the other far from that. Edward had laughed at him. Edward could put on a personality to suit all men. That was something Richard could never do.

Yes, he had brought things to a good pass, for while he had interested himself in trade he had not neglected the arts and his had become a cultured Court. He had furnished his Court so lavishly that he acquired some of the most beautiful works of art in Europe. His gold plate alone was worth a fortune; he had sets of arras representing the histories of the past – Nebuchadnezzar, Alexander and biblical subjects; he was a constant customer at the goldsmiths' shops in London and all their best pieces were first shown to him.

He had started to build a new chapel at Windsor which he was calling the Chapel of St George and which he planned should exceed – or at least equal in splendour the buildings at Cambridge, built by his predecessor. He had gathered together some of the finest books in the world and was building up a magnificent library. He had monks in Bruges working on illuminating manuscripts for he particularly admired Fleming art. He had brought William Caxton to England. He had met Caxton during his enforced sojourn at the Court of his sister the Duchess of Burgundy and had then expressed great interest in the art of printing. At the time of Edward's exile Caxton had been working on a translation of the *Receuil des Histoires de Troyes* and as there had been such a demand for copies he had learned the art of printing that he might produce a large quantity. A few years ago Edward had persuaded him to come to England where he had printed *The Dictes and Sayings of Philosophers*. Since then he had printed other books and Edward had let him know that he was always welcome at Court.

So the King had reason to be pleased. These were the good years. The sun was high in the sky; the King in all his splendour reigned over a happy and prosperous country.

The Queen was pregnant again. Elizabeth bore children with ease and her continual confinements left her as beautiful as ever. She seemed to have some special power to remain young. It was small wonder that people said she was a witch.

That spring it seemed as though the country had had too many blessings showered on it for news came to London that there was plague at several ports. People had never forgotten the terrible Black Death which had swept over Europe even though it had happened more than a hundred years before. There had been minor outbreaks since and everyone grew fearful at the very mention of the dreaded scourge returning.

The King and Queen had left for Windsor where the King was absorbed by the work on his chapel. But there was a melancholy atmosphere over the Court. Even Edward was affected by it. He too thought of the Black Death and was afraid that everything he had built up since his second coming to power might be swept away if this bout were anything like that of the last century.

It was not to be so. For one thing, they had learned during that terrible time that the plague was brought in from abroad so the first thing to be done was close the ports. Any inconvenience this caused was trivial compared with having the epidemic raging through the country so fast that it could not be controlled.

Edward's energy in sealing off infected areas was effective and the plague began to die out.

Little Prince George had begun to grow weak. There seemed to be no reason for it. His mother watched over him fearful that he might be suffering from a new form of the plague. The doctors attended him night and day, but they could not save him.

It was a great sorrow when the little Prince died. Elizabeth was deeply distressed for however cold and calculating she might be there was no doubt that she loved her children and could not bear to lose one of them.

Edward comforted her reminding her that they had six healthy children and there would soon be one more. God had blessed them and his beautiful Elizabeth was indeed as the fruitful vine.

She gave herself up to the preparations for the child about to be born.

It was a girl and they called her Catherine.

The King declared he was delighted with her. She had a good pair of lungs, said her nurses, and that was always the best sign.

Apart from the brief visitation of the plague and the death of little George, it seemed that the good times had come to stay.

The King's sister Margaret, Dowager Duchess of Burgundy, was proposing to visit her brother. Edward was delighted, not only because his family feeling was strong and he would enjoy seeing his sister, but because he believed that she might have some proposition to lay before him. Margaret was astute; moreover the situation in France was uneasy. England had been the ally of Burgundy – it was for this reason Margaret had married the Duke – but since Edward's treaty with Louis when he had received his pension and affianced his daughter to the Dauphin there had been a subtle shift.

Margaret had been of inestimable value to Edward when he had been in exile. She had been important to him as more than a sister and when the Duke had been alive she had kept the alliance between Burgundy and England firm. But when he had died and left her childless, his daughter Mary had become the Duchess of Burgundy and moreover the most wealthy heiress in Europe. It was at this time that Clarence had sought her hand in marriage and Margaret who had the strong family feeling of all the House of York had done all she could to bring about that match. The Queen had tried to secure the prize for her brother Earl Rivers, but that of course was not to be taken seriously. One of the reasons why Clarence had so hated his brother was because Edward had appeared to put forward Rivers's suit while he had declined to help Clarence's. This seemed to Clarence the height of family disloyalty though it should have been clear to him that Edward had pretended to help Rivers merely to placate the Queen while he knew full well that the idea of any match between the heiress of Burgundy and Rivers would be ridiculed.

As for Mary of Burgundy, she had declined both English matches and in due course had married Maximilian son of the Duke of Austria and Holy Roman Emperor.

Edward was determined to entertain his sister lavishly. He never forgot what she had done for him when he was in exile so he prepared a series of lavish pageants for her amusement. He sent the fleet over to Calais to escort her to England and she was immediately aware that this fleet was under the command of a member of the Queen's family, Sir Edward Woodville. He was most splendidly attired and his retinue had been fitted out in purple and blue velvet especially for the occasion. A Woodville, of course! she thought. Edward had behaved as though he were bewitched by that woman and now it seemed her entire clan had him in thrall. Her brother George had told her of it, deploring it as undignified in a king. 'It is Woodvilles before York, sister,' he had said. And it seemed that this was so, for Edward had actually dared suggest Rivers for her stepdaughter. He could not have been serious of course, but he had done it . . . to please his Queen, no doubt.

Well, she would soon see for herself, and at least the welcome was gratifying.

She was escorted to London and lodged in Cold Harbour, a house near the Tower and so close to the river that the water washed its walls. The family were there to greet her. Richard had come down from Middleham although his wife was not with him. Poor Anne Neville, she was a sickly creature

Margaret believed yet Richard seemed content. There was one notable absence: her brother Clarence.

Edward was feeling a little uneasy. Margaret had expressed great sorrow and concern at the death of their brother, for oddly enough, he had been her favourite in the family. She had supported him whenever she could; although she had deplored his break with his brother and during that time when Clarence had gone over to Warwick against Edward she had done everything she could to bring them together. It had been unnatural, she had always said, that brothers should fight against each other and that they should be brothers of the House of York was quite unacceptable. Edward had always believed that it had been Margaret's continual pleading which had brought Clarence back to him.

And now Clarence was dead – ordered to be killed by his own brother! It would make a rift between them, Edward feared, for Margaret could never understand.

Margaret embraced her family with great affection. It gave her great pleasure, she assured them all, to be among them. She congratulated Edward on what he had done for England; he had lifted the country out of the troublous state it had been in during the reign of poor weak Henry. It was a triumph for the House of York.

She obviously wished to speak to Edward in private and at length there came a time when this was possible. She mentioned Clarence at once.

'It was such a bitter blow when I heard,' she said. 'I could not believe it.'

'George was the most misguided of men,' Edward replied. 'It was a great tragedy but inevitable, I fear.'

Margaret did understand; she could see that George wanted

the crown and partisan as she was, even she must agree that he would never have ruled the country as Edward did. But it was hard to forget the little brother who had always seemed so charming.

It was no use talking about George. He had come to a most undignified end and there was nothing that could bring him back. He had been reckless and foolish and dangerous and it was because of this last that he had had to die.

She understood. This was a new Edward who stood before her. He had hardened a little. It was natural with the life he must lead, with so many responsibilities. Not that they sat heavily on him. The same ease of manner, the same beguiling charm. He was over-fat of course, which would have been unsightly but his great frame enabled him to carry it off. But it could not be good for him. She had gathered that though he worked hard for his country by day, he pursued his pleasures by night and there were countless mistresses to satisfy his voracious sexual appetite; moreover he was a great trencherman and doubtless needed to be to a certain extent to support that massive frame. He was a connoisseur of wines and could discover the best by a sip.

He was larger than life, this brother of hers. But perhaps he was what men thought a king should be.

First she discussed exports of which her country was in need. She wanted licences to export oxen and sheep to Flanders and she wished to export wool free of customs duty. Edward enjoyed these discussions; he knew exactly what he was talking about. He was as good a merchant as any of his subjects. And because of Clarence, because he wanted to placate her and because he wished to kill that reproachful look in her eyes which was always there when Clarence was mentioned, he granted the licences.

But this was not the main purpose of her visit. What she really wanted was help against the King of France.

'You know, Edward,' she said, 'Louis has one ambition. He wants to bring Burgundy back to the crown of France.'

'It is a worthy ambition, Margaret, and an understandable one. It has always seemed unnatural that Burgundy and France should be at war with each other.'

'Burgundy will not submit to France. There is too much enmity between us.'

Edward nodded. He was thinking: How can I help her? How can I go against Louis now? I have his pension. Moreover young Elizabeth is to marry the Dauphin. On the other hand it was to his advantage to keep Burgundy and France at each other's throats. It was this controversy between them which had been of such value to the English when they had been on the point of conquering France, and doubtless would have done so if a simple country maid had not risen to lead the French to the most miraculous victory ever known.

That was long ago. The picture had changed. Edward had no desire to fight in France. He liked things as they were. He had his pension from Louis – what could be better? As long as Louis went on paying that and kept Edward out of debt, Edward was content. Or would be when his daughter was the Dauphine of France.

'You cannot trust Louis,' insisted Margaret.

'One learns to trust no one, alas,' said Edward with a wry smile. He was wondering how he could refuse his sister without actually saying what he intended to do. He was certainly not going to help Burgundy fight its wars. He was at peace with the King of France and was paid well for it. He was going to let it stay like that. It was not easy to tell Margaret of course. She had come for help, expecting it from him as she had given it to him when he needed it. He would talk round the matter, not saying definitely that he would not help . . . but all the time not intending to.

'So, Edward, what say you?'

'My dear, it is a matter which I have to discuss with my ministers.'

'I seem to feel it is you who makes the decisions.' 'On a matter like this . . .' He smiled at her ingratiatingly.

'You see, my dear, the country is at peace. It has known peace for some time. It has come to realise the value of peace . . .'

'So you will not help Burgundy.'

'My dear, it is a matter I need to brood on. You see, I have an agreement with Louis. My young Elizabeth is betrothed to the Dauphin.'

'And you think Louis will honour his pledges?'

'So far . . . he has appeared to do so.'

'I see,' said Margaret with finality. 'You are making a mistake, Edward. You will see what happens if you trust the King of France.'

He lifted his shoulders and smiled at her.

She had turned despairing away. She knew her brother. He always wanted to please, which was why he had not given her a firm refusal; but he meant it all the same. He was too fond of the easy life; he liked his pension; he liked his growing trade, his prosperous country. He could have told her all this for he had said No to her request as clearly as if he had stated that he would not help, but being Edward he could not bring himself to say so directly. Yet none could be firmer than he when he had made up his mind and she would not be deceived by his smiles and smooth words.

She saw that her journey had been in vain.

She repeated: 'You are making a grave mistake to trust Louis.'

He was to remember her words later.

On a dark November day the Queen gave birth to a daughter. She was to be christened Bridget and the ceremony which was to take place in the Chapel at Eltham was as splendid as any that had been performed for her brothers and sisters. Five hundred torches were carried by knights and many of the nobles in the land were in attendance. For instance the Earl of Lincoln carried the salt, Lord Maltravers the basin and the Earl of Northumberland walked with them bearing an unlit taper. Lady Maltravers was beside the Countess of Richmond who carried the baby and on her left breast was pinned one of the most splendid chrysoms ever seen. The Marquess of Dorset, the Queen's eldest son by her first marriage, helped the Countess of Richmond with the baby; and the child's two godmothers were the King's mother, the old Duchess of York, and his eldest daughter Elizabeth.

As the ceremony was performed the torches were lighted and the little Duke of York with his wife Anne Mowbray together with Lord Hastings were all witnesses of the ceremony. After the baby had been carried to the high altar the most costly gifts were presented and when the processions to the Queen's apartments took place the gifts were carried by the knights and esquires before the young Princess.

There the Queen, a little languid but as brilliantly beautiful as ever, waited with the King to receive those who had taken part in the ceremony.

The baby was taken to her nursery and the company circulated about the Queen and the King. The beauty and good health of the baby were discussed at length and the King sat back watching them all. He was in a somewhat pensive mood on that day. Perhaps it was the birth of another child and the recent death of little George which had made him so. He had a premonition that this might be the last child he and Elizabeth would have. They had eight now – all beautiful, all children of whom he could be proud. His eldest son would be King on his death; his eldest daughter Elizabeth would be Queen of France. He had much on which to congratulate himself.

As in every assembly of this sort there was a goodly sprinkling of Woodvilles. Elizabeth saw to that, and in any case they now held all the key positions in the country. He had been weak about that . . . letting Elizabeth rule him. But he had liked the Woodvilles for themselves; they were handsome and charming; they flattered him blatantly of course but he liked flattery. Dorset, his stepson, was a rake who had even dared make advances to Jane Shore, but he enjoyed Dorset's company. Hastings was there – dear old William, good and faithful friend since the days of their extreme youth. What adventures they had had then, vying with each other, notching up the conquests.

Then a faint feeling of unease came over him. Hastings could never disguise the fact that he deplored the rise of the Woodvilles. Elizabeth hated Hastings. Richard who was not here today disliked the Woodvilles and had never really accepted Elizabeth. He was polite and did all that was expected of him, but beneath the courtesy there was suspicion and distrust. And Elizabeth and her family had not endeared themselves to those of the most noble houses in the country. They were still referred to as upstarts.

For the first time he was thinking of death . . . his own death. He wondered what had put such a thought into his head. Was it the birth of a new child; seeing little Richard there with his wife Anne Mowbray – such babies – and thinking of Edward in Ludlow with a household almost entirely made up of Wood-villes? Would Edward be able to step into his shoes? Not yet. There had to be many years before that happened. Young Edward was not as strong as his parents would have wished. There was a deficiency somewhere which affected his bones and he would never be the size of his father. Edward knew how that great height of his had stood him in good stead.

But why think of these things on such a day.

There was Elizabeth looking not so very much older than she had on the day he had first seen her in the forest, though a great deal more regal, of course, more sleek, accustomed to the homage paid to royalty. They could have more children yet. More healthy sons perhaps to follow young Edward and Richard.

Then his eyes fell on the Countess of Richmond. A comely woman, Margaret Beaufort, perhaps a year or so younger than himself. Married now to Sir Henry Stafford but still calling herself the Countess of Richmond – a title she had acquired through her marriage to Edmund Tudor.

The Tudors had always irritated him. They had been good fighters and always the adversaries of the House of York. Naturally, they considered themselves to be the legitimate off-spring of Queen Katherine and half-brothers to Henry the Sixth. They might be. It was possible that there had been a marriage between Queen Katherine and Owen Tudor. Then of course Margaret Beaufort herself was the daughter and heiress of John Beaufort, eldest son of John of Gaunt and Catherine Swynford.

He wondered if they had been wise to let Margaret come to Court. She had been quiet and showed no desire to do anything but serve her sovereign. But there was that son of hers, born of her first marriage with Edmund Tudor. He was skulking abroad at the moment and he had his uncle Jasper with him.

Somehow it was not very comforting to think of the Tudors free. Surely they would not have the temerity to consider for a moment that they had any right to the throne! No, that would be absurd. But there was something about them ... a singleness of purpose ... an aura of some sort. It had been there in Owen and had stayed with him until the time of his execution in the market-square of Hereford. He had even made a flamboyant exit. Edward remembered how a woman had washed his face and combed the hair on his poor severed head.

An insidious thought had darted into his mind. Beware of the Tudors.

Then it was gone and a warm feeling of well-being followed.

Life was good. All was going well in England. The King of France dared do nothing but send his annual pension and very soon he would be sending for the King's eldest daughter to be the bride of the Dauphin and the future Queen of France.

These were appropriate thoughts on such an occasion. On the birth of one daughter he should be thinking of the glorious prospects which were about to be opened to another.

Two peaceful years had passed. The King had grown a little fatter, the pouches were a little more defined under his eyes and his complexion had taken on a slightly deeper hue; his energy was as unflagging as ever. He could still occupy himself with state matters and commerce with an amazing skill and at the same time spend his nights in luxurious debauchery.

There might perhaps have been a slackening off of his sexual adventures. He had three mistresses now. They were the merriest, the wittiest and the most pious, he declared laughingly; and he was clearly satisfied with them all. It was not that he had given up the stray encounter but he did not go off in disguise as he had in his youth. Hastings and Dorset were still his companions; and each of them had a reputation almost as bad as his own.

But the people continued to love him. They did not want a monk. They had had that with Henry the Sixth. Edward had the reins of the realm firmly in his hands. He was driving along at a steady pace and everyone had come to understand that his method was so much better than those of other kings. They had had great conquerors, but what had happened to the conquests when the conqueror passed away? Some other king lost them. There had been King John, Edward the Second, Henry the Sixth. What had become of their predecessors' victories when they were in power? They were lost, frittered away, and it was as though they had never been. But the wool trade could prosper; a king who had arranged that the King of France should support his country and so relieve his people of exorbitant taxes was a good king indeed.

There had been two sad incidents. The first was the death of little Anne Mowbray. Richard Duke of York had become an eight-year-old widower. The little girl herself had not been quite ten years old and she was with the Queen's household at Greenwich when she had passed away. Elizabeth had been saddened by her death for she had loved the little girl and she had always said it was so charming to see her and Richard together. The child was buried in Westminster Abbey and it was fortunate, said Elizabeth, that the possessions she had brought to her young husband were to remain his even though his wife had died before him and they had no children.

So apart from the unfortunate death of the child, the little Duke of York had come well out of his marriage. That was what Elizabeth liked to see – the most cherished possessions of the kingdom falling into her family's hands.

There had been an even greater blow for the royal family when the Princess Mary died after a short illness. Mary was nearly sixteen and her parents had been planning a brilliant marriage for her with young Christian, the King of Denmark, when she developed a sickness which made her weaker every day.

The Queen was overcome by her grief. Her daughter Margaret had died some ten years before, but she had been with them only eight months and that had been hard enough to bear, but to lose a daughter who had been with them for nearly sixteen years and had been healthy until this time seemed a bitter blow indeed.

They buried her at Windsor and the Prince of Wales attended the ceremony as chief mourner. Elizabeth was comforted a little by her daughters and in particular the eldest Elizabeth who was now known in the family as Madame le Dauphine.

But since the death of Clarence there had been peace in Court circles – at least outwardly, for although the resentment was there between the noble families and the Woodvilles it was rarely allowed to show itself to the King. That was what he wanted. He had never lost the desire to turn away from what was unpleasant as if by ignoring it it ceased to exist.

Richard was a great blessing, and Edward would never cease to be thankful to have the troubles of the North taken from his shoulders by someone as able and loyal as his brother.

Scotland had been a thorn in the side of every English king. Peace would reign for a while and then there would be war. It had gone on like that for centuries and always would unless some solution could be found whereby they could live peacefully side by side. A few years earlier he had agreed to a marriage between his daughter Cecily and the Duke of Rothesay, son of James the Third; and he had been paying annual instalments of the dowry ever since, a fact which pleased the Scots; moreover, Elizabeth had been most anxious to find a royal bride for her brother who had been widowed and a match had been arranged between James's sister, Princess Margaret and Earl Rivers.

Even so trouble continued: raids over the border, pillaging of English towns, raping of women and carrying off booty. Even Richard could not be everywhere at once.

On Richard's last visit to the Court he and Edward had talked at great length about James's young brother, the Duke of Albany.

'Like other younger brothers he is eager to take the throne,' said Edward sadly. He looked with affection at Richard. 'There is so little loyalty in the world.'

Richard met his gaze steadily. 'You will always be able to rely on me,' he said firmly.

'I know it,' said Edward, stretching out a hand and taking his brother's. 'I never forget it. It has been the greatest comfort to me and will always be to the end of my days.'

'I beg you do not speak of their ending. You are the king

England needs and Edward, this country cannot do without you, so I pray you do not talk of leaving us.'

'Lately the thought comes into my mind now and then.'

'Then dismiss it.'

Edward laughed. 'You know my nature well. Yes, I dismiss it, Richard, because it alarms me.'

'There is no need. You are in good health.'

'Oh yes, I have always enjoyed that. The occasional touch of some disorder. Natural enough, I suppose. I must live until young Edward is of an age to govern.'

Richard looked uneasy. 'Let us hope that he will be a worthy successor to his father.'

'You speak with doubt.'

'It would be hard to match you, Edward, and the Prince is . . . smothered by his maternal relations . . .'

Edward burst out laughing. 'My dear brother, you never liked my marriage did you? Too loyal to stand against me of course, but Elizabeth and you were never the best of friends, let's face it.'

'She is a very beautiful woman and she has given you and the country some handsome heirs. She has also set up her own family very well . . . very well indeed.'

'Sometimes I think it is due to Elizabeth and her family that you stay so long in the North.'

'I have duties there.'

'You remind me of Scotland and that is somewhere I would prefer not to remember. But you are happy in the North.'

'I was brought up there. Middleham was my home for so long. Anne loves it. It is her home too. There we can live away from the ceremonies of Court life like a modest noble family.'

'In a way, Richard, you are King of the North.'

'I hold the North for you.'

'And well you do it. You make a fine administrator. I want you to promise me, Richard, that if I should go before young Edward is of an age to govern, you will be close to him . . . you will be beside him, you will govern for him until he is of an age.'

'You have my word on it.'

'Then that is settled. Let us have done with this dismal subject of my demise and speak of the almost equally dismal one of Scotland. What think you of this project concerning Albany?'

Richard was thoughtful. 'Albany is weak, but we could control him. If we helped him to the Scottish throne we could demand all sorts of concessions. We could insist that he break his treaties with France. Scotland has always been there . . . ready to stab us in the back whenever we crossed with our armies to the Continent. Now there are the proposed marriages.'

'There have been several marriages between our two countries but that has brought no permanent peace. I have drawn up a list of concessions we will demand, and let us bring him over. We could have a meeting somewhere . . . I suggest Fotheringay. You and I will see him together and we will discover what we can get from him. He should be ready to give us a good deal. Then we will set him up in place of James and he will be our puppet. It is always best to have a puppet ruler who moves when we jerk the strings.'

'If it works it could be good,' said Richard. 'It will mean getting an army and marching across the border.'

'That, brother, I leave to you. But first let us get Albany.'

The brothers spent several days together discussing how

they would deal with the situation, and during the last days of March messengers arrived with news from across the seas.

Edward's sister Margaret, the Duchess of Burgundy, wrote to her brother telling him that her stepdaughter Mary, the heiress of Burgundy, had been killed while out riding. Her horse had thrown her and she had died soon after.

This was a great tragedy, for Mary was clever and she had been brought up by her father with a sense of deep responsibility. She was married it was true to Maximilian, the son of the Emperor, and they had two young children, a girl and a boy; but Burgundy had been Mary's inheritance and Margaret was fearful of what the reaction of the King of France would be.

'You know,' she wrote to Edward, 'he has always wanted to bring Burgundy back to France. He will now do everything in his power to achieve this. Maximilian would fight but he has no money to do this. Edward, you must help.'

Edward stared ahead of him. He could see the comfortable existence slipping away. Help Burgundy against the King of France! What of his pension? He was in no mood to fight for Burgundy. He had Scotland to think of.

How could he possibly help Burgundy? What? Lose fifty thousand crowns a year! What of the marriage of his daughter and the Dauphin? That was almost as important to him as the pension.

He wrote to his sister commiserating with her for the loss of the stepdaughter of whom he knew she was very fond. But he offered no help for Burgundy.

There were more messengers.

Louis was now claiming that Burgundy should revert to the crown of France. If it did that would affect trade.

Edward was in a dilemma, but he dared not quarrel with the King of France. Ever since Louis had promised to pay the pension, he had paid it and it made all the difference. On no account must it be stopped.

Edward did what he often did in such circumstances, he turned away from what was unpleasant – more than that in this case . . . alarming.

He must think of Scotland.

After the meeting with Albany at Fotheringay, Richard returned to the North and it was not long before the attack began. Richard was a clever commander and in a short time he was besieging Berwick. In the South, Edward expressed great satisfaction with the Scottish campaign and he arranged for special couriers to bring him the news because it was such a pleasure to receive it. He had great faith in his brother and Richard's successes could stop his thinking of what was happening in France.

All through the autumn Edward revelled in the news. Richard was triumphant. He had left troops at Berwick to continue with the siege and marched on Edinburgh. James was at his mercy; the Scots were ready to treat for peace and even promised that if Edward did not wish his daughter Cecily to marry the heir of Scotland they would refund the instalments of the dowry which had already been paid.

There were more messages from Burgundy. Maximilian was fighting valiantly but he needed help. Edward must come to his aid.

Edward turned away to read the despatches from Scotland.

By this time, however, Richard was realising that he could not keep up his supply lines and good general that he was decided that the only sensible action was to return. He had taught the Scots a lesson; there would be no more raids across the border for a while; but there was one thing Scotsmen were determined on. They would not accept Albany as their King.

Richard retired to Berwick where the siege was still in progress; realising that Edward would not want to go on paying a large army he dismissed many of the men, keeping only a strong enough force to take Berwick which he promptly did.

Edward was delighted with the campaign.

He sent a special courier to Richard.

'I want you to come to Court,' he said. 'I want to tell you myself how much I appreciate what you have done. I want to honour you. I want all men to honour you . . . my beloved and faithful brother.'

There should be feasting in Westminster. It was a time for rejoicing. The conquering hero should be fêted.

Richard had more than subdued the Scots, he had given Edward those Northern victories to think of when he might have been very plagued by the news from Burgundy.

They would keep Christmas at Westminster he told Elizabeth and he wanted it to be a season all would remember.

Preparations were in progress, there should be special banquets, balls and a morality play performed in the great hall. The guest of honour should be his brother Richard. He wanted everyone to understand how he relied on his brother.

Elizabeth was a little sullen when Richard's name was mentioned. She would have liked to whisper a word of criticism regarding him in the King's ear, but she was wise enough to know how that would be received.

'I am glad,' she told her brother Anthony, 'that he seems to be so enamoured of his life in the North. It keeps him away most of the time. As for Anne, she is a poor creature; she always looks to me as though she is fading away – and they say the boy is not very strong either.'

'We shall doubtless see them at Christmas,' said Anthony, who was suffering from a disappointment because his proposed marriage to the Scottish princess seemed to be going the same way as that which was once suggested with the Duchess of Burgundy.

Poor Anthony, thought Elizabeth. He needed a wife. She could easily find an heiress for him but she really wanted someone royal like Margaret of Scotland or Mary of Burgundy.

Poor Mary, she was no more now, and her husband Maximilian was not in a very happy state. Elizabeth knew that they were always sending frantic calls for help to Edward and she wondered what would have happened if Anthony had married Mary. Would he be in the same position as Maximilian was now?

She shrugged her shoulders. She could always brush off her disappointments and look for new fields of conquest.

Messengers had arrived with more news from Burgundy.

The King received the despatches but did not open them immediately. He did not want to hear disturbing news.

He talked to Elizabeth of the coming Christmas and as he talked his fingers curled about the papers. He supposed he must see what they contained. Who knew, it might be good news.

Good news from Burgundy! What good news could there possibly be? That Maximilian had miraculously found the arms and money he needed from somewhere. Where? Elizabeth was watching him. She knew that he was delaying reading the messages. She pretended not to notice and went on to discuss a new dance the girls were learning.

'Elizabeth hopes that you will dance with her,' she said.

'Ah yes . . . that I will. She is a delightful creature.'

'Oh, Madame la Dauphine has her fair share of good looks.'

He could delay no longer. He broke the seals. It was from Margaret.

The words danced before his eyes. He was not seeing correctly. It could not possibly be. Maximilian had capitulated. He could no longer hold out. He was making terms for peace with the King of France. In this treaty Louis had agreed that the Dauphin should marry Maximilian's daughter and bring the provinces of Burgundy and Artois under French domination.

Red mist swam before Edward's eyes; his heart was beating with thundering hammer-like strokes.

The Dauphin for Margaret of Burgundy. But the Dauphin was for Elizabeth. He could hear his wife's voice going on and on in his head. 'Madame la Dauphine . . . Madame la Dauphine . . . ' No. His lips formed the word. It must not be. The Dauphin was for Elizabeth, Madame la Dauphine. *His* Elizabeth. His daughter. There could be no other Madame la Dauphine. And Louis had done this . . . arrogantly, insolently, without even warning him. Louis knew how great his desire for this match had been. He knew what it meant to him. Perhaps he had heard how, ever since it had been decided on, young Elizabeth had been known as Madame la Dauphine. Perhaps he had laughed slyly. And he had done this . . . brushed the King of England aside as though he were of no importance!

And what of the pension? What need to pay the pension now that he no longer feared Burgundy? What need to pretend this unnatural friendship existed? Oh he should have acted differently. He should have foreseen this. He should have sent everything he possibly could to prevent Maximilian being beaten by Louis.

At this most important stage of his career he had made a great mistake. He had been too complacent. He should have seen disaster coming. He had but he had refused to look at it. He had pretended it wasn't there. And now . . . it had come upon him. He had lost the marriage. He had lost the pension. An instalment was overdue now. No wonder for the first time Louis had held up payments. He should have seen it coming. And now here it was presented to him in such a way that he could no longer pretend not to see it.

He had failed . . . wretchedly. He felt sick, sorry and ashamed. The old spider had got the better of him at last.

The maddening thing was that he might have prevented it.

'Edward . . . Edward . . .' It was Elizabeth's voice seeming to come to him from a long way off. 'Edward . . . Edward.'

Red mists swam before his eyes and then blackness seemed to envelop him.

The King had had a slight seizure brought on by shock, but his strong body and immense will-power enabled him to shake off the effects and he declared that the Christmas celebrations should go on as planned.

In fact they should be more lavish than ever; he wanted the Court to say that this Christmas was the most magnificent of his reign.

Elizabeth had been thoroughly shaken by the sight of the King unconscious. At first she had feared he was dead and had immediately begun to calculate what this would mean to her and her family. That it would be a major calamity she had no doubt for although her family had been strategically placed in all the positions of power throughout the country they had been like planets revolving round the sun, drawing their power from that brilliant orb, and if it were suddenly removed who could know what would happen?

There was her son, twelve years old, and a minor unable to govern. He was it was true surrounded by his maternal relations who would govern for him, but Elizabeth knew there were many in the country who would rise against that. And Edward would not be there to suppress them.

For Edward himself she had a certain regret also. Theirs had been a happy marriage, and she could congratulate herself on keeping her place – no easy matter for a woman in her position, and with a man of such roving appetites one would have thought it well nigh impossible. But she had done it and proved to the world his continued interest in her by the fact that she continued to bear his children.

When she thought of losing him she looked into a dark future where anything might be likely to happen.

Thus when she saw him there, still and silent, his ruddy face turning a deep purple, his limbs after twitching a moment or two remaining still, she was filled with a desperate fear.

She had shouted to the attendants who came rushing in. They managed to get him to his bed, not an easy matter for he was very heavy; they sent for the doctors.

By the time they came he had regained consciousness and as the days passed it became clear that he would recover;

moreover, although the attack had alarmed him and those about him and the doctors said he must keep to his bed for a week at least, he seemed to have come through unscathed.

So preparations for Christmas went on. The King took a great interest in them. Richard with his family would be present and Edward would be surrounded by his own children – all five girls and the two boys and there should be special revelries.

He wanted to see the new velvets of which he had heard and he himself would select those from which new garments would be made. There was a cloth of gold shot with blue which was most effective. He would have a long gown made of that, and a new purple velvet mantle edged with ermine.

He was deceiving himself. He was feigning an interest in the garments. His thoughts were elsewhere. He knew he had come close to death and now he was looking the future starkly in the face.

His heir was twelve years old, and he had always believed the boy would have grown to a mature age before he ascended the throne. Little Edward was not yet fitted to be a king. He was not prepared at all. He had been kept at Ludlow, living by a set of rules, governed solely by his Woodville relations. He should never have allowed the Queen to have such influence over the boy. Why had he allowed it? Because Elizabeth had always been so understanding about the life he led, had never complained about his numerous mistresses, had never reproached him and had always received him graciously when he came to her; it was a rare quality in a woman. He had repaid her by letting her honour her family, by setting them in high places. So they surrounded the future king. She had made sure that when her son came to the throne his greatest friends would be his maternal relations.

He had shrugged it aside, telling himself that when the boy grew older he would take him in hand. Perhaps when he was fourteen he would supervise his education, take him about with him, guide him, mould him, teach him all of the wily subterfuges which had to be practised by kings. There is time, he had told himself.

And then suddenly it had been brought home to him that there might not be time.

He was going to dance this Christmas as much as he ever had; he was going to drink and be merry. But this was for a reason – to show the people that he was not as ill as rumour might have had it. It was true he had had some sort of attack but it was nothing. He was as strong as he ever was. They must go on believing that. *He* must go on believing it.

He was glad that Richard was coming for Christmas. The sight of his brother did him good. He would confide in him as he could to no other. Poor Anne looked delicate and Edward wondered whether the harsh North was the place for her. He had always marvelled that Warwick – that bold strong man – had only been able to produce two sickly daughters. Richard proudly presented his son – another Edward. A pleasant boy, with clever looks like his father's and the same rather delicate build. So different from the King.

But how glad he was to see him!

Edward was filled with emotion as his eldest son stood before him. He looked so young – rather small for his age which was surprising. People had marvelled at Edward's height when he was his son's age. Young Edward would never match his father in stature. The doctors murmured something about his bones which did not grow as quickly as they should; they thought it was due to something . . . they knew not what.

Richard was almost as tall as his brother. Richard looked more healthy. The brothers were pleased to be together. Perhaps it would have been better for them to have been brought up together instead of putting Edward in that establishment at Ludlow.

His thoughts were in turmoil since the realisation that he could have died suddenly leaving the affairs of the country in anything but a settled state.

He *must* go on living for a few years yet. Edward must be of age before he became King.

The festivities progressed and none would have thought the King was in the least disturbed. It appeared that he had shrugged off the perfidy of the King of France, the loss of a pension for himself and the crown of France for his daughter. He looked magnificent. His colour was a little deeper but that looked like good health. His garments were a wonder to all who beheld them. The sleeves of his handsome robe were very full and flowing, lined with the most expensive furs.

People said that rarely had he looked more handsome. There he was surrounded by five beautiful daughters, his two good-looking sons and his Queen who was reckoned to be one of the most beautiful women in the country.

He danced with his eldest daughter and both he and she seemed to have forgotten that she had just lost one of the most important titles in Europe.

They were all completely entranced by the special Morality which was performed for their enjoyment and the King applauded loudly and rewarded the players more handsomely than they could have hoped for in their wildest expectations.

It was a very happy Christmas. It was only to Richard that Edward spoke of his misgivings.

He made it clear that he wished to be alone with his brother and took Richard to his apartments.

'Richard,' he said when he had assured himself that none could hear them, 'I am deeply disturbed.'

Richard was surprised, having noticed that Edward had been behaving with exceptional gaiety.

'I fear, Richard, that I have failed.'

'Failed?' Richard was amazed. 'You . . . why, you are the most successful King we have had since the third Edward.'

'I have been but I look to what this country is brought to now. If I live all will be well. But Richard, am I going to live?'

'What has happened to you? You are strong . . .'

'I came near to death a short while ago.'

'But you are fully recovered now.'

'I am unusually healthy but I have impaired my health some would say. Too much riotous living. Too much excitement with the ladies. Too much rich food and wine . . . You see how I have grown, brother.'

'You could lead a more abstemious life.'

'I was never made to be a monk.'

'There is no need to be a monk. You could eat less, drink less and be faithful to your wife.'

'Ah, there speaks my good brother Richard. You find it difficult to understand men such as I am.'

'You have lost Louis's pension and he is marrying his son elsewhere. Well, you have had worse setbacks. Do you remember when you had to flee the country? As I recall you were not so very worried then.'

'I was young then . . . not so weighed down with responsibilities.'

'You will live long yet. The fact that you threw off this attack shows how strong you are.'

'That may be so, but I want to be prepared. I am going to use what time is left to me to set my affairs in order. I reproach myself.'

'*You* reproach yourself! You who have brought the country out of anarchy! Order prevails now as hardly ever before. You have brought trade to the kingdom. You scared the King of France into paying you a pension. Forget that he will no longer do so. He did it for a time which was more than we could expect. You have the goodwill of the people. They love and admire you. You have a family of beautiful children and you seem to have remained pleased with the Queen.'

'Ah, I detect the inflection in your voice when you speak of the Queen. You never liked her, Richard.'

Richard was silent.

'Come,' said Edward, 'this is a time for frankness.'

'She was too low-born for you,' said Richard.

'Oh come. Who was Warwick before he married and got his lands and title? Yet you considered Anne a worthy bride.'

'I have not been in the position to grant such possessions to her family that they might take over all the important offices in the land.'

'Ah, the Woodvilles! They are your grievance, Richard, as they are to so many others.'

'They are overbearing and arrogant for the most part as should be expected of those who come up suddenly from little.'

'I like them, Richard. They are good company. Handsome people. I like them about me.'

'And you like to please the Queen.'

'We should all try to please our wives, brother.'

'But now I sense this is the reason for your lack of ease.'

Edward was silent.

'They have brought up the Prince,' went on Richard. 'They have imbued him with the idea that the Woodvilles are the most important people in the country.'

'If I should die,' said Edward, 'there might be trouble between the Queen's family and certain nobles.'

It was Richard's turn to be silent. Edward caught his arm and looked at him earnestly.

'Brother, promise me this. You will be there. You will look after my sons. You will see them safe on the throne.'

'You are going to live for a long time. Young Edward is twelve. Why, in only six years he will be of an age to govern.'

'He will need help and what I want to be assured of is that you will be there to give it.'

'I will be there,' said Richard. 'But put these thoughts from your head. It is unlucky to speak of death. I am certain, brother, that you will not meet it for many years to come.'

'You are a comfort to me, Richard. Were you not always?'

'I have served you faithfully all the days of my life. Remember that.'

'I do remember it and it sustains me.'

'Now, have done with this talk of death. I want to speak to you about Scotland.'

After Christmas the Court went to Windsor but was back in Westminster by the end of February.

Edward had done nothing to change the household of the Prince of Wales. He knew that it would be difficult to explain to Elizabeth. It was still presided over by Anthony Woodville who was constantly with his young nephew. Anthony, disappointed of his marriage to the sister of the Scottish King, had now taken an heiress whom Elizabeth had found for him. This was Mary Fitz-Lewis whose mother was daughter of Edmund Beaufort, second Duke of Somerset. So there was not only money but good family there. However, in spite of his marriage he continued to live at Ludlow with the Prince. Elizabeth would not hear of those arrangements being changed. If Edward had had a shock, so had she and she was more determined than ever that if there were a new king he would be hedged in by Woodvilles.

There would have to be change, Edward supposed. He would see to it in due course.

At the Parliament which was called in January money and supplies were voted for an army which should go into Scotland and the King bestowed on Richard the Wardenship of the West Marches so that he was now indeed the Lord of the North.

February and March were very cold months and towards the end of March Edward went on a fishing trip with some of his friends. The wind along the river bank was piercing and the fishermen in due course decided to abandon the day's sport and return to a warm fire.

The next day the King was ill. He had pains in his side which made it impossible for him to lie comfortably.

The physicians came to him and declared themselves alarmed by his condition. He had lived so indulgently that he had used up his energies they said and lacked the strength to withstand this violent cold he had caught. It attacked his lungs.

April had come with warmer weather but the King remained in his bed for his condition did not improve. He knew he was dying and that the seizure just before Christmas had been a warning.

Time was slipping away and there was so much he should have done. He was leaving a son, a child little more, vulnerable in a situation which he, in his carelessness, had allowed to arise.

There would be warring factions. There were so many who hated the Woodvilles. While he was there he had kept the peace but what would happen when he had gone?

What must he do? What could he do?

Richard was far away in the North. He wanted Richard here but he did not send for him. He was following his old practice of turning away from what was unpleasant. He was not dying, he told himself. He was going to survive this as he had that other attack.

He would not admit that he was facing death.

He was only just forty years of age. That was not old and he had always been in such good health. Until the seizure no one had thought of him and death in the same moment. He was going to get well.

But in his heart he knew that Death was close and that he must hurry to set things right. Conflict, which seemed inevitable, must be avoided. He sent for those nobles whom he thought might quarrel together. Chief among them was Dorset, his stepson, and Hastings, his greatest friend.

Dorset was on one side of his bed, Hastings on the other and with them were those men who supported them. They looked coldly at each other across the bed and with a gnawing anxiety Edward was aware of their hostility towards each other.

'My friends,' said the King, 'I beg of you forget your differences and work together for the good of my son. He and his brother are but children. They need your help. I beg you give it to them. For the love you have borne me and for the love I have borne you, and for the love that the Lord God bears to us all, I beg you love each other.'

He could not sit up and collapsed on his pillows and the sight of this great strong man thus, moved everyone present to tears.

He begged Hastings and Dorset to clasp hands and to promise as they did so that they would remember their King's dying wishes.

Hastings was overcome with emotion. There were so many memories he had shared with the King, and to see Edward lying there while life slowly ebbed from him filled him with a sad emotion – not only for the past and the good times they had shared, but for the future. He well understood Edward's fears for his son.

The boy would have to be protected . . . against the Woodvilles.

'Remember,' went on the King breathing painfully and finding the utmost difficulty in speaking, 'remember they are so young, these little boys. Great variance there has been between you and often for small causes.'

He closed his eyes. He was young himself to die. Not yet forty-one years of age and having reigned for twenty-two of them.

But this was the end. There was nothing more he could do.

So on the ninth of April of the year 1483 great Edward died. The news spread through the city of London and on through the country to the blank bewilderment and dismay of the people. They had looked up to him – the great golden King, the rose-en-soleil, the sun in splendour. And now that sun had set.

What next? they asked themselves.

For twelve hours he lay naked from the waist that the members of the Council might see that he was truly dead. Then he was taken to St Stephen's Chapel where Mass was celebrated every morning for a week, and after that to Windsor and there buried in St George's Chapel in the tomb which he had had prepared for himself.

The country was stunned. He had been with them so long. They looked to him. They relied on him. He had been among them for so long – their brilliant, splendid, magnificent King.

And what would happen now?

They waited in consternation to discover.

SUNSET

🏵 Chapter X 🏵

THE KING AND PROTECTOR

When he awoke that morning there was nothing to suggest to the thirteen-year-old Edward that this was going to be any different from another day. Time glided along smoothly at Ludlow. He had come to regard the great grey castle as home and when he rode out in the company of grooms and very often with his uncle, Lord Rivers, he was always delighted to come back to the square towers and the battlemented walls guarded by the deep wide fosse. He loved the Norman keep and large square tower with ivy clinging to it. In the great hall Moralities were performed at Christmas and when his mother came special balls were arranged. He loved to ride out into the town which itself stood on a plateau overlooking hills and dales of considerable beauty. It would be hard, his uncle Rivers had said, to find a more beautiful spot in the whole of England.

The most important person in his life was Lord Rivers, Uncle Anthony, who was so eager to be with him and explain everything to him and was such an agreeable companion. They hunted together, played chess together, and he had been very much afraid when his uncle had recently married – for he had been a widower – that he would lose him.

'No,' said Uncle Anthony, 'nothing would prevent my being with you, my little Prince. You are my first concern.'

So although he had gone away briefly he was soon back and it was as it had been before. His wife would visit them from time to time perhaps but she would want to please her husband and that would mean pleasing the Prince.

If Anthony was his favourite companion and perhaps the most important person in his life, his mother held a special place.

She was so beautiful. He had never seen anyone like her. And she was always affectionate towards him. When she arrived she could look so cold, like an ice Queen and he liked to watch her when she was greeted by the servants and attendants with the utmost respect because after all she was the Queen; and then she would see him and her face would change; it was like the snows melting in early spring. The colour would come into her face and she would hold out her arms and he would run into them and then he thought he loved her more than he could ever love anyone even Uncle Anthony, although of course he admitted to himself he *needed* his uncle more. His mother was like a beautiful goddess – something not quite of this earth.

Then there was his half-brother, Richard Grey, another of his close friends, who was Comptroller of his Household. His uncle Lionel was his chaplain although he did not see a great deal of him for he had so many other duties to perform being the Chancellor of Oxford University as well as Bishop of Salisbury and Dean of Exeter.

How could he be so many things all at once? Edward had

asked Anthony, who replied that it was possible; and at the same time to be able to keep an eye on his young nephew.

'After all,' said Edward, 'he *is* a Woodville.'

Anthony agreed. He had always taught the boy that there was something very special about the Woodvilles. They were capable of doing what ordinary mortals could not. The King, Anthony explained, had recognised that. It was why he had married one of them and so given Edward his incomparable mother; it was why he had put so many of them in the Prince's household so that his son should have the benefit of their virtues.

Yes, there were many of his mother's family. Her brothers Edward and Richard were his councillors and even Lord Lyle, his master of horse, was her brother-in-law by her first marriage. His chamberlain, however, was not a Woodville. He was old Sir Thomas Vaughan who had been with him since his babyhood. He seemed to be the only one to hold a post in the household who was not a Woodville.

Well, it worked very happily for Edward. He loved to hear of the perfections of his maternal ancestors. He scarcely knew those of his father, although Anthony said that now that he was coming into his teens he supposed his father would wish him to go to Court now and then.

'I don't want to,' said Edward. 'I like it here with us all. We are all so happy together.'

'It gives me great pleasure to hear you say that,' replied his uncle. 'It is what I have always striven for.'

There were his sisters the Princesses and his brother Richard. He liked Richard and his sisters, but he did not see them very often. He had to be kept apart in his own household. He knew why. Anthony had explained. It was because he was the most important member of the family; the heir to the throne.

He had scarcely known his uncles on his father's side. Anthony had told him something of them, of his wicked uncle Clarence for instance who had taken arms against the King and had come to a violent death – drowned, they told him, in a butt of malmsey. Edward could hardly imagine what that was like. He was overcome having already drunk too much of the stuff, his uncle told him, and then he toppled in. That was the end of him. It was a Good Thing.

There were certain events which were Good Things and they were the things that the Woodvilles wanted or caused to happen. Then there were Bad Things which were brought about by the enemies of the Woodvilles.

There was his uncle Richard. He did not know what to think of him. He was cold and stern and he had a son named Edward too, and a wife whom they always called Poor Anne. There was nothing very attractive about Stern Richard and Poor Anne. Moreover although his uncle Anthony did not say anything very revealing about him Edward sensed that he did not like him much. Therefore Edward was not going to either.

So he awoke that day with no premonition of the great change which was about to burst on him. He had heard of his father's seizure for he had noticed that Anthony was a little perturbed and when he asked him why Anthony told him that his father had been taken ill.

That had been hard to imagine. That great big splendid man suffering from the ailments which beset ordinary mortals had seemed impossible.

It was not impossible, said Anthony, his brow furrowed. Men like his father who lived . . . Anthony had sought a word and found 'luxuriously', often had what was called seizures. They lived so fully that they used up as much energy in half a lifetime as some did in the whole of one. Did Edward understand?

Edward did.

'Has he used up all his energy then?' he asked.

'Oh no . . . no. It's just a warning of what could happen.'

The King recovered. At Christmas Edward had seen him looking even larger and grander than ever. He had talked to Edward and told him to obey the rules of his household and grow up quickly. He had pointed out that heirs to the throne had to learn more quickly than others.

He did his best, Edward explained, and he would try.

'Well, my son,' said the King ruffling his hair, 'you can do no more than that, now can you?'

The King had danced with Edward's sister Elizabeth and everyone had applauded and Edward had forgotten all about the King's seizure. Uncle Anthony seemed to have forgotten also for he did not refer to it again.

It was time to rise and his chaplain and chamberlain came in. He must dress at once and go with them to his chapel there to hear Mass. His father had laid down strict rules for his household and one of these was that he must not hear Mass in his chamber unless there was a good reason for his doing so – which, thought Edward, means if I were dying.

After Mass there was breakfast and lessons in between that and dinner. On his father's orders this was a fairly ceremonial occasion; those who carried his dishes to the table were specially chosen and they must be in his livery. No one was allowed to sit at table with him unless his uncle had given his approval that they were worthy to do so. After dinner there were more lessons followed by exercises during which he must learn to carry arms and fence and joust as became his rank. There followed supper and bed. And so, enlivened by the bright conversation of his Woodville relations, surrounded by their affection and very often their flattery, the days had slipped by very pleasantly and with the passing of each one he was more and more convinced by the charm, the grace and the utter wisdom of the Woodvilles.

A week before his half-brother, Richard Grey, had gone to London. There was a certain amount of whispering going on in the household, Edward noticed. He asked Anthony about it and his uncle replied that it was nothing. People were always whispering together and making dramas out of nothing or very little.

But Uncle Anthony was a little different, perhaps even a shade more affectionate.

He forgot it. There was so much to do during the days. He wondered if his brother Richard was as good a horseman as he was. He would ask Lord Lyle if he knew.

His uncle Anthony came hurrying to him when he returned from the stables with Lord Lyle and he did a strange thing. He knelt down and kissed Edward's hand.

Bewildered as he was Edward had a faint inkling of what had happened then because loving as his uncle had always been he had never shown that much respect before.

'Uncle . . .' he began.

But Uncle Anthony cried: 'Long live the King!'

'My father . . .' stammered Edward.

His uncle had risen. He had put his arms about him and held him in a firm embrace.

'Edward, my dear dear nephew, my King, your father is dead.'

'My father . . . dead!'

'Yes, dear nephew, my lord. He has been ailing this last week and now he has gone. It is a terrible blow for us all . . . for the country. But thank God we have a new King and I know he will rule wisely and well.'

'You mean . . . that I will?'

'You are our true and lawful King Edward the Fifth. We knew the day would come but we had not thought it would be so soon.'

Edward was overwhelmed. King! A boy of thirteen who had been living quietly in Ludlow Castle until this day! Everything would be different now. He had come to it not gradually but at one big blow. And his father was dead . . . that big splendid man! It was hard to believe. And his mother, what of his mother?

Anthony put an arm about his shoulders. 'You have nothing to fear,' he said. 'I shall be there beside you.'

'You will tell me what to do?'

'Indeed I will, my little King.'

'Then all will be well.'

His uncle took his hand and kissed it.

'Now we have to prepare to leave at once. We are going to Westminster where you will be crowned.'

The Queen was deeply disturbed for she realised the danger of the situation and the need for prompt action.

It would have been impossible not to be aware of the immense unpopularity of her family. The King had always been there to protect them and in a manner curb their wildest ambitions. Now that he was no longer there she knew their

343

enemies would rise up against them. Thank God, through her foresight she had put her family into high posts. They were rich and influential as no other family was. They could therefore stand firm, and after the coronation of young Edward rule . . . if they were clever, rule absolutely, because her son would be so much easier to guide than her husband had been. Indulgent he had certainly been but he had always kept her ambitions firmly in check, and she had always felt that she had been on a leading-rein and although in his indulgence he had made it fairly long, she would be quickly jerked back if she went too far. Now, if she were careful, there would be nothing to hold her.

She was closest in touch with her son, the Marquess of Dorset. He was now in his early thirties; he had been a great favourite of the King – partly because he had been his companion in vice. His chief companion perhaps. No, Hastings had held that place, but in any case Thomas had been a close runner-up.

As a wife she thought that deplorable, as an ambitious woman with a son through whom she now planned to govern, it was advantageous.

She sent for Dorset. He came with all speed realising the urgency of the situation.

'What we must do,' she said, 'is get the Council with us. I expect trouble from Hastings. A pity we could not exclude him but I fear he was too firmly entrenched. We have the family well represented. We should watch Stanley. I think he will go to whichever side offers the best advantage to himself. We must make sure *we* do.'

'What of Gloucester?'

'He is in the North. On the Scottish border. Far far away.

We must wait until the King is crowned before we allow him to be aware of what has happened.'

'It would be better so as Edward named him as the King's Protector.'

'The King already has his protectors and once a king is anointed and crowned, he is accepted as king.'

'I fear Gloucester.'

'I will deal with Gloucester,' said the Queen. 'Our first act must be to get the King crowned. Let us call a Council meeting in the new King's name. We will show ourselves amenable and carry on as though the King was alive and then we will bring up the important matter of the King's coronation as though it were a matter of course.'

Dorset was certain that his mother would succeed. After all, had she not succeeded in everything she did; and surely only the cleverest of women could have kept a man like Edward as long as she did.

The Council was called and all went as planned until the matter of the King's coronation was brought up.

Dorset said: 'May the fourth would be a suitable day, I believe.' Then the protests started. It was far too early. The Duke of Gloucester would not be at Westminster in time. They should bear in mind that he was defending the Scottish border.

'Then, my lords,' said the Marquess, 'we must needs do without the Duke of Gloucester.'

Hastings was on his feet. 'It would seem that the terms of the King's will have been forgotten.'

'The King wished his son to be crowned at once,' said Elizabeth.

'What escort will bring him to London?'

'That,' replied the Queen, 'is for the King to decide.'

'You mean for Lord Rivers?' asked Hastings. He went on somewhat heatedly: 'The King should come to London with a moderate escort. He should not have more than two thousand men.'

Hastings clearly did not want the young King to march from Ludlow with an army. Very well, thought Elizabeth, let him have his way. Anything to get the King in London and crowned. For once he was crowned he would not need a Protector and therefore the King's instructions that his brother Gloucester should take that role need never be considered.

As soon as the Council meeting broke up, Dorset sent his message to Rivers. The King must come to London with all speed and should arrive not later than the first of May.

Hastings had already sent a messenger to Richard in the North telling him what was happening in London and urging him to come with as many men as he could muster for it might be that he would need them.

With a clatter of hoofs the messenger rode to Middleham Castle. He leaped from his steaming horse and demanded of the astonished grooms to be taken at once to their master the Duke.

It was a stroke of good fortune that Richard should at that time be at home. He had returned only a week or so before from the Scottish border and his thoughts were fully occupied by the conflict with the Scots.

It was two months since he had seen his brother and then they had gone fully into the Scottish question. He should soon be on his way north again and was for this short period enjoying a little respite with his family.

His son Edward was not strong. He knew that Anne worried continually about their son. He had inherited his mother's constitution and sometimes Richard wondered whether he would be better in a more benign climate. There was one other boy in the castle whom Richard watched with interest. The boy was several years older than Edward, and did not know it but he was Richard's own son. His name was Richard and he had been educated by the schoolmaster whom his father had brought into the castle for the purpose. Richard would have liked to acknowledge him and promised himself he would one day. He was a little embarrassed about the situation; he was so unlike his brother and had rarely indulged in sexual relations with women. Strange that this one affair of this nature had produced two children. Catherine was with her mother in London, but Richard he had brought up here in his retinue. One day, he thought, he will be told.

He wished that he and Anne could have had another. The delicate looks of his legitimate son were a source of anxiety as were Anne's own. She had been delighted to see him and heartily wished that the wretched wars could end so that they could all be together in the cosy intimacy of Middleham.

He had decided that he could indulge in a few more weeks of family life when the courier came.

He received the man at once and was astounded by the news.

'My brother . . . dead!'

'My lord I fear so. He went fishing and caught a cold. He did not recover.'

'A cold . . . Edward to die of a cold!'

'He had been ill before, my lord.'

Oh yes, he had been ill. Richard remembered their

conversation. He could almost believe that Edward had foreseen his death. He had harped on it and had extracted a promise from his brother to look after young Edward, to be his Protector until such a time as the boy should be of fit age to govern.

'When did it happen?' he asked.

'On the ninth of April, my lord.'

'But this is a week ago.'

Thoughts passed quickly through his mind. What could happen in a week? A week already passed and by the time he reached Ludlow . . .

'Why did you not come before? Did not the Queen send anyone?'

'The Queen sent no one, my lord. Nor did Lord Rivers. I come from Lord Hastings who sent me as soon as he knew that the King was dead.'

Richard was silent. He had turned very pale. He was seeing it all clearly: Elizabeth Woodville and her brother had withheld the information. They had not wanted him to know until the little King was crowned. The Woodvilles were waiting to take command. They would be planning now to rule the country.

He thanked the rider and told him he must go to the kitchens for refreshment; then he went to find Anne.

'My brother is dead,' he said.

She put her hands to her heart and turned pale.

'And,' he went on, 'the Queen has not told me. Nor has Rivers. I do not like this.'

'Why should they withhold the information from you?'

'They want to get the King into their care. I shall have to leave for Ludlow at once.'

'Oh Richard . . . must you?'

'Indeed I must. Edward left his son in my care. We talked when we last met. It was almost as though he knew. I gave him my promise . . . moreover I can see that the realm will have to be protected from the Woodvilles. Now, I must lose no time. I have to prepare to leave.'

Before he left another messenger arrived from Hastings. There had been a meeting of the Council called by the Queen and it had been declared that the King should be crowned on May the fourth. Hastings had had great difficulty in getting them to agree that the King's escort should not exceed two thousand. When Richard came he must come well prepared to face a company of that number.

Richard knew what Hastings meant. The Woodvilles were determined to rule. They were going to get the King crowned and then declare that there would be no need for Richard to fulfil his brother's wishes that he should be the little King's guardian. Richard could see that his presence was urgently needed and he must go to challenge them; he would take Hastings's advice and go well armed.

Richard was within reach of Nottingham. He had decided that since the King was having an escort of two thousand, he would do the same. He wanted no suggestion that he came for conflict. He merely wanted the people to know that his brother had appointed him his nephew's guardian and if Edward was to be escorted into London he was the one to do it.

In Nottingham a courier arrived from Lord Rivers. He sent courteous greetings to the Duke of Gloucester and condolences for his great loss. Lord Rivers knew of the affection the King had always had for his brother and was therefore deeply aware what Edward's death had meant to Richard. He had left Ludlow with the King and planned to reach Nottingham on the twenty-ninth of April. It might well be that the Duke would be there at the same time. If Rivers arrived first he would await the coming of the Duke of Gloucester if that was his wish.

Richard sent back a message that he would be delighted to meet Rivers and the King at Northampton.

There was a further message from Hastings. He implored Gloucester to make haste to intercept the King. The Woodvilles were in command. They were eyeing him, Hastings, suspiciously because he had reminded them that the late King had appointed Richard as Protector. He believed they would seek to remove him. He begged Richard to come with all speed.

Richard pondered the state of affairs. He saw that he alone could avert civil war. There would be many to side with Hastings. Buckingham was one. He had always hated Elizabeth Woodville ever since he was a child and had been forced to marry her sister. The Queen had managed to make the Council agree to the date of the coronation, so she had many with her for they realised that the Woodvilles had already assumed so much power that it would be difficult to dislodge them. But Richard promised himself that he was going to curb the power of the Woodvilles. He had often warned Edward against granting them so much power. Well, now that Edward was not here, something might be done about it.

He waited with eagerness his meeting with Rivers.

It was a sunny afternoon of the twenty-ninth of April that Richard with his retinue reached Northampton. There was no sign of Rivers and the King's cavalcade.

Enquiries brought the information that they had already passed through the town and had gone in the direction of Stony Stratford.

This was disturbing and looked as though Rivers had no intention of meeting Richard, who decided that he must stay in the town for a night as his men and horses needed a rest. There was good news. Another courier had arrived and this one came from the Duke of Buckingham who was in the vicinity and on his way to join up with Richard.

Richard ordered that his men should be lodged where they could find places to take them while he himself went to an inn with a few intimates and there settled to spend the night.

They had scarcely arrived at the inn when a horseman came riding into the yard.

It could be Buckingham,' said Richard; but to his amazement it was not. It was Anthony Lord Rivers.

Anthony came to Richard and bowed low. 'My lord Protector,' he said, 'I come with all speed to welcome you and to explain why I was unable to keep my appointment here with you. It seemed there would not be enough accommodation here for your followers and those of the King so we agreed that he should go on to Stony Stratford and that I would return and explain the position to you here.'

A neat explanation, thought Richard, but he did not believe it was true. The Woodvilles wanted to get the King to Westminster and crowned so that there would be no need for a Protector.

Richard made a pretence of accepting the explanation and invited Rivers to dine with him. Anthony declared that he would be honoured to do so and while they were talking the Duke of Buckingham arrived.

Richard received him with a show of pleasure. Rivers feigned to do the same but he was disturbed for Buckingham was an enemy of the Woodvilles even though he had married into the family – but perhaps it was because of that that he hated them.

Rivers, going back to the inn in which he was to spend the night, was uneasy.

Richard never betrayed his feelings so it was not easy to know whether he had been duped by the explanation that there had not been room in town, or not. The young King, however, was at Stony Stratford and as that was fourteen miles closer to London this seemed a wise move on the part of Rivers.

It was a friendly supper party. The three of them – Gloucester, Buckingham and Rivers appeared to be in agreement about all they discussed. Gloucester was perhaps a little silent, but then that was his way. Rivers would have been astonished if he had been otherwise. Henry Stafford, Duke of Buckingham talked enough for two men. Volatile and ebullient Buckingham made it a merry party so that Rivers's suspicions were completely lulled. Moreover Buckingham had never greatly interested himself in state affairs. Rivers regarded him as a dilettante, a lover of luxury, somewhat lazy. Until now in spite of his high rank, he had chosen to live in the country away from affairs. He had married Catherine Woodville, sister of the Queen, when he was very young and having been forced into a marriage for which he had had no desire had always been resentful towards the Woodvilles. Rivers knew that he was not friendlily disposed towards the family but he thought that he was too indifferent to state affairs to consider working against them and that this meeting must be, as Buckingham hinted, accidental.

They parted on the best of terms and Rivers went back to the inn which was a short distance from that one in which Gloucester and Buckingham were to spend the night, promising himself that he would be off early next morning before they arose.

After he had gone Buckingham went with Gloucester to his room. They looked at each other very seriously for a few moments and then Gloucester said: 'Well, what is it?'

'He will get the King to London before you,' said Buckingham.

'No, he will not,' replied Richard.

'My lord, the King lies at Stony Stratford. You may be sure that Rivers plans to have him away before we get to him.'

'It shall not be.'

'He will have sent messages to Stony Stratford without doubt.'

'I have stopped all messengers leaving the town.'

Buckingham smiled.

'So the King will stay at Stony Stratford until I arrive to conduct him to London,' went on Gloucester.

Buckingham nodded. 'You are wise, Lord Protector. I came here to join you, to offer my services. The Woodvilles are in charge . . . at the moment. They plan to rule the country.'

'I know that well. They deliberately refrained from telling me of my brother's death although they knew that he had named me Protector of the Realm and the King's guardian.'

'They are determined to get the boy crowned and then he will be surrounded by the Woodvilles who will proceed to rule. It must never be.'

'It *shall* never be,' said Richard.

He was regarding Buckingham quizzically. Buckingham

was fierce in his condemnation of the Woodvilles. He was a considerable ally, representing one of the most noble families in the land as he did. Richard was confident of his ability to conduct affairs in the way his brother would have wished them to go, but the more friends he had the better. Hastings had proved himself an ally; and now Buckingham.

His confidence was growing. Not that he needed support. Richard had always done what he considered right without too much consideration of the cost.

He now said: 'Firm action is needed, firm and immediate action.'

'My lord,' said Buckingham, 'you will know what action to take.'

Anthony had returned to his room in a mood bordering almost on complacency. Gloucester had been affable – rather unexpectedly so. He had never while the King was alive shown any great regard for the Woodvilles and Anthony knew he had made his brother aware that he considered the marriage of the King and Queen most unsuitable. As for Buckingham he behaved as one might expect a brother-in-law to – but it was the first time he had.

Rivers smiled as he settled into his bed. Of course they realised, these two, that he, Rivers, was of greater importance now than he had ever been. The King was devoted to him and anyone who wished for favour in the new reign would have first to consider Lord Rivers. The Queen too perhaps for he had taught Edward to revere his mother. He was certain that there were good times ahead for the whole Woodville clan.

He slept easily for he had drunk rather more deeply than

usual in that affable company, but before retiring he had given instructions that he was to be awakened just before dawn. He must leave then and set out for Stony Stratford where young Edward would be waiting for him. And then . . . off to London and the coronation.

When he awoke the first streaks of light were in the sky. He rose startled. He should have been awakened by now. Hearing a murmuring below and with a sudden feeling that all was not as it should be he went to the window and looked out. Soldiers appeared to be surrounding the inn.

Throwing a cloak about himself he went to the door. He was confronted by a guard.

'What means this?' he cried.

'You are under arrest, my lord.'

'What? This is nonsense. Under arrest. For what reason? Who has arrested me?'

He saw the badge of the Boar on the men's livery and he knew because the man replied: 'On the orders of the Lord Protector, my lord.'

Rivers stepped back into the room. What a fool 'I've been! he thought. How could I have been so duped? I should have stayed at Stony Stratford. I should at this moment be on my way to London with the King.

He dressed hurriedly and said that he wished to speak with the Duke of Gloucester. He sent for his most trusted squire and told him to go at once to the inn where the Duke had his headquarters and tell him that Lord Rivers desired to speak to him without delay.

'And get a message to my nephew, Lord Richard Grey, who is with the King. Tell him to leave at once with the King for London.'

'It is not possible, my lord. No one is allowed to leave the town. The Protector's men are posted on all roads.'

'It is too late then,' said Anthony. 'Then I must see the Duke.'

'I will go at once my lord, and ask if he will see you.'

In a state of great mortification and extreme anxiety Rivers waited and in due course his messenger returned and said he was to conduct him to the Duke of Gloucester.

Richard regarded him sardonically.

'It was not very clever,' he said. 'There was no room for you all in the town! You should have done better than that, Rivers.'

'My lord Gloucester, it was so . . .'

Richard held up a hand. 'I do not wish to parley with you. I know full well what you planned to do . . . you and the Queen. You disregarded my brother's wishes. You sought to keep me in ignorance of his death until you had crowned the King and established yourselves as rulers of the land. That is not to be, Lord Rivers.'

'I assure you, my lord Duke, that the people wish the King to be crowned.'

'Assuredly the people wish their rightful King to be crowned, but in due course, and not in such a manner which will make the most hated family in the country rulers of it. The King will be crowned, I assure you, but it will not be on the fourth of May as you planned.'

'My lord, the King himself may wish . . .'

'The King I have no doubt will wish what his uncle tells him to. He is young. Perhaps he is not aware of the scheming ambitions of that self-same uncle. Nay my lord, your schemes have been foiled. There is one thing the people do not want and that is to be ruled by the Woodvilles. They shall have their King and a proper Council to support him.'

'Headed by my lord of Gloucester I doubt not.'

'Headed, my lord, by the man selected by the late King to do so.'

'I came in peace.'

'Then how do you explain the arms in your baggage?'

'A natural precaution.'

'Precaution against those who seek justice for the King and the realm?'

'Ask the King whom he wishes to guide him.'

'The King has been well primed by his mother's relations. All know that. The King is a child. Children cannot rule. Enough of this. I granted you this interview and now it is over.' He called to the guards. Take Lord Rivers away. He is under arrest. He shall be lodged in Sheriff Hutton until such a time as his case can be judged.'

Protesting, Rivers was hustled away.

Richard with Buckingham beside him and their men behind them rode over in the dawn's early light to Stony Stratford.

The young King, with Lord Richard Grey and his old chamberlain, Sir Thomas Vaughan, was eagerly watching for the arrival of Lord Rivers. He had said that he would come in the early morning when they must all be prepared to leave for London without a moment's delay.

Lord Richard had arrived only the previous day with messages from the Queen to her son. She was longing to see him, she said. He was her King now and she knew that he would understand how important he had become. She had lost his dear father and she needed him to protect her now.

Edward was overcome with emotion. The idea of

protecting his beautiful mother, who always seemed so well able to take care of herself, seemed to him a great task and one he was impatient to undertake. Uncle Anthony would tell him what he had to do. His mother would too, and Lord Richard as well. He need not be afraid with so many to help him.

Lord Richard was a little anxious because his uncle had not yet arrived. He had been so insistent that they leave as soon as it was light. He had said he would be arriving from Northampton in the very early morning. But where was he?

Richard said they should all be ready for when Lord Rivers did come it was certain that he would be in a great hurry and would want them to start off without delay.

Lord Richard was in a quandary. The Queen wanted her son in London for the coronation was fixed for a few days ahead. He decided that they would have to leave without Lord Rivers. They had left the inn and the King had mounted his horse with Richard Grey beside him when there was the sound of horses' hoofs in the distance.

'He is here,' cried Lord Richard. 'Thank God. And I am sure that he will wish to leave without delay.'

Orders were being shouted. No one was to leave the town.

Then into their midst rode the King's paternal uncle instead of his maternal one and with him was the Duke of Buckingham.

Gloucester and Buckingham came straight to the King, dismounted and bowed low before him with the utmost respect.

'Where is Lord Rivers?' asked the King rather shrilly.

'I have news for you of my Lord Rivers,' said Richard. 'Let us retire into the inn that we may talk in quiet.'

Bewildered the King dismounted and Lord Richard Grey and Sir Thomas Vaughan went with him into the inn. Gloucester and Buckingham followed.

Richard commanded that they be taken to a room and when they were there and the door shut he knelt and kissed Edward's hand.

'The greatest calamity which could befall us and this nation has come about,' he said. 'Your father, my brother, is dead and you, my lord, are now the true and rightful King of England.'

Edward nodded. There were tears in his eyes. He was frightened. His uncle Gloucester had always had that effect on him. He was wondering where Uncle Anthony was and why he had not come as he promised.

'It is said,' went on Gloucester, 'that your father might be alive today if he had not given way to excesses. There were certain men surrounding him, notably your half-brother the Marquess of Dorset, who encouraged him in these excesses. It is my intent, as your guardian, named to be such by your father, that you shall be saved from these evil influences.'

Lord Richard Grey cried out: 'My lord . . . I protest. I and my uncle have never had anything but the King's welfare at heart.'

Gloucester waved him aside.

'Certain men,' he said, 'intended to deprive me of the office which my brother in his last words expressed a wish that I should take. They planned to remove me. For this reason I have had no alternative but to arrest Lord Rivers.'

'You have arrested Lord Rivers!' cried the King. 'But he has never done any harm. He is my very good friend . . . my very *best* friend.'

'My lord, they have kept you in ignorance. There is a plot to destroy me and to govern through you. This plot has been fabricated by the Marquess of Dorset, Lord Rivers and Lord Richard Grey here.'

'These are my family . . . my brothers and my uncle.'

'It is for this reason that they have laid these grandiose schemes. They have always presumed on that relationship. The Woodvilles were nothing until the King married your mother. Now they are trying to take charge of us all.'

'I will not believe this of them. I love them all dearly. They have always been my very good friends.'

'My dear nephew,' said Gloucester, 'for years I have shared your father's confidence. None was closer to him than I in matters of state. I have known his mind since he came to the throne. We have worked together; and only a few weeks before his death he spoke to me of this. He told me that he wished me to take the reins of government until you were of an age to do so yourself. He trusted me, Edward, as he trusted no other.'

'He trusted me with Lord Rivers,' said Edward quickly.

'It is true that your uncle was the choice of the Queen but your father was growing anxious about the domination of her family and intended to make changes.'

Edward wanted to shout at this uncle: 'I don't believe it. I love them all. They love me. My half-brother Richard and my uncle Anthony are my best friends. As for you, my lord Gloucester, I don't know you. I don't like you. And I want my uncle Anthony brought back.'

But there was something stern and fierce about Uncle Richard of Gloucester. Edward quailed before him, and was afraid of him. He looked as though he rarely laughed. Uncle Anthony laughed a great deal, although he was a very religious man and sometimes wore a hair shirt under his fine garments. Surely that was a sign of holiness? But Uncle Anthony was fun to be with. So was his half-brother. He wanted to command

Uncle Gloucester to send Lord Rivers back to him but he did not know how to do it.

'My lord,' said Gloucester gently, 'your father left instructions that I, his brother, who was closer to him than any other, should be Protector of the Realm and of your person. Do you give your consent that your father's wishes be carried out?'

Edward looked helplessly about him. He wanted to protest. He looked to Lord Richard Grey but his half-brother knew that there was nothing to be done against Gloucester, for it was true that the late King had named him Protector.

'Y . . yes,' stammered the King. 'I agree that my father's commands shall be carried out.'

'Then, my lord, we shall return to Northampton,' said Gloucester.

'To Northampton! But my mother is waiting for us in London.'

'I must first of all ascertain that it is safe for you to go there.'

'But my mother . . .'

'Your mother could not protect you as I shall. We are returning without delay to Northampton and very soon I am sure my friends in London will let me know what is happening there and as soon as it is safe we shall return and you shall be crowned King of England. We shall leave this place in an hour.'

He left the inn and sitting on his horse he addressed the soldiers.

'Your task is done,' he said. 'The King is safely in my hands which is where his father wished him to be. As soon as I have news from London that it is safe for him to go there I shall accompany him to the capital. I trust, my friends, that ere long our King will be attending his coronation. Now there is no need for your good services. Disperse and go back to your homes. You will be told if and when you are needed.'

There was a slight hesitation and murmuring among them then they turned away and did as they were bid.

Gloucester went back into the inn.

'Where are Lord Richard Grey and Thomas Vaughan?' he asked.

'They are with the King, my lord.'

'As soon as they leave him, arrest them. Let them be sent with Rivers to Sheriff Hutton.'

🏵 Chapter XI 🏵

JANE SHORE

The Queen with her son, the Marquess of Dorset, was eagerly awaiting the arrival of the young King with his uncle Rivers.

She could not understand the delay for she knew that Anthony was at Stony Stratford. That was the last place from which the messengers had come.

'If we are to be all prepared for the coronation on the fourth there is little time left to us,' she declared.

'We will get it done in time, never fear.'

Elizabeth looked with faint exasperation and a great deal of affection at this handsome eldest son of hers. He was like his father who had been an extremely handsome man. She had certainly managed to attract good-looking men, she thought ruefully. Edward had of course been incomparable and royal at that, but her first husband had been a most outstandingly handsome man and Thomas took after him. Thomas of course was not the most steady of men; he was impulsive and she had to confess a little arrogant and quite vain. His stepfather had spoilt him, taking him about with him. Now Thomas was known as one of the biggest rakes in the kingdom.

At first she had been annoyed when he and Edward had gone off adventuring together and then she had thought it was not such a bad thing. Far better that the King should be with Thomas rather than Hastings. Thomas and Hastings did not like each other and she had heard that they were both contenders for Jane Shore now that the King was dead.

What an attraction that woman appeared to have! The King had been devoted to her until his last days. She must have great physical gifts; but there must have been something more than that to hold Edward to her for so long. Hastings, it seemed, was really in love with her – or so rumour went, but she would have none of him. The same rumour had it that she had succumbed to Dorset now that Edward was dead.

Poor Jane! Although he was her son and she was devoted to him, Elizabeth rather pitied the woman who relied too much on him. He was a rake of a different kind from Edward and Hastings. Edward had been a romantic at heart and Hastings most certainly was. There was nothing of that about Thomas. Thomas knew exactly what he wanted and that was the gratification of his sexual appetites which were as voracious as those of the late King – or almost as voracious – for surely none could compare with Edward in that respect.

She was deliberately trying not to think of what might be happening at Stony Stratford because she very much feared something had gone wrong. She had given instructions that couriers were to come in a continuous stream, so anxious was she to be ready when her son arrived.

It had been hours now and there were none. Anthony should be almost in sight of London now.

At last, the messenger had arrived. Something was definitely wrong. The Queen commanded that he be brought to her without a second's delay. He was breathless and stammered out the news.

She could not believe it. Gloucester had the King! He was at Northampton with him! Anthony and Richard arrested!

'Oh God preserve us,' she cried, 'this is disaster.'

She looked at Dorset. He was never at his best in a crisis.

'Gloucester has defeated us,' he cried. 'A thousand curses on Gloucester. A pox on the man!'

'But what are we to *do*?' demanded Elizabeth. 'He has arrested your brother and your uncle. What do you think will happen to us when he comes to London?'

'We must get away . . .' cried Dorset. 'But where can we go?'

Elizabeth was ready. It had happened before. She said: 'We must go into Sanctuary.'

She looked about her at all the rich possessions which she so loved. Leave them . . . go to Sanctuary. How long would she remain there? And yet she must. How could she know what Gloucester would do when he brought the King to London?

'We must prepare to go at once. I will take all the children with me. He cannot harm us in Sanctuary. I lived there before when the King was in exile. I shall do it again. But this time I shall take with me . . . some of my possessions. I shall not go empty-handed as I did before.'

'Then let us start at once to collect what you will take with you. There is little time to be lost.'

Elizabeth frantically called to her servants and began directing them as to what must be packed. Others must go and prepare the children. She thanked God that young Richard was with them. He and the five girls must be prepared at once to leave and as soon as her precious possessions were crated they would sail up the river to the Sanctuary.

Meanwhile Hastings had received the news that the King was in Gloucester's hands. The city was crowded with the nobles from all over the country who had come for the King's coronation and it occurred to Hastings that he should inform Thomas Rotherham Archbishop of York, who was also Chancellor and who by good fortune happened to be in London at this time, that all was well.

The old Archbishop who was sixty years of age was startled from his sleep by the news.

Hastings's words intended to reassure him did nothing of the sort. 'All will be well,' Hastings's message ended.

The old man pondered it. He was a supporter of the Queen and he did not like this. 'All will be well,' he muttered. 'But it will never be as good as it has been.'

No, it was a great disaster that Edward should have died so young before they were prepared for his death and thus to leave this innocent child to carry on the responsibilities of the crown. He hastily dressed and as he did so it was brought home to him more and more what this meant. The Queen's family was too powerful to stand aside and let Gloucester take over what they had decided was theirs.

He must warn the Queen without delay. He set out at once for Westminster Palace. There he found a most extraordinary scene. The Queen was seated on the rushes, her expression blank and despairing; all about her were servants packing crates, taking down tapestries from the walls and putting valuable ornaments into boxes.

'My lady,' cried the Chancellor, 'you must not despair. I have had word from my Lord Hastings. "All will be well", he says.'

'Hastings!' cried the Queen in fury. 'If ever a man was my

enemy that man is. He is determined to destroy me and my family. What he calls good is bad for me, my lord.'

The Chancellor was horrified.

'Oh my lady, my lady,' he cried, 'what shall we do?'

'You will stand by me, my lord? I shall have some friends.'

'My lady, you may rely on me to defend your cause.' He took the Great Seal and placed it in her hands.

Elizabeth took it gratefully and bade the Archbishop go back to his palace. Ere long she, with her family, would be leaving for Sanctuary.

The goods she was taking with her were packed. She sent for her children and they came, bewildered. They had never known the uneasy days. Their lives had all been guarded by their great indulgent all-powerful father. There was lovely Elizabeth, sixteen years old now and who should have been Dauphine of France at this time but for the treachery of Louis, the shock of whose deception had doubtless hastened Edward's death. Cecily, fourteen years old. And Anne eight, Catherine four and little Bridget three. Seeing them together thus the Queen thought of poor Mary and the great sorrow her death had brought them. Elizabeth and Edward had often congratulated themselves that they had been more lucky than most families because although they had lost three children – Margaret, George and now Mary – they had kept the rest and out of ten they had seven left to them and that was a very good number. The Queen embraced them all tenderly. She kept young Richard close to her. He as the boy was very precious. He was ten years old now and he was always asking questions about his brother and wanting to see him. She had often considered sending him to Ludlow, but she had been unable to resist the temptation to keep him with her.

Now she was glad.

'My dear children,' she said to them, 'something dreadful has happened. Your wicked uncle Gloucester has taken the King from my lord Rivers and now holds him. I am afraid of what he will do when he brings him to London and for that reason we are all going into Sanctuary until we know what is happening.'

'Are we taking all these things with us?' asked Richard.

'Yes, my son, we are not leaving them behind for your uncle to have.'

'Will he kill Edward?'

'No, no. Nobody is going to kill anybody. He wouldn't dare. But he wants to rule through Edward and we are not going to allow that to happen.'

'Are we going to fight him . . .'

'We are powerful enough to stop him.'

'The Woodvilles will be able to,' said Elizabeth. 'They are the most powerful family in the country.'

'That is so and rightly,' said the Queen. 'Remember, my dears, that you are Woodvilles too. Now Elizabeth and you Cecily, take care of the little ones. We should be leaving at once. The sooner we are in Sanctuary the more relieved I shall be.'

They went out into the barge and soon arrived at the Sanctuary beside the Abbey.

'I was here once before,' said young Elizabeth.

'Yes,' murmured the Queen, 'and I never thought this could ever befall us again.'

'Well, we are together,' Elizabeth reminded her.

'Not all of us,' piped up Richard. 'Edward isn't.'

'We shall soon have the King with us,' said the Queen firmly.

※ ※ ※

Waiting in Northampton Gloucester received Hastings's message.

The Woodvilles had clearly realised they were beaten. The Queen had fled with her children into Sanctuary. Rotherham, the foolish old man, had lost his head and given the Great Seal back to the Queen though no sooner had he committed this act of folly than he had attempted to retrieve it. He had been too late, however; the Queen had gone and when it was realised what he had done he had naturally been deprived of his office.

It would be fitting now for Gloucester to bring the King to London.

So all was going according to plan. Gloucester could be sure that if Edward could look down from Heaven he would approve of what had been done. He had decided that it would be unwise to send Rivers, Grey and Vaughan to the same place of imprisonment and far safer to keep them separately confined. Rivers should go to Sheriff Hutton as originally intended, Richard Grey to Middleham and Vaughan to Pontefract.

He was now prepared to march on London. The King was a little sullen; he showed clearly that he did not like his uncle Gloucester and deeply resented that the uncle of whom he was very fond should with his half-brother be taken away from him.

Gloucester tried to talk to the boy of his father and how friendly they had been as brothers. Gloucester reminded the young King of his motto *Loyaulte me lie* which he had always adhered to and on which the late King had always been able to rely. Gloucester implied that he would now transfer that loyalty to the new King.

'Why, Edward,' he said, 'you are your father's son, my own nephew. To whom should I owe my loyalty but to you?'

Edward listened politely but there was a sullen line to his mouth.

'Perhaps,' he said, 'you could bring my uncle Lord Rivers to me for I do not know of what he can possibly be accused.'

'He will have a fair trial and then you will understand.'

'I do not need a trial to tell me that he is innocent of all wrong doing,' said the King.

'You are loyal to those you believe to be your friends and that is admirable,' was all Gloucester said.

He was eager to show the King that he wanted to take nothing from him. All he wanted to do was set him on the throne and help him to govern wisely.

On the fourth of May – the day the Woodvilles had selected for his coronation – Edward the Fifth rode into London.

He was attired in blue velvet which became him well and his fair hair falling to his shoulders made of him a pretty sight. The people cheered him, though they had had their fill of Kings who were minors and knew that good rarely came of them. What England needed was a strong king – a man such as this boy's father had been.

Beside the King rode the Duke of Gloucester; he was sombrely clad in black, a contrast to the King's rich garments. And on the other side of the King was Buckingham, clad like Gloucester in black.

Solemnly they rode. The people cheered so wildly that Elizabeth with her children in the Sanctuary of Westminster heard them and she was exultant. It would not be long she promised herself and her family. Soon they would be out of this place and with the King.

The people looked at the Duke of Gloucester, pale, serious and sombre. His brother had relied on him, trusted him.

We have a young King, they thought; but we shall have a wise Protector. Edward in his wisdom has left us well provided for.

News of what was happening outside was brought into the Sanctuary. Elizabeth was desolate. The people accepted Richard; they saw in him a wise ruler, a man who had remained loyal to his brother and had had his confidence. He was serious-minded and had shown that he was a wise administrator by the order he had kept in the North of England. They loved their little King. He was good-looking and youth was always appealing providing there were those who could guide it.

The country unanimously agreed that Richard of Gloucester should be the Lord Protector, and Defender of the Realm.

He was against the Woodvilles but then so was the country. They had watched the avaricious Queen push her family into all the most important houses in the country. Well, that was going to be over now and the Protector had acted promptly and with good sense when he had arrested Rivers and Richard Grey and made Dorset realise that the only place where he would be safe was in Sanctuary.

Dorset was restive. He could not bear being confined in Sanctuary. How could he possibly pursue the kind of life which he had found so necessary to him in such a place? He missed Jane. He laughed slyly to think that she was his mistress. It had happened as soon as the King died – as he had known it would.

He had long had his eyes on Jane and he would not have waited for the death of the King. She was the one who insisted on that. Jane was different from other women he had known; Edward had always said she was and he was right. She was not a natural harlot; she was warm-hearted and amorous by nature, born to it, as Edward had said; and yet there was no question of buying her favours. It is not easy to give Jane anything, the King had said wonderingly. Dorset was cynical; at first he had thought she was just exceptionally clever as his own sister was in her way. But there could not be another woman living less like Elizabeth.

He derived great satisfaction from his affair with Jane for a number of reasons. In the first place she was beautiful and desirable; and for another, and this gave him special pleasure, Hastings had wanted her right from the time when the King had first discovered her. Indeed Dorset was not sure whether Hastings had not discovered her first. Edward had come along and jostled poor William out of the way and of course he dared not anger the King over her and Edward would have been furious in the case of Jane though with any other woman he might have been ready to enter into a kind of tournament with his friend.

Not Jane though. There was something special about Jane. Hastings was gnashing his teeth because Dorset had been the one she had gone to on the King's death.

Dear weak Jane, she had found him irresistible, although she was no fool. She knew his faults. She knew him for the cynical, selfish sybarite he was. She would have no faith in his fidelity; he lacked the kindliness of the late King; that desire in Edward never to hurt people's feelings if he could help it and always to seek a way of smoothing over unpleasantness was no part of Dorset's nature. Dorset cared nothing for others; he did not consider them except in their ability to supply his needs. Jane knew this and it was a double triumph therefore that she had come to him. The truth was he was possessed of extraordinary physical attraction. So many women, hating him for what he was, yet found him irresistible; and that Jane, who had basked in the King's affection and returned it undemandingly for all the years they had been together, should now turn to Dorset was a great triumph – particularly when Hastings was standing by ready to give her the same devotion that she had enjoyed so long from Edward.

To be confined in Sanctuary was unbearable. Yet what would happen if he ventured out? He would immediately be imprisoned for Gloucester would regard him as one of the leaders of the Woodville party.

What a wretched state of affairs to have fallen into so suddenly – and all because one king had died and his brother was determined to rule the country.

'A plague on Gloucester!' he cried. But what was the use of words? He had to find a way out of this miserable situation.

He could see only one way of doing it, and that was to escape.

He began to plan. It would be easy enough to slip out of Sanctuary at dark of night, but where would he go then? There were many houses of ill fame in the city and he was known to them. The point was how far could they be trusted? When he was free, son of the Queen, companion of the King, rich, influential, he had been surrounded by friends. It would be different now. Or would it? He was the sort of man people would be afraid to offend for the fortunes of war and politics changed quickly and he was of a vengeful nature.

He knew of one house where the lady in charge was particularly fond of him. He had great confidence in his power to charm. Should he sound her? No. That would be unwise. What if a message went astray? What if instead of the loving arms of the lady he found Gloucester's men waiting for him? He would find himself in a worse state than he was now.

Nevertheless he must attempt it. He would slip out. He would find his way to the tavern and ask to be hidden there until he could get abroad or away to the North. It should not be difficult. It would be some time before his absence was discovered. His mother would make sure of that.

She listened eagerly when he told her of his plans. She was as weary of this confinement as he was and sure that they could rouse men to follow them. After all was she not the King's mother? And if Anthony could be freed and Richard with him they could immediately begin to rouse the country against Gloucester.

Yes, he must go. So one dark night Dorset left Sanctuary. He made his way through the narrow streets over the familiar cobbles, wrapped in an all-concealing cloak so that his identity was completely hidden. He knocked; he was let in; he asked for the lady of the house.

She came to him, and when he threw off his cloak she expressed her joy. The old magic had not deserted him. She was as enamoured as ever and clearly flattered that he had come to her.

'I need to remain here for a night or two . . . perhaps a week,' he told her. 'Could you hide me?'

Indeed she could and it should be her pleasure.

He kissed her warmly on the lips in his own inimitable way. Old Edward himself could not have done better.

Her response was warm. He knew he could trust her.

Jane Shore was very uneasy. Life had changed so drastically for her within the last weeks that she was quite bewildered. Deeply she regretted the death of the King. Theirs had been a most satisfying relationship. That he was really fond of her there was no doubt and their liaison had been of such duration that some might have said it was habit. That may have been but it was a very satisfying, comforting habit.

Jane had been faithful to the King even though Dorset had often tempted her to stray. She could not explain to herself the terrible fascination Dorset had for her. It was as though he had laid a spell on her. When he was near her that compelling attraction was so irresistible that she had to succumb to it knowing full well that there was evil in it – evil in him.

When the King was alive he had not dared to be too persistent. He had followed her with his eyes and in them had been that burning desire which against her will had drawn a response from her. She had fought it off successfully while the King lived. It was a different matter when he was dead.

Dorset had then claimed her and made her his slave. Jane was both repelled and utterly fascinated by the man. When he was not present she could tell herself that she must break away from him; but he only had to appear and she was lost.

Jane was not naturally a loose woman. She was not meant to be passed from one man to another. She needed a settled and respectable existence and with the King she had had that.

She had loved Edward. Who could have helped it? He had seemed to her – as he did to many – the most handsome man in the world. Moreover he had such charm of manner and such kindliness radiated from him; he was so powerful, so romantic, every inch a king, a perfect lover; he was all that Jane could ever have asked for.

She often thought of the early days, and how it had all come about. Her life had been simple enough in her father's household for he had been a well-to-do mercer and those early days had been lived in the house in Cheapside where she had been born. Her mother had died and left Jane an only child to her father's care, which had been strict yet affectionate in its way. Thomas Wainstead had been eager to do everything for his daughter even to finding her a worthy husband in the goldsmith William Shore.

Perhaps all would have been well if Jane had not been so outstandingly beautiful that she caught the roving eye of one of the Court gallants who attempted to abduct her. That man had been William Lord Hastings and she had for ever after been wary of him. He was good-looking – but a pale shadow of Edward as every other man must be.

He was rich; he had the means to bribe servants and set the stage for abduction; and this might have taken place had not one of the servants – whom he had bribed to help him drug her mistress – not suddenly grown alarmed and warned Jane.

From the beginning marriage with Goldsmith Shore had been a dire mistake. Jane had wanted to be a good wife to him but she was naturally exuberant, full-blooded and romantic; and the goldsmith who was several years older than herself was certainly no hero of romance.

He was a highly respectable man – naturally he would be since her father had chosen him; he served the Court and was even more comfortably placed than the mercer; he was also deeply religious. Jane found him intolerable.

And then . . . it was after the King's return from exile and that must have been some thirteen years ago . . . he had come to the goldsmith's shop ostensibly to look at ornaments but in truth to see Jane of whom Hastings had spoken. Dressed as a merchant he had filled the shop with his magnificent presence and as soon as he saw Jane she had been aware of the glint in his eyes and understood.

It was a short step from then to becoming the King's mistress. She had never regretted it although she was often sorry for William Shore who in his way had been devoted to her. In those first days she had worried about her father, how he had taken the news, for there was no doubt that she had become notorious.

In the early days she had often wondered what would become of her when the King tired of her. Jane had never sought advantages; she delighted to please the King and although she knew she shared that honour with many others, still she did not care. She loved him. If she could please him that was her pleasure. This selfless attitude of hers, together with her amazing beauty which never ceased to astonish however many times the King beheld it, and her witty tongue which was never used unkindly remained a source of delight to Edward during all the years of their liaison.

For thirteen years they had been lovers. She was part of his life and a part he never wanted to change.

She had had standing at Court and the King had insisted that she accept a fine house which was full of treasures which he had bestowed on her. He did not want to visit her in some hovel, he had said. And so she had lived in some state although she had not asked that this should be so.

Even the Queen had been kind to her. Elizabeth had sent for her and talked to her most gently. Jane knew that the Queen was aware of the life her husband lived. Perhaps she deplored it, but she preferred that he should have a mistress such as Jane, a good unselfish woman, by no means a harlot, than a succession of mistresses who would try to usurp the Queen's power.

They had liked each other. Although they were so different – Elizabeth eager to take all she could get and Jane asking nothing – they had one great quality in common: each knew how to handle the King.

They both managed admirably and they were the only two women who had kept their hold on his affections. They respected each other and whenever Jane was at Court she could always be sure that the Queen would treat her with respect. Whether she did this because to do otherwise would have angered the King, or whether she had a real respect for her, Jane was not sure. But she admired the Queen and considered her a clever woman and the Queen clearly had the same opinion of Jane.

And now the pleasant world had collapsed. The King had died suddenly, and Jane had lost her kind protector. She had never felt so alone in her life before.

Then Dorset had come.

She had not wanted another lover so soon. She wanted to mourn the one she had lost – incomparable Edward whom she had loved so deeply and so long.

But Dorset would not wait. He had proved to her without doubt that she could not resist him. He was an impulsive impatient lover. He had long wanted Jane and it had been galling to have to stand aside for that old man his stepfather – King though he was.

How different was Dorset from Edward. There was no

romantic lovemaking, Dorset cynically demanded and took. He was arrogant in the extreme and he wanted her to know that he was the master. Every time he left her she promised herself that it should be the last but when he came again he was as dominating as ever.

And now he had fled into Sanctuary. What would happen next? She hated to think of the proud Queen and her beautiful children in that cold place. She had met them all, and had particularly loved little Richard the Duke of York. She remembered so well his marriage to Anne Mowbray. What an enchanting little bridegroom he had made and little Anne was such an appealing bride. Alas, the little bridegroom had become a widower very soon, a fact which did not distress him for he did not seem to know anything about it.

The new King she had rarely seen because he was kept at Ludlow; and now he was in the Tower of London awaiting his coronation and there was this conflict between his uncle Gloucester and the Queen and her family.

Jane shivered; she had always kept away from state matters. Perhaps that was another reason why Edward had found it so restful to be with her.

It was some days since she had seen Dorset. She was not unhappy about that. He frightened her and she always despised herself for being the victim of her own senses, so there was a certain relief in being away from him. How different it had been with Edward! How she longed to go back to those cosy days, those intimate sessions with that most charming of lovers!

Her servants came to her and said that there was a man without who had a message for her.

Her heart started to beat uncertainly. From whom? she wondered. And somehow she knew it was from Dorset.

She sent for the man; she took the crumpled paper. Yes, Dorset. He had escaped from Sanctuary. He was in a house not far from the Chepe. She knew of the house. It was one which was frequented by the men of the Court and had a reputation for harbouring high-class prostitutes.

They were good to him there. He wanted her to come to him at once. It was important.

She crumpled the paper in her hand. She did not want to go. Dorset would have to understand that she was not like the women he was meeting in that house. But he was in acute danger. If it were known that he had left Sanctuary the hunt would start. The Protector would not be content until he had caught him and brought him to trial.

At the moment the Queen's brother, Lord Rivers, and her son, Richard Grey, were held by the Protector. There was no doubt of what Dorset's fate would be if he were caught.

She pondered a while and then she decided that she must at least see him.

She told the man: 'I will come at dusk.'

He went away satisfied.

She went swiftly along by the river through to the Chepe until she came to the address Dorset had sent her. She was recognised at once by the lady of the house, who took her through several passages to a room at the back of the house and there was Dorset.

He came towards her and seized her hungrily. She tried to hold him off but it was the same as ever and she felt her resistance slipping away.

'Jane . . . my Jane . . .' cried Dorset exultantly. 'I knew you would not fail me.'

'You said you must see me. What are you going to do?'

'I'll tell you later. There is time yet. We have the whole night before us.'

'I must go.'

'What, through the streets at this hour! Come confess it, Jane, when you agreed to come at dusk you knew you would not leave until morning.'

'I will not stay.'

He laughed; and she knew she would.

During the night she learned the real reason why he had sent for her. Of course he had delighted in her body, but there were many handsome women on the premises and any would have been delighted to entertain the mighty Marquess of Dorset even though he was in hiding. The general belief was that the King would soon be crowned and then the Protector would go back to the North; the Queen and her family would emerge into prominence again and they would naturally be the ones who would control the King.

'I shall have to leave here very soon,' said Dorset. 'It's dangerous.'

'I am glad you realise it.'

'Oh yes, Jane, it will be sad to be far away from you, but I have to get away . . . to raise an army to come back and show Edward's little brother that it is not as easy as he thinks.'

'I doubt he thinks it easy,' said Jane. 'Edward talked a great deal about him. He had the highest regard for him. He used to say he trusted him as he did no other.'

'Please, Jane, do not sing Gloucester's praises to me. The man is after power like everyone else. He sees himself as ruling the country through his little nephew King.'

'Edward did not think that.'

'Edward always refused to see ill in anyone. Look at the manner in which Warwick duped him. We have to think of the little King. He is desperately unhappy because my uncle Anthony was taken from him. He frets for my brother Richard. Just think, those fine men are in the hands of that hunchbacked little upstart.'

'He is not a hunchback. One shoulder is a little higher than the other, that's all. Edward used to say that they forced him to wear armour that was too heavy for his bones. Moreover Edward always thought so highly of his administrative power. He trusted him as he did no one else . . .'

'Yes, exactly as he trusted Warwick when the mighty Earl Kingmaker was thinking of unkinging him and remaking Henry.'

'Wait a while,' said Jane. 'See what happens. Go back to Sanctuary where you will be safe.'

'Dear Jane, you are the perfect mistress but do not seek to meddle in matters of which you know nothing. I am going to instruct you and you shall play your part, I promise you.'

'What do you mean, instruct me?'

'I want you to do something for me. You will, won't you?'

'If I can I will, but what is it?'

'Jane. Listen. We need to bring men to our side . . . influential men. Men like Buckingham . . . but I don't know enough of him. There is one other whom I know very well and who is important to us. You could help me here, Jane. You could persuade him. He would listen to you.'

'Who is this man?'

'Hastings.'

'Hastings! You know how I feel about Hastings.'

'Oh come, Jane. You bear him a grudge and that is not like

you. What did Hastings do but admire you? What has he ever
done against you but look at you with longing? I know that at
one time he tried to abduct you and take you by force. Don't
think too hardly of him, Jane. It was the sort of adventure we
all indulged in.'

'I have never forgotten it.'

'But you have forgiven him. He has always been so eager to
show you how pleased he would be for a little notice from you.'

'You think I could persuade him to change sides?'

'Yes, Jane, I do . . . cleverly, subtly . . . as you with your
merry witty talk would know how to.'

'You ask the impossible.'

He took her by the shoulders and shook her.

'Do this for me. I want to be back in power. I do not want to
skulk in Sanctuary afraid of Gloucester's guards for ever.
Come Jane, do this for me. Be my lovely little Jane. It would
be a challenge. Do you fear you could not do it?

'I have not considered doing what you ask.'

'It would be revenge on him. He treated you with scant
respect when he tried to abduct you . . . aye, and would have
done so but for that last minute dash of conscience which beset
your maid. Have your revenge, Jane, and work for me at the
same time. Help me out of this wretchedness into which I have
fallen. Think of my mother, our proud Queen. Think of the
Princesses and the little Duke of York. They are forced to live
in Sanctuary, afraid to emerge. Afraid of their lives. Oh Jane,
help me . . . help the Queen who has always been your friend.
You loved the little Duke didn't you? I think you were a
special favourite of his. The King once said that you had told
him you looked on Richard as your own. And little Catherine
and little Bridget . . . Think of them.'

'I am sorry for what has befallen the Queen, but it is not for me to meddle.'

'So you will not help your friends?'

'I would if I could. But Edward named the Duke of Gloucester as the Protector of the Realm and of the little King.'

'He did not tell him to send the Queen into Sanctuary.'

'The Queen went of her own free will.'

'Because my brother and my uncle have been arrested. For what, Jane? For bringing the King to his coronation.'

Jane was thoughtful. Then she said: 'Lord Hastings was the King's best friend.'

'And you should remember that.'

'He never liked the Queen.'

'Oh that was due to some silly quarrel about the Captaincy of Calais which went to Hastings when my mother thought it should have gone to my uncle.'

Jane continued silent.

Dorset drew her to him and began to make violent love to her.

'Promise me, Jane,' he said. 'Swear you will help. Amuse yourself with Hastings . . .'

'What you suggest is . . . is . . .'

He stopped her with his kisses. He was laughing. 'You'll do it, Jane,' he said. 'You'll do this for me.'

Jane felt half ashamed, half excited. She was glad to escape from Dorset. When she was with him he was irresistible but she fervently wished that she could fight off the violent passion which he inspired in her. She wanted love. She had it astonishingly enough from Edward. There could be none to replace him but he was gone now and it was no use brooding on the past.

Since she had left Dorset she had thought a good deal about Hastings.

She had always told herself that she disliked him. She had never forgotten that experience when she had been about to take the ale which her maid had brought; she remembered still the frightened look in the girl's eyes and then her confession. Often she had wondered what would have happened if she had drunk the ale and gone into a deep sleep while Hastings was let into the house and carried her away.

Hastings himself had often looked shamefaced and had even told her how he repented that act. She had shrugged his apologies aside. She had told herself that was in the past and of no importance now for he would never attempt such an action with her again. The King had laughed at it. 'Forgive poor old Hastings,' he said. 'He's a good friend to me. I trust him and that means a great deal. What he did I am afraid we would all have done if the idea had occurred to us.' She had protested and made Edward see that men who thought they had a right to treat women so were rogues. He agreed with her, and said: 'But then you are so beautiful, Jane. A temptation to us all, and did I not take you away from that virtuous goldsmith of yours?'

She could sound Hastings. He always looked at her with a kind of brooding tenderness nowadays which made her feel differently towards him.

When she next saw him he was on the way to Westminster to talk with the Protector. They were arranging when the coronation should be, she knew. Dorset had said that the Protector would put it off for as long as possible because once the King was crowned he himself would cease to be so important.

She smiled at Hastings. He immediately hesitated. She supposed she had never done that spontaneously before.

He paused and bowed low. 'Greetings, Mistress Shore,' he said. ''Tis a fine day.'

'It is so,' she answered.

He was still pausing, looking at her with that obvious admiration.

'You grow fairer than ever every time I see you,' he said.

'You are gracious.'

'Jane.' She saw the hope leap into his eyes. It had been easier than she had thought.

They supped together. He talked soberly of the death of the King. 'A sad blow to us both, Jane,' he said. 'Nothing will ever be the same for either of us again. You miss him sorely do you not?'

'Most sorely,' she confirmed.

'He was a great man . . . a great King. He possessed all the qualities of kingship. That he should go like that . . . so suddenly . . .'

'He lived too heartily,' said Jane. 'I often told him.'

'He could not help it. He was made like that. Do you know, Jane, I am twelve years older than he was. Think of it, I have had twelve more years of life.'

'My lord, I hope you have twelve more left to you.'

'Now that you are gracious to me, I could wish it,' he said.

That night she became his mistress.

It was easier than she had thought. He was kindly, tender and he loved her. That was obvious. He told her during that first night together how bitterly he had regretted that first approach. He had always felt that if he had tried to woo her as she deserved to be wooed, perhaps he might have been successful before Edward found her.

'I have a feeling, Jane, that you would be faithful to the one you loved.'

'I always was to Edward.'

'I know it well. He knew it. He loved you for it and although he could not repay you in the same vein he often said what joy you had brought to his life. What of Dorset, Jane?'

She shivered. 'He is in hiding. I do not want to see him again.'

'Dorset is not a good man, Jane.'

'I know it well. I am glad to be free of him.'

Hastings seemed well satisfied with that.

🏵 Chapter XII 🏵

DEATH ON TOWER GREEN

So Jane Shore was now Hastings's mistress. It was a matter which was talked of throughout the town. Jane was popular with the citizens; so was Hastings. Gloucester listened with distaste. He had always deplored Edward's way of life and had on more than one occasion told his brother that it was no way for a King to live. Edward had laughed at him, had called him a monk, and said he could not expect everyone to be like himself. Hastings had been such another; it was something Gloucester had always held against him. He had reason to be grateful to Hastings for he had kept him informed of what was happening in London and in fact had been the first to tell him of Edward's death. But now that Buckingham had joined him and had shown himself to be so single-mindedly his man he was moving away from Hastings.

His brother's chief advisers had been Lord Hastings; Thomas Rotherham, Archbishop of York and Lord Chancellor; John Morton, Bishop of Ely; and Lord Stanley. Rotherham had shown himself up as a weakling by handing the Great Seal back to Elizabeth when she was packing her treasures to go into Sanctuary. He was not the kind of man Gloucester wanted about him. Morton was a good man but he had been a staunch Lancastrian and had only become Edward's minister when it was certain that there was no hope of Henry's being restored to the throne. It was a matter of expediency and Gloucester did not like such men. Stanley had not a very good reputation for loyalty and had previously shown himself ready to jump whichever way was best for Stanley; there was one other reason why Gloucester would not trust him too far. He had recently married Margaret Beaufort, that very strong-minded woman, who was descended from John of Gaunt and was also the mother of Henry Tudor. That upstart of very questionable parentage had of late begun to hint that he had a claim to the throne as grandson of Queen Katherine the widow of Henry the Fifth through a liaison – though the Tudors called it marriage – with Owen Tudor. Royalty on both sides, said Tudor, counting Katherine of France as his grandmother and John of Gaunt through his mother.

These had been Edward's men. It sometimes happened that when there was a change of rule there had to be a clean sweep. He wanted none of them – except perhaps Hastings. Buckingham was at his right hand. Buckingham was royal and the second peer in the land after himself. Then on a humbler scale there were Richard Ratcliffe, Francis Lovell, William Catesby . . . men who were his tried friends and had been over the years.

He was going to need staunch and trusted friends. The position was dangerous. If he were defeated by the Woodvilles they would have no compunction in destroying him. He was fighting not only for what he believed to be right but for his life.

It would be good to see Anne who was coming south for the coronation which was fixed for the twenty-fourth of June.

He met her on the outskirts of London and as soon as he saw her he was appalled by her frail looks. She always looked more delicate than ever after an absence. He had hoped that she would have their son with her although he had known that the little boy's health might have prevented his travelling.

Anne smiled as he took her hand; there was sadness in that smile for she noticed how he looked eagerly for their son and the disappointment on his face when he realised he was not with her. 'Welcome to London, my dear,' he said.

'I could not bring Edward,' she told him. 'I dared not. His cough has worsened and I thought the journey would be too much for him.'

He nodded. 'He will grow out of the weakness,' he said with an attempt at assurance, but he added: 'Praise God.'

'Oh yes. He was better in the spring.' She smiled and tried to look excited but all she could really feel was exhaustion. Being with Richard lately had always been something of an ordeal because she must continually pretend that her health was improving – and as that was far from the case it was not easy.

As they rode side by side into the City, he told her that the King was in the Palace of the Tower and that the coronation would be on the twenty-fourth of June. It was now the fifth so there was not much time.

There was a great deal to tell Anne but he did not want to overwhelm her with the detail of events nor did he wish to alarm her. He could see that she was uneasy when she heard that the Queen was in Sanctuary.

He took her to Crosby Place, his residence in London, and as soon as she arrived he insisted that she rest. He sat beside her bed and talked to her, explaining how the Woodvilles had tried to get control of the King, that their ambitions had to be curbed and it was for this reason that he had had to imprison Lord Rivers and Lord Richard Grey. The King was not very pleased about this.

'You see, Anne, they have brought him up to be a Woodville. My brother was too easy-going. He allowed the Queen to surround him with her relations. They have taught him that they are wonderful, wise and good.'

'Does it mean that he turns from you?'

Richard nodded ruefully. 'But I shall change that. He will learn in time.'

'I do wish there need not be this conflict,' said Anne, 'and I wish that you could come back to Middleham.'

'It will be some time before I do, I doubt not. My brother left this task to me and I must fulfil it.'

Then he talked of Middleham to soothe her and he asked about their son's progress with his lessons, for he was clever and his academic achievements made a happier subject than his health.

Anne slept at last and as Richard was leaving her chamber one of his attendants came to tell him that Robert Stillington, the Bishop of Bath and Wells was below and urgently seeking a word with him.

Richard immediately commanded that the Bishop be brought to him. He bade him be seated and to tell him the nature of this important news.

Stillington folded his hands and looked thoughtful. After arriving with a certain amount of urgency he seemed reluctant to explain the cause of his visit.

Richard knew that he was one of those ambitious men who sought advancement through the Church. There were plenty of them about. He had been a staunch Yorkist and in 1467 had become Lord Chancellor, an office of which he had been deprived on the restoration of the House of Lancaster; but it was given back to him when Edward returned. He resigned after a few years and when Edward had been a little disturbed by Henry Tudor's bombastic claims, Stillington had been sent to Brittany to try to persuade the Duke to surrender him to Edward.

He had failed and later he had been put into the Tower at the time of Clarence's death on a matter which had been somewhat secret and of which Richard was ignorant. It had seemed too trivial at the time to enquire about and Edward had dismissed it. In any case Stillington had soon been released.

Now here was Stillington with this urgent news which he prefaced by explaining it was for the ears of the Duke of Gloucester alone, for he himself did not know what use should be made of it.

All impatience Richard urged him to explain and Stillington burst out: 'My lord, the late King was not truly married to Elizabeth Woodville.'

Richard stared at him in astonishment.

'Oh my lord,' went on Stillington, 'this is true. I know it full well. I myself was in attendance on the King when he gave his vows to another lady. She went into a convent it is true but she was still living at the time when the King went through a form of marriage with Elizabeth Woodville.'

'My lord Bishop, do you realise what you are saying?'

'Indeed I do, my lord. I have pondered long on this matter. There is only one other occasion when I mentioned it and I told the one whom I thought it most concerned: the Duke of Clarence.'

'You told my brother this!' Richard stared in horror at the Bishop. 'When . . . when?'

'It was just before his death.'

It was becoming clear now. Events were falling into place. Stillington in the Tower. Clarence drowned in a butt of malmsey. Clarence would have had to die, possessed as he was of such knowledge.

How deeply it concerned Clarence, for it meant that he, not Edward's son, was heir to the throne!

And Clarence had died. Edward had seen to that. At the same time he had imprisoned Stillington and suddenly the Bishop had found himself in the Tower.

But why had Edward let him go free? Wasn't that typical of Edward? He always believed the best of people. He wanted to be on good terms with them. He could imagine his saying to Stillington: 'Give me your word that you will tell no one else and you shall go free on payment of a trivial ransom.' And Stillington would give his word to Edward, which he had kept until this moment. But he was of course exonerated from his promise now.

He was speaking slowly. 'You say my brother married . . . before he went through the form of marriage with the Queen.'

'I say it most emphatically, my lord. For I performed it.'

'My brother had many mistresses . . .'

'The Queen was one of them, my lord.'

'No doubt this was some light of love . . .'

'No, no, my lord. The lady was Lady Eleanor Butler, daughter of the Earl of Shrewsbury. She was a widow when the King saw her.'

'He had a fancy for widows or wives it seems,' murmured Richard. 'Go on. Old Talbot's daughter.'

'Her husband had been Thomas Butler, Lord Sudeley's heir. She was some years older than the King.'

'He liked older women,' mused Richard.

'He went through this form of marriage with her. She was his wife when he went through a form of marriage with Elizabeth Woodville. The Lady Eleanor went into a convent and I discovered that she died there in 1468.'

'So she died *after* he went through the form of marriage with Elizabeth Woodville.'

'Exactly, my lord. You see what this means?'

'It means that Elizabeth Woodville was the King's mistress and the Prince now living in the Palace of the Tower is a bastard.'

'It means exactly that, my lord.'

'My lord Bishop, you have shocked me deeply. I beg of you to say nothing of this to anyone . . . anyone whatsoever, do you hear?'

'I shall remain silent, my lord, until I have your permission to tell the truth.'

'I appreciate your coming to me.'

'I thought it was something which should be told.'

'It must be kept secret. I must ponder on this. I must decide whether or how it should be acted upon.'

'I understand, my lord, and I give you my word.'

'Thank you, Bishop. You have done right to tell me.'

When the Bishop had left Richard stared in front of him visualising the prospect ahead of him.

Jane Shore was happier than she had been since the death of the King. It was a revelation to her that she was actually beginning

394

to care about the man she had intended to dupe and who for years she had deeply resented. But Hastings was very different from that brash young man who had tried to abduct her. She had become an obsession with him over the years when he had watched her with the King and realised her qualities. Now he was finding that kindliness, that gentle wit, all her outstanding beauty was for him.

His friends laughed. Hastings has settled down, they said. His wife, Katherine Neville, daughter of the Earl of Salisbury had long been indifferent to his philanderings. They had had three sons and a daughter so the marriage could be called successful after a fashion. They did not attempt to interfere with each other's way of life and Hastings had been closer to the King than to anyone else on earth. Edward had even said that when they died they should be buried side by side so that, good friends that they had always been in life – apart from that one occasion when the Woodvilles had sought to sow discord between them and had quickly discovered that it was useless – they should not be parted in death.

Jane talked to him a great deal about the Queen. She was rather sad about her; Hastings believed her conscience worried her. Had she wronged the Queen by taking her husband from her? Hastings laughed at that. Edward had had many mistresses and the fact that Jane had been his favourite had not harmed the Queen in any way.

The King was in the Palace of the Tower and no one whom he wished to see was prevented from seeing him – except his mother and his brother and sisters who were in Sanctuary. No one prevented them but what would have happened to them if they had emerged was uncertain.

He was delighted to see Hastings, knowing him as his

father's best friend. He did know that his mother did not like Hastings but he had a vague idea that it was due to the fact that they went out a great deal together drinking and carousing with women. It was understandable. But all the same Edward could not help being attracted by Hastings.

Hastings had a similar charm to that of the late King. He was good-looking, easy to talk to and made a young King who was not very sure of himself feel absolutely comfortable in his presence. He was very different from his Uncle Gloucester who was so serious always and made him feel at a disadvantage. Mistress Jane Shore visited him too. No one stopped her and he had always liked Jane. She was always so merry and at the same time she seemed to understand that he grew tired quickly and that when his gums bled and his teeth hurt he was a little irritable.

Jane would say: 'Oh it's those old gums again is it. Not really our King who scowls at me?'

She understood that he didn't want to be miserable but he couldn't help it; and that made him feel a great deal better.

'I wish I could see my mother,' he said. 'I wish she would come here. Why does she have to hide herself away?'

'I could go and see her in the Sanctuary and tell her you want to see her.'

'Would you, Jane?'

'But of course. There is nothing to stop my visiting her.'

'I am the King. I should be the one to say who goes where.'

'You will in time.'

'Anyone would think my uncle Richard was the King. I wish my brother Richard would come here. We could play together and I wouldn't be so lonely.'

'I will go to Sanctuary and tell them what you say,' Jane promised him.

Later she talked to Hastings about the sadness of the little King. 'Poor child, for he is nothing more, to be there in the Tower with all that ceremony! I don't think he enjoys his kingship very much. He would rather be with his family. I know you don't like the Woodvilles, William, but they are devoted to each other.'

Hastings was thoughtful. He did not like the Woodvilles. They had always been his enemies and particularly so since Edward had bestowed the Captaincy of Calais upon him. If they could have done so they would have destroyed him. He had supported Gloucester because he was so strongly against the Woodvilles, and he had thought he would be Gloucester's right-hand man as he had been Edward's. But Buckingham had arrived – Buckingham who had never done anything before this day. And now here he was firmly beside the Protector so that everyone else was relegated to the background.

Hastings was turning more and more against Gloucester with every day. Perhaps Jane had something to do with this. She liked the Woodvilles; she had this ridiculous notion that she owed something to the Queen because she had taken her husband. The Woodvilles were powerful even though Rivers and Richard Grey were in prison, Dorset in exile and the Queen and her family in Sanctuary.

Then it began to dawn on Hastings – with a little prompting from Jane – that as by siding with Gloucester against them he had promoted Gloucester, so perhaps he could relegate Gloucester to a secondary place by supporting the Woodvilles. His visits to the young King showed him clearly where the boy's sympathies lay. The King wanted to be with his family; he trusted his family; he had been brought up by Woodvilles to believe in their greatness and goodness and he had learned his lessons well. Any who wanted to be friends with the King would have to be friends with the Woodvilles.

This last decided Hastings. He had finished with Gloucester who had taken Buckingham so strongly to his side so that there was room for no one else, although but for him the King would have been crowned before Gloucester even knew of his brother's death. Very well, he would turn to the Woodvilles. He would feel his way with them and the first thing would be to let the Queen know of his change of heart.

'If I went to the Sanctuary it would be noticed at once,' said Hastings. 'Gloucester would hear of it and I should be under arrest in no time.'

'I have promised the King that I will visit his mother,' said Jane. 'Why should I not take some communication from you?'

So it was arranged, and Jane Shore paid frequent visits to the Sanctuary.

Elizabeth was delighted to see her, to have news of the King, and to receive the information that Hastings was turning away from Gloucester and was ready to side with her and her family filled her with hope.

William Catesby was talking earnestly to the Duke of Gloucester. Richard trusted Catesby; there was a sincerity about the man which he had noticed from the first; he was well versed in the law and could offer useful advice on that subject. It was men such as Catesby and Ratcliffe that Richard liked to gather about him.

He was uneasy about Hastings. The fact that Hastings had taken Jane Shore as his mistress seemed somewhat shocking to Richard. Although he had always been dismayed by his brother's

398

way of life and thought that side of his nature to be a flaw in the idol, he had accepted it with Edward; he could not quite do so with Hastings. He himself had lived a comparatively virtuous life – he had been faithful since his marriage and it was only before that that he had had a mistress and two illegitimate children.

He knew that he had to make allowances but Hastings had been licentious and revelled in that state; he had, the Queen had always said, led the late King into wild sexual adventures. And now that he was with Jane Shore who had already passed through Dorset's hands, Richard felt quite disgusted.

This had made him turn away from Hastings. He did not really want the man in his councils. He liked him personally. Hastings was a man who knew how to charm; he was influential but he had to be treated with care.

Now here was Catesby with a disturbing story.

Catesby had worked close to Hastings. It was Hastings who had been a kind of patron to him, who had helped him in his career; he had advanced him considerably in the counties of Northampton and Leicestershire and Hastings it was who had first brought him to Richard's notice.

Richard had liked him immediately and given him a place in his councils. Now it was very disturbing that Catesby should be talking in this way to him of Hastings.

Hastings trusted Catesby. Hastings was a little like the late King in the way he accepted what he wanted to, and looked the other way if something displeased him.

Hastings should not be so trusting.

Catesby was saying that he could not believe this was really true, but he feared it was. Hastings was in communication with the Queen.

'How so?' asked Richard.

'By way of Jane Shore. She visits the Queen in Sanctuary. I have watched her. I have paid people in the Sanctuary to listen to what is said between the Queen and Mistress Shore.'

'And Hastings?'

'My lord, he is ready to betray you, to take sides with the Woodvilles, to get the Queen out of Sanctuary and rouse the people to the side of the King. The King thinks his mother and uncle can do no wrong.'

'I know that well,' said Richard. 'He has made that obvious to me.'

'Hastings has hinted to me what is in his mind,' said Catesby. 'He trusts me. He looks on me as his man. My lord, I owe my allegiance to you . . . not to Hastings. Thus I have undertaken the painful task of telling you what is in his mind and what I have discovered about him.'

'It is a grievous shock to me,' said Richard. 'I trusted Hastings. He was my brother's best friend.'

'My lord you should trust him no more.'

'Rest assured I shall not, and when I have discovered that there is indeed a plot I shall know how to act.'

Catesby said: 'Then I have done my duty.'

'I thank you. This shall be dealt with. And in the meantime watch for me. Let me know if there is anything more passing between them. Find out all you can of how Hastings conducts himself.'

Catesby swore that he would.

After he had left Buckingham called on Richard and was told what Catesby had revealed. Buckingham listened intently.

'Hastings was always a fool,' he said. 'There is only one way to deal with traitors even if they are fools.'

'So thought I,' said Richard. 'But there is more to discover yet. Buckingham, there is something else of great moment that I would say to you. Stillington has been to me with a strange revelation. He says that my brother was not indeed married to Elizabeth Woodville.'

'Can this really be so?'

'So says he. He married my brother to Lady Eleanor Butler,'

'By God! Old Shrewsbury's daughter. Eleanor was my cousin – my sister's daughter. She would have been more suitable to be Queen of England than the Woodville woman.'

'Yes, you are right. Eleanor Butler went into a convent and died there, but several years after my brother's so called marriage with Elizabeth Woodville.'

'Then, Richard, you are King of England.'

'It would seem so . . . if Stillington speaks truth.'

'Why should he not speak truth?'

'These are weighty matters. They must be proved.'

'By God, they must be. And when they are . . . This is good news. We shall have a mature king, a king who knows how to govern. There will be no regency . . . no protectorate . . . no boy King. It is an answer from Heaven.'

'Not so fast, my lord. First we must prove it. There is much to be done. What I fear more than anything is to plunge this country into civil war. We have had enough of that. We want no more wars.'

'But you must be proclaimed King.'

'Not yet. Let us wait. Let it be proved. Let us test the mood of the people.'

'The people will acclaim their true King.'

'We must first make sure that they are ready to do so.'

Richard stared ahead of him. He had let out the secret. That it would have tremendous consequences he had no doubt.

It was a devastating discovery. Men such as Buckingham could act rashly. Buckingham's idea was that Richard should immediately claim the throne. It was what Buckingham would have done had he been in Richard's position. As a matter of fact Buckingham himself believed that he had claim to the throne – a flimsy one it was true but he made it clear sometimes that he was aware of it.

Richard found himself in a quandary. He wanted to be in command because he knew he was capable of ruling. He had proved that by the order he had kept in the North. He wanted to keep the country prosperous and at peace and the last thing he wanted was a civil war.

The young King disliked him more every day and one of the main reasons was that he was imprisoning Lord Rivers and Richard Grey, and the fact that his mother was in Sanctuary. Young Edward blamed Gloucester for this, which was logical enough; but the King did not understand that his mother and his maternal relations would ruin the country if they ever came to complete power. Lord Rivers was indeed a charming man; he had become a champion in the jousts, he had all the Woodville good looks; he was quite saintly when he remembered to be but he was as avaricious as the rest of the family and he wanted to govern the King. That was what all the Woodvilles wanted. So did Richard for that matter. The difference was that Edward the Fourth had appointed his brother as Protector and guardian of the King for he knew – as Richard knew – that Richard alone was capable of governing the country in the wise strong way which the late King had followed.

Yet the King disliked his uncle. The only way in which

Richard could win his regard was by freeing the Woodvilles and to do that he would have to become one of them. There were so many of them and they had gathered so much power and riches during Edward's lifetime that they would absorb him. He would become a minor figure. He would in fact become a follower of the Woodvilles. It would mean too that he would have to sacrifice his friends – Buckingham, Northumberland, Catesby, Ratcliffe . . . It was unthinkable. He . . . a Plantagenet to become a hanger-on of the Woodvilles!

The alternative to all this was to take power himself. It seemed to him that he had every right to do this. In the first place he had been appointed by his brother to be the Protector of the Realm and the young King. And now Stillington had come along with this revelation. If it were indeed true that his brother had not been legally married to Elizabeth Woodville he, Richard of Gloucester, was the true King of England.

He could take power with a free conscience. If the people would accept him as their King, he could prevent civil war. He could rule in peace as his brother had done. It was his duty to take the crown. It was also becoming his dearest wish.

But he must go carefully. He had rarely ever been rash. He liked to weigh up a situation, decide on how to act, then consider the consequences – the good and the bad for there were invariably good and bad in all matters.

This marriage with Eleanor Butler would have to be proved. Its consequences would be so overwhelming that there must be no hurrying into a decision on it. He must have time to think on it.

In the meantime there were other pressing matters to be dealt with. Hastings, for instance. Hastings had great power. He had believed him to be loyal. Hastings had warned him of the King's death and the need to come prepared to London. That had stood him in great stead. Without that warning he might not have heard of his brother's death until after young Edward's coronation and that would have been too late. He owed something to Hastings.

Yet Hastings was in touch with Elizabeth Woodville; he had seen the King. Jane Shore took messages to the Sanctuary. They were plotting against him. Richard hated disloyalty more than anything. He had chosen his motto 'Loyalty binds me' because it meant so much to him.

If Hastings were deceiving him, he deserved to die, and die he must, for he would be the link between the King and the Woodvilles and if his conspiracy were allowed to proceed it could be the end of Richard. They would have no compunction in beheading him, he knew. They hated and feared him; and the King could give his ready consent.

There must be prompt action. He sent for Richard Ratcliffe, a man whom he trusted. Ratcliffe had been Comptroller of King Edward's household and his efficient management of affairs had aroused Richard's interest in him. He came from Lancashire and Richard knew his family in the North. He was a man he trusted.

'I want you to ride with all speed to York. Take this letter from me and it is to be put into the hands of the Mayor. I want him to raise men and come south to assist me, and to do so with all speed.'

He had written that he needed men and arms to assist him against the Queen and her blood adherents and affinity who, he was assured, intended to destroy him and his cousin the Duke of Buckingham, as the old royal blood of the realm.

'This,' said Richard, 'is of the utmost importance. Delay could cost me my life. Impress this on my good friends in the North.'

'I will do this, my lord, and leave at once.'

Richard Ratcliffe took the letters and set off.

But Richard of Gloucester knew that he could not afford to wait for help from the North.

It was Friday, the thirteenth of June, two days after Ratcliffe had left for the North. The Protector had summoned the Council to assemble in the Tower for a meeting. There was nothing strange about this for meetings at this time occurred frequently and the Tower was usually chosen for them to take place.

Among those who were to attend were Archbishop Rotherham, Morton Bishop of Ely, Lord Stanley and Lord Hastings.

Richard knew exactly what he had to do.

It was going to be extremely distasteful, but it had to be done. It was either that or his own head and disaster for England as he saw it. So he must not shirk his duty. His brother had not when it came to the point. Clarence had signed his death warrant when he had taunted Edward with the illegitimacy of his children.

Edward had been strong, as Richard must be.

It was a beautiful morning. The sun dappled the water of the Thames as his barge bore him along. He alighted and looked back along the river and then turned to face the Tower. The King was there . . . in the Palace. He must remain there until the Protector had decided how best to act.

He met Bishop Morton as he was about to enter the council chamber. He was affable though in his heart he was deeply suspicious of the Bishop. A staunch Lancastrian who had changed sides and served Edward of York when it was expedient to do so. Richard could never like such men; he would have had more respect for him if he had refused to serve Edward and had gone into exile. Not the ambitious Bishop. He was very comfortable in his palace in Ely Place, where he had the most magnificent gardens.

'I hear your strawberries are particularly fine this year, Bishop,' said Richard.

'That's so, my lord. The weather has been right for them.'

'I trust you will give me an opportunity to sample them.'

'My lord, it will be an honour. I will have them sent to Crosby Place. I doubt not the Lady Anne will like them.'

'Thank you, Bishop.'

Stanley, Rotherham and Hastings had arrived. They all looked relaxed. It was clear that they had no notion yet as to what was about to take place.

Richard veiled the distaste he felt on beholding Hastings. He must have come straight from Jane Shore. He looked jaunty, younger than of late. He was clearly enjoying the company of the late King's favourite mistress.

The council meeting proceeded and after a while Richard said: 'My lords, will you continue without me for a while. There is something to which I have to attend. I shall be with you ere long.' That was the first intimation the members of the Council had that morning that something strange might be afoot. That Richard should suddenly leave them in this way was unusual. It was almost as though he were preparing himself for some ordeal and wished to steel himself before attempting it.

Hastings was thinking that although Richard appeared to be cool he had seemed a little preoccupied. For instance he had not glanced Hastings's way since he had appeared. But there was all that chat about Morton's strawberries. That was natural enough. Hastings thought: I imagined this. It is because of Jane. She was worried because he was getting very deeply involved in the conspiracy with the Queen.

Richard had come back. He looked quite different from the man who had left the council chamber. His face was white; there was a look of bitter determination in his eyes.

He spoke quietly but firmly. 'My lords, you know well who it was whom my brother set up as guardian of his son, do you not?'

'Indeed yes, my lord. It was you . . . his brother.'

'That is true. But there are traitors who would deprive me of my rights . . . who would destroy me. What punishment would they deserve who are guilty of this?'

No one spoke. They were all so astonished, taken off their guard as they were.

'You do not answer me. My lord Hastings, what think you?'

'Well, my lord, if any have done this they deserve to be punished.'

'Whoever they be, my lord Hastings, whoever they be? I will tell you who have sought to do this to me. I will name these traitors. They have plotted against me . . . The Queen is one . . . and Jane Shore, my brother's mistress, is another. These two have worked together . . . against me.'

Hastings felt limp with fear at the mention of Jane's name. He knew what was coming. He knew her visits to the Sanctuary had been remarked on. Gloucester *knew* . . .

It had happened too suddenly for him to think clearly. He could only stare at the fierce eyes of the Protector glowing in his pale face.

'Now, if these women have conspired against me then they

are traitors . . . What should be the fate of traitors?' There was silence round the table. Everyone's eyes were on Gloucester. He had turned to Hastings.

'You are silent, my lord. Tell us what should be the fate of these . . . traitors.'

Hastings forced himself to speak. 'If they have done these things and if they can be proved against them . . .' he began.

Richard turned to him. 'You answer me with your ifs and your ands. I tell you this, they *have* done it. And you have been with them in this treachery !' He struck his fist on the table with such violence that all those watching drew back in their seats. 'I will make good on your body, my lord Hastings.'

There was a moment of silence. For half a second Richard wavered. He looked at Hastings. He had been fond of this man who had been Edward's greatest friend. Edward had found great pleasure in his company. But that made the remedy ever more necessary. Hastings had known that Edward had appointed him; and yet he was ready to play the traitor not only to Richard but to Edward.

There must be no softening; he must be strong. Everything depended on how he acted at this time.

He looked steadily at Hastings.

'I swear I will not dine until your head is severed from your body. You are a traitor, Hastings, and the reward of traitors should be death.'

He rapped on the table. It was the sign he had told the guards to wait for. They came in shouting: 'Treason.'

Richard looked at the guards and the ashen faces of the men about the table.

'Arrest these men,' cried Richard, indicating Rotherham, Morton and Stanley.

Take them away. But not my lord Hastings. No . . . not my lord Hastings. You, traitor, shall die now.'

It was the signal. The guards seized the four men. Rotherham and Morton were taken to lodgings in the Tower; Stanley went to his home under guard; but Hastings was conducted at once to the Green and a priest was found for him so that he could hastily be shriven.

Hastings, bewildered still, stood on the Green. It was so sudden. This morning he had said adieu to Jane, now his loving mistress, just as he had always wanted her to be – telling her he would soon be with her.

He had been happy. He was dabbling with conspiracy it was true but that added a certain zest to his life. He had been reckless; he had been foolish; he had never liked the Woodvilles. He saw how foolish he had been to think of throwing in his lot with them. Gloucester was a strong man. Edward had seen that when he had named him as Protector.

And now, this was the reward of his folly. This was the end.

There was no executioner's block but men had been working at the Tower and they found a piece of wood which would serve.

The soft and balmy air caressed his face as Hastings laid his head on the hastily improvised block and died.

The cries of treason had been heard in the city and the apprentices had come running into the streets brandishing any weapon they could lay their hands on, while the merchants were prepared to protect their shops, and the mayor was ready to marshal his forces. If there was treason in the air, if there were to be battles then London must protect itself.

Richard immediately sent a herald into the streets who rode along sounding his trumpet and asking the people to listen to what he had to tell them. There was no cause for alarm. All that had happened was that a conspiracy had been discovered and those responsible had received their just rewards. Lord Hastings had plotted to destroy the Protector and the Duke of Buckingham and had himself been beheaded. All knew that Hastings had lured the late King to live licentiously and Hastings was at this time the lover of the late King's mistress Jane Shore – a whore and a witch; he had been with Jane Shore on the previous night and the woman was disclosed as one involved in the conspiracy.

'Put away your weapons, good citizens,' cried the herald. 'Danger has been averted by the prompt action of the Protector.'

The Londoners were delighted to do this. Trouble they did not want. But the crowds stayed in the streets to ask themselves what would happen next. It was an uneasy situation. A King who was a minor was always a source of trouble. The Queen was in Sanctuary and the Woodvilles in decline. That was good. The Londoners had never liked the rapacious Woodvilles. There was the Lord Protector who had proved himself a worthy ruler in the North to look after the country.

'If the Lord Protector took the crown,' said some, 'it would not be a bad thing.'

'There is the little King,' replied some of the women.

'Little Kings cause trouble,' was the answer.

But they were all delighted that there was to be no fighting in the streets.

Richard immediately called a meeting of the Council to

explain the reason for his prompt action. It was always dangerous to execute men without trial.

There was not a man among them who did not realise the need for prompt action. Many of them knew that Hastings had deviated from his loyalty to Richard; they knew too of his association with Jane Shore and it was a fact that the goldsmith's wife visited the King and the Queen. It was all very plausible. Gloucester had done what any strong man would.

Richard was anxious to show that he bore no personal venom towards Hastings. The late King had asked that Hastings be buried beside him so Richard ordered that the body should be taken to Windsor and there buried close to Edward in that chapel of St George's which Edward had started to build and which was as yet incomplete. As for Hastings's widow, Katherine, she should not be deprived of her goods, and Richard would take her under his protection.

Jane Shore, he said, was of little importance robbed of her protectors. She was a harlot and as such should do penance and be deprived of her possessions. He would pass her over to the Church which could decide what her penance should be, and when it was performed she should be forgotten. He would take no action against her. She had been loved by his brother and he would remember that. The penance and the loss of the goods his brother and others had bestowed on her would be punishment enough.

Now to more serious business.

Elizabeth Woodville must be persuaded to come out of Sanctuary. If she would do this she could reside with the King and he and the Duke of York could be together as they wished; and so could the King's daughters.

If, however, the Queen refused to leave Sanctuary – and she

could not be forced to do so – then the Duke of York must be taken from her.

The Council agreed that the choice should be put to her.

There was a great deal of rumour flying round not only London but the entire country.

First there was the spectacle of Jane Shore's walking through the streets barefooted wrapped in a worsted robe, a lighted taper in her hand.

It was the ultimate degradation. They had sought to humiliate her and this they had done indeed.

She was stricken with grief. She blamed herself for the death of Hastings. She had brought him into the conspiracy with the Queen. But for her he would be alive today.

She could see the people as she walked; they crowded about her, eyes filled with curiosity, with malice, and with pleasure! They had envied her once when she was the adored mistress of the King. They had cheered her often. She had always tried to do what she could for the people. They had known it and loved her for it. But on occasions like these it was not those people who came out to gloat; it was the malicious, the envious, those who considered themselves virtuous.

'Harlot,' they called her. Well, she supposed she was. A whore was not a better one because she was a King's whore.

No. She had loved the King; she had loved Hastings. The goldsmith . . . no she had never loved him but she had been forced into that marriage by her father. The relationship with Dorset had not been a good one. She was ashamed of that. But where was Dorset now . . . plotting somewhere against the Protector.

The Protector despised her. She believed he always had. She knew he had deplored the King's fondness for her. The Protector was cold, aloof but just, she believed. He might have sentenced her to death himself instead of handing her over to the Bishop of London.

She was sure that remembering his brother's fondness for her he had been lenient.

This horror would pass.

Her feet were bleeding for the cobbles were sharp; she was aware of the eyes that followed her. Into the Cathedral she went with her taper; and then out once more to make confession at Paul's Cross.

Eyes watched her. All marvelled at her; because she who had so much had sunk so low.

Jane was desolate. Edward was gone; Hastings was gone. What was there left for her?

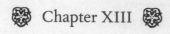

Chapter XIII

'MY LIFE WAS LENT'

It was three days since the death of Hastings. The Council had decided that a proposition must be put to the Queen. With an armed guard they rode up the river to Westminster.

It was decided that the Archbishop of Canterbury, Thomas Bourchier, should head the deputation to the Queen and that Lord Howard should go with him.

Richard and Buckingham would await their return in the Palace.

Elizabeth received them with great misgiving. She had heard of Hastings's execution and that Jane Shore had been set to do penance; she had also heard that Jane had been deprived of her worldly goods.

It was a great setback. Elizabeth had been hoping for a great deal from an alliance with Hastings. She and he had always been such great enemies and the fact that he had sought a reconciliation had been particularly pleasing to her.

Elizabeth had always enjoyed intrigue, and from the moment she and her mother had set out to capture the King and succeeded in doing so, she had believed she had a special talent for it.

She had looked forward to Jane Shore's visits and now of course someone had betrayed them.

She wondered what this deputation meant. That it was of the greatest importance was obvious from the presence of the Archbishop of Canterbury.

He greeted her with respect as indeed he should. Was she not the mother of the King? How she longed to see her son; and how comforting it had been when Jane had brought her messages from him.

The Archbishop came straight to the point.

'My lady, it is the wish of the Protector that you emerge from Sanctuary,' he said. 'You need have no fear. You have the Duke of Gloucester's word that you shall be treated as the mother of the King.'

Elizabeth lifted her head and her eyes glittered.

'What of my brother, Lord Rivers? Richard of Gloucester has imprisoned him. For what reason?'

'My lady, you must know that your brother Lord Rivers and your son Lord Richard Grey attempted to take the King from the Protector. They withheld from him the news of the King's death. It is for this reason that they are now his captives.'

'As I should be if I came out of Sanctuary.'

'That is not so, my lady. You have not committed these offences.'

'I do not trust the Duke of Gloucester.'

'He prides himself on keeping his word. He promised the late King that he would guard his son and that is what he is determined to do.'

'I am the King's mother. It is for me to guard him.'

Bourchier bowed his head and started again. 'The Protector

offers you an alternative. Come out of Sanctuary or deliver to me the Duke of York.'

'Deliver him to you! Why? He is a child. He should be with his mother.'

'His brother is asking for him. He wants him to join him in his apartments in the Tower.'

'I shall not let him go.'

'My lady, you have no alternative. Either you must come out of Sanctuary with your son and daughters – and the Protector promises that if you do you will be treated with the respect due to your rank – or you must deliver up the Duke of York.'

Elizabeth was silent. She did not want to lose her son; on the other hand dared she emerge from Sanctuary? Her great hope lay in trying to raise an insurrection against the Protector which she had thought possible through Hastings.

She must stay in Sanctuary.

What if she let the little Duke go? He would be with his brother. Poor child, he would hate to leave her and his sisters, but he would be going to his brother . . . and it would be good for Edward to have his little brother with him.

Should she leave Sanctuary so that they could all be together? It was what her maternal feelings told her she should do. She knew Gloucester well enough to know that he would not be harsh with her unless she deliberately plotted against him. In truth he had been lenient with Jane Shore. He suspected her of plotting; she had indeed brought messages from Hastings; some would have had her head for that. Penance and confiscation had been enough for Gloucester.

No, he would not be hard on her. He would remember his

brother's affection for her and for that reason he would be kind.

She should leave Sanctuary.

No . . . no . . . that would be the end of hope. She would be safer in here.

She would have to let Richard go.

It was a fateful decision. In later years she often thought of it and wondered what would have happened to her sons if she had left Sanctuary at that time and kept all the family with her.

She sent for Richard. He came running to her. He was a charming little boy, more healthy than his elder brother and of a merry disposition. Poor Edward was often tired, suffering as he did from that strange disease of the bones which, said the doctors, prevented them growing as they should normally. Poor little King, he would never be like his father. It was different with Richard, he was a healthy, normal boy.

'Richard, my little one,' she said to him, putting her arms round him and holding him close to her, 'you are going to see Edward.'

'Oh, my lady, when do we go? Now?'

'We are not going. I and your sisters have to stay here. It is just you who are going.'

'Is Edward coming back to us?'

'No, you are going to stay with Edward.'

'When are you coming?'

'That, sweetheart, I cannot say. It will depend on your uncle.'

'I don't like my uncle.'

'Dearest, none of us do but for a while we have to do as he says.' She held him to her and whispered in his ear. 'It won't always be so. Now you have to go with the Archbishop and he

417

will take you to Edward and you will be able to shoot your arrows together.'

Richard smiled. 'I can shoot further than Edward,' he said.

'Well, you must remember that he is not so well as you are. You will always remember that, won't you?'

'Yes, my lady. But you will come and be with us soon, won't you, and Elizabeth . . . and Cecily . . .'

'As soon as I can I shall be there. You don't think I like being separated from my boys, do you?'

'No, dear Mother, you do not. And you hate . . .'

'Hush . . . Not before these gentlemen.'

The boy put his arms round her neck and whispered: 'Dear Mother, I don't like them much either.'

'This is the Archbishop of Canterbury, my love, and Lord Howard. They are going to take care of you.' She lifted pleading eyes to the Archbishop. 'You will take care of him, my lord? I want your promise.'

'I give it, my lady. I pledge my life for the Prince's safety.'

'Then take him and remember those words. Goodbye, my little one. Say goodbye to your sisters. You are going to be with your brother and I shall be thinking of you both so dearly. Tell him that, will you?'

'Yes, dear lady, I will.'

'And remember it yourself.'

The little boy flung his arms about her. 'I do not want to leave you, dear Mother. I want to stay with you. I don't want to go to Edward even . . .'

She held him tightly and looked appealingly at the Archbishop, who shook his head.

'You could go with him, my lady,' he reminded her.

So she was torn again. She must stay. She dared not go out. How could she know what would happen to her? If she were ever going to regain her hold over her eldest son she must stay in Sanctuary and relinquish his younger brother.

'Dearest baby, you must go. You must be brave, my love. We shall all be together soon. Edward is lonely for you.'

'Yes, dear Mother.'

She kissed him tenderly and sent for his sisters who took their leave of him.

And then the Archbishop took the little boy by the hand and led him out of Sanctuary.

That day he entered the Tower to be with his brother.

In his prison at Sheriff Hutton Lord Rivers heard occasional scraps of news as to what was happening throughout the country. That the Protector was in command was obvious. It had been a masterly stroke to arrest him at Northampton for it had given Gloucester a free hand with the King.

Yet how near the Woodvilles had come to success. Once the King had been crowned none could have taken charge of him, young as he was, and Edward was well enough primed to insist on keeping his Woodville relations about him. That would have been the end of the Protector. He would either have had to join the Woodvilles, and quite clearly become an inferior member of the party, or go back to the north. No, that would have been too dangerous. Gloucester had the north with him. It would very likely have been his head for he – Plantagenet that he was – would never have taken a subsidiary role with the Woodvilles.

Oh yes, a master stroke. But then Gloucester was a master

at the art of strategy and justice. Edward had thought more highly of him than of anyone else. Elizabeth knew that and had always resented it; but she had realised there was no one to change the King's opinion and that he would have turned against her if she had tried to.

Gloucester was indeed capable of governing, Rivers conceded that. But oh how the Woodvilles longed to!

And he, Rivers, was at the head of the family. He would have been chief adviser to the King.

Gloucester knew it; that was why Rivers's fate was inevitable.

Of course Gloucester might have had his head on the spot as he had Hastings's. That would not have been wise. He might have had the country against him if he had. He wanted to go cautiously, which he had done. He had by the arrest of Rivers and Grey taken over the King; he had delayed the coronation; he had set himself up as Protector, and as the last thing the people wanted was a bloody conflict, for heaven knows they had had enough of that with the Wars of the Roses, they had accepted him. They saw in him a good and steady ruler, and that was what they wanted.

So now there was only one logical fate which could possibly await Rivers. The only question was when would it come, and he guessed it was at hand when the Earl of Northumberland arrived at Sheriff Hutton.

The trial was brief. He was accused of treason and condemned.

It would not have been so easy for them to find him guilty if a quantity of arms had not been found in his baggage which indicated clearly that he was ready to do battle.

He spent his last night in making his will, praying and writing poetry.

'My life was lent
Me to one intent.
It is nigh spent.
Welcome fortune . . .'

He wrote and found some pleasure in musing and writing
down how Fortune had treated him and at last brought him to
the state in which he now found himself.

He had been told that he would be taken to Pontefract
where Richard Grey was being held and Thomas Vaughan
would be brought there from Middleham, so that they should
all lose their heads in the same place on the same day.

Lord Rivers then asked that he might be buried beside his
nephew, Lord Richard Grey.

The request was granted and on the twenty-fourth day of
June Lord Rivers, Lord Richard Grey and Sir Thomas
Vaughan were beheaded at Pontefract.

🏵 Chapter XIV 🏵

KING RICHARD THE THIRD

Buckingham was growing impatient. A volatile man, impulsive, always seeking excitement, he wanted events to move fast and if they appeared to lag he was always ready to act in such a way as to speed them on.

Richard told him of Stillington's revelation and Buckingham now suggested that Richard should make this known to the people and then take the crown.

This was a big step which Richard had had in mind for some time, but he hesitated to take it. In the first place it seemed disloyal to the brother whom he had revered for to declare his sons illegitimate would have enraged the late King. On the other hand he must have known the truth – who more than he? And he had had Clarence despatched when Stillington had let the truth slip to him; and Stillington himself had been imprisoned in the Tower.

It was the truth and the fact was that Edward the Fifth had no right to the throne.

The trouble with the country now was that there were rival factions conspiring against each other which was due to the minority of the King. But if the true King were proved to be a grown man, a man who had the ability to govern, what a boon that would be for the country!

Buckingham was right. He should state the truth and tell the people; then he would be proclaimed Richard the Third.

It would save the country from possible civil war – and the country had had enough of that.

He discussed the matter with Buckingham; he pondered the position deeply. It was right that the truth should be known. It was best for the country.

How should the secret be revealed?

'Let the Lord Mayor of London make the announcement from Paul's Cross,' suggested Buckingham. 'The Londoners will listen to their Lord Mayor as to none other and Sir Edmund Shaa is a good man for the job.'

'My brother knew him well and thought highly of him.'

'Indeed he did. Shaa is a prosperous goldsmith and you know how your brother liked such men. Didn't he find Jane in a goldsmith's shop? Shaa is a member of the Goldsmiths' Company and now Lord Mayor, so let us see him and tell him what is required of him.'

'Yes,' said Richard. 'Send for him.'

Sir Edmund Shaa came to Baynard's Castle for the Protector had moved there from Crosby Place about the time when young Edward had taken up residence in the Tower.

Shaa listened. He had known the late King at the time of his obsession with Eleanor Butler and he could well believe that a marriage had taken place. Yes, he saw that if that were so, the true King was Richard and what a good thing it would be for the country if this was generally accepted to be the case.

'There is another matter,' he said. 'I had heard that your brothers, Edward the King and George Duke of Clarence, were not the sons of the Duke of York, and that so incensed was the Duchess of York when the King married Elizabeth Woodville that she said she would make it known that she had taken a lover while the Duke was away on his many campaigns and that Edward and George were the result of this liaison.'

Richard shook his head, but Buckingham was excited. 'It strengthens the case,' he said. 'Both the late King and his son bastards! My lord, we have to think of the country. We want a good case. We must end this strife, for if it goes on it could well result in civil war.'

'That,' said Richard, 'must be stopped at all events. England is more important than anything. A boy King is the biggest danger which can threaten us.'

Buckingham nodded to Sir Edmund. This was tantamount to the Protector's consent to give the full details at Paul's Cross.

Buckingham was exultant. The plot was going to work. Within a few days Richard would be proclaimed King of England.

'I would not wish it without the people's consent,' said Richard.

'My lord, they will be begging you to take the crown.'

From St Paul's Cross the Lord Mayor spoke to the people. He had grave news for them. A great discovery had been made. The little King who had not yet been crowned as Edward the Fifth was not the true King after all. King Edward the Fourth had already been married when he went through a form of marriage with Elizabeth Woodville.

This had been proved and the King's real wife was none

other than the Lady Eleanor Butler, daughter of the Earl of Shrewsbury — a lady of higher rank than Queen Elizabeth Woodville at the time of her mock marriage. Of course everyone knew how the Woodvilles had risen since that time but let the people consider, they owed their rise to a ceremony which was invalid and should never have been performed at all. The truth was that the young boy whom they called King Edward the Fifth was a bastard and therefore should never have been called King.

There was only one true King of England. They knew him well. He had done good service in the North and held back the Scots. He had served his country and brother with absolute loyalty and devotion. And he was the true King of England.

There was one other matter. Edward himself had been a bastard. The Duchess of York had taken occasional lovers during her husband's frequent absences. Both Edward the late King and George Duke of Clarence were bastards. The Duchess herself had threatened to reveal this at the time the late Edward the Fourth went through a form of marriage with Elizabeth Woodville, so shocked had she been that one of what she called such low birth should marry her son. She did not, however, for that would have meant exposing her own dishonour; but now that the King — and make no mistake he had been a great and good King — was dead, they need not despair. What was past was done with. They had a new King, one who had proved his ability to serve them well.

They had King Richard the Third.

There was silence in the crowds about Paul's Cross. This was the most astounding revelation and if anyone but their Lord Mayor had made it they would have thought he was a madman.

The King married already! The little King a bastard! And those slanderous things they were saying about the Duchess of York!

They wanted to get away to talk together. It was astounding. They did not believe it.

Sir Edmund Shaa watched them walking away, whispering together.

In Baynard's Castle Buckingham and Richard discussed the people's reactions.

'What did their silence mean?' asked Richard.

'That they were shocked of course. Although we have heard the rumours they had not. They will take a little time to get used to the idea.'

'I like it not,' said Richard. 'The announcement should never have been made. I liked not the slander against my mother. I'll swear it is a lie.'

'The important thing is the King's pre-contract. You believe that, I'm sure.'

'I do.'

'Stillington must be brought forward to show proof.'

'There is no proof. Only Stillington's word.'

'What reason should he have to lie?'

'He might think it would bring him advancement in a new reign.'

'He would never dare to lie in such a matter. We must strike again quickly. I will take some of my men with lords and knights to the Guildhall on Tuesday. There I will make a declaration. The people will have crowded into the hall and will have assembled outside. There I shall state the facts again.'

'I forbid you to mention my mother.'

'There is no need to. All that matters is that the boy is known as a bastard, and that you are the rightful King of the realm.'

Buckingham went to the Guildhall as he had said he would. There he spoke with the utmost eloquence on the situation which had arisen through the disclosure of Bishop Stillington, and when he had assessed Richard's claim to the throne, he cried out: 'Will you accept Richard of Gloucester as Richard the Third of England?'

There was a heavy pause in the crowd which as Buckingham had predicted filled the Guildhall and spilled into the streets outside.

Then some of Buckingham's men shouted from the back of the hall: 'Long Live King Richard.'

Buckingham appeared to be satisfied.

The next day the Parliament met. The facts were presented; the marriage discussed, as was the illegitimacy of Edward the Fifth and of Edward the Fourth and the Duke of Clarence. Buckingham reminded the peers that Edward had been born in Rouen and Clarence in Dublin. Richard was a true Englishman for he had seen the light of day at Fotheringay Castle in Northamptonshire. Would they agree that a deputation should be sent to Baynard's Castle and ask Richard to take the crown? They agreed and the following day, Buckingham led the deputation to the castle where Richard, with a show of reluctance, agreed to accept the crown. The reign of Edward the Fifth was over. That of Richard the Third had begun.

Anne had arrived in London with her son Edward. She was uneasy for she was sure that Edward was not fit to travel.

However, on such an occasion she must be present and so must their son, for now she was the Queen . . . Queen of England. On the journey down from Middleham her apprehension had increased. She had grown accustomed to the quiet life at Middleham; she had wished, naturally, that Richard could be with them, but since the death of his brother she had scarcely seen him. It had been something of a shock to her to learn that he had been offered the crown and for what reason.

She thought often of Queen Elizabeth Woodville and imagined her wrath at the turn events had taken. And here was she, in Elizabeth's place. She wondered what those who had departed would think if they could look back and see what was happening. She could imagine her father's delight. His daughter a queen!

Dear father, who had been good to his family when he had time for them, but he had sought the glittering prizes of life and had in time met his death. What were all those prizes worth now? But she smiled to think how he would have rejoiced to see his daughter Queen. He would have thought everything worthwhile and she wished that she could share those feelings. Alas, the prospect filled her only with misgivings.

She knew that Richard would be uneasy too. He would be a worthy King; he had the gift of governing well; but to think that he had come to power through the dishonour of his brother and his young nephew would disturb him greatly she knew.

He brought her into London by barge but as soon as he had greeted her she noticed the fresh furrows on his brow. He was delighted to see her and their son of course though the looks of both of them added to his anxieties.

She had commanded her women to brighten her complexion for she did not want to alarm Richard with her pallor. There was nothing she could do, though, to disguise the boy's wan looks.

'So,' she said, 'you are the King now. You were a mere Duke when we last met.'

'It has all happened quickly, Anne. I want to talk to you about it.'

The people cheered them as they sailed up river to Baynard's Castle. There was little time, Richard explained, for the coronation was fixed for the sixth of July.

'So soon?' cried Anne.

'Coronations should never be delayed,' answered Richard.

He talked to his son and was at least pleased with the boy's brightness. It helped to compensate for his frail health.

He sought an early opportunity of being alone with Anne for he could see that she was bewildered by the astonishing turn of events.

'You have heard the story. Young Edward was a bastard because of my brother's previous marriage.'

'The whole country talks of it.'

'Everyone of good sense wants a stable country and that cannot be with a King who is too young to govern. There are certain to be rivals – different people eager to get the King in their control. If Edward had been of age I should have subdued the fact of his bastardy for my brother's sake.'

'Yes, Richard, I believe you would.'

'It is not that I wish for the crown . . . for the arduous duties of a sovereign. Power is enticing but it brings such burdens, Anne. We were happy at Middleham, were we not?'

'So happy,' she said. 'But such happiness does not last.'

'And you are worried about the boy?'

'His health is not good.'

'We will make him Prince of Wales.'

'I do not think that will improve it.'

'Anne, he *must* get well.'

'I wish we could have more children. I'm afraid I am not a very good wife for you, Richard. You should have had someone fecund, vital . . . someone like Elizabeth Woodville.'

'God forbid. I dislike that woman as much as she dislikes me. I thought Edward demeaned himself by marrying . . . or rather going through a form of marriage with her. It was from that that all our troubles started. The Woodvilles . . . the cursed Woodvilles . . . they brought your father against my brother.'

She laid a hand on his arm. 'Richard, that is all over now. Don't let us brood on the past.'

'You are right. But let me say this one thing, Anne. I was begged by the lords to take the crown. I hesitated but I saw my duty, though if the people had raised a voice against me I would have refused.'

'Of course the people did not raise a voice against you. They want you, Richard. They want what you can give them . . . a stable, prosperous country . . . the kind they had when Edward ruled. They cannot get that without you. If it were not for you the Woodvilles would rule the country now. All know their cupidity. They had done nothing but enriched themselves since Edward made Elizabeth his Queen. They want you, Richard. They are determined to have you. And do not forget, because of Edward's previous contract, you are the rightful King.'

'I know it, Anne. It is for this reason that I have taken the crown.'

'Then, let us give our thoughts to the coronation for there is very little time.'

On the day before that fixed for the coronation ceremony the people crowded out on the river bank to see the King with his Queen and his son go by water to the Palace of the Tower.

Edward the Fifth and his brother Richard Duke of York had been transferred from the royal apartments as soon as they had been declared illegitimate and lodged in the Garden Tower. They did not, of course, attend their uncle's coronation.

There in the precincts of the Tower the son of Richard and Anne was formally created Prince of Wales, and the next day the coronation took place.

It had been short notice but as a great many preparations had been made for the coronation of Edward the Fifth it had been possible to make use of this. A coronation and its festivities would not have to change because the King to be crowned was not the same one for whom all the pomp had been originally created.

The Duke of Buckingham carried Richard's train while the Duke of Norfolk bore his crown before him. Then came the Queen with the Earl of Huntingdon bearing her sceptre and Viscount Lisle the rod with the dove while the honour of carrying her crown was assigned to the Earl of Wiltshire.

Anne, splendidly clad, weighed down with jewels, felt tired before the ceremony had begun. Walking under a canopy, to each corner of which had been attached a golden bell which tinkled as they moved, she hoped that she did not show how she was longing for it all to be over. But it had only just begun. The anointing had to take place and afterwards the crowning.

'God Save the King. God Save the Queen.'

The cries rang out clearly and Richard was straining his ears to hear one dissenting voice. There was none.

Afterwards they dined in Westminster Hall, Anne and Richard seated on a dais overlooking the rest of the guests at their tables while the Lord Mayor himself served the King and Queen with sweet wine as a sign of the capital's desire to do homage to them.

When the champion of England rode into the hall and challenged any to combat who did not agree that Richard was the rightful King, Anne was aware of her husband's tension; and when there was not a single voice raised against him, she was aware of his sinking back into his seat with an over-whelming relief; and she hoped that had silenced his fears for ever. The people had chosen him. The people wanted him. He was the rightful King; and he must stop thinking of those little boys in the Garden Tower. Their claim to the throne was null and void. The rightful King was at last crowned.

Darkness fell and the torches were brought in and one by one the nobles and their ladies came to the dais to pay homage to the King and Queen.

And when that ceremony was over they could retire to their apartments and make their preparations to depart for Windsor where they would go when the festivities were over.

Richard was already planning a tour of the country. They would go to the North. He had no fear of what his reception would be there. The North was his country. He had served it well and they were with him to a man.

Chapter XV

BUCKINGHAM

The Duke of Buckingham was displeased. The excitement which he so enjoyed had abated considerably. Richard was King and he had been accepted by a docile people. Secretly Buckingham had been hoping for trouble. He revelled in trouble. He found life dull without it.

Moreover Richard had angered him. It was over the matter of the Bohun estates. These had come to the crown on the marriage of Mary de Bohun and Henry the Fourth and now that he was Lord High Constable of England, which was the ancient hereditary office of the de Bohuns, he believed he had a right to the estates.

Instead of enthusiastically agreeing to this, Richard had demurred; and that angered Buckingham. He looked upon himself as a Warwick, a Kingmaker. Who had suggested that Richard should claim the throne? Who had made the announcement at Paul's Cross and whose men had shouted for Richard at the Guildhall? The answer to that was Buckingham's, and Richard it seemed, now he had achieved the goal, was ungrateful and was reminding him that he was King. Richard would do well to remember his old friends. In a fit of pique Buckingham left Court and decided to go for a while to his Castle Brecknock on the borders of Wales and which had come to him with his post of High Constable of England. He was looking forward to having conversation with a most interesting guest . . . well hardly a guest, a captive in fact.

He was thinking of John Morton the Bishop of Ely who had been arrested at the same time as Hastings during that fateful meeting in the Tower. Morton with Rotherham had been confined for a while in the Tower and being interested in the man – for they had love of plotting in common – Buckingham had asked Richard if he might take care of Morton. The Bishop could not stay all the time a prisoner in the Tower and his rank as churchman demanded that certain respect be shown to him, so Richard agreed that Buckingham might make him a sort of honoured captive in his castle of Brecknock.

This Buckingham had done and had become on good terms with the Bishop. He enjoyed his conversation. Morton was a clever man – shrewd and devious, and as such he appealed to Buckingham.

That he was at heart a Lancastrian, the Duke knew; he also knew that he was not averse to changing sides when expediency demanded it, but he would be pleased of course to put forward the side he really supported while he tried to live amicably with its enemies.

In spite of this he had been one of the last King's chief advisers; he had helped to arrange the treaty of Picquigny which had brought such good fortune to England at the expense of the French; he had negotiated for the ransom the King of France had paid for Margaret of Anjou. Edward had thought highly of him. Of course Edward had a habit of believing the best of everyone until their perfidy was proved.

434

Morton had gone from strength to strength until the meeting in the Tower.

That his head was full of plans, Buckingham had no doubt, and that they were not for the good of Richard the Third he was certain.

That suited him in his present mood, and so he was looking forward to seeing the Bishop at Brecknock.

When he arrived he went to the Bishop and greeted him warmly, asking if he lacked anything he needed for his comfort.

'The captive has nothing of which to complain,' the Bishop told him.

'You must not think of yourself as a prisoner, Bishop.'

'My lord Duke, you are kind. But what else am I?'

'A friend I hope.'

'I doubt a friend of Richard of Gloucester would be a friend of mine.'

Buckingham sent for wine and they drank together. The wine was good and warming and Buckingham enjoyed his wine.

The Bishop watched him closely. He knew that something had happened between the two who had been so close together. Buckingham had been Richard's first man. Now what? Morton asked himself. He felt gleeful. He summed up Buckingham – feckless, unreliable, friend today and enemy tomorrow. He was surprised Richard had put so much faith in him.

Morton had not been idle during his captivity. He had been making plans. He was going to stir up trouble for Richard of Gloucester and he felt he knew how to do it. It was not that he wanted to support the Woodvilles although he might have to make a pretence of doing so. That was not important; he was rather good at making a pretence. He had his eyes on someone over the seas, someone who could be said to belong to the House of Lancaster. Morton would like to see the red rose win the final triumph over the white. A great excitement gripped him as he wondered how he could use this rift which had clearly sprung up between Buckingham and Gloucester. Gloucester was a strong man; it would not be easy to fault him; but Buckingham was weak and vain; he was over-excitable and impulsive, and could not see very far ahead. He was the ideal dupe.

Buckingham had turned to the Bishop.

'I have been a good friend to Gloucester,' boasted Buckingham. 'I have put him on the throne.'

'That is so,' agreed Morton. Flattery was what the Duke wanted. That was easy. 'But for your good services methinks we should not have this King set above us.'

'I put him up . . . I could put him down.'

'There may be something in that, my lord.'

'He has a claim to the throne it is true.'

'When he declares his brother's children bastards, yes.'

The two men surveyed each other. Did they want to put Edward the Fifth back on the throne?

Morton knew that was not the aim of the ambitious Duke. Nor was it his.

As soon as he realised that Richard was aware of his infidelity to him he had begun to plot. And he was in touch with a very resourceful lady who was very clever and had had one idea in her head since the death of Edward when it had become clear that there was going to be considerable conflict while a boy king reigned.

This was Margaret Beaufort, Countess of Richmond, whose third husband was Lord Stanley. But Margaret's first marriage had been to Edmund Tudor and the result of that marriage was her son, Henry Tudor, and it was on this son that Margaret's hopes were fixed.

Margaret's ambitious plan was to make him King of England. That he was worthy, she insisted. His grandfather was Owen who had married Katherine widow of Henry the Fifth, and his mother Margaret Beaufort was the daughter of the first Duke of Somerset, John Beaufort, who was the son of another John Beaufort who himself was the son of John of Gaunt and Catherine Swynford. Margaret insisted that her son Henry Tudor had royal blood from both sides and if there were questions of his legitimacy on both sides she would brush that aside. The Beauforts had been legitimised by Henry the Fourth; and she insisted that Katherine of Valois had married Owen Tudor.

In Margaret's eyes Henry Tudor had a claim to the throne.

Morton was interested in the idea. If Henry Tudor became King he would bring back the House of Lancaster. It would be the triumph of the red rose over the white – and possibly the final victory.

Richard stood in the way.

Morton had been in touch with Margaret Beaufort. She had not been idle. She was busily sounding possible recruits to her cause. That was how she had come into contact with Morton. She was married to Lord Stanley who would it seemed likely be ready to change sides at the vital moment. He had always had an eye to the main chance and he was clever enough to have ingratiated himself with Richard – until of course that fateful council in the Tower when he had been arrested. But he had quickly been released being able to give a plausible account of his activities, and was now back in the Council.

Well, he was Margaret's husband and presumably she must know that he could be relied upon when the time came. In the meantime it was useful to have him appear to be Richard's friend.

This was the plot into which Morton hoped to lure Buckingham but he could see that the noble Duke had ideas of his own.

He would have to go carefully, but he did not anticipate a great deal of trouble from the emotional Duke. His support would be the greatest help. The whole country would be aghast if Buckingham, who had done so much to put Richard on the throne, were openly to turn against him.

'It would seem,' went on Morton, 'that my lord has regrets at the turn of events.'

'I begin to think the country has acted with some haste in offering Richard the crown.'

The country! Morton was secretly amused. Wasn't it Buckingham who had done that? But for that meeting in the Guildhall and the applause of his men which they had clearly been ordered to give, would Richard have taken the crown?

'It is only when a man comes to power that he emerges as himself.'

''Tis true, my lord. But you had a foresight, eh, at the Tower that day.'

'I did, my lord. When Hastings, his friend, lost his head . . . without trial . . .'

'It was shameful. And Rivers and Grey.'

'He is a tyrant.'

'I agree.'

'My lord, could something be done about it?'

Buckingham's eyes gleamed. 'There are others with equal claims to the throne.'

He was preening himself. Already trying on the crown.

This would need care, thought Morton.

He wanted Buckingham's help to further Henry Tudor but how could he get that when the conceited Duke saw himself as a contender for the throne?

'You know of my royal descent?' said the Duke.

'I do, my lord.'

'The Woodville children are disqualified on account of their bastardy. If Richard were dethroned . . . well then.'

He was smiling and Morton smiled too.

God forbid, he thought, but he pretended to be excited and he allowed a new but subtle deference to creep into his manner when he looked at and spoke to the Duke.

Of course it would take a little time. He would go along with Buckingham; and when he judged the moment ripe he would show him how impossible it was for him to reach for the crown.

They had many discussions. Subtly the Bishop sowed the seeds of doubt in Buckingham's mind.

'If there was no truth in this Eleanor Butler story,' the Bishop pointed out, 'Richard would be exposed as an usurper.'

'Then the people would claim young Edward as their King.'

'And,' the Bishop pointed out, 'they would accept no other.'

They looked at each other intently. Inwardly they decided that the illegitimacy of the late King's children must be adhered to otherwise there would be too many to come before the next King. Myself, thought Buckingham. Henry Tudor, thought Morton.

'There is Stillington,' said the Bishop. 'He will cling to the story. It must be true. Stillington would not have lied about such a matter. He places himself in great danger by doing so. Moreover he is a man of the Church.'

That made Buckingham smirk but he hid his cynicism because he wanted to remain on good terms with the Bishop.

'There is no doubt that Edward went through that marriage with Eleanor Butler,' he said.

They talked of possibilities but whichever way they looked Richard was the true King and the only way to depose him would be to murder him.

They spent days in discussion. Buckingham could not tear himself away from his fascinating companion. Morton had ideas there was no doubt of that. He played on Buckingham's feelings to such an extent that within a week, the Duke's hatred of Richard had so increased that to destroy him became an even greater obsession than to seize the crown for himself.

'We need an army to oppose him,' said Morton slyly.

'I could raise men.'

'Enough?'

Buckingham considered.

'Henry Tudor is working in Brittany. He could do a great deal. He would have the Welsh with him.'

Buckingham was silent. Henry Tudor was a claimant to the throne.

'It is a pity that you are married, my lord,' said the Bishop.

'Aye. Married to a Woodville . . . forced into it when I was a child. I have never forgiven the Woodvilles for that.'

'Nay. That is one thing we shall have to be careful of. We don't want the Woodvilles back in power. I was going to say that if you were not married and could marry the late King's daughter . . . that would please a great number of people. There are still some who crave for the old days and even if he did foist his bastards on the nation people still admire King Edward the Fourth.'

'You mean that if I were unmarried and married Elizabeth of York it would be a sop to the Yorkists?'

'I mean that exactly, my lord.'

There was silence and after a few moments, speaking slowly and carefully, Morton said: 'Henry Tudor plans to marry Elizabeth of York.'

Buckingham was thoughtful.

After a while the idea began to take form. It was true that his claim to the throne was slight. He could not really see himself being accepted. But this Henry Tudor . . . *if he* married Elizabeth of York then he would unite the houses of York and Lancaster. That was something which would win the applause of the people. They would see in such a marriage a real end to the Wars of the Roses for although there had been no battles for a number of years the rival factions were still there. There would always be Lancastrians ready to stand against Yorkists until the houses were united.

Buckingham began to see a great deal of hope in the plan. It would ruin Richard and that was what he wanted.

He wanted Richard deposed and dead; and he began to see that the best hope of bringing that about was to support the Tudor.

Very soon his enthusiasms were won over. It was a superb piece of diplomacy on Morton's part. He could be thankful for his imprisonment which had brought him to Brecknock. This was the beginning of his power. He was going to put Henry Tudor on the throne and win his eternal gratitude.

Ambition had brought him to the Church not religion, for the Church offered opportunities to a man who had great ability and few influential relatives.

And now he had been given this great opportunity. He

arranged a meeting between Buckingham and Margaret Beaufort who was delighted to have Buckingham on their side. This was a great breakthrough and Buckingham's help could be decisive. She told him that her son was lying in wait until the moment was ripe. He was leading a very precarious existence on the Continent. Francis Duke of Brittany had been his friend but Francis was now in his dotage and was eager to be on good terms with Richard the Third.

'Francis would have given up my son had Richard sent his men to take him, but good Bishop Morton warned him in time and Henry escaped with his uncle Jasper who has been his constant companion for so many years. He brought him up. We could never have survived without Jasper. But my son Henry is coming back and he will rule this land, I promise you. It will not be long . . . '

'Amen,' said Buckingham, now one of Henry Tudor's fiercest supporters.

'We have good friends,' said Margaret, 'and Bishop Morton is one of the chief among them. He has brought us you, my lord, and now that you are with us that brings victory very close.'

Buckingham was flattered and eager. He wanted to go into action. There should be no delay.

There were more talks with Morton.

One day Buckingham said: 'Henry Tudor when he has defeated Richard of Gloucester in battle will marry Elizabeth of York. Will it be meet and fitting for a King of England to marry a proclaimed bastard?'

'No,' said Morton. 'It will not.'

'In that case if Elizabeth is not a bastard then neither are her brothers.'

'You speak truth,' said Morton, and hesitated wondering

whether to tell the Duke the plan which had been forming in his mind for some time.

'If Henry Tudor married Elizabeth of York it would have to be that she was the heiress to the throne in the eyes of those who did not accept the Stillington story.'

'How could she be while her two brothers lived?'

There was another pause. Then Morton said slowly: 'It could only be after her two brothers were dead.'

'Dead! The elder – King Edward the Fifth – is something of a weakling I believe. But even if he died there is his brother the Duke of York.'

'When Henry gained the throne they would have to be removed . . .'

'Removed!'

'There is no need to go into details. The position has not arrived just yet. The Houses of York and Lancaster must be united as they would be by Henry Tudor and Elizabeth of York. Elizabeth must be seen to be the true heiress of York and Henry of Lancaster. Of course if the Princes are alive . . . they would be heirs. Edward first and if he had no children – and we know he is too young for that – there is Richard, Duke of York. Only if they are removed and Elizabeth proved to be legitimate can she be the heiress to the throne. Henry on one side for Lancaster, Elizabeth on the other for York. It would be the perfect unity.'

'But there are the Princes . . .'

'My lord, sometimes it is necessary to take certain action.'

'You mean that if Henry Tudor landed here and defeated Richard, killed him in battle, that time would come.'

'You see that it is so, my lord.'

'I see it is so. I see that King Henry Tudor could not marry a bastard, therefore Elizabeth must be legitimate. I see that she can only be heiress to the throne if her brothers are dead.'

'Then you see my point exactly.'

'But the children . . . those two boys in the Tower.'

'The time is not yet ripe. We should not consider that yet. Rest assured it will be taken care of when the time comes.'

'What will the people say of a King who murders children?'

'They will say nothing for they will not know. My lord Buckingham I am talking of things which may never come to pass, but we know you and I that it is sometimes necessary to take actions which are obnoxious to us. But if they are performed for the good of the greater number of people they are acceptable in God's eyes. What this country needs is the unity of York and Lancaster, an end to the conflict which will never really cease until this comes about. The unity of York and Lancaster can be brought about by the marriage of Henry Tudor and Elizabeth of York.'

'That I understand but . . . '

'You concern yourself with the children. It is a minor matter. It may not be. It cannot be until Henry Tudor lands on this island and proclaims himself King and Elizabeth of York his Queen. Thank God she is in Sanctuary and no husband has been found for her. No husband must be found until Henry Tudor comes.'

Buckingham was thoughtful, and the Bishop said no more that day.

Later he told the Duke that if the Princes were removed the blame must be attached to their uncle Richard.

'On what grounds?' asked Buckingham.

'That he fears them.'

'Why should he? The people accept their bastardy. They have therefore no claim to the throne and Richard is the true heir.'

'That is true. But we must ensure the peaceful reign of the new King. It will never be so if people blame him for removing the Princes.'

'But you say they must . . . be removed.'

'They will be a menace to him because he must in marrying their sister accept their legitimacy.'

'Exactly, and they provide no threat to Richard who does accept their bastardy.'

'People forget. There are ways of dealing with these matters. If you tell the people something constantly and forcibly enough in time they believe it. I propose to begin now. I am setting some of my servants to whisper in the shops and the streets and the taverns . . . not only here but all over the country and particularly in London. I am going to tell them to spread the rumour that the Princes have been murdered in the Tower.'

'People can see them shooting their arrows in the gardens of the Garden Tower.'

'I know. But all will not see them and those who do not may believe. Rumour may be a lying jade but she can be a useful one.'

'I don't like it,' said Buckingham.

Morton was uneasy. Had he gone too far?

'It is nothing. The boys are safe enough. It is just a theory I had in mind. Perhaps the people would not object to the bastardy. Perhaps the marriage between Henry Tudor and Elizabeth of York will not take place after all. I was just looking ahead to the possibilities. The first thing is to depose Richard. Let us give our energies to that.'

'That is what I am most eager to do and I think the time has come for us to go into action.'

When Richard heard that Buckingham had put himself at the head of an insurrection to come against him he was deeply shocked.

Buckingham, who had been his friend, his Constable, and the one who had been closest to him in the struggle. He could not believe it.

He immediately set about calling an army together and gave instructions that they were to meet at Leicester. He was quiet and calm, hiding how deeply wounded he was. He did say that Buckingham was the most untrue creature living and everyone knew that if ever the Duke fell into the King's hands that would be the end of him. He was declared a rebel and a price was put on his head.

Richard was supported by his good friends John Howard, Duke of Norfolk, Francis, Viscount Lovell, Sir Richard Ratcliffe and William Catesby . . . all men on whom he could rely. But then he had thought he could rely on Buckingham. No, Buckingham had come up too quickly. It had been an error of judgement to have relied on him to such an extent. Then there was Stanley. He did not trust Stanley. He was after all the husband of Margaret Beaufort, mother of the Tudor. He was watchful of Stanley and must make sure that he was given no opportunity to be false.

There were risings in Kent and Surrey and East Anglia. These were quickly suppressed and Richard marched on to Leicester.

Buckingham was in difficulties. He had moved towards the east with a force made up mainly of Welsh troops but when he came into Herefordshire he found the rivers Wye and Severn in flood and impassable. There was no help for it but to attempt to retreat but that became out of the question for he found he was hemmed in by enemy troops. He was forced to wait and the men grew restive. The expedition was ill-timed and ill-planned. Men began to desert and the Duke saw that there was nothing left to him but escape.

There was a big price on his head. If he fell into Richard's hands there would be no mercy. He could not expect that. Therefore he must escape.

Perhaps he could get across the Channel and join Henry Tudor. Then they could plot together and come back in triumph.

One of his retainers, Ralph Bannister, who had a house near the town of Wem, took him in and Buckingham stayed for a few days at his mansion of Lacon Park.

Everyone was talking about the débâcle and the price on the Duke of Buckingham's head. It was a large price for Richard was very eager to get the traitor into his hands.

For a day or so Bannister resisted the temptation but after a while it became too much for him. He advised Buckingham to leave his house and showed him a hut where he could stay for a while until he could make good his escape. But no sooner was Buckingham in the hut than he was arrested and taken to Salisbury by the Sheriff of Shropshire.

He asked to see the King. He wanted to talk to him. He confessed that he had been a foolish traitor. He had wronged the King who had been his friend. But if he could but see the King, if he could talk to him, if he could explain . . .

It was no use. He could hardly expect Richard to see him in the circumstances for never had a man more blatantly played the traitor.

It was the second of November, a dark day and a Sunday, when Buckingham was taken out to the market-place and there laid his head on the block.

🏵 Chapter XVI 🏵

RUMOURS

The insurrection was over. Henry Tudor had not landed. Of the fifteen ships which the Duke of Brittany had given him all but two had been destroyed by storm. He had come close to the coast with those two but seeing the soldiers on land had thought it wiser to return and try another time.

Richard was triumphant, but he had received a warning.

Another matter which had deeply disturbed him was the rumour of the death of the Princes and that he was named as their murderer. Of what purpose would their death serve? They were no menace to him. He was the true King. The bastard sons of his brother did not threaten his position.

The only way in which they could do so would be if they were his brother's *legitimate sons*. And if they had been it would never have occurred to him to take the throne. He would have remained as Protector of the Realm and guardian of the little King until he was of age to govern.

It was a disturbing rumour. Did it mean that there was a plot afoot to murder the Princes and lay the blame at his door? It was a feasible plan, the logic behind which became clear to him when he heard that in the Cathedral at Rennes Henry Tudor had sworn to marry Elizabeth of York and thus unite the houses of York and Lancaster.

He thought a great deal about the matter and the more he thought the more certain it seemed to him that some harm was planned for the Princes. They were in the Garden Tower at the moment and his very good friend Sir Robert Brackenbury was the Constable.

He decided he would warn him to guard the Princes well, and he summoned to him his Master of Henchmen Sir James Tyrell. He told him that he wished him to take a letter to the Constable of the Tower and that he should prepare himself to leave at once.

Richard then wrote the letter in which he asked Sir Robert to guard the Princes well. He feared for their safety. He thought it would be a good idea if they were removed from their present lodging and put into a secret one until such time as it would be safe for them to emerge.

He would explain his fears to Sir Robert sometime when they were together. For the present he knew he was his very good friend and could trust him.

The year passed uneasily. Richard was aware that the Bishop of Ely was one of his greatest enemies and he heartily repented putting him in Buckingham's care. After the débâcle Morton had escaped to Flanders and now had probably joined Henry Tudor.

It was difficult to govern as he would have wished with so much to deter him. How lucky Edward had been to have the people with him. After the defection of Buckingham Richard felt he could never trust anyone again.

He wished that everyone would forget their grievances, that

they would try to work with him for a prosperous state. He was sorry that Elizabeth Woodville remained in Sanctuary. He wanted her to come forth – she and her daughters.

He sent word to her telling her that if she came out no harm should befall her.

Elizabeth was wary. She could not forget that her brother Anthony and her son Richard had been beheaded at Richard's orders. He had answered that they had deserved their fate and they would have had his head if events had gone the other way. It was no use going over the past. That was done with. She had five daughters; she should think of their future.

He did not remind her that she had a son, the Marquess of Dorset, who was now on the Continent with Henry Tudor.

A letter was delivered to her in Sanctuary which Richard had written himself.

'I swear,' he wrote, 'that if the daughters of Elizabeth Grey, late calling herself Queen of England, will come to me out of Sanctuary and be guided and ruled by me I shall see that they shall be in surety of their lives and that as they are my kins-women, being the undoubted daughters of my brother, I will arrange worthy marriages for them . . .'

He also offered to pay an annual pension to Elizabeth herself.

Elizabeth considered the offer. He could hardly dishonour it, she said. And she was anxious about her daughters.

On a bleak March day she emerged from Sanctuary and decided that she must accept the offer and rely on the mercy of the King.

During that month Richard left London for Northampton. It seemed certain now that Henry Tudor would make another attack with the coming of better weather. Richard must be prepared. Until Henry Tudor was dead there would be no peace for him, he realised. Henry Tudor wanted the throne and he was going to do everything he could to gain it. Moreover there were many who would help him in this endeavour. Richard was surrounded by people whom common sense forced him to doubt.

Norfolk, Lovell, Ratcliffe, Catesby, Brackenbury . . . those he believed he could trust with his life. But there were others who filled him with doubt. The conduct of Buckingham and Hastings had made him distrustful, suspicious of everyone.

He longed for peace. He was a born administrator. He wanted to encourage trading as Edward had. That was the sure way to prosperity. A country wasted its substance in war.

There were other anxieties. Anne's health was failing. She was so easily tired. He was worried about his son too. Anne had sent him back to Middleham because she thought it was better for him to be there. Her thoughts went with him though, and although she made a great effort to accompany Richard and smile at the people and appear to be merry he was aware of what a great effort it was and how very tired she felt.

They were halfway through April when the messenger came from the North. He was brought immediately to the King and Richard knew at once that the news was bad.

'Have no fear,' he said. 'Tell me quickly.'

'My lord, it is the Prince.'

'He is ill . . .'

The man looked at him silently.

Richard turned away to hide his emotion. 'He is dead,' he said slowly. 'My son is dead.'

'My lord, I fear . . . it is so.'

'I will tell the Queen,' said the King; he waved his hand in dismissal and the messenger glad to escape hurriedly left.

Anne valiantly tried to suppress her desolation. It was impossible. For a time she gave up all pretence that she was well. She sank to her knees and covered her face with her hands.

He tried to comfort her, but there was no comfort. This delicate boy, whom they had loved even more tenderly because they had suffered constant fear for him, was lost to them.

He had suffered from the same disease which had afflicted both Warwick's daughters, and meant that they could not hope for any but a brief life span.

They had cherished him – their Prince of Wales, their heir to England . . . and now he was gone.

And looking at Anne, so desolate in her grief, Richard wondered how soon it would be before he was mourning his wife.

The future was grim. The Scots were giving trouble on the border now that Richard was no longer there to keep them in check. The King of France was showing friendship to Henry Tudor. Richard knew he must get his hands on that man. If he could capture him and bring him to England, get rid of him, then they might settle to peace. He sent men to Brittany to capture Henry Tudor, but Morton had his spies in England. Among them was Rotherham who was able to inform Morton of what was planned. Morton then warned Henry Tudor in time so that he escaped into France. Morton was a dangerous enemy. Richard knew that now and cursed himself for not destroying him when he was in his hands. He was far more dangerous than Hastings would ever have been.

He was indeed more dangerous than Richard knew. He had heard of Richard's instructions to Brackenbury and thought that if everything went according to plan that act might be of considerable use to him.

Morton had staked his future now on Henry Tudor's victory and if he could bring about the marriage between Elizabeth of York and Henry Tudor he would be delighted with his plans. If that marriage ever came about and it was to be effective those little Princes would have to be disposed of. So they had been kept out of the way at Richard's request. Well, that might be useful. It would give credence to the story that they were already dead. He was sorry that Elizabeth Woodville had come out of Sanctuary with her daughters. That was unfortunate on two counts. First if she had believed that Richard had murdered the Princes – her little sons of whom she was so fond, for whatever else she was she was a devoted mother – she would never have put her daughters in his hands. Another fear – and perhaps an even greater one – was that Richard might find husbands for the girls. Then the marriage between Elizabeth and Henry Tudor could not take place and would the people accept Henry Tudor if by doing so they were not going to unite the houses of York and Lancaster?

We need to move fast, thought Morton. And yet how could they? They must be absolutely sure of success when they came in.

The weary year was passing. Henry Tudor had made no attempt to land. Clearly he was not ready.

Richard guessed there were traitors all about him. One morning there was discovered on the door of St Paul's a rhyme which could only spell treachery:

It was a criticism of the King and ran:

'The Cat, the Rat, and Lovell our dog
Rule all England under a hog.'

The Cat was Catesby, the Rat Ratcliffe and Lovell – a name frequently used for dogs – was Francis Lovell – all faithful friends. And the hog was himself taken from the sign of the Boar on his staff.

The rhyme was traced to William Colynbourne who had been an officer in the household of the Duchess of York. Richard was deeply wounded not only by the criticism of his rule but because this man had been one of his family's servants. Colynbourne had committed a greater sin than writing seditious doggerel verse. He was found guilty of sending messages to Henry Tudor giving the state of the defences of England.

He was accorded the traitor's death and suffered cruelly on Tower Hill.

One urgent need was staring Richard in the face, and that was the importance of getting an heir. There had always been anxiety about Edward's health and he and Anne had longed for another child. She had been so delicate that he had begun to feel that they would never have another and while they had the young Prince they could put their hope in him. But now he was gone. Moreover Anne's health had deteriorated rapidly since the death of Edward. It was clear that a great interest had been taken out of her life and she felt so ill now that she could no longer disguise it.

Richard called in the doctors.

Could they not *do* something? Surely their skill was not beyond helping her.

They shook their heads.

'It is a disease of the lungs, my lord. The Queen cannot recover. She can only grow progressively worse.'

The physicians were uneasy and he was aware that there was something else they wished to say to him. They hesitated, each waiting for the other to speak.

At last one of them said: 'My lord, the Queen's disease in these stages is contagious. You should no longer share a chamber with her.'

The implication of this was obvious. He and Anne would never have another child.

He explained gently to Anne. She understood. She said: 'I can't have long left, Richard. Bear with me for these few weeks. Then when I am gone you must marry again . . . marry a healthy young woman who can give you sons.'

He shook his head. 'There would never be anyone else I could love as I do you. Oh I know I have not told you often enough, not shown you. It is my way.'

'I know . . . I know and I would not have had you otherwise. You have been good to me always . . . and it was always you I wanted. Do you remember, Richard, when we were together in those early days at Middleham?'

'I have never forgotten them. For that reason I have always loved Middleham. I would we could be there now . . . together . . . with our son . . .'

'Time passes, Richard. We have had some bad times . . . I shall never forget those days I spent in that hot and foul-smelling kitchen . . . Sometimes it comes back to me now . . . I dream . . . and I wake up and am thankful that that is over. But we must look to the future. When I am gone . . . I want you to be happy, Richard.'

'I could not hope to be.'

'You will be. You will succeed. You will be a great King – even greater than your brother. Oh Richard, I want you to be happy. If you are, everything that has gone on before will be worthwhile.'

'You are going to get well,' he said firmly, 'and when you are we will have children, sons . . . sons and daughters.'

'Yes,' she said to comfort him. 'Oh yes.' And she tried to pretend that she believed that possible.

Christmas had come. It was spent at Westminster and in order to keep his promise to look after his brother's daughters, Richard had them brought to the celebrations. He had said that they should have gowns suitable to their rank and Elizabeth of York was attired as magnificently as the Queen.

She looked beautiful and her stay in Sanctuary had clearly done her no harm. She was sparkling, merry and clearly delighted to be free at last.

She showed marked appreciation to the King who was very gracious to her. She was very beautiful with her long golden hair flowing about her shoulders – a marked contrast to the Queen who, although she made a brave effort, looked as though she were visibly fading away.

Morton's spies at Court noticed Elizabeth's deference to the King and that he paid her due honour. They sent word to Morton who was horrified at the thought of Elizabeth's being at Court and clearly enjoying it, and at the accounts of the King's graciousness to her and her willingness to please.

Any marriage of Elizabeth of York not to Henry Tudor would render the scheme of making him King impossible. Elizabeth must not marry . . . until Henry Tudor came to claim her.

Morton did not like all this talk about the King's gracious-ness to Elizabeth. His task was to win the throne for Henry Tudor and he, shrewd plotter that he was, knew that slander against Richard would be of as great importance as winning a battle. Elizabeth must not marry.

In the meantime there was a chance to defame Richard further.

Why not send out hints that he was contemplating marrying his niece? He was married to Anne yes, but a little dose of poison would soon remove her and then he would be free.

Anne would be dead soon, according to reports. She was weaker every day. So that story could sound plausible.

Richard could not understand why people should hate him so, why they should continue to send out these evil rumours.

Catesby and Ratcliffe said that it was because Henry Tudor had people working for him secretly and slander was one of the weapons they were using against him.

Events weighed heavily upon him. He must be prepared for the coming of Henry Tudor and each day he saw Anne growing weaker and weaker.

On the sixteenth of March Richard was summoned to her bedside. He sat there holding her hand while the chamber was filled with darkness.

Outside the people stood about in the streets staring up at the sky for the sun's face was slowly being obscured.

It was the greatest eclipse of the sun which the people of England had ever seen and they thought it must have some-thing to do with the passing of the Queen.

Anne was unaware of it. She knew only that Richard was with her, holding her hand and that she was slowly slipping away from him.

'Richard . . .' she tried to say his name.

He bent over. 'Rest, dearest,' he said. 'It is best so.'

'Soon I shall be at rest,' she murmured. 'Soon I shall see our son . . . Oh Richard, I shall be with you . . . always . . .'

His cheeks were wet. He was surprised. It was long since he had shed a tear.

An utter desolation had come to him.

She had gone . . . this companion of his youth, this faithful wife; the one he had loved even more deeply than he had loved his brother.

There would never be anyone else. He did not change. Loyalty bound him.

The rumours were at their height. He was going to marry his niece.

Elizabeth of York was agreeable and Elizabeth Woodville would welcome the marriage. It would settle differences. The Woodvilles could hardly be against a King who was the husband of one of their daughters.

Marry his niece! It was incest.

Typical of him, they said. He was without scruples.

Richard knew that he must think of marrying.

Rotherham had pointed out that a King without an heir was storing up trouble. He should marry. People were saying that his niece was a strong and healthy woman.

'She is indeed,' replied Richard, 'and I doubt not that she will bear strong children when the time comes.'

Rotherham reported to Morton that the King was contemplating marrying his niece.

Sir William Catesby and Sir Richard Ratcliffe took an early opportunity of speaking to the King.

He must not marry Elizabeth of York. They themselves were very anxious to keep out the Woodville influence for they feared it would go hard with them if ever that family crept back into power. They had placed themselves on Richard's side so clearly against the Woodvilles. But that was not all. They served Richard faithfully and they feared that a marriage with his niece would damage his reputation even further. They had no doubt that the Pope could be induced to grant a dispensation. But it would be wrong and if Richard was going to look for a bride he must do so elsewhere.

'My dear friends,' said Richard, 'you have no need to warn me. I had no intention of marrying my niece. It is just another of those evil rumours which have suddenly started to circulate about me.'

Catesby and Ratcliffe were greatly relieved.

Richard smiled at them. 'Surely you did not believe I would marry my niece? I tell you this, I am in no mood for marriage. I still mourn the Queen and have other matters more urgent. Spring is coming. The Tudor is certain to make an attempt some time this year.'

'That's so,' said Catesby, 'but all the same I should like to find the source of these rumours.'

Richard sighed. 'My good friends,' he said, 'I agree with you. It is the insidious enemy who can harm us more than the one who comes in battle. I long for the day when I shall face the Tudor on the battlefield. I pray God that the task of taking him may fall to me.'

'In the meantime, my lord,' said Ratcliffe, 'we must put an end to this rumour.'

'I will send Elizabeth away from Court,' said Richard. 'It is not fitting that she should be there – in view of the rumours – now that the Queen is no longer with us.'

'Where should she go, my lord?'

'Why not to Sheriff Hutton. She will be away from the Court there. One or more of her sisters could go with her. It shall be for them to decide. My Clarence nephews are there, Warwick and Lincoln. She will be company for them and they for her. Yes, to Sheriff Hutton.'

Catesby and Ratcliffe were well pleased. They hoped they had stopped the rumours about Richard and Elizabeth.

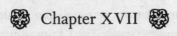 Chapter XVII

BOSWORTH FIELD

August had come and Richard knew that across the Channel plans were coming to a climax. It seemed certain that Henry Tudor would attempt a landing.

Richard was prepared. He was feeling philosophical. Soon the test would come and it was going to be either victory or death for him, he knew.

He faced the future with a kind of nonchalance. He had lost his wife and son. There was nothing left but to fight for the crown.

If he defeated Henry Tudor he would plan a new life. He would try to forget the sadness of old. He would try to be a good King as his brother had been. But that could not be until he had cleared the country of this evil threat of war.

Wars had clouded his life. These incessant Wars of the Roses. He had thought they were over — all had thought so when Edward rose so magnificently out of the horrors of war and took the crown. If Edward had lived . . . If his son had been a little older . . .

But it had not been so and now he was faced with this mighty decision. He would do his best and he would emerge from the struggle either King of England or a dead man.

At the end of July Thomas Lord Stanley had come to him and asked permission to retire to his estates. He was very suspicious of Stanley. Stanley was a time-server. He was a man who had a genius for extricating himself from difficult situations. Such men were born to survive. They lived by expediency. They swayed with the wind. Richard had little respect for Stanley and yet he needed his help.

He had been arrested at the time of Hastings's execution but after a very short time had been freed, in time to carry the mace at Richard's coronation.

He had married Margaret Beaufort, the mother of Henry Tudor, but he had continued to serve Richard.

Richard did not trust him but he was too important to be ignored and it seemed to the King that to have him close at hand was better than to spurn him and send him right into the ranks of the enemy.

That his wife had played a part in the Buckingham insurrection was undeniable. When Buckingham had been beheaded Stanley had expressed his agreement that the Duke had deserved his fate. It would have been a different story, Richard was fully aware, if Buckingham had been successful.

At the time Stanley had promised to restrain his wife. He would keep her quietly in the country, he had said.

Now he wished to go to his estates as they urgently required his attention.

Ratcliffe and Catesby put it to the King that Stanley could turn against them and the wisest course was to watch him. After all he was married to the mother of Henry Tudor.

'I know,' said Richard. 'If he is going to turn traitor it is better for him to do so now than on a battlefield.'

So Stanley left but Richard said he must leave his son behind to answer for his loyal conduct.

There was nothing for Stanley to do but comply.

And on the seventh of August Henry Tudor landed at Milford Haven.

Richard was at Nottingham when news reached him that Henry Tudor was near Shrewsbury.

He sent for the men he could trust: Norfolk, Catesby, Brackenbury, Ratcliffe.

Stanley had not returned but had sent an excuse that he was suffering from the sweating sickness. His son, Lord Strange, had attempted to escape but on being captured had confessed that he and his uncle Sir William Stanley had had communication with the invaders.

The Stanleys would betray him, Richard thought, as he had known they would.

There was no time to be lost. They must march now and on the twenty-first of August the two armies arrived at Bosworth Field.

Richard spent a sleepness night. He was fatalistic. Would there be victory on the following day? He felt no great confidence, no great elation. Sorrow weighed heavily upon him. But this should be the turning-point. If Fate showed him that he was to go on and rule he would be a great King. He would learn from his brother's successes and mistakes and he would dedicate himself to the country.

They were there . . . his good friends. Brackenbury – his

good honest face shining with loyalty – Catesby, Ratcliffe, Norfolk. . . the men he could rely on.

And the Stanleys – where were they?

He mounted his big white horse. No one could mistake him. It was indeed the King's horse. And on his helmet he wore a golden crown.

'This day,' he said, 'decides our fate. My friends and loyal subjects remember that victory can be ours if we go into this fight with good hearts and the determination to win the day. At this day's end I will be King or a dead man, I promise you.'

The trumpets were sounding. The moment had come and Richard rode forth at the head of his army.

The battle waged. The sun was hot and the Lancastrians had the advantage because it was at their backs. The Stanleys waited. They would decide which side they were on when the decisive moment came. In the meantime they had no intention of fighting for Richard.

They were Henry Tudor's men and had worked hard for his success. They were ready now . . . waiting for the precise moment which would be best for them to depart.

That moment came. The Stanleys were riding out crying: 'A Tudor. A Tudor.'

Richard heard them and smiled grimly.

Catesby was urging him to fly. He laughed at that. He rode forward brandishing his axe.

He saw Ratcliffe go down and Brackenbury.

My good friends . . . he thought. You gave your lives for me . . . for truth . . . for righteousness . . . for loyalty.

A curse on the traitor Tudor!

'Treason!' he shouted after the retreating Stanleys who were making their way to the Tudor lines.

He would find Henry Tudor. He should be his special prey. He would take him in single combat. It was their fate which was being decided. Plantagenet against Tudor. If Richard did not succeed it would not only be the end of a King, it would be the end of a line. Glorious Plantagenet supreme for generations would give way to the new House of Tudor – begotten by bastards . . . with none but the flimsiest claim to the throne. And the rule of the proud Plantagenets who had governed the land since the glorious days of Henry the Second would be over.

It must not be. It was for him to save it.

'God help me,' he cried. 'I must find Henry Tudor. The fight is between us two.'

In spite of his small stature he was an impressive figure as he rode forward, the sun glinting on his golden crown, his white horse galloping forward.

His friends called to him but he did not heed them.

'I shall find Henry Tudor,' he shouted.

With his small band of followers he rode right into the midst of the enemy's cavalry.

Now he had seen it – the Welsh banner held aloft by William Brandon, Henry Tudor's standard-bearer. There was the Tudor. He was well protected, surrounded by his men, by no means in the thick of the fight. Trust the Tudor for that.

'I have come to kill you, Tudor,' he muttered. 'It has to be one of us.'

It was folly he knew. There were too many of them but he was there. He had glimpsed Henry Tudor . . . He struck at William Brandon, and the man went down.

He saw Ratcliffe who was trying to protect him. His horse had collapsed under him but he was immediately on his feet.

'My lord . . . my lord . . .' It was Ratcliffe again. But Richard did not hear. He had seen Henry Tudor. He had come close enough to strike down his standard-bearer. He was going to take Henry Tudor.

He went forward wielding his battle-axe.

'Treason!' he cried. 'Come, Henry Tudor . . . Come out and fight.'

His men were falling about him, Ratcliffe was down now, but Richard fought on valiantly, the crown on his head. He was determined to storm his way through to the Tudor. If he were going to die he would take him with him.

They were attacking him now. The blows were coming fast. Then he was sinking into darkness. He fell to the ground and his crown rolled from his head.

It was the end. The battle was over. It was victory for Henry Tudor. Of Richard's loyal friends Norfolk, Ratcliffe and Brackenbury were slain. Catesby was captured and hanged; Lovell escaped to live on into the new reign.

It was Lord Stanley – to whose treachery Henry Tudor owed his victory – who found the golden crown in a hedge and placed it on Henry Tudor's head.

So ended the battle of Bosworth, the last in the Wars of the Roses. So ended the rule of the Plantagenets. A new reigning family had come to England with the Tudors.

Stephen, Sir Leslie and Lee, Sir Sydney *The Dictionary of National Biography*

Stratford, Laurence *Edward the Fourth*

Strickland, Agnes *The Lives of the Queens of England*

Timbs, John and Gunn, Alexander *Abbeys, Castles and Ancient Halls of England and Wales*

Vickers, K. H. *England in the Later Middle Ages*

Wade, John *British History*

Walpole, Horace *Historic Doubts on the Life of Richard III*

🏵 Bibliography 🏵

Aubrey, William Hickman Smith *National and Domestic History of England*

Clive, Mary *This Sun of York: A Biography of Edward IV*

Costain, Thomas *The Lost Plantagenets: The Pageant of England 1377–1485*

Gairdner, James *History and Life and Reign of Richard III*

Gairdner, James *Life and Papers of Richard III*

Green, John Richard *History of England*

Green, Mary Anne Everett *Lives of the Princesses of England*

Guizot, M. Translated by Robert Black *History of France*

Halsted, Caroline *Richard III, As Duke of Gloucester and King of England*

Hume, David *History of England from the Invasion of Julius Caesar to the Revolution*

Jenkins, Elizabeth *The Princes in the Tower*

Kendall, Paul Murray *Richard III*

Kendall, Paul Murray *Warwick, the Kingmaker*

Kingsford, C. L. *Prejudice and Promise in the Fifteenth Century*

More, Sir Thomas, *Life of Richard III*

Oman, Charles *Political History of England*

Oman, Charles *Warwick, the Kingmaker*

Ramsey, J. H. *Lancaster and York*

Ross, Charles *Edward IV*

Scofield, C. L. *The Life and Reign of Edward IV*